THE
BEACH HUT
MURDERS

An absolutely gripping cozy mystery filled with
twists and turns

PETER BOLAND

The Charity Shop Detective Agency Mysteries
Book 2

Joffe Books, London
www.joffebooks.com

First published in Great Britain in 2023

Cover art by Nick Castle

ISBN: 978-1-83526-026-5

PROLOGUE

Annie smelled smoke. Carried on the damp night air, its unmistakable tang whispered its way to her nostrils.

She'd noticed it as soon as she'd opened the door and stumbled dozily outside. Not much, just a whiff, but a whiff was all it took to alert the strongest of primeval responses — the survival instinct. Hardwired into the genes, handed down through countless generations. A message that could not be ignored. Smoke meant danger. Smoke meant fire. And fire meant death.

A winged irritant interrupted her involuntary thoughts. A mosquito. Invisible in the darkness, its high-pitched whine was the only noise save for the gentle lap of water nearby. Her clumsy arms windmilled, hoping to bat it away. The whining faded. Satisfied that she had repelled the insect, Annie shuffled along the sand barefoot and soporific, still sniffing the smoky air.

The only person up at this ungodly hour, she shrugged off her instinct to run or raise the alarm. Remembering where she was, the smoke was nothing to worry about. Nothing new. It was like this all the time.

She was on Mudeford Spit. Home to the poshest, priciest and possibly largest beach huts money could buy. At the end of each afternoon, as day-trippers, weighed down like packhorses, reluctantly dragged themselves back home, beach hut owners would pop corks and fire up

1

their barbecues and firepits along the length of the spit. A miniature series of medieval beacons, the fires would often smoulder long after their owners had drawn their curtains and retired for the night. Inside their adult-sized Wendy houses, all mod cons were squished into every available space: tiny fridges, cookers and, most importantly, a low-ceilinged bedroom, hidden on a platform in the roof space — a crucial difference that separated these larger huts from the smaller, garden-shed beach huts lining every British coastline.

For that very reason, Annie had had no problem getting her kids to bed every night since they'd arrived. Climbing up a set of wooden stairs, steep as a stepladder, it was like sleeping in a treehouse. Every night was an adventure, and Sam and Millie couldn't wait for it to begin. Plus, it helped that they were exhausted from all that fresh air. Annie had to make do with a converted sofa bed downstairs. She didn't mind. It was comfy enough and the thrill of waking up with the sea a few feet from your door was worth it. Mudeford Spit was the best childcare a parent could get. A place where kids could still be kids, having adventures and mixing with others their age, going off in their little gangs. That's what every parent wanted for them, wasn't it? To prolong their innocence. To stretch out the days of making their own fun, before the artificial world of social media had them in its digital clutches.

As she edged along the cold beach, shivering in her ratty jogging bottoms and T-shirt, Annie mused that the only drawback to this idyllic place was the one she was experiencing right now. The beach huts had no toilet.

That evening, she'd had a couple of very large glasses of well-deserved chilled Chardonnay, sitting with her feet up on the deck, revelling in the sheer joy of watching Sam and Millie squeeze the last drop of fun out of the day. It had warmed her heart to see them frolicking in their wetsuits in the gentle waters of Christchurch Harbour as the sun slipped towards the horizon, throwing dashes of orange and red onto the priory's stained-glass windows. Life didn't get much better, except now those two large glasses of wine were coming back to haunt her. A full bladder meant reluctantly dragging herself out of bed, leaving her kids slumbering upstairs while she made the short trek to one of the public toilet blocks.

Despite it being July, she had her arms wrapped tightly around herself. Surrounded on both sides by water — sea on one side, harbour *on the other — the air could get pretty cold and dank here, especially at three thirty in the morning. She soldiered on past the regimental rows of beach huts. During the day, their vivid colours reminded her of sweets lined up ready to eat. Tonight, under the cloudy, starless sky, thick with darkness, they appeared grey. All she could make out was the silhouette of their little pitched roofs, the collective outline forming a jagged jaw.*

Up ahead she glimpsed the lonely light of the toilet and shower block, signalling that salvation was near. Sniffing the air, she noticed the smoke seemed stronger now, headier, assaulting her senses rather than caressing them.

As she neared the toilet block, it became harder to hold the call of nature. Annie broke into a jog, the jigging not helping her predicament. Finally reaching the entrance to the toilet, she crashed through the door. The automatic energy-saving light sensed her arrival and popped on, blinding her momentarily. She made for the nearest cubicle, slamming the door and bolting it behind her.

A few minutes later, she emerged feeling far more comfortable than when she had entered. Annie looked forward to climbing back into the warmth of her bed, snuggling beneath her duvet, closing her eyes, and not opening them until the sun came up or her kids woke her demanding breakfast — whichever came first.

She blinked as something caught her eye. Impossible to ignore against the black of night, a glowing orange dot floated above her head, bright as a firefly. Another followed. Then several more, aimlessly drifting past her. The smell of smoke, more pungent now, was accompanied by a faint crackle and a glow. The instinct she had suppressed earlier now screamed at her. She darted around the corner and gasped.

On the other side of the toilet block, further down the beach, one of the huts was ablaze.

She hurried towards the dancing flames, the heat and panic increasing with every step. Someone was in there.

CHAPTER 1

Three weeks later

Fiona watched the woman sitting in her car outside the charity shop. She'd been there since opening time at nine o'clock
on the dot. It was now nine twenty-five and the woman had
not moved a muscle. She just sat there, staring through the
windscreen, unmoving. Fiona noticed a cardboard box beside
her on the passenger seat, while a pre-schooler, perhaps aged
three or four, strapped snugly into a car seat, slept with her
head tilted to one side.

Assuming she was there to make a donation, Fiona
had a pretty good idea why this woman was reluctant to
exit her car and drop off the box. Being a seasoned volunteer for Dogs Need Nice Homes, Fiona had come to know
the types of customers who frequented charity shops, the
various characters who thrifted along Southbourne Grove.
She had names for all of them. For example, there were the
'casual browsers', who had no idea what they were looking
for, as long as it was a bargain. Usually buying something
they didn't really need, they just had to snap it up at that
crazy price — it would be rude not to. Then there were the
'eBay resellers', who wanted to stock up on goods at vastly

4

discounted prices so they could sell them online for more, making a healthy profit. The 'antique hunters' were similar, but for them it was all about quality rather than quantity, the hope they would stumble on that one rare item of incredible value that had somehow slipped through the net. Intense and determined, they'd snuffle in boxes, rummage along racks and rifle through shelves to uncover a hidden gem. That first edition of *The Lord of The Rings*, or that vintage Matchbox car, miraculously still in its box. Highly unlikely, these days. With the internet, people knew what everything and anything was worth. It was only a quick Google search away. The closest Fiona had come to finding anything of value was the odd folded-up fiver or tenner stuffed in the pocket of a pair of trousers, which would go straight into the till.

However, this woman was different. She was donating, not buying, and if Fiona's instincts about her were right, then she would belong to a very small category known as the 'sorrowful donors'. They had to be treated with a kind and gentle touch, a great deal of sensitivity and respect. There would be a very powerful, emotional reason why this woman would have great difficulty parting with the contents of the box that sat beside her.

The car door opened. The woman slowly emerged, her dark-grey overcoat flapping in the breeze, a woolly hat pulled down tight over her ears. Though it was the height of summer, the beginning of August no less, the weather had had other ideas. After a long spell of sunshine, and just as everyone had acclimatised to the heat, an unseasonal cold snap had barged summer out of the way. An arctic northerly wind had taken up residence over the UK, stripping back the temperature until it barely reached double figures, forcing everyone to retrieve their winter clothes from the back of the wardrobe.

As she rounded the car, Fiona saw the woman more clearly. She appeared to be in her late twenties or early thirties, with a makeup-free face that looked as if it would never be happy again. A pair of Deidre Barlow glasses perched on her nose gave her an owlish expression, albeit a very sad one.

She paused by the passenger door, head bowed. Fiona wondered if she should go out and help but decided against it.

Outside, the woman shook her head as if disagreeing with herself, then opened the passenger door to lift out the box. She stood on the pavement, back to Fiona for several seconds, still indecisive, arms hugging the box as if her life depended on it. Slowly she turned and headed towards the shop, eyes still cast down. Before she entered, she checked her child was okay, then shunted the door open with the box in front of her.

Fiona desperately wanted to hold the door open, but experience had taught her not to make a fuss. So when the little bell above the door tinkled and the woman negotiated her way in, Fiona simply looked up from the counter, smiled and said, "Morning."

The woman hesitated.

"Still cold out there?" Clearly it was, judging by the icy blast chilling her stockinged legs. She wrapped her trademark chunky-knit cardigan a little tighter around herself.

"Sorry?" the woman replied, her mind still elsewhere. "Oh, yes. Very cold." She bit the side of her lip self-consciously, not daring to venture any further.

Slowly, so as not to spook her, Fiona came out from the side of the till. "Would you like me to take that for you?"

The woman took two tentative steps into the shop, letting the door close behind her. "I have some things I wish to donate."

Fiona met her halfway. "Yes, of course. Thank you so much." She stretched out her hands, ready to take the box. The woman didn't respond, reluctant to let go. They stood in this awkward stalemate for a second or two until the woman slowly extended her arms towards Fiona and relinquished her grip.

Fiona placed the box reverently on the counter. It was sealed up tightly with brown parcel tape, more than was really necessary, as if the woman was frightened its contents might escape.

Fiona turned back to face her. The woman appeared to be traumatised by their simple exchange. Eyes on the edge of tears, they flicked nervously outside to check on the state of her slumbering child.

"Are you okay?" Fiona asked. "Is there anything I can do?"

"Yes, yes I'm fine." Her voice wavered. She wasn't fine.

"Pardon me. But I was wondering. Are you sure you're ready to part with these items?"

Once again, the woman didn't respond, just gazed at the floor. Eventually she looked up with a pair of red-rimmed eyes. "I'm not sure," she managed to say. "It's some of my late grandfather's things. He passed away recently, and I've been meaning to get rid of them. It's nothing that I want to keep. Nothing sentimental. But I still feel like I'm betraying his memory . . ." Her voice trailed off. She let out a sob.

Fiona snatched a couple of clean tissues from a box by the till. The woman took them and dabbed the corners of her eyes from beneath her glasses. Fiona gave her a reassuring squeeze of the arm, not wishing to be too intimate but also wanting to signal that she had her support. The poor woman was in a no-win situation. Letting go of a lost loved one's belongings was never easy, even the trivial stuff that you had no need for. They all had value, imbued as they were with the departed's essence. Throw them out too soon, and it felt cold and uncaring. Hold on to them and you might never get rid of them, like keeping a wound open.

Fiona couldn't tell her what to do with the contents of the box and when would be the right time to part with them. There was no advice she could offer. It had to be her decision. However, there was something she could do to ease the process very slightly, a little service she had provided from time to time for other bereaved customers who had stood where this woman was standing, facing this difficult situation.

"Might I make a small suggestion?" Fiona asked gently. "Why don't I keep this box behind the counter? I won't open it and I'll write a note telling other volunteers not to touch

7

it. You can come and take it back any time you want, but if I don't hear from you after a couple of months, I'll assume it's safe to donate the items to the shop. How does that sound?"

The woman's face brightened a little. "Really? Would that be okay?"

"Of course. Not a problem."

"Oh, my gosh. That would be great. If it's not too much trouble."

Fiona smiled warmly. "I'd be happy to. I've done this before for other people in your situation. It really helps. It's like a halfway house, and you can still come back any time to get your grandfather's things."

The woman nearly collapsed with relief. "That makes me feel so much better. Thank you, thank you so much."

"It's my pleasure. Let me just take your name. First name is all I need."

"M-Mary," the woman stuttered.

"Perfect. I'll be sure to write it on there to make sure no one touches it."

"Thank you." Mary's voice quivered as if the tears might return at any second. She left the shop, climbed back into her car and pulled out into the traffic.

Fiona knew she would not come back. They never did. But knowing she could return at any time within the next two months would allow her the space and time she needed to part with her grandfather's things.

Watching her drive away, Fiona slowly lowered herself into a chair at the small table they kept in the shop for customers and staff to have coffee. A crushing sadness forced her into the seat. Fiona didn't know that woman. But something about her pain had triggered 'It'. 'It' was the name she gave to her depression, which had haunted her since retiring. Most of the time she could handle it. 'Stay busy, keep mind and body occupied' was her mantra. Hence why she'd become a charity-shop volunteer, and it had worked up to a certain point. However, sometimes the corrosive feeling snuck under her defences, taking her by surprise, just as it was doing now.

She cuffed a tear and called for Simon Le Bon, her small, scruffy terrier cross. Ears pricking up, he bounded out of his bed by the till to see what the fuss was about. Dogs are sensitive animals. He could probably smell the sadness radiating off her.

Instinctively, he leaped onto her lap and pushed his warm furry body into hers. Though not erasing it completely, her canine comforter took the edge off her depression, offering temporary respite to that overthinking brain of hers. It had been fully engaged when she'd worked for a busy London publisher, pushed to the limits every day, overwhelmed and tangled up with too much to do and too little time.

After retiring, Fiona had thought she'd enjoy giving her brain a rest. She did at first, luxuriating in not having anything to think about. But after a while, her brain cells stood idle. The thing about depression is that it loves a vacuum. Thrives in it. Rushing in when her work had vacated the space, it took up residence and had stayed ever since. No number of crosswords or sudoku or hours spent managing a charity shop would shift or distract it. What she really needed was something big to occupy all that surplus mental energy. An investigation. A crime to solve, big enough to consume that overactive brain of hers, to fully occupy it so it would think about nothing else.

For now, she'd have to make do with the three comforters that never let her down: her friends, Simon Le Bon and cake. She had one, and the other two were on their way.

CHAPTER 2

The parking space outside the shop didn't stay vacated for long. Another car filled it, rattling to a halt. It was the battered Fiat Uno belonging to Partial Sue, who was partial to saying partial a lot.

Simon Le Bon jumped down off Fiona's lap as she got to her feet. Snatching up a donated mirror labelled with a three-pound sticker, she checked her face for signs of puffiness. She didn't want any of her co-workers to see her distress. Didn't want them to worry. She ran her fingers through her short, dark hair, noticing a few new white streaks. Satisfied with her appearance, she put on a brave face, as she always did.

Every day, Dogs Need Nice Homes had a ritual. They would start the morning with a nice cup of tea and a slice of cake, selling any leftovers to customers for a pound a slice. A warming prospect to begin the day, even if it had begun in a dark place. However, today was Partial Sue's turn to provide the cake, which always made Fiona a tad nervous, as she was partial to saving a bob or two. Fiona, on the other hand, maintained that corners should never be cut where cake was concerned, only slices.

Partial Sue's slight and skinny frame burst through the door, a bag for life in one hand. Far too lithe and animated for this early in the day, her bright, alert eyes fixed on Fiona from beneath a severe grey fringe. "Morning!"

"Morning, Sue. How are you?"

"It's brass monkeys out there. What happened to summer?"

"Don't know. But you know what this country's like. We get a couple of good weeks at the beginning and that counts as summer."

"True, true."

"Did you get the cake?" Fiona asked.

Partial Sue was about to answer when the Wicker Man from next door entered, lured as usual by the possibility of scrounging free cake. His name was Trevor, but everyone called him the Wicker Man because he sold old-school seventies'-style wicker furniture. Though he never seemed to actually *sell* anything, which had led the ladies of Dogs Need Nice Homes to conjecture that his dodgy, cash-only business was some sort of front for money laundering.

"Cold enough for you?" he said heartily.

Fiona had never understood why anyone uttered that question when the weather turned bitter, as if the person it was aimed at had put in a request for the temperature to be lowered on their behalf and were now being asked if it suited them. When the temperature rose, if it ever did, he'd undoubtedly start asking the opposite.

"I've had to throw on a cravat to keep the old neckular region warm." He adjusted the folded silk, which was tucked into his shirt beneath a V-neck sweater. The Wicker Man had taken to sporting a cravat on a daily basis but continued to make weak excuses for wearing one, it being all part of his plummy, eccentric Englishman act, despite originally hailing from Clacton. He pulled out a chair and slotted himself around the little table.

"Anyone for a cup of tea?" Partial Sue was about to head for the storeroom to put the kettle on when she halted abruptly, her magpie eyes spotting the box on the counter. "Oh, are those new donations? I am partial to a first rummage." She made a beeline for it.

Fiona stopped her. "Hands off. I'm keeping those safe for a customer. Which reminds me, I need to write her name on it." She found a marker pen by the till and scrawled Mary's name and the date on top of the box, along with *Do Not Touch*.

"Can't I just have a peek?" Also partial to a bargain, she couldn't stand the thought of missing out on something good.

"It's for a sorrowful donor," Fiona replied in a whisper. She placed the box on the floor behind the counter.

"Ah, okay. Fair enough." Partial Sue backed away into the storeroom and filled up the kettle.

Ears like a bat's, the Wicker Man questioned, "Sorrowful donor? What in the Dickens is one of them?"

Thankfully, Fiona didn't have to answer. The doorbell rang, and in staggered Daisy in her trademark maxi dress, except she'd added a thick duffle coat over the top and a wide-brimmed hat on her head, forcing her thick mass of curly grey hair to explode out of the sides. "Sorry I'm late."

"I've only just got in myself," Partial Sue remarked. "I like the outfit. I am partial to a duffle coat. You look like Paddington's Aunt Lucy."

Daisy, who liked all things cute and cuddly, blushed happily. "Oh, thank you."

"Would you like a cup of tea?" Partial Sue asked.

"I wouldn't say no." She sat next to the Wicker Man.

"Cold enough for you?" he asked for the second time today.

"Um, I don't understand the question," Daisy replied innocently.

"It's just an expression. You know, like 'many a mickle makes a muckle'."

"I don't understand what that means either."

"I don't think anyone does," Partial Sue called out above the bubbling kettle.

Fiona filled them in. "It means many small things can add up to a lot. It's Old Norse, I think."

"Like 'stack 'em high, sell 'em cheap'," the Wicker Man declared. "That's my business motto."

It would be, if you actually sold anything, Fiona thought to herself.

Partial Sue brought out the teapot clad in a thick, home-made crocheted cosy. She placed it in the middle of the table and gave everyone a cup and saucer. "Let it brew for a while."

Daisy rubbed her hands, relishing the highlight of the day. "So, what cake did you get? It was your turn, wasn't it?"

"Oh, yes. Almost forgot." Partial Sue retrieved her bag for life and delved inside. Those assembled around the table leaned in, eager to see what baked delight she'd brought them. After rummaging around, she pulled out her hand and held aloft a small rectangular pack. "Ta-da!" She placed it on a plate in the middle of the table.

The awaiting faces dropped.

"Oh," said the Wicker Man, not hiding his disappointment.

"What's that?" asked Fiona.

"Malt loaf."

"I can see that," she replied.

Daisy winced. "I don't like malt loaf. It's too gooey. Sticks to the roof of my mouth."

"Is it bona fide cake?" asked the Wicker Man.

"Course it's cake," Partial Sue replied.

"It's a loaf, not a cake," Daisy pointed out, distress creeping into her voice. "Victoria sponge is cake, lemon drizzle is cake, coffee and walnut is cake. This is a . . . a . . ."

"Sweet bread," the Wicker Man chimed in.

To an outsider this might have seemed an overreaction, but to the ladies of Dogs Need Nice Homes and, to a lesser extent, the Wicker Man, cake was a very serious business indeed. They were connoisseurs. Not pretentious, but they did like to chomp into a slice of something moist, light and half decent. But now it seemed that standards were slipping in the cake-purchasing department. A poor-quality cake would have been bad enough, but did this even class as the right food group?

"Have you been to the twenty-pence shop again?" Fiona demanded.

"No," Partial Sue replied. Then, after a beat, she said, "Well, yes. Sort of."

"How can you 'sort of' go to the twenty-pence shop?" asked Daisy.

"Because it's now the twenty-five-pence shop. Cost of living's gone up. But how did you know I'd been there?"

"Because it's not even a proper Soreen," Fiona added. "The logo's the same, but it's called Moreen." Brand appropriation was rife at the twenty-five-pence shop, formerly known as the twenty-pence shop.

The Wicker Man drained his tea and made himself scarce, not wanting to wade any deeper into this sticky conundrum. Just as well, because the is-malt-loaf-a-cake debate continued all morning and well into the afternoon, neither side budging. Google had never had so many hits about the culinary status of malt loaf. With two against one, Partial Sue resorted to asking customers their opinion on the matter, hoping for a bit of support, until Fiona pointed out that it wasn't appropriate to include them in their little debate, besides the fact that no one wanted to buy a slice of malt loaf for a pound. They couldn't give it away. For the rest of the day the shop was quiet, and it wasn't just the lack of customers put off by the cold. Partial Sue's malt-loaf faux pas had put them all in a bad mood.

Fiona's depression refused to budge, not helped by being denied the daily fix of sponge and customary sweet, sticky filling. Stubbornly, Fiona and Daisy refused to get a replacement, believing that Partial Sue had not fulfilled her obligation. Partial Sue also refused on the grounds that she had. In the end they came to an agreement and drew up a spreadsheet on the shop's ancient laptop, listing what constituted as acceptable cake. Malt loaf didn't make the cut. Neither did lardy cake, and Jaffa Cakes didn't count either. Technically, they had been proven to be a cake and not a biscuit (by the fact that they hardened when stale, as did cake, while biscuits went soft). They all loved Jaffa Cakes but agreed that they didn't give you the same sense of wonder and ritual as proper cake. It was more of a stopgap, an emergency substitute you bought at a newsagent or a petrol station when the real thing wasn't available. The twenty-five-pence shop as it was now known was also blacklisted as an acceptable cake-purchasing establishment. They all felt much better now that clear lines had been drawn and everyone knew what was expected of them.

Towards the end of the day, just before closing, the doorbell tinkled, and a smartly dressed man in a grey suit entered. He had a plain, round face, making it difficult to place his age. Fiona would have guessed anywhere between thirty-five and fifty. His eyes were small, but not unkind.

"We're just about to close," she informed him. "Do you know what you're after? Maybe I can help you find it."

"Oh, my apologies," he replied. "I'm not here to buy anything, although your shop is very charming." He glanced around at the rich dark-wood panels. "My name's Owens, Antony Owens. I'm the liaison officer for the Beach Hut Residents' Association on Mudeford Spit. I'm here seeking the assistance of the Charity Shop Detective Agency. I was wondering if you might help me solve a murder."

CHAPTER 3

Fiona gave the nod, and the Charity Shop Detective Agency sprang into action — although their version of 'action' involved making a fresh pot of tea, spreading chocolate digestives on a plate and placing them in front of their guest. After introductions, they scooched their chairs in closer, collective midriffs squishing against the table. Daisy poured. She could have done with leaving it to brew longer but they were all keen to hear what Antony Owens had to say.

Before speaking he carefully added a considered measure of milk, stirring it precisely three rotations. He then took a small, delicate sip, possibly testing its temperature, leading Fiona to conclude he was perhaps a fastidiously cautious man who didn't like surprises and wanted to be prepared for every eventuality. Carefully, he repositioned his cup on the saucer and adjusted the cuffs of his suit.

"Firstly, I think I should point out that 'liaison officer' is not my day job. I'm a solicitor — conveyancing. I just do this as a little sideline. Beach hut owners pay me a small subscription and in return I represent their needs, making sure they have a say about what happens on Mudeford Spit. I used to have a beach hut myself so I know the kind of things that rattle them."

"Like a murder," Fiona said.

"Yes, I'm afraid the murder has sent a cold shiver down everyone's backs."

"It was on the front cover of the newspaper," Daisy shuddered. "A man got burned alive. *In his own beach hut*." Daisy tended to read only the headlines of newspapers, and only those publications that were most liberal with the truth, twisting and wrestling everything into the most shocking version of what had happened.

"That's not what I read," Partial Sue pointed out. "He died later of smoke inhalation."

Antony shifted in his seat. "That's right. A very brave mother of two named Annie Follet risked her own life. Knocked down the door and dragged the poor man out. Malcolm Crainey was his name. He died a few minutes later from smoke inhalation, before the ambulance could get to him. She tried to resuscitate him."

Daisy slapped a hand over her mouth. "Oh, my gosh. That's terrible."

"Then she started trying to put the fire out with a bucket," Partial Sue said. "Real hero, that one."

"I read the police are treating it as murder," Fiona said.

"That's right," Antony replied. "The fire was started on purpose."

"Do they have any suspects?" Partial Sue asked.

Antony shook his head. "Police are tight-lipped, but there have been no arrests. So my guess is no."

"Who's leading the investigation?" Fiona asked.

"DI Fincher and DS Thomas, or smart cop, scruffy cop, as I call them."

"We know them well," Fiona said.

"You do?" Antony looked pleased at this. "That should make things a little easier."

Partial Sue made a *meh* sound, then clarified. "We sort of get along, but I think DI Fincher would rather we stuck to running a charity shop."

Antony looked worried, his forehead a matrix of creases. "Will you still help me find who did this? I know it only happened three weeks ago, which isn't long in terms of an investigation, but I'm getting a lot of pressure from the owners. They don't feel safe, but they're also losing a lot of money."

"Losing money?" Fiona questioned.

"Yes, a few beach hut owners rent theirs out in the summer for the odd week or two, or longer. Bookings have been cancelled left, right and centre because of this. Annie, for example, the woman who pulled Malcolm out of the burning hut, she was a renter. Planned to rent a beach hut for the whole of the summer holidays with her kids. She cancelled. So have a lot of others. This incident has scared them off. I really need to find who did this."

Fiona looked around the table at her friends, throwing them a questioning look, making sure they were both on board with taking this case. Eyes bright and wide, Daisy and Partial Sue looked eager to get started. Fiona turned her attention back to Antony. "Yes, we'll help you."

Antony physically sagged in the middle with relief, then quickly regained his shape, as if someone had reinflated him. "Thank you. But first I must ask what your fee is? The beach owners have clubbed together a little sum of money to pay for this private investigation. It's not much."

"Oh, there's no fee," Partial Sue replied.

Antony glanced at the faces around the table. "What?"

"There's no charge," Fiona answered. "All we ask is you make a donation to Dogs Need Nice Homes. Whatever you think is appropriate."

Antony's face broke into a smile, not quite believing his luck. "Well, I'll donate the whole lot if you find the killer."

"Deal," Fiona said.

Antony's smile grew wider. "Consider yourselves hired."

CHAPTER 4

A smart and shiny vinyl folder with reinforced brass corners slid across the table in Fiona's direction. She picked it up and examined it, flipping open the stiff cover. Antony Owens' business card was slotted neatly inside, together with two pages secured by a spring-loaded metal bracket; a little overengineered to house only a couple of sheets of paper and a rectangle of card, leading Fiona to deduce that Antony Owen had a fetish for stationery, a-place-for-everything-and-everything-in-its-place kind of guy. She'd bet her life he used to be one of those annoying kids who got a thrill at the end of the summer holidays when the Back-to-School posters went up in WHSmith. Still, Fiona couldn't talk. She had alphabetised the bookshelves in the charity shop and had never looked back.

Fiona scanned the two pages in the folder. They were computer printouts listing names, numbers and addresses, nearly 200 at a guess, maybe more. Some were marked with a bright yellow highlighter using a ruler, no less, each regimental stripe of yellow perfectly parallel to the next. She passed the folder on to Daisy and Partial Sue to examine.

"Those are the contact details of everyone who owns a beach hut on Mudeford Spit," Antony informed them. "The highlighted ones are the people who were in their huts on the fateful night. Although I doubt they'll be much use."

"How come?" asked Fiona.

"No one saw anything. Police interviewed all of them. Wouldn't let anyone set foot off the spit until they'd taken a detailed statement. Everyone claimed to be asleep until they were woken up by fire engine and ambulance sirens."

"Apart from this Annie Follet," Fiona said.

"Yes, she claims to have left her beach hut at around 3.30 a.m. to go to the loo. Beach huts don't have toilets, you see."

Partial Sue nearly choked. "They don't have toilets! They cost an arm and a leg, and they don't have toilets!"

"I heard one went for half a million pounds recently," Daisy added.

Partial Sue snorted her disapproval. "A fool and his money are soon parted."

"I don't know . . ." Daisy smiled. "I'd love to have a beach hut down there."

"Yeah, so would I." Partial Sue rubbed her fingertips together. "If I had a spare five hundred grand lying around, but not if I had to pee in public."

Fiona didn't have the energy to point out that peeing in public was something very different from peeing in a public convenience.

Daisy continued with her beach hut fantasy. "You could all come around for hot chocolate with little marshmallows and squirty cream on top — you included, Antony. I'd make it all cosy with a log burner and a big squishy sofa."

Before Daisy's imagination could embellish things further, probably incorporating finer details such as choice of soft furnishings, throws and which ornamental dolls she'd handpick from her main collection, Fiona brought the conversation back on track. "And when Annie went to the toilet, that's when she saw the fire?"

"Yes, that's correct," Antony answered.

"Did she see anyone else?"

Antony shook his head. "Not as far as I know."

"No one running from the scene?"

"It's very dark down there at night. Police have interviewed her repeatedly. She saw nothing."

Partial Sue poured everyone more tea. "We'll speak to her ourselves, but how come she's not a suspect? I mean, if she was the only one up at that time, and saw no one else?"

Antony declined the offer of tea, placing his hand over his cup. "That I don't know. I'm afraid my knowledge is limited. Only bits and pieces I've managed to glean from the police, and the newspapers. Then there's the second- and third-hand hearsay from the beach hut owners. Not the most reliable source. Plus, they don't know Annie, as she was only renting. It's a little community down there. Gossip travels fast but only if you're in their circle."

Fiona got a shiver down her spine. The way Antony described it made the place sound like some insular community wary of outsiders. An us-and-them culture. Shades of *The Wicker Man* (the film, not their cravatted neighbour). Mudeford Spit wasn't isolated, but it certainly had the potential to be closed off. She dismissed the idea for now. Had to be led by facts and evidence, not preconceived prejudices. One thing was sure, Annie Follet had been a local hero for risking her life to drag Malcolm Crainey out of the burning beach hut. She remembered the papers being full of it for a day or two, until they'd moved on to something else. She smiled and reassured Antony. "Don't worry, we'll get to the bottom of this."

"Wonderful. The beach hut owners will be pleased." Relief crept into Antony's voice. The owners must have been leaning on him heavily to get a result. He celebrated the positive outcome by selecting a chocolate digestive. Taking his time, his hand hovered over the plate even though they were all identical. He picked one up with his thumb and forefinger and nibbled rather than biting it. With his other hand, he cupped any stray crumbs to prevent them from falling onto his smart suit.

When he'd finished his biscuit, he dusted his hands of crumbs and rose to his feet, tugging on his cuffs and smoothing down his suit. "Well, I'd better be going. You have my details. Call me if you need anything."

"Oh." Fiona was a little surprised at the abruptness of his departure. There was more they needed to know. "Could you spare us a few more minutes of your time?"

"I'm supposed to meet my wife. But, yes, okay." He reluctantly sat back down, glancing outside the shop, possibly searching for his spouse.

Fiona continued, "The victim, Malcolm Crainey. Do you know if he had any enemies?"

The network of creases was back on Antony's forehead. Fiona could see why he'd been so keen to leave, perhaps hoping to make his exit without having to answer the most important question of all: why would anyone want to kill Malcolm Crainey?

Antony straightened his cuffs again, giving each one a little tug, then another after that, followed by several more: a nervous tic. "I don't believe he did."

"What was he like as a person?" asked Daisy. "What did he do for a living?"

Antony smiled weakly and took a deep breath. "Malcolm didn't work. He was a one-off. Eccentric. A local character, you might say. Great big beard, masses of long grey hair. Reminded me of a taller, skinnier Billy Connolly."

His description didn't seem to fit the type who would have the means to own a beach hut on Mudeford Spit. "How could he afford a hut?" asked Fiona. "Was he an eccentric millionaire?"

Antony snorted at the idea. "Gosh, no. I think a relation left it to him. But I can't be sure of that."

"How old was he?" Daisy asked.

"Seventy-one, I believe."

"And what did the genteel beach hut owners all think of this ragamuffin in their midst?" asked Fiona.

"They all loved him and his hut. It was a bit of a local landmark. Front of it was covered in shells and junk he'd collected and beachcombed."

22

Daisy gasped. "Oh, my gosh. Yes, I remember seeing the picture in the newspaper before it burned. I loved that beach hut. Covered in little knick-knacks."

"And big ones too," Partial Sue added. "I think he had giant clam shells fixed to the deck like seats."

"That's right," Antony agreed. "He'd let kids sit in them while their parents took pictures."

Even Fiona, who was a relative newcomer to the area, had walked to the end of the spit many a time and knew of the infamous hut with its kleptomaniac style.

Daisy did a Google search and held her phone around for everyone to see. The search engine was littered with pictures of the eccentric hut. Number 117, probably the most photographed and Instagrammed hut on the whole of the spit. Every inch of its frontage was peppered with shells, foraged sea glass, figurines and little statues, bits of old boat and pieces of broken china stuck on with glue. The multifarious mess spread down the wall and onto the deck, right down to the sand. At the opposite end, crowning off the top of the whole mad ensemble was a huge pair of deer antlers adorning the apex of the pitched roof.

"Did anyone take exception to its appearance?" Fiona asked.

Antony hesitated and then chose his words carefully. "There is nothing in the rules that says you can't add a bit of character to your hut, as long as it stays within the regulations for height and width, et cetera."

It wasn't the answer to the question she had asked. Fiona tried again. "What did other beach hut owners think of it?"

Antony hesitated again. "Er, I've heard a few people were a bit grumpy."

"Who in particular? Can you give us names?" Partial Sue asked.

"I wouldn't know who exactly," Antony replied. "But you know how people are."

Fiona did. Her neighbours, though lovely, would often give her sideways glances if she left her bin out past twelve o'clock after it had been emptied on collection day. Not toeing the line was frowned upon. Any deviation from the norm or anyone who was different or stood out from the crowd would stir up strong feelings in a population that wanted everyone to be just like them. The who-do-you-think-you-are response was a strong one in this country. Mudeford Spit would undoubtedly be a microcosm of this, perhaps even worse as Fiona imagined there would be an unwritten etiquette to follow in the compact community. Would that be a powerful enough motive for murder? She hoped not. But she was determined to find out.

A woman appeared at the shop door, peering through the window, squinting to make out who was inside.

"Oh, there's my wife," Antony said. "She probably got fed up waiting for me." Before he could get up, she had elbowed the door open and stepped in, her smart heels clacking on the ancient parquet floor. In one hand she clutched a neat brown parcel.

"There you are," she said. Like her husband, she was immaculately dressed, but far more glamorously in a red double-breasted overcoat with large black buttons. Her face looked professionally made up and her blonde hair was as straight as dried spaghetti.

Antony got to his feet and introduced her. "This is my wife, Olivia."

"Hello. Pleased to meet you."

"Fiona, Sue and Daisy are going to help solve the beach hut murder," Antony announced.

Olivia smiled but her eyes betrayed her. They darted erratically around the shop, surveying the counter and everything on display as if some preowned object might reach out and grab her. Judging by her appearance, Fiona would wager that Olivia had never owned anything second-hand in her life and didn't want to start any time soon. Drawing her arms up close to her body, she looked genuinely terrified that her hand might accidentally brush against something unclean.

"We really must be going, Antony." She held up the small parcel. "Apologies for dragging my husband away, but I need to drop this off at one of those automated postal locker thingies and I simply hate putting my fingers on the touchscreen."

Maybe she wasn't a snob, just a germophobe.

"Oh, would you like a disinfectant wipe?" Daisy instantly produced a packet from somewhere on her person. Like some hygienic ninja, Daisy always seemed to have cleaning products hidden in the folds of her clothes.

"No, that's very kind of you," Olivia replied. "No matter how clean they are, I can't bear touching them. Antony has to do it for me."

"It's the only drawback to Depop," Antony said.

"What's Depop?" Daisy asked.

"It's like eBay but just for fashion," Olivia answered.

"It's a great little money-spinner," Antony enthused. "Olivia sells a lot of her unwanted clothes on Depop. She's great with all this new technology. Whereas I'm useless. Olivia just doesn't like public touchscreens."

She glared at him, a mixture of shame and annoyance. He'd clearly shared too much. So, Olivia didn't mind things being second-hand, as long as they were heading in someone else's direction.

"Well, I'd better be going. Please call me if you need anything else." Antony did his cuff-tugging and headed towards the door with his wife.

"Oh," said Partial Sue. "Before you go, do you have a copy of the fire investigation report?"

Antony turned. "No, I'm afraid I don't. I tried to get one, but the fire service keeps stuff like that close to their chests. You have my number. Please call me if you need anything else and thank you once more for taking this case on."

"You're very welcome." Fiona smiled.

"One last question," Partial Sue piped up. "Where do you stand on malt l—"

"Not now," Fiona cut her off.

They said their goodbyes and were gone.

25

"What do you make of all that?" Fiona asked.

"Yeah, I'd say definitely got money problems," Partial Sue remarked, carrying on before Fiona could mention that she was referring to the case and not the couple. "Seen it before a million times. He's got a second job and she's selling stuff online to keep the wolf from the door." Partial Sue had been an accountant before she retired and knew the signs. Although, you didn't need to know how to fill out a tax return to notice they were living beyond their means, with their expensive clothes, well-manicured fingers and, undoubtedly, his Staples account.

Fiona felt a tinge of sadness for the pair. Money worries were guaranteed to send your life into a tailspin, but there was more to it than just lack of funds. "I don't like to make snap judgements, but I get the feeling he's intimidated by the hut owners."

Daisy took a chocolate digestive and snapped it in half. "Yes, but can you blame them?" She took a neat little bite. "Their peaceful haven is no longer a peaceful haven. It's a murder scene."

Fiona got biscuit envy and helped herself to one. "Yes, I suppose they're scared, and scared people act rashly."

Partial Sue completed the trio of digestive gobbling. "I imagine that liaison job was a cushy little number before this. Getting people to agree on the colour of the recycling bins and sending polite notices telling people to flush the public lavs properly."

Reluctantly Fiona voiced her theory. "I know it's early days, but from an initial perspective, it would seem like a case of someone taking an exception to Malcolm and his eccentric beach hut."

"You think it's one of the owners?" asked Partial Sue.

"Or maybe a group of them. It seems like the classic genteel neighbourhood not tolerating the homeowner who paints their picket fence pink instead of white."

"Do you think someone would commit murder over a few shells and bits and bobs?" asked Partial Sue.

"It's just a theory, but think about it. These people have paid hundreds of thousands of pounds for their little square of tranquillity, only for it to be disrupted by someone who not only didn't pay for it, but then covers it in all sorts of detritus."

Daisy gawked. "Well, I wouldn't call it detritus. More of a life-size collage. Maybe they didn't want to actually kill him. Maybe it was just his beach hut they wanted to destroy, and they didn't know he was in it."

"That's a strong possibility." Partial Sue crunched into another digestive. "We need to speak to this Annie Follet. Pity we can't get our hands on that fire investigation report."

Fiona got out her phone. "I think I might know someone who can."

CHAPTER 5

A narrow ribbon of tarmac unravelled in front of them, just wide enough to fit a single car. The only traffic that troubled its windy bends were cyclists, scooters and a rattly Noddy train. All other vehicles were banned. To the left, the docile waters of Christchurch Harbour, fringed by golden reed beds, ruffled in the bitter evening breeze. A lone dinghy skittered across the shallow water, leaning at a jaunty angle. To the right, the sleeping sandstone giant of Hengistbury Head loomed above them. People had lived here since the Palaeolithic times; nowadays it was an unspoilt walkers' dream. Tufted with quivering heather and flanked by yellow cliffs, the flattish summit of the headland offered 360-degree views over the English Channel and the harbour, and was dotted with a single, lonely building: a sturdy, stone-built coastguard station. From there the plateau of Hengistbury Head gently sloped towards the ladies' destination: a long shelf of sand separating the sea from the harbour with a parade of colourful beach huts in between. Mudeford Spit.

"How long's this going to take?" asked Daisy. "My legs are already famished."

Fiona was sure she meant to say fatigued. Daisy often got her words confused and would conjure up some truly bizarre expressions. Although, in this case, Fiona wouldn't rule out the possibility that legs could be hungry.

"It's about half an hour to the spit," Partial Sue answered. They'd only been walking for about ten minutes.

"Half an hour!"

Realistically it would probably take a lot longer, what with Simon Le Bon halting them every five minutes to do his 'wants' or investigate a compelling smell, but Fiona held back this detail. "You've done this walk before, haven't you?" she asked.

"Yes, lots of times," Daisy answered. "Well, on the Noddy train."

A shrill bleeping interrupted their discussion, like an anxious piccolo. An orange-beaked blur of black and white skimmed over the dark waters of the harbour.

"That's an oystercatcher, that is," Partial Sue remarked. "I am partial to a spot of twitching. I wish I'd brought my binoculars."

"This place is teeming with birds," Fiona replied.

"It's usually teeming with people," Partial Sue said, "and we're the only ones down here. Where is everyone? It's August, for crying out loud."

Daisy did up another button. "Cold weather's keeping everyone away. That, and the murder. Can we have a hot chocolate at the restaurant to warm us up?"

"If it's open," Partial Sue replied. "I doubt they're doing much trade in these temperatures."

Ten minutes later, the footpath made a ninety-degree turn, and the idyllic harbour views became camouflaged by dense woodland. Trees arched above them, creating a tunnel of green. Branches hung low in places, heavy under their own weight, as if beckoning passers-by to come and climb. Normally kids would be clambering all over them, but today their limbs were bereft of small hands clutching at their bark.

"These woods give me the creeps," Daisy said with a shiver.

"I know what you mean," Fiona replied. "Especially as we're the only ones here."

The blast of a horn from behind made them jump. Simon Le Bon whimpered, and they all leaped out of the way. Once they'd recovered, they spied the cause of their alarm. Sophie Haverford had stopped up ahead and was standing triumphantly with one foot perched on an electric scooter. Somehow she'd managed to control the thing wearing kitten heels, bizarrely paired with thick socks and a forest-green jumpsuit, with a blanket-like pashmina encircling her neck. Nobody else would have been able to pull off that look.

Sophie was Fiona's nemesis who managed the Cats Alliance charity shop across the road from Dogs Need Nice Homes. Sophie thought she was better than everyone else, but she thought she was particularly better than Fiona, and sought to prove it at any opportunity. Throwing back her perfect, black-bobbed head, she guffawed with a little too much gusto for Fiona's liking. A hearty pantomime thigh slap was added, just in case they didn't know how much she was enjoying this. "Your faces! What a picture!"

Fiona failed to see the funny side of it. "Sophie, you stupid idiot! You nearly ran us over!"

"Relax, I was in control the whole time."

"You bloody maniac," Partial Sue shouted. "You're going to kill someone with that thing."

"It's an e-scooter, dear." Sophie replied. "I rented it from the council. I'm doing my bit for the environment."

"What, by killing people?" Daisy remarked.

The scooter hummed into life and Sophie whizzed towards them. The three ladies darted for the edge of the footpath again. Simon Le Bon growled at the oncoming contraption.

Sophie braked at the last moment, skidding slightly. "You three are such a bunch of nervous Nellies. What are you doing down here, anyway?"

"None of your business," Fiona snapped.

"Mm." Sophie rubbed her chin. "Oh, don't tell me. Is it a bit of amateur sleuthing?"

"Might be," Partial Sue replied.

Sophie looked pleased with herself. "It is, isn't it? There's that burned-out beach hut down there. That's the case you're working on. I got it right, didn't I? Pretty good detective, huh? You should hire me. I'd solve the case in a heartbeat. I'm sure I could have landed the role as a TV detective, you know, if I hadn't decided to become a PR maven."

Sophie had a habit of convincing anyone who would listen that if she hadn't been the world's best PR guru (her words) then she could've been the world's best actress/ballet dancer/composer/surgeon/peace negotiator/Nobel Prize winner (delete as appropriate).

"What are *you* doing down here, while we're on the subject?" asked Fiona, swiftly derailing the woman's ego trip.

"I'm so glad you asked. I'm off to see my good friend Bitsy. She's summering down here, for a bit of a change from the South of France. Hired a beach hut."

"How long has she been here?" asked Fiona.

Sophie jerked her head back, taking offence at Fiona's question. "She's not the beach hut murderer, if that's what you're thinking. She only arrived today. But she's a hoot. She used to be an It girl in the eighties. You simply must come and meet her."

Behind them came the slow, tired squeak of a regular bicycle.

"Hurry up, slowcoach," Sophie called out.

They all turned to see Sophie's assistant, Gail, red-faced and huffing as she pedalled painfully slowly on her old-school shopping bike, wearing a wonky helmet and smudged hi-vis vest. Gail was a person of few words. Fiona liked her, had a lot of time for her. They all did. What she lacked in syllables, she made up for with her talent for technology, which made Fiona wonder why Sophie would want her anywhere near her socialite bestie.

Gail pulled up with a whine of brakes. "All right?" she gasped, leaning on the bars for a respite. Her wooden hiking cane was secured to a rickety rack on the back.

"Hi, Gail," the ladies replied.

"Gail here is going to be our drinks server for the evening," Sophie announced.

Now it was clear. Gail was on skivvy duty. Fiona hoped she was being paid for her time.

"Your drinks server?" questioned Partial Sue. "How many of you are there?"

"Oh, just me and Bitsy. Come on, Gail. No time to hang around. We've got merry to make. Well, I do." Sophie giggled, hit the accelerator button and executed a perfect 180-degree turn. "Remember to join us for a drink when you've finished all your private dicking. It's hut ninety-eight, facing the sea. Come on, Gail. You've got drinks to pour. Toodle-oo."

Gail barely had time to snatch some much-needed gulps of air before she was off pedalling after her boss.

"Poor Gail," Daisy said. "She looks exhausted."

Partial Sue nodded. "And having to pour drinks for Sophie and this Bitsy all night, who, by the way, sounds awful. Worse than Sophie, if that's even possible. We need to avoid that hut at all costs."

They all nodded but Fiona secretly had other ideas.

Eventually, they emerged from the trees, and the harbour reappeared on their left. The tarmac path was swallowed by soft, velvety yellow sand, heralding the start of Mudeford Spit and its two poker-straight rows of colourful beach huts: one facing the harbour and one facing the sea. Before these, as if nudging them together, stood a larger, more sprawling building: Tides Restaurant, flanked on the other side by dipping grass-covered dunes. Flat-roofed and built of salt-scarred and sun-bleached wood, the restaurant straddled almost the whole width of the spit. A generous deck lay out front, commanding glorious views over the harbour and the priory beyond that dominated the skyline. Today, however, the restaurant's tables and chairs sat vacant, its windows dark and lifeless. In what should have been the busiest month of the year, there was something unsettling about a freezing cold August and a deserted restaurant.

Daisy's face contorted into a mask of disappointment. "Darn it. Restaurant's closed. I'm gasping for a hot chocolate."

"They've got something better than that." Fiona pointed to a corner of the roof, clustered with CCTV cameras at various angles.

Partial Sue stepped up onto the empty deck. One by one, she positioned herself beneath the cameras and aligned herself with the direction they each faced. "All angles are covered. And that bottom one has a clear line of sight down the fronts of all the beach huts on this side."

"Wait there." Fiona darted around to the back of the restaurant to the side that faced the sea and the Isle of Wight beyond. A minute later she returned. "It's the same round the back. Four cameras. Every direction covered. Uninterrupted view down the front of the beach huts facing the sea. Plus, there's a camera covering the narrow gap between the backs of the two rows of huts."

Partial Sue gasped. "That means you can't get on or off the spit without being caught on camera."

They exchanged blank glances, this new revelation not making any sense. Anyone with a mind to commit arson would've been captured either coming or going, or emerging from their hut, so long as all the cameras were functional.

Daisy scrunched up her face. "Can anyone hear a steam train?"

CHAPTER 6

Fiona cocked her head to one side. Daisy was right. The heaving and chuffing clatter of a steam train reached her ears, growing louder all the time. But they were nowhere near a railway line. "Maybe it's the Noddy train?"

Partial Sue strained to listen. "That's not the Noddy train. Sounds like a real train to me."

"It's coming from over there." Daisy pointed down the spit. They followed the direction of the bizarre sound, complete with piercing whistle, which startled the seabirds near the shoreline, forcing them to take flight. Up ahead, the noise suddenly increased as the French windows of beach hut number seven swung open. Out stepped a sturdy man in safari shorts, hiking sandals and a multi-pocketed fishermen's vest over a blue-checked shirt. His meaty calves were swathed in woolly socks pulled up to his knees. With thick, wiry, salt-and-pepper hair, and moustache to match, he plonked himself down in a deck chair, travel mug in hand, face content as the symphony of steam washed over him.

Noticing the three pairs of eyes staring at him, he jerked up. "I can turn it down if it's bothering you."

"Is that a steam train?" Daisy asked.

Almost offended by Daisy's simplistic description, he replied, "It's an LNER Class A4 4468 Mallard. World's fastest and most beautiful steam locomotive." He produced a remote control from one of the many pockets in his vest and reduced the volume. "I have it on my iPod dock, plus fifty other steam locomotives. I can name them all just by their sound. Unique, they are. I didn't realise anyone was here, or I would've used my headphones."

"Yes, people are a bit thin on the ground at the moment," Fiona remarked.

"Have been since the fire," he replied. "It's frightened a lot of them off, but not me."

"Were you here that night?" Fiona asked.

"No, I wasn't."

Surreptitiously, Fiona slipped the list of beach hut owners from her pocket, the one that Antony Owens had given her, minus the fancy folder. Glancing down the list she found beach hut number seven. Owner: Frank Marshall. His details weren't highlighted.

"Any ideas who did it?" Partial Sue asked.

Frank Marshall made a fist with his free hand. "No, but if I get my hands on them, I'll give them what for, I can tell you. Burning down Malcolm's hut like that. Shattering our peace. I've had this beach hut since 2008 and nothing like this has ever happened before. It's unforgivable."

"Did you know Malcolm?" Daisy asked.

"Oh, everyone knew Malcolm. Local character and all that."

"Was he liked?"

Frank Marshall hesitated. "I would say so, yes."

"What about that hut of his?" Partial Sue remarked. "Bit over the top, wasn't it? All that paraphernalia. Must have ruffled a few feathers."

Frank Marshall smirked, his moustache twitching. "Well, that was Malcolm, for you. He got away with a lot of things the rest of us wouldn't."

"Like what?" Fiona asked.

Frank Marshall hesitated again, probably not expecting to be pressed on the subject. "Oh, er, only trivial stuff. Like not pulling his bike over when the Noddy train wanted to go past. Dumping his empty bottles in the recycling bins at six in the morning when everyone's asleep. That's a definite no-no around here, seeing as most of the hut owners like to sleep in. Not me. I'm an early riser. Got to make the most of the day."

"Anybody have a problem with him? Any altercations? Any enemies?" Partial Sue made a fisticuffs action.

Frank Marshall shifted in his seat, then slurped from his travel mug. "No, I don't think so. Nobody I know. And I know everyone down here. I mean, for all his eccentricities, he made up for it in other ways." He nodded to the little wind turbine on the roof of his hut, twirling in the cold breeze. "He fixed that for me. Malcolm was a dab hand at anything mechanical, kids' scooters, bikes — you name it, he'd fix them all for free, but he was especially good at boats." He leaned back, settling into his topic. "You see, every beach hut is allowed to moor a boat in the harbour for free. So you get a lot of people suddenly buying little motor dinghies and RIBs to muck about in. Which is great until they go wrong. Malcolm would fix them for nothing. He could regularly be seen sitting on his veranda ankle-deep in bits, tinkering with someone or other's outboard motor."

"So, if he did all those nice things, why would anyone kill him?" Daisy asked.

Frank Marshall swallowed more tea down. "You want to know my theory? Random arson attack, that's all. You know what teenagers are like these days. Bored. Can't think of anything to do, so they come down here and spoil things for the rest of us. Make our lives miserable."

"Let's hope they're caught soon." Fiona ended the conversation.

Frank Marshall grunted his assent. They said their good-byes and carried on towards the end of the spit. When they were out of earshot, Partial Sue asked, "What do you make of him?"

"His name's Frank Marshall, according to the list," Fiona replied. "He was telling the truth about not being here on that night. His name's not highlighted. But there's something off about him, and it's not because he listens to steam trains."

Daisy stopped to pick up a shell and popped it in her pocket. "I quite like the sound of steam trains."

"I'm also partial to a steam engine or two," Partial Sue said. "But did you notice, he was more worried about the peace and quiet of this place being disrupted than he was about Malcolm losing his life?"

"That was cold, I thought," Daisy added. "Speaking of being cold, he didn't offer us any tea."

Fiona agreed. Frank Marshall's priorities were definitely out of whack. He seemed more outraged that a delinquent or delinquents had dared to come down here shattering the bubble of tranquillity than he was about the fact that someone had died. That this precious, sweet little preserve of sand and sea had been sullied more by arson than it had by murder. What sort of man was Frank Marshall to place his quality of life above the value of human life? Plus, like Daisy said, he hadn't offered them any tea. Always the giveaway of a wrong 'un. Fiona felt her sinister theory about the small, insular community protecting itself gain a little more ground.

CHAPTER 7

They trooped along the sand, past the rows of cheerful beach huts adorned with silly hand-painted name plaques, mostly themed around eye-watering seaside puns such as *Don't Get Tide Down*, *Looney Dunes*, *Seas The Day* and — Fiona's personal favourite — *Resting Beach Face*. Cute little verandas sat out front, each one littered with all manner of outdoor furniture. Some had stuck with traditional picnic benches and deck chairs while others were slung with loungers, hammocks or hanging seats twirling in the breeze. The ones facing the harbour side were treated to glorious sunsets, while the row behind them woke up to spectacular sunrises over the sea. Well, they would be if anyone were there to enjoy them. All the huts were locked up tight.

Daisy held up her phone, continuously filming every beach hut they passed. "Which one would you prefer, a hut by the harbour or one by the sea?"

"Neither," Partial Sue replied. "I'd save my money and invest it in a low-risk portfolio. Guaranteed return."

Daisy harrumphed at Partial Sue's cynical answer. "What about you, Fiona?"

Fiona's mind was elsewhere. Something was still bugging her. Something that hadn't made sense since they'd

38

arrived. "If there's clear CCTV at the restaurant covering the only access on and off this spit, why haven't the police released footage of the arsonist?"

Partial Sue thought for a moment. "Maybe the cameras weren't working, or the arsonist or arsonists are beach hut owners, and were already here on the night in question."

"Let's assume the CCTV was working," Fiona replied. "At three thirty in the morning, the arsonist would've been caught on camera coming out the front of their hut before they lit the fire."

Partial Sue picked up a stone. Her bowler's arm sent it skimming over the water, bouncing off the surface seven or eight times. "Maybe they prepared everything earlier in the day, when they could melt into the crowds. This cold snap hadn't started back then. The weather was better, and the place was busy. They could've casually left an incendiary device next to Malcolm's hut on a timer. Disguised it in a cool box or something that wouldn't have raised suspicion."

"Or maybe they hid it in one of the little knick-knacks Malcolm had on display when he wasn't looking," Daisy suggested. "Lots of places to hide things."

"That's what we're about to find out," Fiona replied.

Up ahead, they could see the huge square shape of Martin, a part-time fireman, who also happened to be Fiona's window cleaner. His bright red hair and beard stood out like a beacon next to the blackened carcass of beach hut number 117. Police tape flapped in the wind, encircling the burned-out hut and the ones either side of it, which were largely undamaged, apart from a little charring.

Fiona smiled. "Hello, Martin. Thank you so much for meeting with us."

"My pleasure," he replied, not shivering, despite only being clad in a short-sleeve T-shirt revealing his beefy freckled arms.

After Fiona introduced him to her two co-workers, Partial Sue jumped straight in, eager to hear how the fire started. "Did you manage to get us a copy of the fire investigation report?"

Martin shook his head. "No, but I did read it."

"So what's the verdict?" asked Fiona.

"It makes no sense."

"How come?"

Martin began gesticulating with his hands. "Well, generally speaking, arson is not a complicated crime. Someone lights a fire then scarpers. First thing we do is discover the point of origin, where the fire started. But this has a very weird point of origin. Let me show you."

Martin ducked under the caution tape, followed by the three of them.

"Er, you shouldn't be doing that," an authoritative voice boomed from behind. They swung around to see Frank Marshall standing there, hand on one hip, the other still clutching his travel mug. Fiona wondered if it was the same cup of tea, or if he'd had time to make a fresh one. Either way, she had serious tea envy.

Looking none too pleased, he pointed at the hut. "I used to own a security firm. And that is still a crime scene."

"It's okay," Martin replied, "I'm a fireman. And these ladies are private investigators, looking into the murder."

Frank Marshall relaxed his furrowed features. "Well, why didn't you say? Who hired you, if you don't mind me asking?"

"Antony Owens," Fiona replied.

Frank Marshall's tone dropped to disdainful levels. "Oh, him. I heard he was getting investigators on the case."

"What's wrong with Antony Owens?" Fiona asked, then wished she hadn't.

His finger waved around accusingly. "How can you represent beach hut owners if you're not a beach hut owner? That's what I want to know."

Partial Sue attempted to speak but Frank held up a hand to shush her. "I know what you're going to say, Owens used to own a beach hut, but he doesn't now, does he? He's not in the thick of it like the rest of us. That's why I started the Beach Hut Owners' Association to properly represent the needs of all hut owners."

"Isn't that what Antony Owens does?" Partial Sue questioned.

Frank Marshall sniggered derisively. "No, that's the Beach Hut Residents' Association. Completely different organisation. If you want something done right, you have to do it yourself, that's my philosophy. Like I said to you ladies a minute ago, it was teenagers, them hoodies. Had to be. Coming down here causing havoc. Ruining our peaceful haven. As chairman of the Beach Hut *Owners'* Association, I want to propose a curfew down here after 6 p.m. No one apart from hut owners would be allowed—"

Martin interrupted what promised to be a diatribe about the long-suffering struggle of being a luxury beach hut owner having to slum it with the riff-raff. "Would you mind if we press on? I have a shift starting soon."

"Certainly," Frank replied. "I have great respect for the fire and rescue service. I probably would have become a fireman myself if I hadn't got into security. I'd like to tag along. Hear what you've got to say. Police have told us nothing." He ducked under the tape without waiting for an answer.

"Er, I don't see why not," Martin replied.

They stood staring at the sorry sight of Malcolm's burned-out hut. The main structure, though completely blackened, was intact with all four walls still standing. However, the windows had shattered, and parts of the roof had gone. Out the front on the deck, Malcolm's collection of statues and keepsakes had either melted or turned to charcoal and ash. Up above, the antlers held on defiantly, still clinging to the apex of the roof.

Martin continued. "I wasn't on duty that night. We know Malcolm sadly lost his life due to smoke inhalation. My colleagues managed to put out the fire before the hut burned down completely, which means we have a pretty good record of the nature of this fire. Like I said, generally, arson is not a complicated crime." He leaned in and pointed to the broken front door. "An arsonist will choose the simplest and easiest way to start a fire. In this case, here, where the door meets the deck . . ."

41

Frank Marshall butted in, "To start a fire, they'd set light to some flammable material or some oily rags." Fiona could tell he desperately wanted the position of alpha male in this particular situation, perhaps all situations, and was of the high opinion that his amateur mansplaining was superior to Martin's professional expertise. "Then Bob's your father's brother — you have yourself a fire. That's how I would've done it."

Everyone stared at him, slightly shocked at the last sentence.

Frank Marshall shrank slightly, realising he'd run his mouth too much. "Not that I would ever do anything like that, of course. Please continue."

Martin waited a beat, gathering his thoughts after having them interrupted. "So, if it had started here, I'd expect to see a classic 'V' shape that a fire makes against a vertical surface. The other way to do it would've been by pouring petrol there, giving you a circular burn pattern on the deck where the petrol would have pooled against the door."

Frank Marshall clicked his fingers. "Malcolm used to fix outboard motors on his veranda. He probably spilled petrol or oil on the deck, the daft apeth. That's what happened. It all makes sense now. It's probably not arson at all. The silly old fool must have burned his own hut down."

Martin winced at Frank's unfounded theory. "Trouble is, the fire didn't start on the veranda. Maybe the arsonist was reluctant to start anything on the wooden deck in case it creaked—"

Frank clicked his fingers. "And woke Malcolm up." His interruptions were becoming more annoying by the second, causing a hiss of tinnitus to rise in Fiona's ears.

She made a swift suggestion. "Maybe we should let Martin finish what he's got to say."

Frank nodded. "Of course."

Martin continued. "Yes, in case it made a noise. If that's true, there's a gift of an opportunity that other buildings rarely offer." He crouched on the sand and pointed underneath the hut. "All the huts are built on piles, raised up about two or three feet above the sand. Most of them have had the space beneath boxed in, to use as extra storage. Clearly, not this one. There's room under there just begging to have a fire lit with all that dry timber. Two perfect places to commit arson, but our killer has ignored them both and chosen the most difficult spot to light a fire. Follow me."

Martin got up off his haunches and walked around to the narrow gap between the huts. They followed him.

"Fire's been started here, round the side on the right."

"That makes sense," Fiona remarked. "I mean, the arsonist would be hidden from view."

"True, but wait until you see this." Martin indicated a high patch of wall, an elongated 'U' shape where the fire had been more intense. The cladding had fallen away, revealing the stud wall behind, the frame exposed like burnt ribs. "It started here, about a foot above our heads. You can tell because the timber here has had a lot more time to burn, causing more damage."

"But why is that difficult?" Partial Sue asked.

Martin regarded her. "It's a lot harder to start a fire on a vertical surface. And even more difficult to start it that high up."

For once, Frank Marshall was speechless.

"What about the old trick with the can of aerosol and a lighter? Or maybe they used a blowtorch," Fiona suggested. "You know, one of those little handheld ones. Pointed it at the wood to get it going."

Martin shook his head. "Burn pattern is too big for either of those. But if they did, why start it so high? Why not just hold it at waist or chest height? Why hold it above your head?"

Frank chimed in. "Why stand there holding it at all, when you risk being discovered? You could set the torch on the ground with the flame pointed at the wood or prop it up on something. Leave it going and make your escape." Finally, Frank had made a good point. Choosing the most awkward

43

way to light a fire when there were so many easier options available seemed completely counterintuitive. The ladies of the Charity Shop Detective Agency had no answer and neither did Frank Marshall. They stood there dumbfounded.

Martin shrugged. "That's all academic, though. Blowtorches use either butane, propane or liquefied petroleum gas, as do household aerosols as a propellant. Report said none of these were present. Common or garden unleaded petrol from a filling station was the accelerant in this fire."

"What about a flamethrower?" asked Daisy. "Don't they use petrol?"

"That's true," Martin replied. "Except a flamethrower would be problematic. They're big, hefty things with tanks that strap to your back, and you can't use a flamethrower in such a confined space. The amount of heat that thing would kick out would end up burning the operator, unless they were wearing a great big asbestos suit and helmet. Burn pattern would be huge with one of those things."

Fiona stepped forward examining the large area of damage above her. "So someone brings a can of petrol down here, splashes it against the wall, admittedly a little higher than expected—"

"Above their head, unless they were seven feet tall," Martin corrected.

Fiona nodded in agreement. "Okay, someone very tall with no common sense splashes petrol against the wall, then sets it alight. That sounds quite straightforward, if a little unorthodox."

Martin sighed. "Now it gets weirder. Liquids always obey gravity. If that were the case, we'd have a vertical burn pattern, a column of damage, if you like, where the petrol ran down the wall before it was lit. But it's as if the petrol has defied gravity, puddled on a vertical surface and stayed there without running down. Burn pattern is a large circle about the size of a beach ball, then it burned upwards, creating this 'U' shape."

"Could it have been some sort of incendiary device?" Daisy asked.

"No evidence of devices whatsoever," Martin replied.

All five of them stood silently, scrutinising the devastation before them, hoping a clue might reveal itself. All they observed were varying degrees of blackness, some deeper and harsher than others. The hut gave up no clues, revealed no secrets. It stood mute, frozen in its incinerated state, stubbornly refusing to offer any answers, only more bewilderment.

CHAPTER 8

Fiona and the team said their goodbyes to Martin and thanked him for his time with the offer of unlimited tea and cake whenever he was passing the shop. He rushed off to start his shift but had promised to keep thinking about the arson attack and share any thoughts or anything he heard at work. Frank Marshall, satisfied that his nose had been poked far enough into their business, scuttled off back to his beach hut.

Insight into the origin of the fire had shed no light on the murder and had only confused them further. The evidence baffled rather than resolved anything.

Partial Sue, saddled with irritation and defeat, had wanted to turn back and head for home but Daisy wanted to continue onwards to the end of the spit as it tapered to a sandy arrowhead.

"I thought your legs were tired," Partial Sue protested.

"They are." Daisy held her phone aloft, continuing to film the last few huts. "But I want to capture all of them."

"What for?" Fiona asked.

"You'll see." She smiled mischievously.

The rows of beach huts came to an end and the ominous shape of the Smuggler's House loomed in front of them. With walls of thick, ancient grey stone and squinting black-framed windows, it had stood stoically against the worst that nature could throw it for nearly two centuries.

"Looks like something out of a Daphne Du Maurier novel," Partial Sue remarked.

Fiona had to agree. The funereal look and creepy name seemed ripe for the setting of a sinister novel. If Tides Restaurant bookended all the beach huts at the start of the spit, then the Smuggler's House was the emphatic full stop at the end. It stood guard over the Run, a narrow, treacherous neck of water that flowed out of the harbour into the sea.

Daisy swung her phone camera round to capture the house in all its gothic-horror glory. "Did you know, the locals used to think the place was haunted because they'd hear banging coming from inside the house, even when no one was home. But when the tide was really high, the cellar would flood, and the empty rum barrels would knock together."

"Er, I heard it was really a boatbuilder's house," Partial Sue said, "and that tale about the barrels knocking together is nicked from *Moonfleet*. Bit of historic embellishment to attract visitors down here."

"Well, I think it's more romantic," Daisy replied.

Whatever its history, like most traditional beachfront buildings it had been pleasantly refurbished and divided up into holiday flats, which managed to blunt the edges of a sinister past.

"Speaking of smugglers," Daisy said. "What if the arsonist came over by boat from Mudeford Quay?"

On the other side of the Run, the sweet hamlet of Mudeford Quay was a hotchpotch of fishermen's cottages, a café, a pub and a lifeboat station. Tatty fishing boats alighted there, and mountains of netted lobster pots were piled up high along its length, drying in the cool air.

Partial Sue looked longingly across at the quayside. "I used to go crabbing there when I was little. Spent hours at it."

Daisy joined her. "Me too. Dangling my little orange line over the rail. Bacon was always the best bait. We'd catch dozens of crabs then throw them back before we went home."

"My dad would never let us use bacon," Partial Sue replied. "'That's far too good for the likes of crabs', he'd say. We had to make do with leftover chicken carcass instead."

Daisy scrunched her nose up at the thought, then pointed. "Hey, there's a boatyard over there." Behind all the buildings, little dinghies and rowing boats squatted along the edge of the harbour. "Maybe someone stole a boat, rowed over here in the dead of night, set fire to Malcolm's hut, then rowed back."

Fiona shook her head. "Same problem with all of this. They'd still have been caught by CCTV."

"Surely not this far down," Daisy replied. "Would the cameras on the restaurant be that powerful?"

"Not the ones on the restaurant." Fiona pointed to the Smuggler's House. A cluster of cameras clung to its walls, just above head height.

They did the same exercise, checking the sight lines of each one. Cameras guarded every corner of the building. Every angle was covered, including an uninterrupted straight view down the spit, along the fronts of every hut and the narrow corridor of sand in between the backs of both rows.

"It's possible someone could have landed on the spit unseen by boat from Mudeford Quay," Fiona said. "But once they'd set foot on here, they'd have had to cross the sand to get to the huts. And then they'd have been caught by the cameras."

"Assuming they work," Partial Sue said once more.

Fiona glanced at the cameras above her head. "That's what we need to find out."

Just then, a shadow flitted across one of the uppermost windows. A figure.

Someone was up there. Trying and failing to stay out of sight.

CHAPTER 9

Fiona hurried over to the one and only entrance to the building. Black, heavy and impenetrable, the thick, studded, wooden door said 'medieval stronghold' rather than 'welcoming holiday home'. Attached to the wall was a somewhat incongruous modern door entry system with four glowing buttons and an intercom. Three were for the holiday flats, but the fourth was titled *OWNER*.

Fiona tried the button. No answer.

Then she tried all the buttons of the holiday flats. Again, nothing.

She held her finger down on the button marked *OWNER*. No response.

"I could've sworn I saw someone up there," she said. "And we really need to look at that CCTV." She stepped away from the door, peered up at the window and called out, "Hello. Hello? Is anybody home?"

No response.

Partial Sue picked up a stone, preparing to chuck it. "I could get their attention with this."

"Not with your right arm," Fiona replied. "I think it'll go through the window."

Fiona called out one more time and got the same non-response. "We'll get that footage somehow."

Light had drained from the sky, so they decided to give up and head back home along the seaward side, Daisy filming every hut she passed, each one quiet and lifeless.

All except one.

Up ahead, dance music thudded its way towards them. One solitary beach hut was open for the business of merriment. A brightly lit cube, it stood out, a beacon of amusement in the dimming light. Multicoloured fairy lights were strung up, criss-crossing above the veranda, and palm trees, most probably fake, stood at each corner. An array of patio heaters bathed everything in a warm orange glow and a barbecue smouldered on the sand in front. Apart from the patio heaters, it reminded Fiona of a beach club in Ibiza. Not that she had ever been to one, but she'd worked with plenty of interns who had, and had seen the pictures.

Three figures were out on the veranda: Sophie Haverford, sprawled out on a lounger, and Gail, perched on a high stool, ready to serve at a moment's notice, while the third swayed between them, attempting to dance, champagne flute clutched in one hand.

This must be the infamous Bitsy. Fiona had imagined her to be a refined socialite, chicly dressed for every occasion, but Bitsy wore a huge, shapeless pink changing robe, drowning her from head to foot. With her erratic, drunken jigging, she looked as if Bez from the Happy Mondays had had a fight with a blancmange, and the blancmange currently had the upper hand. Her movements were odd and disjointed, but she was clearly enjoying herself. Raucous cackles drifted across the sand, bouncing off the adjacent beach huts. Lucky that they were out of earshot of Frank Marshall, or he'd be marching over to tell them to turn the racket down, even though he had no issue playing his steam trains at full volume.

Partial Sue grabbed Fiona's arm, panicking. "We need to get out of here fast before they spot us. We can still escape if we cut across to the other side of the spit."

Fiona pulled her arm back. "I'd like to meet Bitsy."

"Me too," Daisy added. "She looks fun."

Abject horror passed over Partial Sue's face. "You're joking. I don't think I can handle two Sophie Haverfords in one evening."

Fiona disagreed. Sophie was conniving and calculating, and all about image, whereas Bitsy seemed like she didn't give a jot about anything — unless she wasn't aware she was being watched by three charity workers. Plus, if she was staying here for the summer, it wouldn't hurt to have a contact on the spit, keeping an eye and ear on things.

"Bitsy is going for a spin," Bitsy declared loudly, as they got closer. She abandoned her dancing and her champagne, stumbled down the steps of the veranda and onto the beach where Sophie's rented e-scooter stood.

"Oh no," Partial Sue groaned. "She's referring to herself in the third person. I'm really not partial to people who do that. Please can we go?"

Dragged by Simon Le Bon, who'd caught the meaty fumes from the barbecue, Fiona headed towards the beach hut. "Come on, it'll be fine. Maybe Gail will make us a hot chocolate."

Daisy followed. "Yes, I'd like that."

Judging by Bitsy's extravagantly decorated beach hut, Fiona would expect she'd brought half of Harrods with her. Reluctantly, Partial Sue caught them up.

Bitsy started up the scooter. Sophie sat upright, relinquishing her previously relaxed pose. "Please don't break it. I don't want to walk home."

"Don't worry, Bitsy has perfect balance." Bitsy hit the button and the thing jerked forward, ploughing through the sand towards Fiona, Daisy and Partial Sue.

"Er, are those things supposed to go on sand?" asked Daisy nervously as the contraption surfed from side to side.

Just before she reached them, the e-scooter's front wheel bogged down, sending Bitsy soaring over the handlebars straight towards Partial Sue.

CHAPTER 10

Partial Sue looked aghast as Bitsy landed on a soft pile of sand in front of her, legs akimbo, changing robe hitched up around her waist. She had revealed a little more of herself than she had intended, being bereft of clothes beneath her robe.

"It's like *Basic Instinct* meets Mudeford Spit," Partial Sue remarked.

Bitsy threw her head back laughing then caught sight of herself. "Uh-oh, Bitsy's flashing again." The 'again' implied that this must be a somewhat regular state of affairs, leading Fiona to wonder if this was the origin of her moniker, because she had a habit of inadvertently showing her bits.

Bitsy hastily snatched the changing robe and forced it down into a more modest position. The three of them dashed to her side.

"Have you broken anything?" asked Fiona.

"Only a few marriages," she guffawed. "What a rush! I'm going to do that again." She swiped away her blonde highlights to reveal a delicate, pixie-like face. Factoring in a facelift or two, Fiona would put her in her early sixties.

Before she could get to her feet, Simon Le Bon was up on his hind legs, licking her face and wagging his tail.

"And who's this handsome fellow?" Bitsy nuzzled her head next to his.

"That's Simon Le Bon."

"Oh, what a perfect name. His hair looks just like dear Simon's, too, round about 'Rio'."

"Do you know Simon Le Bon?" asked Daisy.

"Oh yes, and Yasmin. But we fell out. I beat him at Pictionary, and he's never got over it. He's very competitive at board games. Whereas Yasmin's a boss at Twister."

"I am partial to a bit of Pictionary," Partial Sue replied, warming slightly to Bitsy at the mention of one of her favourite board games.

Bitsy's face lit up. "Then let's have a game. But I have to warn you, I'm like Tony Hart with an HB pencil." She kissed Simon Le Bon's furry head. "Oh, drat, I don't think I packed it. None of you have it on you, do you?"

They all shook their heads. A spare set of Pictionary wasn't something any of them regularly carried on their person, although perhaps it should be — at least a travel version for occasions such as this.

Sophie huffed and harrumphed her way over. But instead of coming to Bitsy's aid, she went straight to the e-scooter, lifting it up and checking that it still worked.

"Oh, I'm fine, Soph. Thanks for asking." Bitsy got to her feet. After brushing the sand off her robe and out of her hair, she made a beeline for the e-scooter.

Sophie stepped between it and her. "Oh, no. Scooter's off limits."

"Oh, please, Sophie. Please. I promise I won't crash it again."

"No. I'm not taking you to hospital if you break your neck. I've had enough of waiting in A & E because of your alcohol-related injuries."

"So boring."

Fiona didn't like making snap judgements, but she had met people like Bitsy before in London on the rare occasions she'd rubbed shoulders with the one per cent. Bitsy was a child, that much was clear. A very rich and impulsive child in a sixty-something body and a pink changing robe, who wanted thrills and experiences to stave off the tedium of having unlimited money and no purpose in life other than to have fun, and whose greatest fear was being bored.

"These are the ladies I was telling you about." A smirk played on Sophie's face. "Fiona, Daisy and Sue enjoy solving murders."

Bitsy gasped without a hint of cynicism. "I insist you come and have a drink and tell me all about it. I simply adore a murder mystery."

CHAPTER 11

They found themselves sinking into a low, modular outdoor sofa, with thick and squidgy cushions as soft as marshmallows. Bitsy had had it delivered from London, today, judging by all the discarded packaging stacked up beside the beach hut. Fiona noticed a tasteful logo on the edge of a cushion made by a company called Quiet Storm of Chelsea. She Googled them and found that they only made furniture to order, mostly for people with yachts and swimming pools. There were no prices on the website, broadcasting that if you had to ask how much it was, then you probably couldn't afford it.

"So how long are you renting the beach hut for?" Daisy asked, snapping off a few shots for Instagram. "It looks fabulous by the way."

Bitsy smiled warmly. "Oh, thank you. I've decided to buy it. Gave the owner an offer he couldn't refuse just this morning. Solicitors will hash it out tomorrow."

"But you only just got here," Sophie replied. "That's impulsive, even for you."

"I know, but I simply love it. I knew I would. Had to have one all to myself so I put a bit of my inheritance to good use. And I'm desperate to get away from all those stuffy people in London, have a bolthole down here. You know, a back-to-basics experience. Rough it now and again." Without looking, Bitsy threw her arm back, holding her glass aloft. "Gail, be a dear and pour me another G & T, will you. Now, more importantly, tell me about this murder."

Taking it in turns, Fiona, Daisy and Partial Sue filled her in on the events so far.

Bitsy gave them her undivided attention, hanging on their every word. "So nobody knows who did it? No clues?"

"Nothing yet," Fiona answered.

"It's a gang of hoodies," Sophie interrupted. "Has to be."

Like Frank, the simple, knee-jerk answer was to blame this on delinquent teenagers.

"Stop interrupting, Sophie!" Bitsy snapped.

Fiona glanced at Sophie to gauge her reaction. Normally Sophie would have several barbed comebacks primed and ready to fling back, but her forked tongue stayed firmly behind her filled lips, leading Fiona to deduce that the balance of power in their relationship was firmly in Bitsy's favour.

Bitsy turned her attention back to Fiona. "Any theories?"

"Malcolm Crainey was an eccentric," Fiona replied. "A one-off. Bit of a bohemian."

"I like him already," Bitsy said.

"He covered his hut in all sorts of trinkets," Daisy added. "Maybe someone took exception to it."

Gail put a G & T in Bitsy's hand. She took a big slug and said, "Ah, yes, I saw that beach hut when I first got here. Couldn't exactly miss it. Well, that's simply awful if someone killed him for being individual. For being himself. Everyone should be allowed to be who they want to be. That's a human right, that is."

"It's a gang of teenagers," Sophie blurted. "Hoodies vandalising property, nothing more. That's my theory. You should investigate that."

Bitsy threw her friend the filthiest of looks. "Oh, do shut up, Soph. It's not all about you. And nobody calls them 'hoodies' anymore. Go on, Fiona."

"Well, I think someone in this little community down here is bound to know something." Fiona glanced at her watch and got to her feet. "Oh, my gosh, is that the time? We'd better be going. We have work tomorrow."

Daisy and Partial Sue joined her.

Bitsy was having none of it. "What? No, no. Stay for a bit longer . . . *please*. This is fun. Have another drink. I can order food in."

"We can't. It's a school night," Partial Sue said.

"I'll make a big donation to your charity. What's it called, Dogs Do Nice Things? Then you can go in late tomorrow."

Fiona shook her head. "I'm afraid it doesn't work like that. But we'd love you to make a donation anyway. I'm sorry we have to go."

Bitsy groaned like a child being told they had to go to bed. She continued not taking no for an answer, right up until the point they stepped off the veranda onto the sand. "If there's anything I can do to help . . ."

Fiona stopped and spun around. "Well, now you mention it, there is one thing."

CHAPTER 12

Next morning, Fiona had her key poised to insert in the lock of the charity shop's front door when her phone rang. It was Bitsy. No greetings came forth, just serious and straight-to-the-point information conveyed in hushed, conspiratorial tones. "I have eyes on the target. Repeat, I have eyes on the target."

Last night before leaving, Fiona had set Bitsy a little task. She'd asked her to keep an eye on the Smuggler's House and call her if she glimpsed the owner either coming or going.

"He looks shifty," Bitsy added.

"What makes you say that?" Fiona needed details and facts, not personal opinions.

"He's tall."

"Just because he's tall doesn't make him shifty."

The line went quiet, Bitsy thinking through her answer. "Tall people can look over stuff like fences, hedges and whatnot."

"That's a bit heightist, Bitsy. What's he doing?"

"There's a tradesman with him. Looks like he's fixing the lock. If you want to question him, now's the time."

"I'll be there ASAP."

"Want me to keep him talking? I'm very good at that."

"No, just wait there. Observe."

Fiona hung up and texted Partial Sue and Daisy to inform them she'd be late. Leaving the locked-up shop behind, she hurried back home with Simon Le Bon and grabbed her old Brompton fold-up bike out of the garage, the one she used to commute on when she worked in the capital. A bike was undoubtedly the fastest way to get there. She carefully lifted Simon Le Bon, placed him in the basket on the front and set off for Mudeford Spit.

Simon Le Bon enjoyed the change in plans, that wet nose of his keenly sniffing the cold, damp morning air as they cycled along. The only thing she regretted was not dabbing a bit of 3-in-1 oil on the chain, as it whined with every turn of the crank. Still, at least walkers along the footpath would hear her coming and promptly move out of the way.

Twenty minutes later, Fiona propped her bike against a rock near the Smuggler's House to take stock of the situation. She lifted Simon Le Bon onto the sand who wasted no time sniffing around and then having a quick lift of his leg. To all intents and purposes, Fiona looked like just another visitor to the spit, which suited her fine. She wanted to observe the owner of the Smuggler's House before approaching him, get the measure of the situation and what type of person he was, and whether he'd appreciate being pounced on by an amateur sleuth.

Just as Bitsy had described him, the owner was tall, easily six feet four, possibly five, and as skinny as the day was long. With thinning, limp black hair, he stood with a slight stoop as he talked to what looked like a locksmith, who was crouched at the front door, going at it with a hammer and chisel. Fiona was about to approach the pair when a voice made her jump.

"Are you going to question him?" Bitsy appeared beside her, still drowning in her pink changing robe. At least she'd added some jogging bottoms. "Can I come? Be your backup, just in case things go pear-shaped."

"I'm only asking if I can look at his CCTV." Fiona wanted her approach to be subtle. She feared that 'subtle' wasn't a word Bitsy had much use for.

Bitsy frowned. "Well, you never know. He could turn nasty."

"He could refuse. I don't have any right to see his CCTV. It's private property."

Bitsy's eyes pleaded with her.

"It only takes one of us to ask him," Fiona said.

She did the zipping her mouth action. "I won't say a word."

Fiona relented, hoping she wasn't about to regret this. "Well, okay, but just as moral support. I'll do the talking."

Bitsy improvised a little happy dance. Simon Le Bon bounced around her on the sand, thinking it was some kind of new game.

"We need to keep a low profile," Fiona said.

Bitsy stopped. "Yes, yes. Of course. I'm just excited."

Keeping a low profile would be a challenge, not helped in any way by Bitsy's oversized pink changing robe. Fiona wondered whether she'd just made a big mistake inviting an exuberant socialite with too much time on her hands and too little self-control for what would be an important conversation. "Let me do the talking, okay?" Fiona reminded her.

"Okay." Bitsy nodded eagerly.

They made the short walk across the sand to the Smuggler's House. As the locksmith hacked away at the wood, he looked sweaty and uncomfortable. Partly from the physical exertion, but mostly, Fiona guessed, because the owner was standing behind him supping on a cup of tea, scrutinising everything he did.

"Security upgrade?" Fiona offered by way of a conversation starter, but also curious as to why he needed a new lock.

Both men turned their heads simultaneously to survey them. The workman turned straight back to his job. The owner eyed Fiona and Bitsy suspiciously, then said, "No, door's a bit stiff. Keeps sticking. Been having a job opening it." His demeanour eased slightly and he attempted a weak smile. "If you're enquiring about the holiday flats, you're in luck. All three are vacant, so you can take your pick. I might be able to do a small discount too."

Fiona remembered Antony Owens' words about people losing money down here. The murder and the bad weather had put visitors off in droves, and the owner was desperate to make a sale.

"Can I have a little peek inside first?" asked Bitsy. So much for her keeping silent.

"Are you interested?" asked the owner, perking up.

"Not for me." Bitsy edged past the workman, surveying the interior, followed by Fiona and Simon Le Bon, straining to sniff in every corner. The hallway was bright and airy, tastefully decorated in whites and pale blues, a complete contrast to the stark outside. "It's for my friends in Richmond. I want them to come and stay but I don't want the bother of putting them up, if you know what I mean. Being their barista for a fortnight is not my idea of fun."

"I know exactly what you mean." The owner stepped in after them, ducking his head and diving straight into full sales-pitch mode, although he hastily modified it to incorporate how his holiday homes were, rather bizarrely, perfect for guests who you'd rather keep at arm's length.

Fiona had to nip his spiel in the bud before he went too far and got annoyed when he realised that they had no intention of renting the place.

"Does the CCTV work?" Fiona asked.

"Oh, yes," the owner enthused. "This is a very secure place to stay. Will be even more secure, once the door's fixed."

"I thought you said the door sticks, won't open?" Bitsy questioned.

"That's right."

"Wouldn't that make it less secure, once it's fixed?"

Fiona wasn't sure where Bitsy was going with this. Before he could answer, Fiona said, "My name's Fiona Sharp, sorry, what's your name?"

"Seb," the owner answered.

"Hello, Seb. I've been hired by the liaison officer of the Beach Hut Residents' Association to investigate the death of Malcolm Crainey."

All Seb could utter was a noncommittal, "Oh."

Fiona waited a beat, assuming he might want to add to his monosyllabic reply. It never came, so she continued. "Yes, well, I was wondering if I could have a copy of the CCTV footage of the night in question."

Seb became sheepish, not looking either of them in the eye. "The police have already examined it. Found nothing."

"I'd still like to have a look," Fiona replied. "If it's not too much trouble."

Seb huffed. "So let me get this straight. You're not here to enquire about the holiday homes?"

Fiona shook her head. "No."

He began ushering them out, shooing them towards the door as if they were cats. "I'm afraid the answer's no, and I'll have to ask you to leave."

Fiona stood her ground. "Please. It would really help with our investigation."

"Like I said, the police have found nothing so I can't see how that would help."

"What have you got to lose?" Bitsy asked.

"The time it would take to sift through the files on my computer, find the right segment, and transfer it onto a data stick, which I don't have, and it's too big to email."

Fiona produced a data stick from her bag. "I have one."

"As you can see, I'm a very busy man."

"Yeah, busy watching someone else work," Bitsy snapped.

Fiona swore silently at Bitsy's rudeness. That wasn't going to get them anywhere.

"Yes. Exactly," Seb retorted. "It's called project managing. Now, please go. I would slam the door in your face but as you can see, I don't have that luxury. So you'll just have to use your imagination."

Fiona desperately tried to think of a plan B, but nothing sprang to mind. The only thing that did was what Bitsy had mentioned earlier — there was definitely something shifty about the owner of the Smuggler's House.

CHAPTER 13

Fiona pushed her bike along the sand to the start of the spit, with Simon Le Bon snoozing in the basket. Bitsy walked alongside her, apologising every step of the way. "I think I cocked that up for you. I'm really sorry, Fiona."

"Don't be. I don't think he had any intention of giving me that footage, whatever we'd said. But you did get one thing right."

"What's that?"

"He's shifty. Definitely hiding something."

"I know right? Shifty."

"And I'm wondering why he needed the locks changed. Was it really the door sticking, or did someone try to break in?"

"Well, he's certainly got enough CCTV to catch them."

Up ahead, they were surprised to see a waitress clad in a thick fleece on the empty deck of Tides Restaurant, wiping down the tables.

"Look," said Bitsy. "The restaurant's open. Let me buy you brunch to make up for it."

Fiona was about to do the that's-really-not-necessary routine, when she remembered the restaurant also had CCTV. If she couldn't obtain the footage from Seb at the

Smuggler's House, there was still a chance she could acquire it from the restaurant.

"Sure, why not? Thank you."

They selected a table outside on the decking, as dogs weren't allowed inside. The waitress shivered as she handed them laminated menus the size of hymn sheets.

"You haven't been open for a while," Fiona remarked.

"No," the waitress replied. "This arctic weather's made it pointless but it's supposed to turn in the next day or two. Owner wanted us open and ready for when it does."

Fiona ordered a pot of tea and a teacake while Bitsy went for the full monty: eggs, sausage, bacon, fried slice and beans. "All this fresh air makes me ravenous," she said.

Fiona got up. "Would you excuse me for a moment? Just need to pop to the loo."

Fiona had no intention of going to the toilet, she just wanted to shake off Bitsy while she did some more digging. Inside, she caught up to their waitress. "Can I speak with the manager or the owner please?"

Someone behind them heard Fiona's request. "I'm the owner," said a man with a round, ruddy face and wearing a casual jumper that was an odd montage of pastel colours and far too tight for his equally round body. "Is there a problem?"

The waitress made herself scarce. Fiona introduced herself and went through the same routine as she had just a few minutes ago at the Smuggler's House. Unfortunately, she received a carbon-copy response.

"The police have already examined the footage," the owner replied. "Found nothing."

"Sorry, what's your name?" Fiona asked.

"Marcus."

"Hello, Marcus. Yes, I'm sure they have but I would like to review it for myself, just so I can cross it off. Otherwise, it looks like I'm not being thorough — the beach hut owners are relying on me and my colleagues to find out who did this, as are the businesses down here, yours included, presumably."

Marcus chewed the inside of his cheek and then said, "I just don't have the time. I'd have to sift through the files on my computer, find the right segment, transfer it. And I don't have a data stick and it's too big a file to email."

His answer was almost identical to Seb's at the Smuggler's House. Almost as if they'd got together beforehand and prepared what they were going to say like a couple of shady co-conspirators. Or was that purely coincidence? No, it was too precise. Too rehearsed. Did these two know each other and, if so, what reason would they have for not wanting her to see the footage? Surely it would've been in both their interests to catch the killer and attract people back to the spit so they could make money.

Definitely shifty.

Once again, Fiona produced a data stick from her bag. And once again she got another stock answer. "Sorry, I'm a busy man. Now, if you'll excuse me." He disappeared into the kitchen.

Fiona shrugged off her disappointment, slotted the data stick back into her bag and rejoined Bitsy.

"Are you okay?" Bitsy asked.

"I'm fine. Just had another knock-back. I asked the owner of the restaurant if I could see his CCTV. Got the same response, almost word for word."

"Two shifty characters."

Just when Fiona thought it couldn't get any worse, Marcus came out onto the deck and stood over their table, arms folded. "I'm very sorry, but I'm going to have to ask you to leave. Your order has been cancelled."

Fiona couldn't hide her shock. "Whatever for?"

"I don't need a reason," Marcus sneered. "I reserve the right to refuse service to anyone I feel is unsavoury."

"Unsavoury?" Fiona would never have classed herself as unsavoury. Perhaps a bit scruffy around the edges but never unsavoury.

"Business a bit slow, is it?" asked Bitsy out of the blue.

"What's that got to do with it?" Marcus replied.

Bitsy fixed him with a cold stare. "How would you like it to be even slower?"

"*What*?"

She prodded her phone and shoved her Instagram account in his face. "I've got a thousand followers — some of them would love to know how bad this place is."

Marcus chuckled. "Are you trying to threaten me with a thousand Instagram followers? A thousand is nothing. It's peanuts."

Bitsy smiled wickedly. "It's quality, not quantity." She scrolled through her list of followers, watching as Marcus's face dropped. "I'm sure Nigella, Gordon, Delia, Jamie and Heston would all love to hear about how simply awful this place is, you know, so their *millions* of followers can avoid it. Social media is such a cruel mistress. Now you and your tasteless jumper are going to go inside and transfer footage from the whole month of July onto Fiona's data stick — just to be on the safe side."

Fiona pulled the data stick from her bag and handed it to Marcus. He took it, said nothing and began a slow shuffle back towards the restaurant.

"Wait!" shouted Fiona.

He turned slowly, his expression one of dread at what was coming next.

"You don't happen to know Seb who owns the Smuggler's House, do you?"

He slowly nodded.

"Oh, that's very handy — could you go down there first and get him to do the same with his footage, if you please."

Marcus's skin paled. He turned ninety degrees and dragged his feet in the direction of the end of the spit.

"Bit quicker. Fiona's a busy lady." Bitsy cackled.

They watched the joyous sight of the pretentious restaurant owner dawdling into the distance to do their bidding.

Fiona couldn't suppress a massive and — even though she was reluctant to admit it — smug grin. "Bitsy, that was incredible."

She laughed. "Bitsy does have her uses. They're not many, granted, but Bitsy does have them."

"I hope the whole month will fit on the data stick. I only really need the night of the murder."

"Well, I figure they've been rude to us, so no harm in giving them some extracurricular activities. Make them pay their dues."

Fiona decided it was time to break her rule of a lifetime. She held up her palm and high-fived Bitsy.

Next, Bitsy clicked her fingers, and the waitress came scuttling back out to retake their order.

CHAPTER 14

Pedalling her bike back along the tarmac path, Fiona held onto the handlebars with one hand while Simon Le Bon enjoyed the ride in the basket, the wind raking his fur. In her other hand she gripped the data stick for dear life. Not the safest way to ride but she didn't want to let it out of her grasp for one second. All she wanted was to get back to the shop and review what it had captured. She was sure it would hold the key to everything. However, there was one more stop she had to make.

Branching off the tarmac path, several small tree-lined lanes ran alongside of Hengistbury Head, converging at the top. She picked one and pedalled up it but had to stop almost immediately as it was too steep. Stepping off her bike, she lifted Simon Le Bon out of the basket and onto the ground. He stared at her with two questioning eyes, as if to say, *Is that it? What, you want me to walk now?* After Fiona had pushed her bike a few feet, he cottoned on that that was the end of the free ride and trotted after her.

On the plateau of the windswept headland, a carpet of heather stretched before her, trembling in the breeze, while above, intense black clouds held the sky to ransom. Fiona half-expected to glimpse a lovestruck heroine dashing barefoot over the wild Brontesque landscape. But nothing of a romantic nature was happening on this cold, dank, late morning, just a couple in matching cagoules shouting complicated instructions at a black Lab called David. The man was bellowing at the disobedient dog to cease and desist clawing the dirt, demolishing some poor creature's underground habitat. Simultaneously, his wife was threatening to put the dog back on its lead. Fiona could only just disassemble their dual rants. The dog would have no hope and instead chose to ignore them both, continuing its dig.

Fiona gave them a wide berth and Simon Le Bon gave David the side eye, as they headed towards the clifftop on the opposite side, overlooking the sea. Her destination was a lonely, one-storey stone building. Standing defiantly against the wind, the coastguard station resembled a box-like turret plucked straight from a castle and plonked on top of the headland.

Fiona had decided that while she was on a roll gathering evidence from surveillance equipment, it wouldn't hurt to call in at a place that appeared to be covered in the stuff, most significantly a mast of zigzagging metal tubes rising from behind its castellated roof at least fifteen feet into the sky. A halo of sharp prongs stuck out the top, prodding the air, giving it the appearance of a giant medieval mace. Fiona got a good feeling. Despite its Tolkienesque appearance, this station was tooled up with hi-tech sensory equipment to monitor even the most insignificant nautical comings and goings out in the channel and across the harbour. Could it detect anything else? Perhaps a fire set in the early hours of the morning? She was about to find out.

She leaned her bike against the building, put Simon Le Bon on his lead, climbed a set of stone steps and knocked on the one and only door at the side.

A smiley man appeared. He had a round face and chin-strap beard, which matched the shape and shade of the hair on his head, giving his face an odd, hirsute symmetry. His torso was chunky, nearly bursting out of his white epauletted shirt, bearing the initials *BCS* embroidered into the top pocket. Fiona hazarded a guess that it stood for British Coastal something or other. Society? Syndicate? Survey? Service? Service seemed the most likely. She'd go with service until she heard otherwise.

"Good morning," he said cheerfully.

"Sorry to bother you."

"No need to be sorry, we love having visitors."

"Who is it, Steve?" came a jolly voice from inside.

"We've got a visitor, Beryl."

Beryl appeared beside him, all red cheeks and warm smiles, decked out in the same uniform. Her short hair formed tight, bouncy red curls, reminding Fiona of a 1940s floral swimming cap. "Would you like a cup of tea?"

Fiona was taken aback by their hospitality. She had no idea why, but she had prepared herself for the cold shoulder, probably because of the reception she'd received from Marcus and Seb. Still, she hadn't asked to see their surveillance footage yet. Plenty of time for that.

"That's very kind of you," Fiona replied. "But I've just had brunch."

Steve looked wistful. "Ah, brunch. What a great invention. An equidistant mini meal. Hey, we should have brunch up here, tomorrow."

"We can make egg and bacon sandwiches," Beryl suggested.

"That sounds more like a standard packed lunch to me," Steve remarked. "I was thinking of maybe hard-boiled eggs, cold sausages . . ."

"What if we brought the camping stove up here? We could have a proper fry-up."

Steve beamed. "Now there's an idea. We could cook whatever we wanted."

"We could make hearty soups for days like today."

"A warming paella."

"Beef stew."

Fiona stood on the doorstep listening to the foodie couple, their excitement rising with every new culinary suggestion.

"Oh, my gosh, so sorry," Steve apologised. "We're neglecting our guest."

Beryl ushered her and Simon Le Bon inside. "We do get sidetracked when it comes to food and drink."

"That's okay. My friends and I often have long discussions about cake. It can get quite heated."

"Oh, don't get us started on cake." Beryl giggled. "You'll never hear the last of it."

Dominating the front of the station, below its generous windows, an array of technical equipment, dazzled. The main feature was a wide control desk equipped with various radios, radars, monitors and displays, with lines of switches and lights, while above it all, fixed to tripods and pointed out to sea, were several giant sets of binoculars and a powerful telescope. But it was the rear of the station that caught Fiona's attention. The back of the space couldn't have been more at odds with the front. Firmly intended for rest and relaxation, two citrus-yellow easy chairs sat in each corner separated by a glass-fronted mini fridge stocked with booze and food. In front of this, on a seagrass rug, stood a low, whitewashed wooden coffee table furnished with mugs, a kettle, teabags and little sachets of biscuits as if they were in a West Country B & B. Two folded-up deck chairs nestled in the corner together with a bright parasol and a portable barbecue. A framed picture on the wall showed an embroidered seagull saying, *If I lived by the bay would I be called a bagel?*

Steve noticed Fiona's curious expression. "As you can tell, we like the good things in life, even while we're coastguarding. We'd sleep here if we could."

Beryl grinned gleefully. "Sometimes when our watch is over, we break out the champers, sit outside and indulge. It's the perfect spot. Views to die for."

"Obviously, we never drink when we're on duty," Steve added. "Molly, our daughter, joins us sometimes — she loves it here, and so does our granddaughter. We have a jolly nice barbecue together. Part of the reason we took the job, but don't tell anyone." He winked.

71

"Well, it does look cosy. All you need now is a wood burner," Fiona suggested, then wished she hadn't.

Beryl got the same look in her eyes as when the camping stove had been mentioned. "I wonder if the BCS would let us install a wood burner?"

Steve tapped the side of his nose, mischievously. "Better to ask for forgiveness than permission."

The pair of them tittered like naughty children.

Beryl's eyes misted over. "Can you imagine having a wood burner going on the stormy days up here?"

Fiona had to cut this off at the root before it grew out of hand. "I was wondering if I could ask you about your surveillance equipment."

The two coastguards halted their animated conversation, slightly surprised at her request.

Fiona continued. "I'm investigating the beach hut fire on the spit. I've just acquired CCTV footage from the restaurant and the Smuggler's House, and while I was at it, I thought I might as well check in here and see if any of your equipment picked anything up."

Steve adopted a more professional tone. "Unfortunately, we don't have any CCTV, if that's what you're after."

"What about all this other equipment?" Fiona asked.

"We're VRR," Beryl explained. "Visual, radio and radar. We watch and radio the ships out there, mark their position with the radar, and report it to search and rescue organisations if they get into trouble."

"SPR," Steve stated. "Spot, plot and report." These two definitely liked their memorable three-letter abbreviations, possibly acquired from a training seminar. Steve pointed out the window. "This stretch of water is treacherous. There's Old Harry Rocks in the west. The Needles on the Isle of Wight, Beerpan Rocks off the coast of this headland, and the Run may look gentle but its currents are evil."

"That's the entrance to Christchurch Harbour," Beryl clarified.

"Radar is great," Steve said. "But it can't tell if someone's in difficulty."

Beryl pointed to her eyes. "You need a pair of these for that. That's where we come in."

"What about the fire on the spit, did you see that?" Fiona asked.

"We're volunteers, only here from nine in the morning until five in the evening," Steve answered.

"Unless we're barbecuing." Beryl made prodding and flipping actions with her hands, as if tending an invisible grill. "But even then we're never here later than nine. I like to be in bed by ten. Light off by ten thirty."

Steve nodded. "Me too, especially on a school night. Now, if they'd let us sleep here then we wouldn't need to leave. Be much better all round. I really don't see why we can't have a few beds in here. A bunkbed."

Beryl's eyes lit up. "Oh, wouldn't that be fabulous."

"It's just a question of height." He rubbed his chin, examining the ceiling.

They were off again on another cosy flight of fancy. Fiona reined them back. "What about the equipment. Is it left on?"

"Oh, yes," Beryl said. "The radar's all automated. Sends the info direct to HM Coastguard, twenty-four seven."

Fiona asked, "Would it have detected anything that night? A person moving about?"

Steve shook his head. "No. Our equipment isn't geared up for people, I'm afraid. It's marine radar, designed to detect sailing boats, motorboats and ships out at sea. I mean, it's possible for radar to pick up anything, if you have the right type, but it must be specifically designed for that job, calibrated in the right way."

"Oh, well. It was worth a try." Fiona thanked them for their time and made her excuses to leave, despite their best efforts to get her to stay, offering to ply her with tea, biscuits and basically the contents of their mini fridge. She declined as politely as possible. As she pushed her bike away, Simon Le Bon by her side, the quirky but gregarious couple of coastguards stood on the steps of the station, waving her off, as if she were a long-lost friend they hadn't seen in ages.

"Come back soon," they chorused.

"We might have a wood burner next time," Steve shouted after her.

Fiona left empty-handed. Well, one hand empty. The other was still firmly clutching the data stick. She placed Simon Le Bon back in the basket, ignoring his grunt of displeasure at being swept up, threw her leg over the crossbar and cranked the pedals as hard as she could. There was simply no time to waste on walking. After her small, uneventful detour, she needed to know what was on that stick.

CHAPTER 15

The familiar and reassuring tinkle of the doorbell sounded as Fiona and Simon Le Bon dashed into the charity shop. Clutching the data stick in her fist for dear life, she desperately wanted to shove it in the shop's old laptop and review the footage immediately. However, Partial Sue and Daisy were embroiled in a heated discussion at the till with a man whose head had become rather red. A pair of smart, patent leather Oxford dress shoes sat on the counter in front of him.

"I told you, I can't wear them, they pinch my feet. I have to get a refund. Do you think I'm lying?"

"No, we believe you," Daisy replied. "It's just, you didn't buy them from this charity shop."

The man acted dumb. "So?"

Partial Sue waved the receipt in front of his face. "Which bit of 'you didn't buy them from this charity shop' did you not understand? You bought them from End Global Hunger in Westbourne, the receipt says so."

"Yeah, but it's a bit of a trek over there, innit. I thought I could just drop them off here. I mean, it's all charity. All goes to good causes." The man had the impression that charity worked like some giant Willy Wonka sack of money, coins and notes constantly dropping into it from a huge purple pipe above, presumably connected to a network of smaller pipes, linked up to the tills of all the charity shops nationwide.

Fiona didn't have time for this. "How much did you buy them for?"

The man jerked around at the sound of her voice. "Five pounds."

"I'll give you a couple of quid for them."

He thought for a moment, then said, "Yeah, all right, then." He accepted his payoff and was gone.

Partial Sue became indignant. "Fiona, you shouldn't have done that. He was trying it on—"

Fiona held up the data stick and smiled.

Daisy's eyebrows rose so high they almost disappeared into her hairline. "Is that what I think it is?"

Fiona was only too pleased to answer. "Both sets of CCTV. Smuggler's House and Tides Restaurant. From the entire month of July, no less."

"How did you manage that?" Partial Sue asked.

"Not me," Fiona replied. "It was Bitsy. She can be very persuasive when she wants to be, and it doesn't hurt that she's extremely well connected."

"I'm growing more partial to her by the day." Partial Sue wasted no time grabbing the laptop and setting it up on the counter.

Fiona pushed the stick into a slot on the side as the other two gathered round. "I also went to see the coastguards in their station on top of Hengistbury Head, quirky couple called Steve and Beryl, to see if their equipment had captured anything."

"Any luck?" Partial Sue asked.

"No, it's all marine radar. Dead end."

Two little file icons appeared on screen. Fiona clicked on both and began sifting through the various camera angles. There were a lot to choose from but only three they were really interested in: the one that covered the front of all the beach huts on the harbourside; the one that covered the same view but on the sea-facing side; and the one that covered the narrow corridor between the backs of the two rows of huts. Tides

76

Restaurant offered all three views looking down the spit, while the Smuggler's House offered the same but looking back up the spit. No one could have gone anywhere near Malcolm Crainey's hut without having been caught by one of these six cameras.

Fiona found the fateful day, 15 July, then arranged all six feeds so that they covered the entire screen in a neat grid, allowing them to be viewed side by side simultaneously.

"Wait, this is far too small." Partial Sue went to a shelf at the back of the store, near the DVDs, where a few IT relics sat waiting for a new home. This made them sound old, but these days, anything electronic older than a year was considered an antique. Selecting a black-framed computer monitor emblazoned with an unpronounceable brand name no one recognised, she lifted it off the shelf with its leads dangling below. She set it up on the counter and connected it to the back of the laptop. It worked instantly. The images popped up on the screen, perfectly recreated, only twice the size.

"Now the rabbit can see the dog," Daisy declared.

"I think it's the other way around," Partial Sue corrected.

Fiona peered at the time stamps of all the feeds, syncing them up. "Annie Follet claimed she came out of her hut at 3.30 a.m. to go to the loo. Shall I go back, say an hour, and start from there?"

They all agreed.

Fiona set all the feeds playing from 2.30 a.m. Three heads all peered into the screen, anticipating that some sinister, hooded figure would appear, scurrying across the sand with a petrol can in one hand and perhaps a lighter in the other. Scanning every second of the footage, no one appeared. Nothing stirred. Not a grain of sand was disturbed. The images remained unchanged apart from their time stamps in the corner, slowly ticking towards Malcolm Crainey's fateful demise.

Then they saw it. At 3.21 a.m.. The faintest of glows, creeping out of the edge of one of the frames. Only the front of Malcolm's beach hut could be seen from the Smuggler's House camera, but clearly the fire had already started, round the side, where Martin said it had and was now spreading to the front.

By 3.22 a.m., the glow also appeared in the feed from the Tides Restaurant, but captured from the other direction.

Fiona halted the footage. "I don't understand. Fire's already started. But we didn't see anyone."

"That's impossible," Partial Sue said. "They'd have had to cross one of these camera views to get to his hut, right? Wind it back. We must have missed it."

Fiona reversed the footage back to 3 a.m. and pressed play, slowing the footage right down. All eyes were on the screen, desperately scanning for evidence of a person or persons cutting across the sand to reach Malcolm's hut, or even just someone skulking in the shadows. No matter how many times they replayed the footage, or how far back they rewound it, or how much they slowed it down, nobody appeared, hooded or otherwise. They examined the footage right back to the daytime, to make sure that someone hadn't darted into the narrow gap beside Malcolm's hut and lingered there until nightfall, hiding until the opportune moment. They tracked everyone who came near Malcolm's hut, following their movements on screen. With multiple camera angles they were able to follow the comings and goings of everyone, accounting for each and every person. At no point did anyone suddenly dart into the little gap between his hut and the one on the right. They checked all the other camera feeds just in case they offered any sort of clue, but nothing materialised or emerged. The spit was deserted. A wasteland barren of clues.

Fiona sighed. "I don't understand."

"So," Daisy said, "we're looking for someone who's not only tall and has no common sense, they're also invisible."

"It would seem so," Partial Sue replied. "Let's carry on. Watch what happens when Annie Follet appears."

Fiona set all the feeds in motion again. Right on time, at 3.30 a.m., a beach hut door opened further up the spit. Annie Follet emerged on the veranda, carefully shutting the door behind her. Jerking her head suddenly, she appeared to swot away a fly, arms flailing, almost sending her toppling over. Regaining her balance, she took carefully measured steps onto the sand, still dozy with sleep. Awkwardly hunched over, she shambled down the spit towards the toilet block near Malcolm's hut.

"That definitely looks like someone in need of the loo," Partial Sue remarked. "I've had to do that walk many a time."

"The glow of the fire has increased. How come she doesn't see it?" asked Daisy.

"Cameras are higher than her eyeline," Fiona replied. "The roofs of all the other huts and the toilet are blocking her view. Plus, her head's looking down, probably concentrating on where she's going. At this point she's just desperate to get to the loo."

Annie's pace increased as she neared the toilet block. Then she disappeared through the door.

The next moments were traumatic to watch.

After she reappeared, Annie Follet gazed up at a burning ember then caught sight of its terrifying source: Malcolm's blazing hut. She ran towards it, nearly tripping over, her feet catching in the sand. Pausing momentarily outside, she hesitated, presumably shocked at the inferno in front of her. In those few short moments the flames had grown higher, more intense.

It was now or never. Snatching a drying towel from the hut next door and throwing it over her head, she dashed onto Malcolm's veranda, then shouldered the French doors open, disappearing into the burning structure. Several seconds later, she re-emerged, backside first, her body bent over at an awkward angle, wrenching Malcolm by his wrists.

Heaving him inch by inch, progress was painfully slow. At times, it appeared the effort was too much for her, but she persevered. Eventually she dragged him out, across the veranda, and onto the safety of the sand.

It was the most heroic and selfless act Fiona had ever seen, leaving her breathless and her hands shaking.

No one spoke. The shocking images had turned them mute. But it was what happened next that had them all baffled.

CHAPTER 16

They'd elected Fiona to question Annie Follet alone after seeing what the poor woman had been through in the footage. No one thought it would be appropriate or practical to have all three of them turning up *en masse* on her doorstep, overwhelming her. Besides, they needed someone to stay and look after the shop.

Annie Follet's home was surprisingly modest for someone who had rented a beach hut on the most expensive strip of sand in the country. The little downstairs flat, with its claustrophobic back garden, just big enough for a netted trampoline, huddled in the middle of a terrace near the shops in Winton. Fiona watched through the patio doors as Annie's kids Millie and Sam squealed with delight at the ceaseless joy of tossing a ball for Simon Le Bon, who never tired of the game. They seemed like gentle, well-mannered children and, crucially, happy. Annie Follet seemed determined to keep them that way, despite what had happened on 15 July, which is why Fiona was surprised when she agreed to answer her questions, and on the same day of asking.

The tea was going cold as Fiona cupped it in her hands. She hadn't touched it once, enrapt by Annie's account of how she came to be staying on Mudeford Spit in the first place.

Annie played with her fingers nervously. "I just want to set the record straight." She had kind blue eyes, but Fiona detected sadness hiding behind them. She wondered if it had been there since the events of that night or if it had been lingering for a while. "My ex lives in France with his new woman. So it's up to me to bring up the kids. I work from home, and I was dreading the summer coming. Always do. Trying to work while feeding and entertaining them. It's impossible. So I persuaded Tom . . ."

"That's your ex-husband?"

"Yes. He's loaded but somehow he always manages to give us the minimum in maintenance, thanks to his creative accountant and his divorce lawyer — he came out of our break-up with the house and most of our savings. Anyway, I persuaded him to pay for a beach hut for the summer. He never looks after the kids so I guess I guilt-tripped him into it. I want them to have happy, joyful childhoods. Not to remember them sat on their iPads. So Tom agreed to pay for renting a hut all summer, and that's how we came to be on Mudeford Spit. I was overjoyed. I could work and they could play. It's very safe down there and everyone's friendly, a little community. Like being in the 1950s, I imagine. You know, when all the children played outside in the street and everyone had their doors open. They could have a proper old-fashioned summer holiday, exploring, having adventures, making friends with the other kids. Bit of freedom."

Fiona smiled delicately, attempting to be as sensitive as possible. "And then the fire happened."

Annie Follet swallowed hard. "Yes, that changed everything. We didn't feel safe after that. Well, I didn't. I've managed to keep most of it from the kids. Don't want them to be traumatised. They were gutted to leave, of course. Still are. Keep asking me when they can go back."

Fiona waited a beat. "I know this is probably going to be difficult, but could you talk me through the events of that night?"

Annie Follet hesitated. Blinked several times and sniffed away a tear. "I remember desperately needing the loo. I came out of the hut and hurried to the toilet block at about 3.30 a.m."

"Did you smell smoke?"

"Yes, but that's nothing new down there. Place is full of smouldering barbecues and firepits in the evening. So I didn't think anything of it. When I came back out of the loo, I saw a few burning cinders floating in the air. I was still sleepy, you have to remember. I thought, *that's weird*, moved around the side of the toilet block, and that's when I saw the hut ablaze. I knew Malcolm was in there."

"How did you know?"

"Around nine o'clock, every night, we had a routine. The kids would get into their pyjamas, and we'd trot off down to the toilet block. They'd clean their teeth and have a wee before bed. They thought it was great. Malcolm's hut is nearby, you can't miss it with all the knick-knacks. Kids loved it. Like a magical grotto. They'd want to have a look before going to bed. Malcolm would always be out on his deck. Always. Lived in his beach hut all year round, or so I'm told. 'Take a picture if you like,' he'd always say. The kids would be too shy. He was a nice man. Eccentric but nice." Annie Follet went quiet.

"Are you okay to continue?" Fiona asked. "We can take a break."

She blotted a tear with her cuff. "No, I'm fine. Let's carry on."

"How would you describe the blaze?"

"Whole thing was burning but more on the right-hand side, fiercer. Thankfully, it hadn't reached the French doors. Next second, before I know it, I'm grabbing a damp towel that was drying outside the beach hut next door. Then I'm running towards Malcolm's hut with it over my head. I didn't really think about it, just did it. Barged through the doors."

"And where was Malcolm?"

"Place was full of smoke. I couldn't see. I shouted his name several times. Then I stumbled and fell onto him. He'd been sleeping on the couch. Luckily, he wasn't upstairs in the bedroom. I tried shaking him, but he was unconscious. By this time, I was coughing, eyes watering. I grabbed his wrists and dragged him out. It felt like it took for ever. I kept dragging and dragging him until we were clear and onto the beach. Then I collapsed and had a coughing fit."

The image on the CCTV footage of Annie Follet writhing on the sand next to Malcolm was one Fiona would never forget.

"Was Malcolm still alive at this point?"

"I'm not sure. But I'm told he was."

"What you did was incredibly brave, Annie."

Annie grunted dismissively and wouldn't catch Fiona's eye, preferring to gaze at the chipped laminate.

"It was," Fiona continued. "Don't underestimate it. But one thing puzzling me is the version of events after that. The CCTV shows you, quite understandably, incapacitated after breathing in the smoke. As you said, collapsed on the sand. But the news tells a different story. Said that you tried to resuscitate him, then when that failed, you leapt up and helped put out the fire, almost managed the whole thing."

Annie shook her head. "By that time everyone was out of their huts and either helping to put out the fire or trying to give Malcolm CPR. I wasn't involved in any of it. I was out of the game at that point. Everyone else should take the credit. To tell the truth, all I wanted to do was get back to my kids, but I couldn't move I was retching so much."

"So why the different version of events?"

Annie Follet went quiet once more.

If Fiona didn't know better, she'd say she had the pale complexion of shame on her face.

Annie sighed heavily, "I was told to say that."

Fiona was taken aback. "Who told you to say that?"

Annie Follet's sad eyes narrowed into angry slits.

CHAPTER 17

Fiona waited patiently for the answer, not wanting to put pressure on Annie Follet in any way. Eventually, she spoke. "I'm a fool. I got bad advice."

"Who was it?"

Annie hesitated. "Let me put the whole thing in context. After the paramedics checked me over, the police questioned me. DI Fincher and DS Thomas — they were very nice, I remember. I gave them a full statement, told them the truth word for word, just as I've told you. Everything that happened. The police had sealed off the spit, wouldn't let anyone leave until they'd taken statements from everyone and got what they needed. Once we were free to go, I grabbed everything, cancelled the beach hut and took the kids home. Wanted to forget the whole thing. A man had died right beside me, and I kept replaying it over in my mind. You know, the what ifs. What if I had done this? What if I had done that? Would he still be alive? That was bad enough, but then I got a call from someone asking if I had a media strategy in place. I had no idea what they were talking about, or how they got my number. 'The next few days will be crucial,' she said. I'd be getting a lot of media attention, press and TV. She could handle them for me, keep them at arm's length. You have to realise I was still in shock. Just wanted to be left alone, at home with my kids. Shut the world out. But I knew she was right. I've seen these things on the news. Press camp outside your door. Won't leave you alone. So I asked her to represent me."

"Who?"

"Sophie Haverford."

Fiona grimaced, an acidic taste suddenly flooding her mouth. "Oh, I should have known."

"You know her?"

"Yes, unfortunately. She runs a charity shop across the road from mine. But she used to work in PR."

"That's right. She was very convincing. Very sympathetic and understanding."

"I bet she was. Silver-tongued, that one."

Nervously, Annie scratched the top of her thigh. "I thought it would be a good move having someone like her to handle the PR side of things. Keep us out of the limelight but give the press what they wanted."

"And did she do that?"

"Yes, at first it was great. But then I started seeing the stories on the news and in the paper. It didn't match what had happened. She'd started to embellish things. Making out I was some kind of superhero with superhuman strength who tore open the beach hut, lifting Malcolm above my head and carrying him to safety, then trying to resuscitate him and single-handedly putting out the fire."

"So what did you do?"

"I sacked her immediately. Didn't want to be part of her lies. She pleaded with me to keep her on. Said there'd be lucrative book deals and TV appearances in the pipeline when I was ready. That I could make a ton of money from this. Start working the single parent angle and how I deserved it. I didn't want to make any money. That was the furthest thing from my mind."

Fiona groaned. "Annie, I'm so sorry you had to go through that, on top of everything else. That woman has no scruples, I know from experience."

"Well, I guess you live and learn. It's made me look at people differently. I don't trust so easily anymore."

Fiona changed the subject. "Would you say any of the hut owners had a problem with Malcolm?"

"Not really but we hadn't been there that long. They all seemed very nice, especially this one chap who came up and introduced himself. Now what was his name? Frank, I think."

"Frank Marshall?"

"Yes, that's him. He said if I needed anything to come and knock on his door, or if I had any problems, to report them to him and he could sort them out for me."

"Oh, right," Fiona replied.

"Sorry, that makes him sound like a Mafia boss. It wasn't like that at all. He was sweet, if you know what I mean. Had two granddaughters that would stay with him. Anyway, apart from that, there's not much else to tell about that night. Like I said to the police, I didn't see anyone or hear anything. Well, apart from a mosquito, but that's not much help."

Fiona grabbed her bag and stood up to leave, not wanting to add to the woman's trauma any more than she had to. "Thank you for seeing me. That's cleared up a lot. I can cross that off our investigation."

Annie Follet went pale again, an uneasy expression crossing her face.

"Are you okay, Annie?"

"There is one other thing, but I'm not sure if it's anything. Not sure I should even tell you."

Fiona sat back down.

CHAPTER 18

Fiona decided to follow up on Annie Follet's tip-off immediately. Well, not so much a tip-off but an observation, or maybe a lead. Whatever it was, it definitely demanded further investigation, especially as it was in Talbot Woods, only a stone's throw away from Winton where Annie lived. However, the outlook couldn't have been more different. Unlike Winton, where the streets were tight and congested, and parking spaces were a sought-after commodity, in Talbot Woods, the roads were grand, wide and leafy, abounding with an impressive procession of palatial Victorian mansions with park-like gardens and sprawling driveways, and not one car parked out on its pristine roads.

Fiona pulled on the handbrake and cracked a window open for Simon Le Bon. Cloudy with the temperature still in single figures, she thought it would be safe to leave him in the car, and wiser, seeing as she was turning up unannounced. She was keen to gauge these people's reactions without the distraction of a cute dog.

From her list of hut owners, she knew that the first house she was about to try belonged to the Pullmans, who owned beach hut number 116, the one on the right-hand side of Malcolm's, nearest to where the fire had started. The house was impressive, a façade of red brick and generous leaded windows, topped with a huge pointy roof, thick chimney breasts and generous, shadowy eaves.

She rang the bell. No answer.

She waited. Rang again. Still nothing.

Crunching out of the gravel driveway, Fiona went next door to the house belonging to the Donovans, who owned beach hut number 118, the one on the left of Malcolm's hut. It had already occurred to her that this set-up was a little peculiar. Not only were they neighbours where they lived, they were also neighbours on the spit — or would have been, if it hadn't been for Malcolm's hut sitting in between them.

The Donovans' house was as equally impressive as the Pullmans', another Victorian mansion in a plot big enough to have its own postcode with towering fir trees and what appeared to be a separate guest house.

Fiona rang the bell.

A few seconds later, a pretty, small-framed, blue-eyed woman with a blonde ponytail answered the door, gripping a glass of white wine. It was just after lunch. Fiona wondered what the special occasion was, or if this was a bit of upper middle-class daytime drinking.

"I'm so sorry to bother you," Fiona said. "My name's Fiona Sharp. I've been hired by Antony Owens to investigate the murder on Mudeford Spit. Would you mind if I asked you a few questions?"

The woman swallowed hard. Fiona couldn't tell if this was nerves, or she had a mouthful of wine she needed to dispose of. "Oh, right. Er, yes, of course. Please, do come in."

She showed Fiona into a vast hallway, complete with substantial flagstones, a dark-wood vaulted ceiling and a sweeping wooden staircase just begging for a Disney princess to sweep down it. "Are you Sadie Donovan?" Fiona asked. She already knew that she was, according to the list of hut owners, but she wanted to make sure.

"Yes. That's me. Please come through into the kitchen."

Passing from the dark-wood interior into the kitchen, Fiona almost had to avert her gaze from the vast swathe of white domestic perfection. This majestic realm of symmetrical marble and gold was dominated by an island big enough to land a plane and fitted with a double sink and an elegant, arched gold tap that looked as if it cost more than her car. A handsome man perched on a stool. Judging by the way his sweater clung to his perfect curves, Fiona would've guessed he employed the expertise of a full-time personal trainer. A wine glass, nearly empty, sat in front of him.

"Hello," Fiona said. "And you must be Michael Donovan."

Worry tugged at his perfect features, almost ageing him. "Oh, no. I'm Rich Pullman, Sadie's next-door neighbour."

"My husband's at work," Sadie informed her.

"And my wife is too," Rich added. "We're both stay-at-home mum and dads. Relaxing as it were, before having to pick up the kids."

Sadie put her wine down. "Well, they're dropped off by the minibus. They're at summer holiday club. We don't pick them up. Not after drinking, that would be irresponsible wouldn't it, Rich?"

He muttered a humbled, "Yes, of course."

Sadie continued, "When our partners get home, we reverse roles. They look after the kids together and we get to go out and play."

There was an awkward air about these two, and the alco-hol was certainly making them loose-lipped. Fiona wasn't complaining, but she'd almost go as far to say that there was something a bit wife-swappy about them. As if she'd stum-bled onto the set of a Robin Asquith movie, but perhaps a less common remake — a reimagining, as they called it these days.

Rich must have sensed Fiona's unease, rushing in to justify living in each other's pockets. "We both have big families. We find doing things together keeps the kids enter-tained, makes life easier for us adults. That's why we bought houses side by side."

"Oh, we can afford childcare," Sadie clarified, as though not wanting to give Fiona the wrong impression. With stone floors, vaulted ceilings and a book-matched marble kitchen, there was absolutely no danger of that. "Money's no object. We could have au pairs and nannies, but we just don't like the idea of strangers in the house."

"Oh," Fiona said. "I hope I'm okay."

"Yes. Of course," Sadie replied. "I'm a good judge of character. Now what can we help you with?"

Fiona cleared her throat. "I'd like to ask you about the death of Malcolm Crainey."

"We didn't kill him!" Rich Pullman blurted.

Fiona had to restrain herself from raising an eyebrow.

CHAPTER 19

Rich Pullman's murder denial came with more exuberance than Fiona had expected. Actually, she hadn't expected any denial to come forth. The accusation hadn't been made, hadn't really crossed Fiona's mind, not yet anyway. She was still in fact-gathering, innocent-until-proven-guilty mode with these two. However, Rich had elected to promote them both to prime-suspect status by protesting their innocence unprovoked and emphatically. Did someone have a tortured guilty conscience and absolutely no self-control?

Fiona glanced at Sadie, who glared at Rich, her face reddening. Adopting a calm voice, despite her livid complexion, Sadie said, "Take it easy, Rich." Then she turned to Fiona. "He worries about getting into trouble. He won't even pull up on double yellow lines when he's picking me up from town."

Fiona avoided being distracted by why he would be picking her up and not her own husband. "Rich, why did you feel the need to tell me you didn't murder Malcolm?"

Sadie opened her mouth to speak but Rich got there before her. "I'm sure you've heard the rumours — on the spit, I mean."

91

Sadie's jaw clicked, presumably because she had clenched it so tightly. Clearly this wasn't the answer she had wanted him to give.

Fiona shook her head. She hadn't heard any rumours. Apart from Frank Marshall and a couple of others, there wasn't anyone down there to spread any rumours at the moment, and Frank didn't seem to be one for gossip. "What rumours?" Fiona braced herself for what might be a very sordid confession.

Rich paused uneasily. "Well, that we wanted to swap beach huts with Malcolm Crainey."

Fiona's shoulders relaxed, but only slightly. This was a significant revelation. "I haven't heard anything about this. Tell me more."

Sadie took over explaining. "Like our houses, we wanted our beach huts to be side by side. You know, so our families can be together, kids can nip next door to play, share the childcare duties. It would have just made life easier."

"We offered him a straight swap," Rich added. "Even though he would have been getting the better deal. Our hut had been recently modernised whereas his needed a ton of work. It was in a bit of a state. And let's face it, it's not a massive ask, just moving one beach hut along. But for us it would've made a big difference. But Malcolm refused."

"Why?"

Sadie gulped down her wine. "Because his aunt left it to him. It had been in his family for years, and he wanted to keep it that way."

Fiona puzzled at this. "But he had no kids, no one to pass it to."

"That's right and he said he hadn't made a will either, so who knows where it's going to go?"

"Back to the government if he didn't have a will," Fiona explained.

Rich and Sadie went quiet, clearly feeling an invisible finger pointing at them. If it were the case that Malcolm didn't have a will, then the beach hut would most likely go back on the market, sold off by the government, which would give the Donovans or the Pullmans the opportunity to buy it, getting what they wanted. Two beach huts side by side. Motive if ever there was one, and probably what had prompted Rich's outburst.

Fiona decided to push on, hoping to gather more evidence to support this theory. She brought out the ace that Annie Follet had handed her. "During the night of the fire, I have an eyewitness account that I'd like to clarify. After the alarm was raised, everyone came out of their huts and started to help put out the fire. All except you and your partners, who stood back and watched. Is that a fair account?"

Sadie slowly shook her head. "I see what you're doing. Clever choice of words. 'Stood back and watched' makes us sound like we were enjoying the spectacle of Malcolm's hut burning down because he wouldn't swap with us."

"It was the complete opposite of that." Rich's voice was brittle and flimsy. "We were terrified. Our huts started burning too, you know."

Fiona referred to her notebook. "Yes, but they were quickly put out, thanks to the other hut owners. Minimal damage. Nothing that a quick rub down and a lick of paint wouldn't fix."

"We were still in shock." Sadie's face twisted angrily. "Stood there frozen with fear. Fear for our lives, watching Malcolm's hut burn."

Rich trembled. "We were thinking, that could've been us."

"Can I ask where your kids were that night?" Fiona asked.

"They were staying with their grandparents," Sadie answered.

"Both sets?" Fiona asked.

Sadie and Rich nodded.

Fiona decided to test their consciences. "That was very fortunate. I bet you're glad they were nowhere near the blaze. Not in any danger."

Sadie's anger flared. "Of course we were! Why wouldn't we be? Where are you going with this?"

"I'm just trying to gather information, that's all."

The veins on Sadie's neck stood up like thick blueish worms. "You're accusing us of burning Malcolm's hut down out of revenge, so we could get our hands on it."

Fiona shook her head. "I'm not saying anything. But to an outsider, that's what it might look like. Plus, Mudeford Spit beach huts come with a hefty price tag. I'm sure a burned-out one is far cheaper to buy than one that isn't."

"We'd still have to rebuild it," Rich mused.

Sadie glared at him. This was becoming a habit. Neither of them were adept at trying to prove their innocence.

"Sounds like you've thought it through," Fiona remarked.

Rich panicked. "We haven't. I swear. I was just following your logic. Burning it would've cost us more in the long run. Wouldn't add up—"

Sadie butted in. "This is all academic. The police interviewed us for hours and hours. Same line of questioning. Same accusations. Motivations or whatever you call it. Bottom line is, there's no proof that we did it. That's. Because. We. Didn't. We were asleep in our huts when it happened and the CCTV backs that up. We never came out until we heard all the commotion. I'm sorry, Fiona, I know you're just trying to do your job but you're barking up the wrong tree."

"Can I ask if you knew Annie Follet? The woman who pulled Malcolm out of the fire."

"No, we didn't know her," Sadie replied. "She was a renter, wasn't she?"

"Her hut was further up the spit. We don't mix with anyone up there." Rich sounded dismissive.

Inside, Fiona groaned. Was this some new subset of hut snobbery? That huts further up the spit weren't as good as ones near the end. Like a beach hut north-south divide. "What's wrong with that end?" asked Fiona.

Sadie was quick to clarify. "Oh, nothing. It's just geography. We didn't cross paths with her, that's all."

"To be fair, it is a bit quieter down our end," Rich said, not helping Sadie's argument.

"Do hut owners look down on renters?" Fiona asked.

Sadie smiled, but her eyes didn't join in. "Don't be silly. Why ever would we do that? We're not monsters. But one thing I would say, Annie Follet still hasn't replaced our towel."

"Towel?"

Sadie sneered. "She grabbed a damp towel that was drying on our deck. Put it over her head when she went into the hut. It's ruined now. She hasn't replaced it."

Fiona cleared her throat. "Let me get this straight. Annie Follet risked her life to save the man in the beach hut next to yours, and you're worried about a towel?"

Sadie forced a smile. "Of course, I get how brave she was and all that. Big kudos to her. But you have to understand when all is said and done, she needs to replace what she damaged. I mean, it was from Liberty's."

"That's in London," Rich added.

Fiona had no words. This pair's ice-cold attitude to what they considered to be important in life had caused her to go mute. There were more red flags flying in her brain right now than in a communist-party parade.

Sadie must have clocked her look of horror. "Well, I think it's time for you to go."

Normally, Fiona would've tried to bargain for just a little more time, pleaded that they answer a few more questions, as she didn't know when she'd get the chance again. Not today. Fiona slid off her stool and thanked them for their time. She had everything she needed. More than enough.

CHAPTER 20

Back in Southbourne, Fiona desperately wanted to head straight to Dogs Need Nice Homes and share what she'd learned with Daisy and Partial Sue. She'd made progress. She might even go so far as to class it as a breakthrough. However, before that happened, her conscience steered her feet in the direction of the Cats Alliance. She had a rather large bone to pick with Sophie Haverford, and she needed to confirm Annie Follet's version of things.

"Oh, hello." Sophie greeted her as Fiona entered the charity shop that didn't resemble a charity shop at all. It had the airy lightness of a designer boutique in Mayfair and not an iota of the second-hand odour that troubled every other charity shop up and down the country, Fiona's included. She wasn't sure what brand of witchcraft Sophie Haverford had employed to eradicate it, but she was certain that somewhere in the rural depths of the UK, a coven was missing a member, especially today, as Sophie was decked head to foot in black. On closer inspection, it appeared to be a loose-fitting trouser suit that bizarrely had long tassels down the arms and legs and across the chest.

"You look like you're going to a cowboy's funeral," Fiona remarked. She hadn't meant it as an insult, merely an observation, unfortunately, one that had slipped out unchecked.

However, Sophie took it as the former. Looking down her nose, she eyed Fiona disdainfully from head to foot, lining up a riposte. "Still eating between meals, I see. And for your information, this is Versace."

Before it turned into a back-and-forth slanging match, Gail interrupted. "All right?" she called out through the open door of the back room where she was beavering over some electronic contraption, parts scattered everywhere.

"Oh, hi, Gail," Fiona replied. She turned her attention back to Sophie. "I want to have a word with you."

"But do I want to have a word with *you*?" Sophie scoffed.

Fiona ignored the gibe and pressed on. "Did you manipulate Annie Follet's story for the media?"

Sophie raised her head sagely, about to impart words of wisdom. "Manipulate is too strong a word, dear. In PR we call it 'massaging the message'. It's all part of the art."

"Dark art, more like." Fiona folded her arms abruptly. "You took advantage of someone very vulnerable just to make money and peddle sensational headlines."

Sophie sniggered. "Oh please, do I look like I need money, and spare me the self-righteous routine. I've seen you in M & S reaching to the back of the chiller cabinets to grab the longer sell-by dates."

"What the hell has that got to do with anything? That poor woman's been through enough and you added to her trauma by making up things that she didn't do."

"Aw, so naive. Don't believe everything you read in the news. Every story gets spun, has an angle. If you want clicks, shares and reads you need more than the truth. You need one of the media holy trinity: sensation, controversy or outrage. Preferably all three."

"Doesn't matter how you dress it up, it's still wrong." Fiona turned on her heel. She'd had her fill of sordid bottom feeders for one day. She needed her own peaceful haven, with people she trusted who didn't have an angle they were working or an agenda they were forcing. She needed the solace and comfort of Dogs Need Nice Homes.

CHAPTER 21

The remnants of Fiona's altercation must have still been evident on her face. Her icy exterior jarring with the cluttered and cosy, tea-soaked atmosphere of the charity shop, worrying her co-workers as soon as she stepped through the door. Thankfully, no customers were browsing the shelves, or they may have made a swift exit.

"Are you okay?" Daisy asked the moment she caught sight of her.

An odd, guttural grunt emanated from the depths of Fiona's throat as they sat at the round table. "Urgh. I've just been to see Sophie Haverford. That woman makes my skin crawl."

Sensing her residual rage, Simon Le Bon took shelter in his bed by the till, circled several times, then settled down into a tight furry ball.

"What's she done now?" Partial Sue sloshed cups of tea in front of everyone, spilling drips all over the table's nice clean surface.

Fiona caught her friends up about how she'd tracked down Annie Follet, only to discover that Sophie Haverford had foisted her services on her and then proceeded to add to the poor woman's trauma by embellishing her story.

"What a beastly thing to do." Daisy pulled a surface wipe from somewhere on her person and blotted the puddles of tea.

"She's a fartlighter, that one," Partial Sue added.

Fiona and Daisy regarded her, befuddled.

"What's a fartlighter?" Daisy asked. "Or would it be better if we didn't know."

Partial Sue gulped down a mouthful of tea. "I made it up myself. It's like gaslighting but it's when these stupid attention-seekers in the media say something incendiary just to cause a stink — hence fartlighting."

Fiona nodded. "That's a good name for it — fartlighting. Sophie Haverford is definitely a fartlighter."

"I'd go further than that," Daisy said. "I'm sure the milk goes sour when she enters a room."

"And plants wilt," Partial Sue added. "That's why she's banned from garden centres."

Daisy looked horrified. "Is Sophie banned from garden centres?"

"No, but she should be," Partial Sue replied. "For worrying the wisteria."

"Petrifying the petunias," Fiona suggested.

Daisy giggled. "Terrifying the tulips."

"This banter is making me want to go to a garden centre. I am partial to a good garden centre or two."

"Me too," Daisy agreed. "They do great roast dinners at the one near me. Very good value for money."

Before the conversation fell off a precipice from which it would never return, albeit the most pleasant precipice one could imagine, adorned with fragrant flowers and smelling of roast dinners, Fiona brought it back to more important matters. "There is some good news. I've made a bit of a breakthrough in the investigation."

Partial Sue jittered with excitement. "Hey! So have we. Well, Daisy did. What's your breakthrough?"

"You go first," Fiona said.

"No, you go first," Partial Sue replied.

"No, you go first."

Partial Sue conceded. "Oh, all right, then. Tell her, Daisy."

Daisy made herself more comfortable, fidgeting in her seat as she mentally prepared for what she was about to say. "Well, we've got a bit of a pickle about this CCTV business. No one can get near Malcolm's hut without getting caught on camera, but there's no one to see, which doesn't make sense — the fire couldn't have started all by itself. That's impossible." She clicked her fingers, attempting to recall something. "Oh, what's that phrase now? Once you eliminate the impossible . . . Oh darn it, I can't remember the rest."

Fiona completed the quote from Sherlock Homes. "'Whatever remains, no matter how improbable, must be the truth.'"

"That's it. No one approached Malcolm's hut from any direction. That means that the killer was already there, hiding."

A shadow of doubt crossed Fiona's face. "But we've wound back the tapes, replayed them. Everyone who came on the spit that day also left. And no one emerged from their hut to start the fire, or they would have been seen."

"Precisely. By a series of deduction and elimination—" Daisy had clearly been indulging in a bit of Sir Arthur Conan Doyle — "there is only one possibility. One place where someone can set light to Malcolm's hut unseen and then get back to theirs without ever being caught on camera. The hut on the right-hand side of Malcolm's, number 116. Anyone emerging from any other hut would be seen. Except that one."

A fizz of adrenalin hit Fiona's bloodstream. Hut 116 belonged to the Pullmans, whom she'd just visited. Before jumping the gun, Fiona wanted to hear more. "But how? They'd still have had to come out of the front of their hut where they'd be caught on camera."

"This is where the 'no matter how improbable' bit comes in," Partial Sue warned.

Daisy took a deep breath. "A hidden or secret door, most likely a trap door underneath. Huts are up on stilts, remember? Like Malcolm's hut, the space underneath 116 isn't boxed in for storage — it's clear, see." She held up her phone and played the video she'd recorded the other day. Sure enough, the footage showed the Pullmans' hut elevated on its wooden piles, with at least a two-foot gap beneath it and dark sand underneath. If Daisy's theory was true, one of them, possibly Rich Pullman, who was lithe enough, could have dropped through the bottom of the hut if it had a trap door, crawled along the sand underneath, then emerged in the narrow gap between the two huts — a CCTV blind spot. "Someone could've slipped out, started the fire then slipped back inside that hut. Once the alarm was raised, they filed out onto the beach just like all the other hut owners, joining in, helping to put out the fire like everyone else."

"Except they didn't help to put out the fire," Fiona said. "That's what Annie Follet told me."

Daisy face contorted, puzzled. "Why wouldn't they help put out the fire?"

"Because they had an issue with Malcolm. I went to see the Pullmans and the Donovans after what Annie Follet said. They own the two huts either side of Malcolm's, number 116 and 118. They're two families who like to do everything together. Sort of inseparable. They even have houses side by side on the same street. There's something very cold and vile about them."

"I bet they didn't offer to make you any tea," Partial Sue proposed.

"You know, now I come to think of it, they didn't." That should have had alarm bells ringing before anything else. Was there any better test of someone's character than whether they made you tea or not?

Daisy beamed. "I've always liked the idea of all of us living together. It would be such fun. Like the Monkees or the Golden Girls."

Fiona wasn't ready for that just yet, even though the thought of living in a real-life sitcom did sound appealing. "Anyway, they admitted to pressuring Malcolm to swap huts with them so they could also have beach huts side by side. Malcolm always refused."

Now it was Daisy's turn to gasp. "They burned his hut down because he wouldn't swap with them."

Partial Sue wasn't as quick to jump to conclusions. "But if that's the case, why stand there on the sand watching everyone else put out the fire? It's a bit incriminating. Surely you'd join in, and their huts were burning too."

Fiona swilled the question around in her mind. "Their huts only charred. But who knows? Could be anything. Shock, confusion. Planning a crime in your head and then seeing it actually happen must be disconcerting, especially if it's your first time. Maybe they didn't foresee that their own huts would burn. Went into shock when it happened. I'd say the distance between their huts and Malcolm's is about five feet on either side. They probably didn't even consider their huts would char in that heat. Rich Pullman isn't the sharpest tool in the box. Sadie Donovan seemed a little more switched on. Cold-hearted but switched on. There is the possibility Rich Pullman did it without telling the Donovans about his intentions. Sadie did seem extremely annoyed with him, and he had a guilty conscience — even denied murdering Malcolm without me bringing it up."

"Let's check the CCTV again," Daisy suggested.

Moving over to the till, they fired up the laptop and replayed the scenes of the fire. Beach hut doors flung open as the alarm was raised. Panicked bodies moved frantically in the confusion. Some ran straight to the aid of Malcolm and Annie lying on the sand. Others desperately grabbed anything that would hold water to put the fire out. They'd seen this footage several times but hadn't noticed the Donovans or the Pullmans among the throng of people. After exiting their huts in the confusion, they swiftly moved out of camera shot, close to the shoreline. Not one of them came back into the frame again, armed with a bucket or anything else to put out the fire.

This was indeed a breakthrough. The Donovans and the Pullmans had motive and they had means, and they were certainly nasty enough.

All the Charity Shop Detective Agency needed to find was evidence.

CHAPTER 22

Five thirty couldn't come around fast enough. The ladies of Dogs Need Nice Homes did everything that people in charity shops — and, for that matter, all shops and places of work — do to hurry the time along: cleaning; serving; rearranging; sorting through donations; anything that would make the second hand on the wall clock spin faster. The thing about time is that it doesn't like to be rushed. It likes to, well, take its time. The remainder of the day dragged, as if they were wading through wet concrete in clown shoes. They were desperate to head down to the spit and examine hut 116 for evidence, the only hut from which a stealthy arson attack could've realistically been launched out of sight of any CCTV. Fiona wanted to send Daisy and Partial Sue on ahead while she took care of the shop, but they all agreed that they wanted to do this together.

Finally, at five thirty on the dot, the front door was firmly locked. Forty minutes later, thanks to some reckless driving, followed by some hearty power walking, their feet touched the powdery sand of Mudeford Spit. A few hardy souls were sitting outside on the deck of Tides Restaurant, braving the relentless bitter wind, warming their hands around steaming lattes and cappuccinos. There was no time for a refreshment stop for the ladies of the Charity Shop Detective Agency. Evidence had to be collected and theories needed to be tested.

They'd barely made it past the restaurant when Frank Marshall stepped out of his hut into their path. He was similarly dressed to the last time they saw him, except he had a pint of cloudy beer in his hand. A cacophony of train engine noises filtered through the open French windows of his hut.

"Afternoon, ladies." Frank's greeting was friendly enough, but Fiona got the impression it masked his unofficial role as gatekeeper of the spit. The self-elected sandal-wearing sheriff round these here parts.

"Hello, Frank," they greeted back.

"What's new?" he asked.

Frank could make it very difficult to examine the Pullmans' hut if they didn't have him on side. Might as well come clean, as they wouldn't get anywhere without his blessing. "We're looking for evidence," Fiona answered.

"What kind of evidence?"

"A trap door in one of the beach huts," Daisy replied.

Fiona expected him to cynically screw his face up at their fanciful and far-fetched theatrical theory, followed by a hearty guffaw from his moustachioed mouth.

"Oh, yes," he replied. "Many huts have trap doors. Mine included."

"What?" they chorused in total disbelief.

"Come, take a look." They followed him up onto his deck and into his hut, which was immaculately clean, even by Daisy's obsessive standards. Did he really want to show them his trap door — they would have taken his word for it — or was this an excuse to show off how impossibly put together his hut was? Everything was arranged with military precision, and not one but two dust-busters clung to the wall, one on each side, poised and ready to form a two-handed pincer movement against any stray grains of sand that dared venture past the threshold. He turned down the steam engine noises on the iPod slotted into its dock, put down his beer and then rolled back a plain hardwearing rug. In the middle of the painted timber floor, a square had been cut out — two flat brass hinges at one end and a flush circular ring handle at the other. Slotting two fingers into the ring, Frank flipped up the trap door to reveal a box-like structure beneath. A hidden cupboard. Measuring about three feet deep by three feet wide, it was a miniature beer cellar, stacked to the brim with dozens of bottles of ale on their sides with peculiar brand names, such as Bishop's Finger, Fiddler's Elbow and Fiona's personal favourite, Brews Forsyth — the label sported a caricature of the famous TV presenter knocking back a frothing pint.

"It's a good place for extra storage," Frank explained. "Space is tight in a beach hut, as you can imagine, especially fridge space. It's nice and cool down there. Perfect for my ales. Now you don't want a real ale to be too cold, otherwise it masks the flavour . . ."

Partial Sue cut him off before it became a mansplaining masterclass on real ale storage. "Does that have any access to the outside?"

"Oh, no," Frank replied. "It's completely secure, otherwise you could have all and sundry entering your hut from beneath the floor."

Fiona believed him. However, it wouldn't be too difficult to add a second trap door on the outside of the hidden cupboard, then secure it with a padlock or some sort of stealthy locking device to keep it secure. Or even have the trap door lead straight out onto the sand below — exactly what they needed to locate and identify beneath the Pullmans' hut.

Frank stood proudly, gazing down at his miniature beer cellar. "Yes, I built that myself. Wasn't difficult. I used marine plywood, of course, not that cheap rubbish they sell in DIY stores. Has to be marine ply, otherwise it just rots in the salt air. A lot of people build theirs with ordinary ply — they're just making a rod for their own backs . . ."

This time, Fiona cut him off before it became another mansplaining masterclass, this one on beach hut carpentry.

"Well, we'd better be going. Thank you, Frank. That's been most helpful."

They filed out of his hut and back onto the sand, Fiona pulled by Simon Le Bon, eager to resume their walk.

Frank hurried after them. "Er, you said you were collecting evidence. May I ask from where?"

Fiona hesitated. If she didn't tell him, Frank would only follow them down the spit and find out anyway. "From hut one hundred and sixteen, next to Malcolm's."

"You don't think the Pullmans had anything to do with this?"

Frank knew exactly who owned the hut just from the mention of its number. She was impressed, and slightly frightened at his intimate knowledge of anyone fortunate enough to have a key to a beach hut.

"That's what we want to find out," said Partial Sue.

Frank planted his fists on his hips. "Why ever would they want to burn down Malcolm's hut?"

Fiona answered, "Because the Pullmans and the Donovans wanted to swap huts with him, so they could have theirs side by side, and he refused."

"Yes, I know that," Frank replied. "But they'd never burn his hut down over it."

Fiona took a step towards him. "Wait, you knew about them wanting his hut?"

Frank nodded. "Oh, yes."

Fiona couldn't quite believe what she was hearing. "Hold on. The other day we asked you if Malcolm had any enemies, anyone who had anything against him, and you said no. Now you're telling me you knew all about the Pullmans and the Donovans wanting to get their hands on his hut."

Why would Frank withhold that information? The first solid motive behind the murder. What else was he hiding that they should know about?

CHAPTER 23

Fiona waited for an answer that didn't come. Frank stood there nonplussed, so she repeated the question. "Frank, why didn't you tell us about the Donovans and the Pullmans wanting to swap with Malcolm?"

Frank came out of his stupor, rolled his eyes, as if this were all nonsense, or maybe he didn't like being put on the spot. In his world, he was the one who put people on the spot, not the other way round. "Oh, come on. You're making a mountain out of a molehill. Wanting to swap huts doesn't mean they'd murder Malcolm. It wasn't anything serious, just a suggestion, a proposal. It was all very light-hearted. They even used to call him 'Malcolm in the Middle'. Besides, the Donovans and the Pullmans have had huts here since before their kids were born. Been here about ten years. They'd never do a thing like that."

And there it was. In Frank's mind they couldn't possibly be guilty because they were hut owners. And beach hut owners weren't capable of such things. A circular argument. They owned beach huts on Mudeford Spit, therefore they must be decent and upstanding members of society, incapable of murder. It was the ultimate proof of one's moral fibre. It filtered out the riff-raff, hence Frank's theory that the fire was the work of a bunch of hoodies. Not because he had evidence of this but because in his mind it was unthinkable that it could be one of their own. Therefore, it had to be someone from outside, obviously young people who Frank, no doubt, deeply distrusted.

"People have killed for a lot less than wanting to swap beach huts," said Partial Sue.

"Is there anything else you need to tell us?" Fiona asked. "Any other grudges that we should know about?"

Frank's moustache twitched, a clear indication that his lip was quivering beneath his bristles. "No, no. Nothing I can think of. Not at this moment."

"Well, if you do think of anything, you need to tell us. No matter how trivial you think it is."

Frank smiled. "Yes. Will do. Now, mind if I tag along with you? Make sure everything's as it should be at the Pullmans' hut."

Returning the smile, Fiona opted for diplomacy. "Of course." Strictly speaking, she couldn't stop him. He might even be useful. "Do you have a key to it?"

In reality, Daisy could have had the Pullmans' door open in seconds. With her deft and nimble miniaturist's fingers, she was quite the lockpicker. However, breaking and entering wouldn't have been a good idea with Frank around, and even if he wasn't, there was all that CCTV to catch what they were doing.

Frank shook his head as they started walking. "No, unfortunately I don't have a key. Although I did propose that I should have a copy of everyone's at the last AGM, but people voted against it. Not sure why."

As they trudged towards the Pullmans' hut, Frank had the opportunity to outline his other proposals for the spit, which included having some sort of manned security hut and lifting barrier positioned along the tarmac footpath just before the spit started, forcing people to show their ID before they could venture any further.

"Like a border control?" Partial Sue suggested.

Frank balked at this. "Well, I wouldn't go that far. It's just so we know who's entering our land."

"That's the exact function of a border control," Fiona said. The fact that Frank had referred to it as 'our land', didn't escape her attention either, further fuelling her conspiracy theory that hut owners resented the presence of outsiders disrupting their peaceful haven. Malcolm Crainey wasn't an outsider but he did disrupt the peace somewhat.

Frank sniffed. "This murder wouldn't have happened if we had measures like that in place."

Daisy chimed in. "Hey, wouldn't that make Mudeford Spit a separate country? Like the Isle of Wight. That's always put me off going there because you need a passport, and I've got no idea where mine is."

"Daisy, you don't need a passport to visit the Isle of Wight," Fiona pointed out.

"Are you sure?"

Everyone agreed.

Daisy clapped her hands joyfully. "Oh, wonderful. I've always wanted to go. Now I can see the polar bear up close."

"Polar bear?" Fiona questioned. What bizarre new flight of fancy had Daisy just conjured up? The image of polar bears roaming free across the island's lush green meadows flashed into Fiona's head, followed by the terrifying thought of them wandering into picture-postcard villages, rummaging through wheelie bins and chasing walkers into tearooms, who would have to lock the door behind them until the threat could be neutralised, presumably by the Isle of Wight Bear Patrol, an improbable agency that would certainly need to have been created if such a thing were true. "There aren't any polar bears on the Isle of Wight."

Frank backed up Daisy's odd claim. "Oh, yes there are. Step this way."

Perplexed and slightly alarmed at this weird revelation, they followed Frank, slotting themselves between a pair of huts in desperate need of a lick of paint that didn't escape

Frank's critical eye. "I'd better remind Steve and Gwen that their huts are getting a bit flaky."

Crossing the strip of no man's land between the backs of the two rows of huts, or no man's sand, as Fiona called it, they emerged on the sea-facing side to a magnificent sight. The Isle of Wight rose out of the march of white caps like some green-topped, whitewashed fortress.

Frank pointed to its towering, craggy, white cliffs plunging vertically into the sea. "Polar bear."

"Well, I never." Fiona exclaimed.

Hiding in plain sight, formed from the exposed chalk cliffs of the island's most westerly point, stood the clear and distinct white silhouette of a polar bear on all fours, its pointed snout taking a sniff of the sea air.

"I am partial to a, to . . ." Partial Sue struggled to find the right words. She couldn't exactly say she was partial to finding natural animal forms in cliffs shaped by millions of years of sea erosion — it really wasn't a thing.

"Pleasant surprises," Daisy suggested.

"Yes, yes, that's it," Partial Sue replied. "Big, pleasant surprises. You know, I've lived here all my life and I've never known he was here. He's wonderful."

They all stood in awe, admiring nature's sculptural ability combined with pure chance and a great deal of time.

"Yoo-hoo!" A bright and sunny greeting broke their solace. Bitsy bustled across the sand towards them, drowning in a new, grossly oversized blue changing robe, instantly reminding Fiona of Violet Beauregarde from *Charlie and the Chocolate Factory*, when she blows up into a giant blueberry. "Admiring the polar bear?" she asked. "He's great, isn't he? Wonderful sight to wake up to with your morning coffee."

"I like your new changing robe," Partial Sue remarked.

"Thank you," Bitsy replied. "I love these things. I'd never get away with it in Richmond. I'd wear one all the time if I could. It's like living in a sleeping bag."

"I'd like to live in a sleeping bag," Daisy said wistfully.

Fiona introduced Bitsy to Frank. After a brief exchange of pleasantries, he went straight into uptight sheriff mode. "Now, I've been meaning to have a word with you about your music. On the spit we have a noise-level etiquette . . ."

"Don't you play your steam trains at full volume?" Partial Sue pointed out.

"Ah, now steam trains are different from rave music, and I only play it loud when no one's around . . ."

"It's not rave music," Bitsy protested. "It's progressive Swedish trance."

Frank's moustache twitched. "Yes, well, whether it's progressive Swedish trance or, er, non-progressive Swedish trance, we like to keep things quiet here after 10 p.m."

Fiona was curious to see how a no-holds-barred bohemian like Bitsy would react to having her freedom restricted.

Bitsy flashed him an irresistible smile. "Hey, why don't you come over tonight for drinks and canapés? We can chat about it. I love steam trains and railways, by the way — my grandfather used to have one."

Bitsy's charm combined with the mere mention of steam trains melted Frank's resolve. "Oh, really, what gauge was it? I'm a double-O man myself."

Without any trace of guile, Bitsy said, "Oh no, it wasn't a model railway. It was a real one, in Devon, I think. Only a small one. Or was it in Hampshire? It had an odd name, celery or something."

"The Watercress Line?" Frank spluttered, almost having to hold onto one of the ladies to steady himself.

"That's the one."

Franks' eyes became so wide they were in danger of toppling out of his head. "Your grandfather used to own the Watercress Line?"

"Yeah, I think so, or a massive share in it."

Frank wobbled, his head spinning, no doubt. He would have probably been unimpressed by the celebrities clogging up Bitsy's phone contacts, but her grandfather owning a real, working railway had turned him into a starstruck teenager. He tried his best to keep a lid on the overwhelming joy that was threatening to get out and turn him giddy. "Oh my. Well, yes. I would most certainly like to take up your offer of coming over tonight. You know, it was renamed the Watercress Line because it originally carried locally grown watercress to London."

"I never knew that. I'd like to hear more," Bitsy replied with equal enthusiasm.

Fiona had the impression that by the end of the evening Bitsy and Frank would be best of friends, and she would subtly change his mind about her music, perhaps even turning him into an unlikely fan of progressive Swedish trance.

Partial Sue rubbed her hands together eagerly. "Right, shall we continue? We've got evidence to check."

Now it was Bitsy's turn to act like a starstruck teenager. "Evidence? Are you on detective duties? Can I come? Please!"

"Sure, why not." Frank assumed authority, muscling in on what was technically the Charity Shop Detective Agency's investigation. Fiona didn't care. Let him have his little bit of superiority. Whatever got the job done.

They trudged back across the sand to the harbour side of the spit, Frank leading the way, of course. A few minutes later, the unlikely little party of mismatched sleuths stood in front of the Pullmans' hut, to the right of Malcolm's burned-out one, still swathed in police tape. Sure enough, as Daisy's camera had faithfully recorded, there was a two-foot gap underneath the structure. However, what it hadn't revealed was that the sand had piled up high underneath like a snow-drift, leaving very little crawl space. "We need to see if there's a hidden trap door under there," Fiona stated.

"I don't think I'll fit," said Daisy.

"Me neither." Frank patted his considerable beer belly. "I'm never one to shy away from getting my hands dirty but I fear my girth might be too much to get under there. I've had too much Bishop's Finger."

Bitsy sniggered.

Judging by his blank expression, the innuendo hadn't registered with him.

"I could probably fit," Partial Sue said. "But I'm really not partial to confined spaces."

Fiona didn't understand this as almost every room in her house was a confined space due to all the junk that she couldn't bear to part with.

"I'll do it," Bitsy said. Before the matter could be discussed, she'd ducked beneath the tape and had flipped onto her back and slipped under the structure like a mechanic sliding underneath a car. Using her phone torch to light her way, she frog-legged her way forward.

Frank gasped and averted his eyes as he glimpsed more than he should have. "Oh, my word!"

"Sorry," Bitsy called out, as she slowly disappeared from view. "Bitsy likes going commando."

Various grunts and groans echoed from beneath the bottom of the hut. Thankfully the only other flashes they caught sight of were from the phone torch, as Bitsy manoeuvred around the sand.

"Can you see anything, Bitsy?" Fiona called out. "Any doors or hidden panels?"

"Nothing yet," she replied.

After a few minutes, Bitsy emerged, covered in sand with cobwebs in her hair and on her face the colour of beetroot. "That was fun. But no dice, I'm afraid. Not a sausage."

"Are you sure?" asked Frank, in a tone that really wanted to question whether Bitsy had performed the task up to his exacting standards.

She held up her phone to silence any further doubt. "I filmed the whole thing. You can see for yourself."

From the shaky footage they glimpsed thick, rough, heavy-duty floor joists, crossed with solid timber floors, screwed down tight. No sign of any secret trap doors or means of stealthy entry. "It's solid under there," Bitsy said. "Impregnable."

"What about the side of the hut? A hidden door perhaps?" Partial Sue suggested.

A bizarre sight ensued. The whole party set about tapping the side of the hut that faced Malcolm's, feeling their way along its surface, banging, knocking and pressing, desperate to locate some hidden panel. Partial Sue even got on Frank's shoulders, swaying around to inspect the roof in case there was a secret hatch up there, but to no avail. It was a solid construction. No means of entry or exit.

Fiona clicked her fingers. "There is another way."

Everyone turned to face her. "What if someone came from a trap door in the Donovans' hut on the other side of Malcolm's. Same thing. They drop down onto the sand, crawl to the right, emerging in the gap between the two huts, but they keep crawling all the way under Malcolm's hut, coming out where the fire started. They'd still be hidden from view."

"But why go to all that trouble?" asked Partial Sue. "If that was the case, surely they would have just started the fire on the left-hand side of his hut, rather than the right-hand side?"

"Who knows?"

"It's worth a look." Bitsy was eager for another mission.

"No time like the present," Frank said.

Making the short trek around to the left-hand side of Malcolm's hut, they watched as Bitsy darted underneath the Donovans' hut, phone torch lighting her way. She re-emerged several minutes later shaking her head. "Same deal. Solid wood."

Fiona sighed deeply. They were back to square one.

CHAPTER 24

One week later

The front window of Dogs Need Nice Homes blurred with rain, distorting the view of cars and people outside as they frantically hurried to work. Then it did that thing that rain often does. Just when you think it can't get any worse, it decides to show off its dreary prowess, almost as if it's saying, 'Think that's bad. Wait until you see this.' The racket of raindrops violently increased, sounding like a million pea-shooters firing at once. So much for the prediction of an improvement in the weather. Now they could add wet to the exceptionally unseasonal cold and windy weather — the full miserable package.

Fiona was glad to be inside, a steaming cup of tea by her side, Simon Le Bon at her feet, and the promise of a full day ahead of her, although that was where the pleasantries ended. She'd come in early before opening, as she always found a solace in the mornings. The fledgling hours of the day were when she did her best thinking. Her unfettered mind had yet to be clogged up with the inevitable distractions. How much is this? Do you have this in a large? Are you accepting toys as donations? Will you do this for a fiver? (People were always trying to shave money off items that were already at hugely discounted prices.) Can you change watch batteries? A hangover from when the place had been a jewellers. It had ceased that function in the noughties when its smart dark-wood panelled interior and elegant glass cabinets became home to second-hand charity goods rather than reliable timepieces and delicate jewellery.

Despite the booming of the rain outside, Fiona managed to focus her brain, peering into the notebook on the table. She stared down the list of possible suspects, making notes as she went. If she were honest, she didn't have much to go on, just hunches and thoughts rather than hard evidence. Frank Marshall, unofficial sheriff of Mudeford Spit, was at the top. Nothing happened on that stretch of sand without him knowing or without his approval. Did he preside over his kingdom of huts like a dictator, ousting anyone who didn't measure up and didn't toe the line? A distinct possibility. Fiona put a big tick by his name. Rich Pullman and Sadie Donovan, and perhaps their spouses. Their collective noses out of joint at not getting their hands on Malcolm's hut, had they torched it out of revenge? Destroying his hut and all its beloved paraphernalia so they could then nab it for themselves and rebuild it to their exacting standards. Highly possible but not probable. Their desire to swap huts wasn't exactly common knowledge but it wasn't hidden either, seeing as Frank knew about it, and there was no way they could have got to Malcolm's hut to set it alight without being seen. Nobody could, thanks to the CCTV. Bitsy had put paid to any theories of secret trap doors they could slip through undetected. Plus, they had inadvertently put their own huts at risk. Reluctantly, although they were awful people, Fiona put a cross by their names.

Next on the list was Annie Follet. She had been there and awake when it had happened. The only person who had. She'd tried to save Malcolm's life by risking her own. She was a hero, and heroes are never suspects. Fiona didn't want to admit it because she liked Annie, respected her. But she had to ask the question, was her story a little too good to be true? The very fact that Fiona felt uncomfortable questioning it, also indicated that she could be onto something. The brave, hardworking single mum had the ultimate alibi. A story that newspapers had fed off. The shiny PR gift that Sophie Haverford had scooped up like a magpie had immunised Annie against having the finger pointed at her. Given her a cast-iron alibi and made her above reproach. Fiona didn't like that. You'd have to be extremely brave, foolhardy or have some cracking evidence to challenge that narrative. Had Annie set the fire earlier, only to re-emerge from her hut, claiming she was on the way to the loo to give herself an unshakable alibi? How she could've pulled this off without being spotted by the CCTV, Fiona had no idea, but she still put a question mark by her name.

At the bottom of the list Fiona had written a number and underlined it several times. Two hundred. A number that made her insides ache. This was the number of people who had been on Mudeford Spit on the night of the fire, all tucked up tight in bed, minding their own business until the alarm had been raised, or so they claimed. She'd been putting off the mammoth task of interviewing them all. Actually, if she were being honest, the thought of interviewing two hundred beach hut owners made her light-headed. One, because of the sheer complexity and gargantuan amount of time and effort it would take to arrange, setting up appointments and then getting around to visiting and interviewing each person. Many didn't live locally. Some lived as far afield as London and Birmingham. It could take months. She could probably do it over the phone or by Zoom, but it wasn't the same as speaking face to face. Gauging people's reactions and noting their nervous tics was harder over a screen and nearly impossible down a receiver. It had to be done in person, with them sitting in front of you.

The other reason she had been reluctant to embark on this all-consuming assignment was because she thought it might be a fool's errand. A complete waste of time and effort. The police had interviewed each of them in great detail. It had revealed nothing. No clues or leads or killer had emerged. Would their own amateur line of questioning get them any further? It seemed highly unlikely. But, then again, it had been over a month now since the murder. If the killer was among them — a member of the beach hut community or perhaps a cabal led by Frank Miller — one of them might get complacent. The conspiracy of silence might be a little less guarded now it had time to settle. Someone might let something slip. No matter how big the task and how small the likelihood of success, if there was a sliver of a chance they could uncover a clue, then the effort would be worth it.

But there was another, more pressing, reason that she didn't want to embark on a mass questioning spree. The CCTV. It had become the great leveller in all this. The elephant in the room that currently trampled over every theory or any suspect that emerged. There was no trace of anyone up and around at that time. Okay, there was Annie Follet, but she had been nowhere near Malcolm's hut when the fire started, and the CCTV backed up her story. It didn't really matter who Fiona suspected, what motives they had or what evidence she found or what her gut was telling her, everything got cancelled by the CCTV. Any potential suspect, if she had one to point the finger at, would just point their own finger back at the CCTV and say, "So if I did it, why wasn't I caught on camera. How can you have arson and no arsonist? There was only one possible conclusion . . .

The doorbell tinkled, snatching Fiona from her thoughts. A dripping silhouette of a woman stood in the doorway, preceded by a pushchair swathed in plastic like a tent on wheels, keeping the rain off her snoozing child. Almost merging with the pushchair, the woman was clad in a vast hooded cagoule complete with gloves and wellingtons. She squelched inside, closing the door behind her, a pool of water instantly forming by her feet. "I hope you don't mind," she said bashfully. "I've come to take you up on your offer."

Fiona attempted to hide her confusion, slightly embarrassed that she couldn't place who this woman was. Then Fiona noticed her glasses, oversized ones, almost covering the whole of her pale face. But it was the sad, sorrowful eyes behind them that caught her attention. It all came back to her. This woman had wanted to donate her grandfather's things but felt uncomfortable, distressed even, at the thought of losing them for good. "It's Mary, isn't it?"

"Yes, that's right," she answered. "I was wondering if you still had my late grandfather's things. There's something I'd like to take back, if that's okay?"

"Yes, yes. Of course." Fiona disappeared behind the counter. The box was where she had left it on the floor, untouched, still sealed with tape. Although she did notice it had a small hole in the side that she hadn't noticed before. Had Partial Sue been up to her old tricks? Poking a little spyhole so she could get an illicit peek at what was inside. She wouldn't put it past her. Fiona set the box on the counter. "There you go. I'll . . . er, be in the back if you need me." Fiona thought it best to give her a little privacy, especially if she were recovering something of great sentimental value.

It hadn't been a minute when she heard Mary calling out her thanks. By the time Fiona had emerged from the storeroom, she'd gone and the box was back behind the counter, tape restuck. This would have been a painful exercise for her. Clearly, she didn't want to make a fuss. Had simply wanted to get that sentimental item back in her possession without any song and dance, before it got emotional. Fiona could understand completely. She would be the same.

Partial Sue burst through the door, a jittering, wet stick insect of caffeinated energy, her saturated grey hair smeared about her face. "I've had a thought. A conclusion. The only conclusion that's left to us. The CCTV must have been faked. That's the only possibility."

Fiona grinned. It was exactly the same conclusion she had come to just moments before Mary had interrupted her thoughts.

CHAPTER 25

They were desperate to get the footage checked for signs of tampering, which is why their geographical position dictated the choice of specialist. Thankfully the rain had eased off a little and Freya's computer repair shop up the road was closest, only a few doors along Southbourne Grove.

Not known for analysing digital footage for signs of sabotage, its regular stock in trade ran along the lines of cleaning up hard drives, replacing cracked screens and updating laptops with the latest version of Windows. However, Freya, who ran and owned the place, punched well below her weight. After leaving university, her programming talent had secured her a job with a major tech company in London. She'd left after three years to take over her dad's computer repair shop once he'd retired, partly to keep the family business going, but mostly because she missed the beach. That was the curse of being brought up by the sea. Salt water never stopped running through your veins. And there was nothing like being your own boss, even if she could do the work with her eyes closed and standing on one leg, whistling the theme tune to *Coronation Street*.

Daisy had elected to stay at the shop. She had no problem staying behind as she would rather avoid Freya, who made her uneasy. It wasn't difficult to see why. A loud bang made them jump as they pushed open the door to the computer repair shop. Freya had made some big changes since taking over. Most noticeably a huge wooden structure that had taken over one half of the whole length of the interior, a roughly sawn timber construction that appeared to have been thrown up over a drunken weekend. Essentially, it was a long narrow corridor, like a vastly elongated voting booth, easily twenty feet long, open at one end, but enclosed top, bottom and sides. A large target stood at the other end with a brightly painted, albeit wobbly, bullseye.

Freya stood with her back to them, poised with a small axe in her hand. "Be with you in a minute." She was over six feet tall, with Celtic tattoo sleeves down each muscular arm and black spikey hair on top. She lifted weights, regularly attended kickboxing classes and if she'd been born a thousand years ago, would have probably raided monk-filled islands off the north-eastern coast of England and made off with holy relics. Though possibly not while wielding an axe. She raised the weapon above her head with both hands, then flung it at the target.

Cartwheeling through the air several times, it slapped uselessly against the target then clanged to the floor. "Damn it! I keep missing! I don't understand. I'm usually good at this sort of thing."

She turned to face them both and smiled with her black-painted lips. "Oh, hi, guys. What can I do you for?"

Fiona produced a USB drive. "I know this is a little unorthodox, but I don't suppose you know how to check if CCTV footage has been tampered with."

Freya's face lit up. "Oh yeah!" She took the stick from Fiona's hand and went behind the long counter, which was strewn with laminated price lists, outlining the costs of their various services, none of which included detecting fake footage. Stacks of refurbished beige computer hardware stood at one end, which hadn't shifted since the last time Fiona had been in, presumably because like second-hand underwear, people were reluctant to buy them as they didn't know where they had been. Fiona wondered about the logic of having delicate old computer equipment next to a place where heavy, sharp metal objects spun through the air. It seemed as sensible as having a lion and lamb petting zoo. But then, that was Freya for you. Highly intelligent but extremely unconventional and individual, and that was a good thing. Perhaps she should introduce her to Bitsy.

Freya slotted the stick into a towering upright desktop computer the size of a small skyscraper. It hummed menacingly as if it were about to explode or bring down the global banking system. She rubbed her hands together while everything loaded. "This is better than repairing slow laptops," she said. "It's totally moat!"

Fiona and Partial Sue looked at each other. "What's moat?" asked Partial Sue.

"Sort of vibey."

Neither of them was any the wiser. Freya was the first to use any new hip word that had just appeared on the scene. Although Fiona was sure she sometimes made them up, just to see if she could coin a new piece of slang that would slip into common parlance and then get added to the dictionary by the time it had gone out of fashion. Not so easy to achieve in gentle Southbourne, where they'd only just got 4G.

Freya typed furiously on the keyboard. "Okay, there's a lot of footage here. A whole month of it. Can you narrow it down?"

"Yes," Fiona replied. "It's just the night of the fifteenth of July."

"Where's it from?" Freya asked. "Do I need to sign some sort of NDA?"

"It's the footage of the beach hut burning on Mudeford Spit," Partial Sue informed her.

"That's right. Some of it's a bit disturbing." Fiona doubted whether Freya found anything disturbing. "No need for an NDA but if we could just keep it between us."

Freya agreed eagerly. "Oh yeah. Hundred per cent. Right, let's see if we can find some jiggery fakery. This might take a little time. Have a go on the axe throwing while you wait."

Partial Sue didn't need to be told twice. A natural-born bowler, her right arm had propelled her cricket team to the championships when she was at school. She snatched up an axe, took aim, and sent it flying. The blade embedded itself into the target with a loud thud, splintering the wood.

Freya came rushing out from behind the counter. "Did you just land one?"

"Yeah, but I didn't hit the bullseye."

"Who cares? I've been trying to land one all week, haven't managed it yet. Massive respect." The Amazonian computer expert held her fist out for a bump. Partial Sue regarded it curiously for a second, probably because it was the first time she'd ever been offered a fist bump. After a beat she accepted the offer and their knuckles nudged. Freya grinned then returned to her work.

Fiona stood a safe distance away while Partial Sue continued to punish the target, mercilessly sinking axe blades into the wood. She was in her element.

"This is fun. You should have a go, Fiona."

"No, I'm fine." Fiona smiled back, although she wasn't smiling inside. Like all the investigations they'd embarked on, a recurring feeling plagued her, that most of their efforts were just doubling up on where the police had already been. It was the same feeling she'd had when she thought about interviewing the 200 people on the spit that night. Why bother when the police had already been through the very same exercise and found nothing?

It was the same with the CCTV. Her suspicion that it had been faked had been growing in the back of her mind for quite some time — ever since they'd obtained the footage. But their tech officers would have analysed it on that fateful night, pulled it apart and found nothing. No jiggery fakery, as Freya put it. Was there any point if the police had already been there, done that, and come up with a blank?

She couldn't assume anything. Had to follow it through. See for herself.

Half an hour later, Freya called them over. "Okay, I've got good news and bad news."

"What's the good news?" Fiona headed over to the counter, joined by Partial Sue minus the axe.

Freya swivelled the screen around so they could both see. Impenetrable computer programming language covered it from top to bottom. "Part of the footage has been manipulated, using video-masking software — it's hidden in the data. Not particularly well, but hidden, all the same. Feeds from several cameras have been manipulated, edited so everything looks normal."

Fiona got a hit of adrenalin. At last, a breakthrough. However, she sensed a 'but' was coming. A rather large one.

"Do you know what was there before it got edited?" Partial Sue asked.

"No. That's been cut and deleted, I'm afraid."

Fiona braced herself. "What's the bad news?"

Freya sighed. "The bit that's been manipulated is not from the night of the fire."

"What do you mean?" Fiona asked.

"I mean that the video footage from the night of the fire was untouched. So I scanned the rest of the month just to be on the safe side and found a manipulated section from two weeks earlier, first of July. Same time of night, but a little earlier, about two in the morning."

Fiona's stomach plummeted, as if she'd just swallowed a bowling ball full of disappointment and confusion.

Partial Sue frowned. "This makes no sense at all."

"Which camera feeds were manipulated?" Fiona asked.

"Three from the Tides Restaurant. One covering the approach from the footpath, the other two are the cameras covering the sea-facing side of the restaurant, looking down the spit along the fronts of the beach huts. The fourth camera is the same view but from the Smuggler's House camera, looking up the spit. Here, let me show you." She hacked away at the keyboard and four camera feeds appeared, filling the screen. Fiona and Partial Sue peered in as she hit play. There was nothing really to see. Just the same night-time view of empty sand and beach huts, devoid of people or anything. "The fake footage starts at 2.10 a.m. and ends at 3.36 a.m."

"And it's like this the whole way through?" Fiona asked.

"Pretty much. I mean, I quickly whizzed through it on fast-forward. You might want to watch it normal speed just to make sure. But I can tell you, nothing changes. Nothing happens. Whatever went down on the first of July has been deleted and replaced with this bit of footage."

"What footage did they replace it with?"

"Don't know. I could do more investigation. But usually with these things it's an earlier period, an hour before, or it might be from the night before, same time, copied and pasted into the gap left by the deleted footage. Do you want me to check? It will take a bit longer."

Fiona's shoulders slumped. "No, that's okay. And you're sure the night of the fire hasn't been faked in any way?"

"Absolutely positive."

Rather than answering any questions, the CCTV footage had opened up more. Their theory had been proven but only to unearth evidence that appeared to have no bearing on the case whatsoever. "Thank you for doing this," Fiona said. "How much do we owe you?"

Freya closed down all the files on her screen and handed her back the USB stick. "Nothing," she said, then looked at Partial Sue. "As long as you show me how to throw them axes like a boss."

CHAPTER 26

As Fiona and Partial Sue left Freya's, their eyes were fixed on the wet pavements, the walk back down to the charity shop considerably slower than the walk up. Disappointment does that to you. Puts the brakes on and robs you of your enthusiasm and energy. The drizzle running down their faces didn't help either.

"Well, at least we got a result." Partial Sue attempted to put a positive spin on things. "It just wasn't the one we were expecting."

Fiona shook her head, not to disagree with her but to remove the logjam clogging up her brain. "We got that footage from Seb at the Smuggler's House and Marcus at the restaurant. They faked it. They're in this together somehow. That's the only explanation. But why?"

"Surely it must have something to do with the murder. It's too coincidental. Do you think the police know about it?"

Fiona avoided stepping in a puddle, taking the long way round. "You know, I wouldn't bet on it. Why would the police bother examining footage from two weeks before, when nothing happened then? We just got lucky that we had the whole month and that Freya is very thorough."

"So what are they trying to cover up, and what does it have to do with the fire? Do you think we should tell the police?"

"Not yet." Fiona suspected that it had nothing to do with the fire but didn't want to voice that opinion, didn't want to admit that they had hit yet another brick wall. "I do know one thing — after work, we're going straight up there to question Marcus and Seb to find out."

Up ahead they caught sight of the Wicker Man helping Daisy carefully carry something very large out of the back of her car. Cumbersome and swathed in billowing bin liners, it took two of them to manoeuvre it from her hatchback and into the shop. Since the malt-loaf incident, the Wicker Man had taken to only setting foot in the shop when it was either Fiona's or Daisy's turn to buy cake, thus avoiding exposing his taste buds to something Partial Sue had dragged in. Regardless of the new cake regime and the twenty-five-pence shop embargo, he still didn't trust her patisserie choices. Today was Daisy's turn. Fiona wondered if maybe a monstrous confection lay waiting under that black plastic. If so, it looked big enough to feed a wedding party. Good job too. The way Fiona was feeling right now she could do with all the cake she could lay her hands on.

Inside the shop, the Wicker Man and Daisy carefully positioned the mound of black on the table, taking up the whole of its surface.

"Whatever is that?" Partial Sue asked.

"I hope it's a giant cake," Fiona added. Both of them shrugged copious amounts of rainwater off their coats.

"Wet enough for you?" the Wicker Man commented.

Fiona gave a groan and ignored him. She really wasn't in the mood.

"It's not cake." Daisy fussed around the black mass, eyeing it from different angles and making micro-adjustments here and there. "It's something far better."

Partial Sue frowned. "You haven't forgotten the cake, have you? We're in dire need of baked therapy."

Daisy ignored the question. When she was satisfied with its position, she produced some nail scissors from her pocket and began carefully slicing around the bottom edge of the black bin liners. She took her time, one miniature snip after another.

"Do you know what it is?" Fiona asked the Wicker Man.

He shook his head. "Haven't the foggiest."

Finally, Daisy completed the delicate task, slicing a clean line around its rectangular base. Standing upright, she stepped back and grasped the top with her thumb and forefinger and plucked off the bin liner in one swift flourish. "Ta-da!"

Everyone gasped and crowded round, leaning in to get a better look.

"Careful," Daisy said. "It's very delicate."

There in front of them, perfectly recreated in painstakingly minute and accurate detail, was Hengistbury Head and Mudeford Spit, complete with each and every beach hut painted in its distinct and individual colours, bright and happy — all except Malcolm's, which was a blackened pitched-roofed cube. The detail was breathtaking. Tiny deck chairs and barbecues perched on verandas, and boats and dinghies sat idle on the sand. Some huts even had a seagull or two waiting atop roofs to snatch up stray ice-cream cones. At one end, as if shunting all the huts together, was the Tides Restaurant, complete with tiny figures drinking coffee on its wooden decking. The ominous form of the Smuggler's House sat at the other end and, in between, little figures in brightly painted beachwear walked dogs, dug holes, threw Frisbees and paddled in the sea.

Fiona had needed her spirits lifted and Daisy had achieved that, at a scale of one to 200, she guessed. "Daisy, this is incredible."

"You can say that again," added Partial Sue.

"What a beguiling creation!" the Wicker Man blurted theatrically. "You are truly gifted!"

"Thank you," Daisy said bashfully. "I thought it might help with the investigation. You know, give us a different perspective."

"A giant's perspective." The Wicker man guffawed.

Fiona peered closer, marvelling at the extraordinary detail. "That's why you videoed all the beach huts the other day."

Daisy nodded. "That's right, and I used Google Earth to get the position of everything right. It's all completely accurate."

"I don't doubt that for a second," Partial Sue said. "What an inspired idea."

"I can't take the credit for that," Daisy confessed. "I've been reading *All the Light We Cannot See*."

"Oh, I love that book," Fiona gushed.

"The blind girl's father builds a model of their neighbourhood in Paris, to help her find her way around," Daisy continued.

Partial Sue stuck her fingers in her ears. "La, la, la, la. I haven't read it yet!"

Daisy reassured her. "It's okay. That's the first line of the blurb. It doesn't give anything away."

The Wicker Man made himself scarce, seeing as there was no cake to be had. They spent the next half hour admiring Daisy's model, examining it from every angle and, if they were honest, not giving customers their full attention. Not that it mattered. The customers were similarly distracted, enraptured by her beautiful piece of miniaturist handiwork.

"You'll be getting commissions from architects soon," Partial Sue said, "to make models of their ugly buildings."

"Hey, guess who I saw in the model shop yesterday," Daisy said.

"Who?" Fiona asked.

"Well, I was buying some moss, to finish off the top of Hengistbury Head." Subconsciously Daisy's fingertips delicately tended the foliage on the model, bedding down the springy moss. "When Olivia walked in, Antony Owens' wife."

"What was she doing in there?" asked Partial Sue. "I wouldn't have thought that was her scene — glamour puss like her."

"I know. She looked just as shocked to see me too. I think she was worried about damaging her image. I mean, what do I care?"

"So, what was she doing there?" asked Fiona.

"Buying a model train for her nephew, apparently."

"Oh," Fiona replied, a little disappointed that it was fairly innocuous. Though trains seemed to be a recurring theme in this investigation, she thought. Frank, Bitsy and now Olivia — all into trains. Well, Olivia wasn't exactly what you'd class as a trainspotter having just bought one for her nephew, and neither was Bitsy, but was there a connection there? She wanted to dismiss it as nonsense, but she knew never to do that. Sometimes the most trivial connections had significance.

"Hey, we've got some news too." The CCTV had completely slipped Fiona's mind since the appearance of Daisy's model. She filled her in about the footage being faked, but not on the night of the fire.

Daisy screwed up her face. "Why would it be faked two weeks before?"

Partial Sue nudged the Noddy train on the model, testing to see if it moved. It didn't. "That's what we're going to find out tonight. We're marching up that spit to confront Marcus and Seb. Force them to spill the beans."

Fiona looked down at the full majesty of the model. Surely they would get some answers about what had happened on that narrow finger of sand. But would it relate to Malcolm's murder? She had her doubts. But something odd was going on with those two, she was sure of it.

CHAPTER 27

The bean-spilling would have to wait. The three women stood in the miserable rain, staring at the Tides Restaurant, closed up tight. They should have realised it wouldn't be open on an evening like this. Nobody would want to make the hike down to Mudeford Spit in this weather to sit in soaking wet clothes for a drink and a bite to eat, only to have to walk back and get soaked all over again.

"We should have called ahead," Partial Sue suggested.

Fiona shivered. "I really wish I had one of Bitsy's changing robe thingies. I'm drenched."

Nobody was in a very good mood. Nobody wanted to be there, Simon Le Bon included. On cue, he shook himself, corkscrewing water off his little body. Fiona really should have put a coat on him. Maybe they did changing robes for dogs. "You two go back. I'm going to press on. Call on Seb at the Smuggler's House."

"Oh no," Partial Sue said. "Not on your own, you're not. If he's the killer, then you need backup."

"That's right," Daisy agreed. "We're coming too."

The trio of drenched women trudged towards the end of the spit along the wet sand. They were the only people who did. Not even Frank Marshall stepped out to confront them

131

and ask them what they thought they were doing. His hut was locked tight and empty. In fact, every hut they passed had the same closed-up standoffish appearance. Mudeford Spit had truly shut up shop for the time being.

"It still looks beautiful, though, even in the wet." Daisy cast her eyes over the dark, shadowy water of the harbour as it was relentlessly pelted with raindrops, angled by the icy wind. The vibrant greens and yellows of trees and reeds around the harbour's edge contrasted starkly with the bruised sky.

Fiona had to agree. She could see why this place was so precious to those fortunate enough to own a beach hut. Dreariness had no effect on it. Indeed, the bleak emptiness only seemed to improve its beauty.

When they reached the Smuggler's House, Fiona approached the front door and held her finger down on the intercom buzzer. She waited a minute. No answer came.

She buzzed again, pressing the button so hard and for so long it was in danger of becoming stuck. "Damn it. Why isn't he answering?"

"Maybe he's out," Daisy suggested.

"On a night like this? I think he needs more persuasion." Partial Sue stepped back and craned her head up at the top floor, cupped her hands around her mouth and shouted, "We know you faked your CCTV footage."

A rumble came from above. Clumsy feet hurtling down a staircase. A clatter of locks spinning and sliding back.

The huge, studded, wooden door flew open. Seb stood dressed head to foot in a light beige tracksuit. With his elongated frame and dark blob of hair he looked like a startled matchstick. "You'd better come in."

They sat in his lounge, tastefully decorated in trendy Farrow & Ball colours combined with antique furniture and sprawling potted plants. The whole ensemble went well together and wouldn't have looked out of place in an interior design magazine. He set a pot of tea in front of them together with a plate of biscuits. Fiona really wanted to dislike Seb, but she had to admit it, apart from Bitsy, he had been the only one on this spit to make them tea.

"I've just called Marcus. He won't be long." Seb took a seat, sitting with his hands slotted between his knees.

"Can we just ask you—" Fiona began.

"I'd rather wait until Marcus gets here," Seb replied. "This involves him. Involves the both of us."

So they sat waiting. Not speaking. Just sipping tea and nibbling biscuits, admiring Seb's interior design skills, which Fiona couldn't really comment on, not when they were about to interrogate him about faking CCTV footage. Flattering his choice of colour palette and fixtures didn't seem appropriate when you were about to give someone the grilling of their life.

Eventually Marcus arrived, out of breath and wet through. His cheeks were rosy and his hair slicked back with moisture. He must've run or cycled here. He declined the offer of tea.

"So," said Fiona, "now we're all here, the CCTV footage — there's a period of just over an hour on the first of July that's been faked, or masked, as I'm told."

"Who told you that?" Marcus asked.

Partial Sue jumped straight in. "Doesn't matter. It's a fact, so speak. What has this got to do with Malcolm's death?"

Seb panicked. "Nothing, nothing at all. I swear."

"So why would you fake your CCTV footage?" asked Daisy.

Fiona followed up that question with another. "Was it a dry run? A test to see if you could get away without being seen two weeks later?" She knew this wasn't true, as the footage on the night of the fire hadn't been tampered with, but it didn't hurt to put them on the spot.

They both denied it vehemently.

Fiona and Partial Sue took turns firing a barrage of questions at the two men, who became more and more uncomfortable with each one posed.

Among the maelstrom Marcus suddenly blurted, "All right, all right. We'll tell you. We were poaching, okay?"

The ladies fell silent. Stunned. Not in a million years would they have guessed that this was the answer.

"Poaching?" Fiona said.

"Yes. Both of us," Seb answered.

Marcus continued. "It's hard running a business down here. Profit margins are on a knife edge. It's so weather dependent, as you can see. My restaurant has hardly opened this season and Seb's holiday flats are empty. Plus, the cost of living's gone up."

"That's the same for everyone," Fiona pointed out.

Marcus ran his hands through his wet hair and sighed. "Look, I realise that, but we were getting desperate. Our businesses were on the line. We needed to supplement our income."

"What was it you poached?" Daisy asked.

"Lobster," Marcus replied.

"Lobster?" the ladies chorused.

"Yes, I can sell it in the restaurant for sixty pounds a pop. We split what we make, seeing as it's a two-man job."

"We take a small rowing boat out when the tide is low and there's no wind. Makes it easier to row out and pull the pots in."

Fiona wondered if the radar at the coastguard station had ever detected them. Possibly too small, and even if it had, a rowing boat staying within a safe distance of the beach and then returning to shore would hardly set alarms ringing.

"How many lobsters do you take in a night?" asked Daisy.

Seb became sheepish. "About six."

"Six!" Partial Sue cried. "That's three hundred and sixty quid you've stolen out of a fisherman's pocket."

Marcus made a weak excuse. "Well, obviously they wouldn't get that for them wholesale. And we take from several different fisherman. We don't take from just one."

Partial Sue became agitated, the accountant in her furious that they were literally eating away at hardworking people's livelihoods, knocking masses of profit off their balance sheets. "That's disgusting. Do you think they can afford to lose that money? Well, it stops now."

"Yes," agreed Fiona. "It stops now."

"Yes, yes, of course," Marcus replied. "We're very sorry."

"Please don't tell the police," Seb pleaded.

"Is that why you changed the footage?" Fiona asked.

Marcus sighed. "We don't normally bother, but when the fire happened, the police asked to see our CCTV. I checked the legalities. Luckily, they don't have a right to see it, unless they have a warrant, although it would look suspicious if we withheld it. But we didn't have to hand it over straight away. It bought us some time."

"I'm not too bad with IT," Seb added. "So I downloaded some software and deleted and pasted over us poaching. They haven't come knocking on our door, so it must have worked."

Fiona shook her head. "It didn't. Our IT expert found it in half an hour."

"You got lucky," Partial Sue said. "Police probably didn't look that far back."

Marcus held up both hands. "We're so sorry. We won't do it again, we swear."

Seb nodded eagerly in agreement.

"We won't go to the police," Fiona said.

"We won't?" Partial Sue questioned.

"No. However, we want something in return."

Seb and Marcus looked more worried than they had before.

CHAPTER 28

Marcus and Seb sat bolt upright on the particularly nice sofa. Two unlikely partners in crime awaiting their fate, surrounded by tasteful soft furnishings. Their faces had paled and Marcus chewed the inside of his lip. Seb obviously couldn't stand it any longer. "What do you want?"

Deliberately slowly, Fiona retrieved her notebook and pen from her bag. Opening it out to a fresh page, she clicked the top of her pen, holding it poised above the paper, ready to write. "You are going to tell us about every little secret on this spit."

"Dish the dirt," Partial Sue said with some relish.

Daisy couldn't help joining in. "Spread the muck." It wasn't a phrase commonly used when referring to divulging the truth, but the two men understood all too well what she meant.

"Yes," Fiona agreed. "All the little whispers and conspiracies, we want to know about them."

Marcus and Seb exchanged puzzled looks, then turned their attention back to the three ladies. "What secrets? We don't know any."

Fiona smiled. Not a nice smile, more of a threatening one. "Oh, I'm sure you do. Otherwise, I pick up the phone and call my friends DI Fincher and DS Thomas."

"Wait, please!" Marcus had his hands up again. "We don't know any secrets, I swear."

"What about Frank Marshall?" Fiona asked.

"What about him?"

"He seems to be in charge down here," Partial Sue answered.

"Yes," Seb replied. "He thinks he's the king of the spit but that's nothing new."

"What else?"

Marcus nervously scratched the side of his neck, clearly racking his brains, searching to find some morsel that would satisfy them. His face brightened. "He doesn't like Antony Owens, the beach hut liaison officer. Doesn't rate him. Badmouths him every chance he gets."

Fiona was getting impatient. "He's already admitted as much. Come on, tell us something we don't know. Is he behind a conspiracy of beach hut owners to oust anyone who doesn't fit in?"

"Maybe," Seb said without thinking. "I don't know. We're not beach hut owners. I run a restaurant and Seb owns holiday flats. We don't mix in their circles. Pretty sure they would rather we weren't down here."

"They never use our businesses," Marcus added.

"Why's that?" asked Daisy. "Is the food not very good?"

Marcus became indignant. "My food is excellent. Beach hut owners don't need us. By and large they prefer to do their own cooking — have barbecues and the like. Besides, they think we're overpriced, and attract the riff-raff, who come down here and drink and make a noise."

"Same here," said Seb. "People who stay in my flats aren't hut owners. They're general public. Hut owners would rather it were exclusively theirs. Closed off, a gated community."

Fiona thought back to Frank's suggestion about having a checkpoint. "See, we kind of know that already. Tell us something new." Fiona pulled out the USB stick. "Otherwise this goes straight to the police."

"Tell them, Seb." Marcus nudged him in the ribs.

"Tell us what?" Fiona prompted.

Seb swallowed hard and gripped the edge of his seat cushion with both fists.

CHAPTER 29

Seb reached over and poured himself a cup of tea. It must have gone cold, the pot had been standing there for so long. He didn't care and took a long, deep gulp, almost downing it in one before taking a deep breath. "Malcolm Crainey and I were cousins. Nobody knows about it because we never mentioned it to anyone."

"He was your cousin?" Fiona blinked several times, taking in this new information. Now this was something she didn't know, nor anyone else apparently.

Seb nodded, drained the dregs in his cup and placed it carefully back on its saucer.

Fiona offered her sympathies, as did the other ladies. "I'm so sorry for your loss."

"Don't be. There was no love lost between us. We had a falling out. Bit of bad blood. When my mum died, she left her house in Southbourne to Malcolm, not me. I mean, she also owned a beach hut down here, which I inherited. But back then in the late eighties, a beach hut on Mudeford Spit wasn't as valuable as it is now. They were far cheaper. Her house was worth four times what the beach hut was worth. I was so annoyed and angry at her. She'd favoured Malcolm over me, her own son. Always had done when we were growing up.

Malcolm Talcum, I used to call him, because in her eyes he was whiter than white, couldn't do anything wrong because he was always so easy going and laid-back, never any trouble. In reality, he grew up to be a slacker and never amounted to anything. I tried to contest the will, but it was impossible, set in stone. Anyway, a close family friend said there was a method behind my mum's madness. Malcolm's never been very good with money. Slips through his fingers like water. Hasn't got a clue how to make it or hold on to it. Have you heard he used to fix everyone's broken bikes and outboard motors for free?"

The three ladies nodded.

Seb continued. "He could have been onto a nice little earner with that one. Made a living for himself. No business sense whatsoever, hence why he lived like a pauper. Plus, his parents had passed away years ago, and left him nothing but debt. So this friend said that she'd heard my mum saying she thought Malcolm needed a house more than I did, as there were rumours he'd had an illegitimate child, a son. She thought he should have the house in case he needed to bring him up."

Fiona frantically wrote this in her notebook. If Malcolm had a son, he could potentially be a suspect. A descendant, even an illegitimate one, could be set to inherit a very valuable property. Combined with abandonment issues, there'd be plenty of bitter motivation there. Fiona tested that theory. "How often did he see this son?"

"Like I said, it was just a rumour. I'm not sure he even existed. Back then I confronted him about it. He denied having a child. Then said he didn't even want the house. Too much responsibility, even though he loved it dearly. It was a very special house, you see, for a lot of people."

"How so?" Fiona asked.

"I'll come to that in a minute. Malcolm offered to do a straight swap. The house for the beach hut. He wanted it because it would be far easier, less maintenance for one person. So we swapped. I thought my luck had changed, but it

139

turned out Malcolm wasn't as stupid as I thought. When I took over ownership, I found out the house had all sorts of problems: subsidence, dry rot, leaking roof — structurally, it was unsafe."

"Did Malcolm know about that?" Partial Sue asked.

Seb shook his head. "He denied it. Said he didn't know about that sort of thing, which, looking back now, was probably true, but at the time I thought he'd engineered it all, that he'd double-crossed me. Bottom line was the cost of the work was more than the house was worth. I only had one option — to sell it to the local council as a tear-down to put flats on. It's a clifftop residence so the land fetched a good price, more than the beach hut was worth. I made a nice wedge of cash and bought the Smuggler's House for a song — place was empty, had been for years. I did it up and turned it into what you see today. However, now it was Malcolm's turn to get angry because I'd sold his auntie's house, a house that he and thousands of other people adored. He thought I was responsible for destroying a beloved Bournemouth icon."

"What icon?" Fiona asked.

"The Sea Garden."

Partial Sue and Daisy both slapped hands over their shocked mouths. Fiona wondered what heinous crime had prompted such a response. It wasn't as if he'd killed someone, although that was yet to be proven. "What's the Sea Garden?"

"I loved the Sea Garden." Daisy almost had tears in her eyes.

"I was so partial to a trip to the Sea Garden when I was a little girl." Partial Sue's normally firm and stern manner had become fragile and vulnerable.

Fiona asked again, "What's the Sea Garden?"

"Ask anyone born before the nineties," Partial Sue replied, "and I guarantee you they will become misty-eyed at the mention of the Sea Garden."

"That's right," Seb agreed. "It was a landmark. My mum and dad's life work. They turned the vast front garden of their house at West Cliff into a giant grotto of shells, collected from their trips abroad over the years, with wishing wells and little statues, fountains and shrines. Every inch was covered in shells big and small. Opened it to the public, completely free of charge, although you could drop coins in its wishing wells, which they'd give to charity."

Daisy Googled images to show Fiona. It was just as they'd described. A delightfully haphazard and eclectic, maze-like garden of cement embedded with shells but also coloured sea glass, mosaics, broken crockery, crazy paving and statues. Faded family album shot after faded family album shot had been uploaded onto Google images of a more innocent time. Little boys and girls with sensible haircuts dressed in itchy shorts and dresses, holding their mums' and dads' hands, wandering around a wonderland of curiosity and dishevelled eccentricity. It had that rare and enticing mix of magic and madness. It reminded Fiona of a larger, more sprawling version of the front of Malcolm's beach hut.

Seb cleared his throat, almost certainly a little choked at the memories of his family home. "There was massive outrage in the local news when it got out that the Sea Garden was to be demolished. Protests, even. Malcolm wouldn't talk to me. Felt I'd destroyed his childhood, plus thousands of others' who'd grown up besotted by the Sea Garden. Strangely, the public didn't point the finger at me, but at the council, specifically a local councillor at the time who led its destruction."

"Who?"

"Malorie Granger."

Now it was Fiona's turn to gasp, along with her colleagues.

CHAPTER 30

They knew Malorie Granger all too well, from run-ins with her in the past. She was a hardy perennial of a woman who now managed the local community centre, which she ruled with a rod of iron — a rod swathed in chintzy Laura Ashley wallpaper. Fiona was unaware of her past as a councillor, but it didn't surprise her. Thick-skinned and built to withstand the harshest storms of criticism, like a sturdy, well-waxed jacket, Malorie bulldozed people into doing what she wanted, hence, her nickname: the Bulldozer in Barbour.

"The protesting didn't bother her, not in the slightest," Seb recalled. "I think she liked it. Thrived on conflict and liked the attention."

"Fartlighter," Partial Sue proposed, hoping, like Freya in the computer shop, to get her new saying coined and into common usage.

Seb didn't pick up on her peculiar comment. "No matter how much the public harassed her it only made her more determined to tear down the Sea Garden and get her flats built."

"Why do you think that was?" asked Fiona.

"Who knows? But a prominent councillor awarding a contract to a private developer . . ." Seb whistled and made a motion that suggested someone receiving a backhander. "But there was one thing that did get her goat. Without her knowledge, Malcolm visited the building site as it was being pulled down. The foreman took pity on Malcolm and allowed him to spirit away bits of the Sea Garden. Every afternoon, just as they were about to knock off, he'd ride up there on his bike and fill his rucksack with whatever would fit and whatever hadn't broken. The foreman even went as far as to instruct his guys to take lots of care around two giant clam shells. Chipping away with chisels, they managed to pull them from the concrete unbroken. Malcolm made two trips cycling back with them under his arm. He began transforming his hut into a miniature version of the Sea Garden. A shrine to it. Malorie was furious when she found out. Took it personally."

"Why was that?" asked Daisy. "If she was so thick-skinned."

Seb rubbed the bridge of his nose, thought for a second or two. "This is only a guess, but I'd say she doesn't like people challenging her authority, but also she didn't want there to be a public monument of what she'd destroyed. She thought he was doing it to annoy her. Funny thing is, he was doing it to annoy me, not her. Wanted me to be continually reminded of what I'd done. Anyway, Malorie was on the warpath. Tried everything to get rid of the detritus on his hut, as she called it, citing this bylaw and that bylaw. But she was powerless against the Beach Hut Residents' Association and its liaison officer."

"Antony Owens?" Fiona asked.

"No, it was someone different back then. Old fella, nice guy. Passed away now. Anyway, strictly speaking, Malcolm wasn't breaking any rules. Huts are allowed to be personalised as long as other beach hut owners don't object. The shells could only be removed by a vote if all the other owners objected. The spit was different back then. Owning a beach hut wasn't the status symbol it is now, and the huts were far more affordable, owned by all sorts of different people, not just rich ones. They all had great affection for the Sea

Garden. Saw it as part of the area's heritage just like the spit itself. When they put it to the vote the result was unanimous. Malcolm got to keep his shells."

Fiona closed her notebook. "Okay, I think we have enough. You're off the hook."

"You're not going to go to the police?" Marcus asked.

"No," Fiona replied. "On the understanding that the poaching stops and never starts again."

"Yes, yes, of course." Seb and Marcus agreed eagerly, slumping in their seats, daring to let relief spread over their faces.

"Just one other thing," Partial Sue said.

The worry snapped back into their eyes, concern that this wasn't over yet.

"Say this illegitimate son of Malcolm's can't be found or doesn't exist. Let's also assume Malcolm doesn't have a will. If that's the case, as his cousin, you'd be his last remaining relative. You would inherit his beach hut."

"It's an empty shell — pardon the pun." Seb replied. "What's left to inherit?"

"So was the Smuggler's House when you bought it," Fiona pointed out. "And the hut's not worthless. The plot would still be worth a small fortune."

This riled Seb. "Look, I didn't kill my cousin for his beach hut, if that's what you think. I'm quite happy with what I got out of our swap. Even if I had killed Malcolm, I'd have been caught by my own CCTV cameras." He held his hands up. "Okay, I know I doctored the footage when we were poaching, but the night of the fire is intact. The police have checked it and I'm sure your IT expert has too. I didn't set fire to his hut. Didn't go near it."

Once more the CCTV had given another likely suspect a cast-iron alibi, ruling them out before they'd even got started. Fiona had no counter argument for that one.

However, Partial Sue wasn't done yet. "If you and Malcolm disliked each other so much, how come you lived within a few feet of each other? That must have been awkward."

Seb didn't hesitate to answer. "Malcolm may be remembered as this Bohemian layabout, but he was stubborn and so am I. Neither of us would budge an inch. Childish, I know. But that's family rivalry for you. After a while we just got used to ignoring each other. Became natural. That's all."

"The only thing we're guilty of is poaching," Marcus said.

"That's right." Seb added.

Reluctantly, Fiona had to agree — for now. Besides, they had bigger fish to fry. A big, wriggling pike that wouldn't take kindly to being on the hook and questioned: Malorie Granger. Especially as last time they spoke, she had banned them from the community centre.

CHAPTER 31

Next day, the rain had stopped but Fiona's mood hadn't improved. It had deepened. The thought of confronting Malorie Granger did that to a person. At least she'd have Partial Sue by her side for a bit of moral support, although she did wonder if they should both be wearing stab vests beneath their comfortable clothing to protect themselves from Malorie's barrage of legendary well-bred bolshiness.

Daisy had wanted no part of it. Quite understandably, the woman terrified her. Quick as you like, Malorie would have her agreeing to volunteer for something she had no desire to do, like clearing marshland of shopping trolleys. Malorie had a habit of publicly getting behind noble causes but recruiting others to do the dirty work, showing up at the last minute when the task was complete to take the glory. No, thank you. Daisy's skills would be better suited to staying at the shop with Simon Le Bon and scouring the internet for signs of Malcolm's illegitimate offspring.

"Gird your loins," Partial Sue warned as they stood outside the community centre, poised to go in.

"I'm girding everything at the moment." Fiona pushed open the stiff double doors and entered Malorie's kingdom, a land of disinfectant-smelling floors, suspended ceilings (hopefully not asbestos, although if they were, Malorie would probably dismiss it as a load of fuss about nothing), fold-out tables and gallons of tea, interspersed with Scrabble, knitting, card games and gentle chit-chat. Its inhabitants looked happy enough, but that's what happened when you had a dictator who kept everyone in line. Better to be feared than loved.

Fiona and Partial Sue wended their way through a forest of Blue Harbour and Country Casuals. Though they were loath to admit it, Malorie had done a good job. The place had a buzz to it. There was energy here, positive and happy. People enjoying one another's temperate company.

But that all changed as Malorie emerged from her office at the back. Everyone's demeanour altering slightly, a collective flinch brought on by simultaneous tensing. The volume of happy banter dropped to reverential tones, less relaxed and more guarded, as if people didn't want to appear to be enjoying themselves too much. Fiona noticed that nobody made eye contact with Malorie as she marched through their midst. Rather like a hostage situation, your chances of survival were better if you kept your head down.

Catching sight of Fiona and Partial Sue, Malorie's friendly but aggressive face transformed into plain aggressive. "What are you two doing here? I thought I'd banned you."

"We need to ask you some questions," Fiona replied, drawing closer.

"Nope, too busy. I've got far too much on my hands with this lot." She gestured to the community centre members, who now felt guilty for simply existing. "Kindly leave."

Fiona knew how to handle Malorie. She'd done it before, and she could do it again. Rattle some skeletons. "Whatever happened to the Sea Garden?"

If someone had been playing a piano at that moment it would have stopped abruptly. Even the people at the tables went quiet, terrified but also curious as to how this standoff would go down. Some would have dived under the tables if they hadn't been on NHS waiting lists for knee and hip replacements.

Malorie fixed Fiona with two icy brown eyes, cold enough to freeze off verrucas. Fiona returned the stare, watching as the cogs clicked away in Malorie's mind — was this a fight she could win in front of all her subjects? Her answer was swift and economic. "Follow me. As you were, ladies and gentlemen." Malorie became all sweetness and light once more, making friendly comments as she passed each table, sending out nothing-to-see-here vibes. "That's a double word score, Reg. I do like that cosy you're knitting, Betty. Your tea's getting cold, Bill."

Malorie was never normally this nice. *Clearly overcompensating*, Fiona observed.

Inside her office with the door firmly shut, Malorie took to her leather-seated throne in front of a messy desk strewn with paper, folders and leaflets, which she would probably argue was the sign of a genius. Fiona and Partial Sue sat on the other side on a pair of sticky orange plastic chairs.

Malorie opened the batting. "What do you want? Dredging up the past, are we?"

"Yes, we are, actually," Fiona replied. "You've heard of Malcolm Crainey's death on Mudeford Spit?"

"I have."

"Care to tell me about your relationship with him?"

"Relationship!" Malorie guffawed. "We weren't going out with each other. Where do you get your information, *Hello* magazine?"

"No," Partial Sue answered. "A source tells us you demolished the Sea Garden to make way for flats."

Malorie rolled her eyes. "Well, that's not exactly a secret. That was common knowledge at the time. The whole town was predictably outraged. Local papers ran stories on it every day. I was public enemy number one. They even hung an effigy of me outside the Sea Garden as a protest, although it wasn't a very good one. Made me look like Colonel Gaddafi."

"How did that make you feel?" asked Partial Sue.

"What, looking like Colonel Gaddafi?"

"No, being vilified like that."

Malorie leaned forward, laced her fingers together. "Look, you don't get into local politics to make friends. It doesn't work like that. You get into local politics to—"

"Accept backhanders," Fiona interrupted.

Malorie's face suddenly reddened as if someone had blow-dried it on the highest setting. "How dare you? That's libellous. I could sue you."

"Well, prove us wrong," Fiona replied.

Malorie slapped the table, sending the mess of paperwork jumping in the air. "I am grossly offended by your comments."

Her fake outrage may have worked on the community centre, but they weren't going to work on Partial Sue and Fiona. They were prepared for her intimidation tactics.

"Well, did you accept backhanders?" Partial Sue asked. "It's a straightforward question that you seem to be avoiding, which is not a good look when you're protesting your innocence. Was it in your financial interest to tear down the Sea Garden and put up flats?"

"No, it most certainly wasn't," Malorie replied. "I have principles. I have integrity."

"All very well saying it. But how do we know that's true?" Fiona asked.

Malorie glared at them. "Because I can prove it. I tried to save the Sea Garden. I bet your source didn't tell you that. You can look through the public records at the time. We carried out feasibility studies, exploring how to keep it going if it were council run. It was impossible. Every scenario we modelled proved to be fruitless. Firstly, we would have had to find nearly a quarter of a million to repair the house to make it safe — more than it was worth at the time. Then we tried to figure out how we could make money out of it to pay for its upkeep. You can't open the house itself to the public. It's nothing special, and who's going to rent a house where the front garden is made of concrete and open to anyone?"

"Lots of stately homes manage it," Partial Sue pointed out.

149

Malorie sighed. "This was a fairly standard 1930s, detached, four-bedroom home, not Chatsworth House. Look, I know it held great affection for everyone, me included. But it only works if it has private owners who let people browse for free. If nobody lived there, we'd need staff to run it and a warden on site twenty-four hours a day to keep it secure. By that time the place was being regularly vandalised and its wishing wells emptied of coins. Plus, to help pay for staff, a warden and its upkeep we'd needed to have charged an entrance fee of three pounds, and that was back in the early nineties. Nobody would have paid it — not to see a bunch of old shells, especially as it had been free before. The public would accuse the council of ripping them off as they do with everything. But it all has to be paid for. So you see, there would have been outrage either way, whether we kept it or demolished it. I made a decision. It was put to council vote and the thing was demolished. It's all in the records."

"Okay," Fiona said. "But what about Malcolm? He salvaged bits of the Sea Garden from under your nose, made his own mini version on Mudeford Spit. That must have been a thorn in your side."

Malorie shook her head, folded her arms. "Rubbish. It was the other way around. I felt sorry for him. He wanted to save some of it for posterity. I can understand that."

"But didn't that smart?" Partial Sue persisted. "Having a reminder of what you'd destroyed for all to see."

"Not at all. I was happy some part of it survived. Like I said, I didn't want to see it disappear, but in local government you have to make hard calls. Ones that aren't popular with people."

The diplomatic answers were a little too convenient for Fiona's liking. She needed to rattle Malorie a bit more. Provoke that anger of hers. When she lost her temper, she often lost control of what she was saying. Fiona knew just the thing. "Did you kill Malcolm Crainey?"

Malorie's lips tightened into two thin lines, like the stretched opening of a balloon. "Don't be ridiculous! Do you think I would kill someone over a bunch of crusty old shells and broken china?"

"You said you had great affection for the Sea Garden," Partial Sue replied. "Crusty shells and broken china don't sound like it."

Malorie paused. Fiona couldn't tell whether her top was about to blow and she was just building up the pressure, prepping herself for a violent outburst.

"All right." She kept a lid on her temper, wheeled her chair backwards, spun it through 180 degrees, and scanned an overflowing stack of shelves rammed with folders and books wedged at all sorts of angles. Selecting a black volume, she returned to the desk and opened it out at the middle. Fiona noticed that it wasn't a book, but a portfolio with clear plastic wallets for holding a myriad of business cards, collected, no doubt, over the years from the various contractors and companies she had done business with.

"Ah, here we are." Malorie plucked a battered, yellowing card covered in basic graphics, bearing the name and details of a company called Edgeware Demolition and Site Clearance. She flipped the card over, called a number that had been handwritten on the back, and put it on speakerphone.

A gruff but not aggressive voice came on the line. "Hello."

"Eddie, its Malorie Granger."

"Malorie? Oh Malorie, from the council."

"Yes, that's the one. Although I'm not at the council anymore. I manage the community centre. How's retired life treating you?"

"Oh, can't complain," Eddie replied.

"You should join us at the community centre. We're a happy breed." Malorie never ceased the hard sell.

"I don't know about that. I'm enjoying the peace and quiet for now."

Malorie laughed. "Good, good. Listen, I'm trying to remember something about the Sea-Garden demolition. Do you remember that fellow who would go through the skips after you knocked off work?"

"Yep, sure do. Malcolm. We told him to clear off, but you told us to let him have whatever he wanted."

"Ah, yes, that was it." Malorie flicked a look at Fiona that said *I told you so*. "And didn't I ask you nicely if you could remove the giant clam shells from the cement so he could have them?"

"Yep. Pain in the arse that was, 'scuse my French. But we got 'em out without splitting them. Tough old things, they were."

"Well, you did a good thing that day. Thank you so much for your time, Eddie, and I'll keep a seat reserved for you at the community centre. Enjoy the rest of your day."

"You too."

Malorie put the phone down, leaned back in her chair, a smug expression spreading across her rosy-cheeked face.

It wasn't proof that she didn't do it, but it didn't make the case against her very strong. Unbeknown to either Malcolm or Seb, Malorie had allowed a small portion of the Sea Garden to survive, contrary to what was written in the paper about her being the destroyer of fond childhood memories. Malcolm's little shrine to the Sea Garden had been enabled by her, not hindered. Not the actions of someone who wanted him dead. Unless it was the best alibi anyone had conceived for a long time, and she'd set up Eddie to say those things before they'd arrived. Highly unlikely.

"Okay, point taken," Fiona conceded.

"What, no apology? No 'sorry for accusing you of murder'."

"Nope," Fiona replied. Malorie would see apologising as a sign of weakness, and that would not stand them in good stead for their next meeting, seeing as whatever nefarious things went on around here always seemed to involve Malorie in some shape or form. Fiona decided that instead of an apology, she would throw her own words back at her. "When you're investigating a case, you have to make some hard calls. Ones that aren't popular with certain people."

Malorie regarded Fiona through narrowed eyes, appearing to be more offended that she'd commandeered her own words than of being accused of murder. "I see. Will that be all?"

"Do you know anyone else who could have had it in for Malcolm?" Partial Sue asked.

Malorie snorted an abrupt laugh. "Any one of those hut owners, I'd say. Bunch of snobs in my book. Especially that Frank Marshall. Always pestering me when I was a councillor to put a stop to whatever thing was currently offending him. You know, the new Noddy train that replaced the old green one used to have a face on it. Bit like Thomas the Tank Engine. Kids loved it. You know he got that taken off, citing an ancient bylaw that no advertising was allowed on the spit. It was only a painted face, for crying out loud! Anyway, he did propose a new bylaw once and it got accepted, and Malcolm broke it. You should look into that."

Now it had become interesting. Fiona wanted to shift to the edge of her seat, but its tacky surface prevented her. "What law did he break?"

"It was after my time. You'd have to ask Antony Owens about it. He'll tell you."

"Can't you tell us?" asked Partial Sue.

"Nope, you've had enough of my time already. And it's better if you hear it from the horse's mouth, as it were."

Malorie got up and showed them to the door. Reluctantly, Fiona and Partial Sue rose from their seats, wondering what Antony Owens had been keeping from them. Whyever had he held this back if it involved Malcolm and Frank Marshall?

"Just one more thing," Fiona asked. "Did Malcolm have a son?"

Malorie held the door open. "Not that I know of."

153

CHAPTER 32

Daisy hovered over the model of the spit, dabbing a seagull's beak with a paintbrush that had bristles as small as a pinhead. Simon Le Bon jumped out of his bed, greeting Fiona and Partial Sue with a stretch and a waggy tail.

"How did you get on?" Daisy asked without glancing up or losing concentration as she applied yellow paint.

"Good," answered Fiona. "We have something. Nothing to do with Malorie, she's in the clear for now."

Partial Sue made a beeline for the storeroom and put the kettle on. "Antony Owens is in the spotlight now."

"Oh." Daisy jerked upright. "He called earlier. Asked if he could come in for an update at three thirty. I said yes. I hope that's okay."

"That's more than okay," Fiona replied. "That's perfect. We need to question him."

Daisy cleaned her brush off with a wet wipe. "Question him? What about?"

"He's been keeping something from us," Fiona replied. "Something about him, Frank Marshall and a bylaw that Malcolm broke."

Daisy began tidying up her brushes and paints. "Oh my gosh. Whatever could that be?"

"Not sure," Fiona replied. "But Antony Owens' timing couldn't be better."

Partial Sue put a cuppa in everyone's hands. They sat down around the model being careful to not put their tea anywhere near it.

"How did you get on with finding Malcolm's secret off-spring?" Partial Sue asked Daisy.

"Not a sausage, I'm afraid. It's incredibly difficult to track down anyone online when you don't know their name or where they live and, of course, Malcolm wasn't online either, making it almost impossible. I did find a site called the National Will Register, checked with them on the off chance that Malcolm had a will and left his beach hut to this long-lost son. But there was nothing there, so I think it's definitely safe to say he never made a will."

"That fits," Partial Sue remarked. "I can't imagine some-one like Malcolm having the foresight to make a will, which would work in Seb's favour. Under intestacy rules, if there's no will and no son, Seb gets what's left of Malcolm's hut. Highly suspect."

Fiona shook her head. "I think that's far too risky for Seb. It's not a hundred per cent guaranteed. Plus, as his cousin, he'd know the finger would be pointed straight at him. But like everything in his case, the CCTV doesn't lie. Well, it does, just not on the night in question."

Partial Sue harrumphed.

"Okay," Fiona said. "I think we need to ask around the spit about this illegitimate son. Might be a good little task for Bitsy. She'd be perfect at teasing out the gossip down there."

"But even if we find his son, and we think he's the killer, we're back to the same problem with the CCTV. Besides, there's hardly anyone down there at the moment to ask," Partial Sue pointed out.

"Well, maybe we'll have to wait until the weather clears up. But I think we have to follow this lead." Fiona gazed out the window at the endless canopy of grey stretched across the sky, tugged along by the ceaseless and bitter northerly. It could be a very long wait.

"We should also ask Antony Owens," Daisy suggested. "He might be able to shed light on it."

Fiona took a swig of tea. "You'd think, wouldn't you? But I'm just wondering what else he's been holding back on."

Partial Sue agreed. "Does seem a bit strange when he's the one who hired us to find the truth, but he's not been telling us the whole story."

"We shouldn't be too judgy," Daisy said. "Let's see what he's got to say for himself when he comes in."

* * *

At three thirty precisely, the doorbell tinkled. The fastidiously smart figure of Antony Owens bedecked in a well-tailored suit stepped in, his equally dapper wife behind him. The pair of them contrasted starkly with the ordered chaos of the charity shop. With her perfect hair and her face camouflaged in pristine make-up, Olivia slipped into the shop, swiftly shimmying sideways through the door before it shut, hands tucked tightly around her midriff, ensuring she made no contact with it.

Antony Owens smiled. "Good afternoon. I hope you don't mind our little intrusion."

Fiona smiled back. "Not at all. Technically it's not an intrusion if you've been invited."

"Like a vampire," Daisy commented.

Olivia silently nosed around the edges of the shop, staring at the counter, then moving on to the bookshelves and clothes, curious about the stock they kept but always cautiously keeping a safe distance from anything that might contaminate her. Surprise caught her off guard when her eyes alighted on Daisy's model. Clip-clopping her way over, as fast as her spiked heels would allow, she cooed and wowed, taking in the wonder of Daisy's miniature marvel.

"This is incredible!" Olivia gushed. "I love it."

Antony joined his wife, examining the model. "Who made it?"

"Daisy did, single-handedly," Partial Sue said.

Olivia clasped her hands together in delight, heaping praise on Daisy. "I can see how much work you've put into this. It's wonderful. So detailed. That's why I saw you in the model shop, you were buying moss for this."

Daisy blushed. "That's right."

"May I take a picture?"

"Of course. That'll be five pounds," Partial Sue said.

Olivia's face became stern.

"I'm joking," Partial Sue reassured her.

Olivia released a breath and clutched her chest. "Oh, I thought you were being serious for a moment." She gave a nervous laugh, then pulled out a slab of a phone that had five lenses.

"That's a smart-looking phone," Fiona remarked.

"Thank you," she replied.

"Olivia loves having the latest gadget," Antony Owens said. "Gadget mad, she is."

"No, I just like nice things, that's all."

Fiona could see that. But she'd level the same observation at her husband. The pair had expensive tastes.

"Shall we press on?" he asked.

They gathered around the counter, seeing as the table was taken up with the model and Olivia was exploring all sorts of creative angles to take shots. Antony declined the offer of tea as did his wife. Fiona outlined their progress or lack of it, mostly dead ends and things that didn't make sense, most notably the spontaneously combusting beach hut with its gravity-defying fire, and that the CCTV had failed to capture anyone at the time, apart from Annie Follet.

Antony Owens rubbed his chin. "How strange. And you're sure of this?"

"Oh yes," Fiona replied. "My window cleaner Martin is also a part-time firefighter. He met us at Malcolm's hut and talked us through the whole thing."

"And you say no one was caught on CCTV, either coming or going?"

"That's right," said Partial Sue. She neglected to mention about Seb and Marcus's night-time lobster antics two weeks prior.

Antony Owens stood beside the counter nonplussed, digesting the information. By the grimace on his face, it didn't appear to be sitting too well in his stomach. "None of it makes sense."

"Yes, you can see why we're in a bit of a pickle," Fiona remarked. "But there's more. Have you ever heard a rumour about Malcolm having an illegitimate son?"

He shook his head.

"What about Seb who owns the Smuggler's House? Did you know he's Malcolm's cousin?"

He raised both eyebrows. "That's also news to me."

Fiona paused for a moment, then carried on. "We need to ask you about something involving Frank Marshall."

Olivia stopped taking pictures and swung around to face them. "Frank Marshall is a pompous twit. Looks down on us. Looks down on everyone. Thinks he's the self-appointed guardian of Mudeford Spit."

Antony smiled timidly, the mere mention of Frank's name producing a red rash around his neck. "Frank can be challenging at times."

"Challenging?" Olivia snapped. "Antony, you're being too generous. That man makes your life difficult. Makes everyone's life difficult. And it's not at times. It's all the time."

"Er, Olivia," he asked politely, "would you mind if I discussed these matters alone with the ladies?"

"Fine," she replied. "I'm going to look in the shutter shop."

"Oh, are you getting some of them smart tilting shutters for your house?" asked Daisy.

Olivia hesitated, temper not ebbing in the slightest. "Just browsing." And then she was out of the door, using her elbows to nudge it open.

Antony fiddled with his cuffs. "My wife gets angry at even the mention of that man's name. He can be very . . ."

"Patronising? Condescending? Belittling?" Partial Sue suggested.

"I'll stick with challenging." Antony loosened his tie, presumably to release some of the heat around his neck.

Fiona cleared her throat. "Tell me about the bylaw business involving him and Malcolm."

Antony Owens became even more nervous, swallowing hard and rearranging some paper clips scattered on the counter, placing them side by side in a neat row. "Back in 1998 when illegal raves were springing up everywhere, Mudeford Spit didn't escape. During the winter months when nobody was around, ravers would club together and rent out a beach hut, then use it to have an illegal rave."

"Aren't they a bit small for that?" Daisy remarked.

"The raves would be outdoors on the sand, but they'd use the beach hut for the DJ to set up their turntables and speakers, keep them dry, face them out through the open French windows. Frank Marshall caught wind of this. Wanted to stop it, so he suggested to the council that the only people who could have access to the spit were hut owners. Nobody else would be allowed. No renters, no members of the public. He wanted to turn it into a gated community. This was rejected instantly by the council. So he came up with another more reasonable idea. Proposed a new bylaw to ban anyone staying overnight in beach huts during the winter months, from the start of November to the end of March. This wasn't really a problem for hut owners, as they didn't really use their huts during the winter months, and they'd usually use this time for maintenance and fixing them up. And people rarely rented them out due to the weather. However, it would deter the ravers. The bylaw was accepted. However, there was a victim to this new bylaw."

"Malcolm Crainey," Fiona said.

"That's right. Frank managed to kill two birds with one stone. He'd got rid of the illegal ravers while knowing full well that the misfit Malcolm Crainey would be turfed out of his beach hut for five months. Made homeless. Probably forcing him to sell his beach hut so he'd have to find somewhere else to live. You see, the poor guy didn't have any money to rent a flat during the winter."

Frank Marshall's heartlessness sent shocks around the table. "So what happened?" asked Daisy.

Antony Owens straightened his cuffs. "I got a call from the council, asking if I'd represent someone in danger of losing their home. I hadn't been qualified long as a solicitor. I was still very idealistic about the law, convinced it could help the little guy get justice. Did some pro bono work on the side. So I said yes. I put forward Malcolm's case that he would be made homeless by this new bylaw, and that unlike all beach hut owners who had nice big homes to go to in the winter months, Malcolm Crainey did not."

"What happened?" Partial Sue asked.

"I won the case. Malcolm was made the one and only exception to the bylaw due to his unique predicament. He was allowed to stay on all year round. Much to the annoyance of Frank Marshall."

Partial Sue smiled. "I bet he didn't like that."

Antony frowned, taking no pleasure in Frank's defeat. "No, he didn't. He's disliked me ever since. But then he got even worse a few years ago. I was offered the part-time job of liaison officer for the Beach Hut Residents' Association by the council. I needed the extra cash so it seemed like a good fit, as we'd had a beach hut for a while. Frank's been trying to get rid of me ever since. The owners could vote me out, but it has to be unanimous. Frank knows that, and he hasn't managed it yet. Thing is, by and large, I do a good job down there."

There was a natural pause.

After a while, Fiona said, "Who was it from the council who asked you to represent Malcolm?"

"It was Malorie Granger."

Daisy flinched at the mention of the woman's name. "Malorie?"

Antony Owens nodded. "Yes. I know she can be a bit of a bully. But I think at heart she has a good moral compass, even if that compass sometimes feels like its strapped to a sledgehammer. Plus, it doesn't hurt that she doesn't like Frank either. I mean, she'd never say that, but when she was a councillor, he'd never stop pestering her to do something about this or that."

Fiona cleared her throat. "Can I ask why you didn't mention this bylaw business with Malcolm and Frank right at the start of this investigation?"

Antony Owens ran his hand over his head, exhaled heavily. "I didn't want to influence your investigation. I've had my difficulties with Frank Marshall in the past, still do. However, I knew I couldn't mention this to you or you'd think I was trying to point the finger at him. Make him a suspect, which he may well be. I preferred that you found out organically, as it were."

It hadn't been a helpful stance to take but it made sense in Fiona's mind. She understood that Antony Owens needed to be careful, especially in his position and with his history with Frank. He had to rise above it all and act impartially, even though Frank hadn't.

The quiet returned. Only the sound of Simon Le Bon snoring at their feet and the ticking of the clock troubled their ears.

Partial Sue had something else on her mind. "Speaking as an individual and not as the liaison officer, did you hear anything conspiratorial when you owned a hut? Any plans to get rid of Malcolm or anything else for that matter, from Frank or anyone?"

Antony shook his head. "Much as I'd like to say yes, no I didn't. Oh, there was plenty of moaning among them all. A lot of uptight tutting at this and that."

"What sort of things?" asked Fiona.

"Mostly trivial. A few of the owners agree with Frank and don't like the fact that members of the public are allowed on the spit. They think it should be exclusively for hut owners. So their complaints would be, for example, about visitors and day-trippers spreading their beach blankets too close to their huts. And they hate anyone taking short cuts between huts to get to the other side of the spit. Wanted me to propose an exclusion zone around the huts, making it a no-go area for ordinary members of the public. Ridiculous, of course, the council wouldn't even entertain the idea. However, I would say that the feeling of us and them is strong down there, as you've probably already encountered."

The three ladies nodded.

Antony took a deep breath and continued. "Thing is, over time, they've realised I'm only going to represent them on serious matters that need my attention. Not them getting their knickers in a twist because they don't like mixing with the public. This has led to them going to Frank more and more to complain. He always listens. Sticks his oar in. For instance, he once told a group of youngsters to get lost because they were having too much fun and it was disturbing the peace. Another time it was teenagers swimming in the harbour with all their clothes on. He said he was worried that they might drown, weighed down with all that wet clothing. The harbour's only about two or three feet deep, apart from a channel in the middle. The real reason was that some hut owners didn't like the fact they weren't wearing correct bathing attire. That's the level of snobbery some of these people have, and it's led to Frank being the guardian of the spit, the chieftain."

"Or self-appointed cult leader," Fiona added. "He calls himself chairman of the Beach Hut Owners' Association — an unofficial title and group."

Antony Owens rolled his eyes. "The ego on that man. Now it's all out in the open, I can say this — I'm convinced he's involved in some way. But I don't have any evidence. Just a gut feeling."

Fiona and no doubt Partial Sue and Daisy also had that same feeling. Whichever way this investigation went, all roads seemed to lead back to Frank Marshall. If nothing happened on that spit without his say-so, then surely that could include a murder.

CHAPTER 33

Late Saturday afternoon the unthinkable happened. Just before five o'clock the impenetrable canopy of dark clouds that had taken up residence over the whole country slid back and the sun appeared. An intensely emotional event. A long-lost friend you didn't realise how much you'd missed until you clapped eyes on them, or squinted at, in this case, as the sudden increase in bright yellow light blinded everyone, unaccustomed as they were to it.

The raw, arctic wind ceased its relentless assault. In its place, a far more conducive and friendly balmy southerly caressed the air. The mercury rose at a rate of knots.

Out on Southbourne Grove people shed their coats and tied their heavy jumpers and sweatshirts around their waists, hurrying to empty the supermarkets of beers and barbecue food, seizing the opportunity for an evening spent in the garden rather than around the telly with the heating on. Summer was back.

The ladies of Dogs Need Nice Homes stared in wonder through the shop window at the sight of the sun, as if some giant yellow UFO mother ship had just entered the atmosphere. Gleefully, Daisy pulled out her phone and checked the Met Office weather forecast: nothing but sun icons for the days to come. She wobbled with excitement. "Tomorrow I'm going early to M&S to load up with summer food, then I'm going to sit in the garden all day and read my Kindle."

Fiona smiled. "Did you know that a kindle is the collective noun for a group of kittens?"

Daisy became overwhelmed with the cuteness of it all. "Oh, that's simply adorable!" she gushed.

"I thought you'd like that."

Partial Sue brought the conversation back to food. "Scrummy grub in the sunshine, is there anything better?"

Warmth enveloped Fiona at the thought of doing exactly the same with the addition of an early-morning stroll along Southbourne beach before the crowds took up every inch of sand with their picnics. Fiona didn't mind people on the beach per se, it was just that it played havoc when exercising Simon Le Bon off his lead. He'd hopscotch from one picnic blanket to the other, doing his sad orphaned-dog routine in a bid to snaffle the odd cocktail sausage. She was about to share her plans with the other two, when a nagging thought snapped her back from her indulgence. "Er, you know, I think I'm going to head to the spit tomorrow."

"Ah." Partial Sue nodded sagely. "Going to relax down there, eh?"

"Not relax." Fiona didn't want to force them into investigating on the first good day of full sunshine for what seemed like months on end, but the opportunity to glean information was too good to pass up. "I figure nearly every beach hut owner will be down on that spit tomorrow. A good opportunity to question them, all in one place."

Partial Sue gulped. Daisy looked at the floor. The expressions on their faces demonstrated that they knew it made sense.

Fiona reassured them. "Please don't feel you have to come with me. Honestly, have a day off." Whichever way she said it, it came across as though she were guilt-tripping them into joining her, but that really wasn't the case.

"We want to come too," Daisy said.

"We do?" Partial Sue wasn't happy about being included in that sentence.

Daisy smiled. "Fiona's right. We should strike while the iron's hot, or the beach is hot. Plus, we have our evenings to relax and read. The forecast is the same for the next couple of weeks. A heatwave."

"My garden goes into shade in the evening," Partial Sue grumbled. "It's north facing."

No one said anything.

"Oh, all right then," she conceded. "I'd hate to miss out on a breakthrough."

The other two ladies gave her gentle pats on the back, happy that the Charity Shop Detective Agency would be at full strength for what could be a challenging investigation. Out of 200 beach hut owners, someone had to know something.

"Put on plenty of sunblock," Fiona advised. "And bring lots of water and snacks. It could be a long day."

CHAPTER 34

Next morning, the harbour and headland looked resplendent in vibrant colours, turned up to full brightness and drenched in sunlight. It was picture-postcard perfect, and being a Sunday morning, the bells of Christchurch Priory rang out, the cheerful sound wending its way over the calm waters.

Fiona, Partial Sue and Daisy joined the seemingly endless procession of day-trippers schlepping along the tarmac path towards the spit. A bright caterpillar of primary-coloured beach paraphernalia: cool boxes, striped windbreaks and surreal-shaped inflatables. A happy gathering of people prepared and ready for a day of fun, sun and relaxation on Mudeford Spit. Although some of the beach hut owners probably wouldn't see it that way. They'd regard it as an invasion, a rabble of unwelcome visitors sullying the sands of their beloved haven.

Perhaps this wasn't a bad thing. Misery loves company, and Fiona hoped that grumbling beach hut owners might also be loose-lipped when it came to Malcolm's death.

"Can we get an ice cream before we start?" Daisy asked from beneath a straw hat so wide it kept flopping down in front of her face; she had to hold it up with one hand to see where she was going. "I'm boiling already."

Fiona had opted to leave Simon Le Bon at home for that very reason. It wouldn't be fair on him, out all day in this searing heat. She'd walked him earlier that morning when the air was cooler on his little furry body, and she would walk him again later in the evening, although he'd still be grumpy at being left behind.

A dull hum like a low-flying bomber rose up behind them. In one smooth simultaneous movement, the whole procession of people shifted to the side to let the Noddy train past.

"And can we get the Noddy train on the way back to save our legs?" asked Partial Sue.

Fiona felt like one of the many parents walking beside them, constantly herding children and fielding questions. She wasn't about to take up that role with her two friends. They were grown adults. "You don't have to ask my permission."

"Oh, goody," Daisy enthused, not sounding much like an adult at all. Although, Fiona had to admit, the thought of sinking her teeth into an ice-cold strawberry split made their trek along the hot tarmac far more bearable. That was until they reached the spit and saw the queue for the little kiosk attached to the side of Tides Restaurant snaking its way around the building as if it were a cinema in the seventies showing a blockbuster movie.

"Oh," Daisy said.

"I am not partial to queues," Partial Sue complained. "Not ones that big."

Fiona spotted a familiar figure hurrying back along the line of hungry holidaymakers. She stood out from the shorts and bikini-wearing masses in her black-and-white uniform. Flustered and red-faced, Beryl the volunteer coastguard clutched two gigantic double ninety-nines. The yellow ice cream had already begun running down the cones and over her knuckles. Her concerned expression at the failing solidity of her purchases immediately improved when she spotted Fiona. "Oh, hello. What a nice surprise. Bit different to the other day." She gestured to the sun with her ice creams.

Fiona returned the greeting and introduced Beryl to her friends.

Partial Sue wasted no time interrogating her about the expediency of the queue. "What would you say is the ETA on ice creams?"

"I'd say it took me twenty, maybe twenty-five minutes to get these," Beryl replied.

Daisy didn't look happy. Fiona noticed both pairs of flakes starting to lose their battle to stay upright. "We should let you go, otherwise you and Steve are going to be left with two cones of runny yellow stuff."

Beryl noticed the wilting chocolate. "Oh gosh, yes. I'd better get going. Drop by any time you want. You're all welcome."

They watched her scuttle off towards the steps that led up the side of Hengistbury Head.

"She's nice, isn't she?" Daisy remarked.

"Oh, yes." Fiona agreed. "She and Steve love their food."

"I don't fancy her chances of getting back to the coast-guard station before they've melted," Partial Sue said.

"Me neither," Daisy said.

"We should leave the ice creams until later," Fiona suggested. "Maybe the queue will improve." This seemed like wishful thinking, judging by the number of people thronging onto the spit and tagging straight onto the end of the queue, which had increased in the short space of time they had been standing there. But Fiona was keen to get started. They had a lot to do, and she didn't want to delay proceedings by waiting. Reluctantly the other two agreed.

Fiona pulled out the list from her bag. "The first high-lighted name is the Segensworths. Hut number nine. Let's see if they're in."

The three ladies had barely taken a step when Frank Marshall materialised beside them, almost out of thin air, travel mug in one hand. "Morning, ladies, and what a glorious day it is."

Fiona wanted to return the greeting but became distracted, her brain befuddled by the bizarre sight in front of her. Frank had his shirt off, exposing a considerable rotund midriff, resembling a large white bin liner that had been over-filled with cookie dough, the ill-gotten gains of all that real ale, no doubt. But it was his chest that Fiona found herself unable to tear her gaze from. Two bluish tattooed portraits adorned each pectoral muscle. A pair of wrinkled and distorted inked faces stared back at her, smiling, or was it grimacing? She couldn't tell, but both had the artistic merits of partially melted waxworks.

Frank noticed her curiosity, and that of Partial Sue and Daisy as they all contemplated the strange sight on his torso. "Ah, I see you've spotted Mabel and Gracie, my two grand-daughters." He pointed to each tattoo in turn.

Fiona swallowed hard. She desperately wanted to say what lovely granddaughters he had but wondered what terrible calamity had befallen the two little girls who appeared to resemble Judith Chalmers and Gloria Hunniford having very bad hair days. Fiona turned to her friends for help, but they too had similar expressions of confusion on their faces.

Saving the ladies from further awkward embarrassment, two angelic little blonde girls appeared by Frank's side.

"Ah, speak of the devils," Frank said. "Here they are."

Fiona nearly collapsed with relief. Mabel and Gracie hadn't grown old before their time and bore no resemblance to two octogenarian TV presenters. Frank's tattoos were a stark warning about the dangers of shoddy tattoo artistry and cutting corners when it came to having one's skin permanently inked.

"Mum says do you want a bacon sandwich?" asked one of the little girls.

"No, no, my little angels," Frank said. "I'm fine. Tell her I'm going to be busy with some friends for a while. Would you take this back for me?" He handed one of the little girls his empty travel mug. Mabel and Gracie scampered off.

Fiona wondered if Frank knew of their plans to question the entire spit. Possibly not. She should have been used to the fact that whatever they did here, Frank always had to be involved. That was just the way things were.

"You have two beautiful granddaughters," Fiona remarked. Daisy and Partial Sue nodded in agreement.

"Thank you," Frank said. "Now, what can I help you with today?"

No point beating about the bush. "We want to interview everyone on the spit," Fiona said. "About Malcolm's murder."

"Looks like the whole gang's here." Partial Sue gestured to the packed spit, buzzing with holiday energy.

"I'm not sure that would be such a good idea." Frank folded his arms, distorting Mabel and Gracie's faces more than they were already. "People just want to relax. Take it easy. Not sure they would take too kindly to being questioned for hours and hours about a murder while they're spending quality time with their families."

Fiona produced a computer printout listed with ten questions. "Won't take long, we only have a few things to ask them." She handed him the list.

Frank examined each of them one by one. At the end, he handed her back the list and blew out through both nostrils, clearly not happy but not really having a good enough reason to deny them this simple request. "Well, okay then. But I will accompany you."

Fiona played along, once again, appeasing the badly tattooed silverback to get what she wanted.

"Follow me," he said, striding off across the hot sand.

CHAPTER 35

As they trudged along the spit, signs of joyful occupation could be seen along its entire length. Strewn in front of every beach hut various outdoor toys lay ready to be picked up and played with: kayaks, paddle boards, swingball sets, Frisbees and balls of all shapes and sizes — what a traditionalist like Frank would describe as good, wholesome fun. Paddle boards appeared to be the latest must-have. There were more of them than any other item, with each hut having at least two parked out front, some tiny, some big enough to double as a swimming platform. The harbour was full of them, pointing this way and that, ridden by lifejacketed tweens, teens and adults stabbing the water with their paddles and wobbling to stay upright. Their endeavours were not always successful and they'd topple off into the shallow water that only made it up to their thighs.

The popular pastime didn't escape Daisy's attention. "I do fancy having a crack at that waterboarding."

A collective gaze swung in Daisy's direction. The ladies were used to her words coming out a little unintended, but Frank was not. "Waterboarding?" he asked.

"Yes," Daisy replied. "I think I'd be brave enough to do it."

Frank's moustache twitched nervously.

"I think you mean paddle boarding, Dais," Partial Sue corrected.

Daisy appeared confused. "Oh, what's waterboarding then?"

"You don't want to know," Fiona replied.

Before Daisy could Google it, Frank filled her in about the controversial torture technique. A nauseated Daisy was not pleased. "Why has it got such an innocent name? Waterboarding sounds like something you'd get as a gift voucher — an experience day waterboarding in Sussex."

Their debate about the appropriateness of waterboarding as a title halted abruptly as they arrived at their first highlighted name on the list, the Segensworths at beach hut number nine.

Three well-behaved junior-school-aged children, a girl and two boys, were playing quietly out the front of the hut. The two boys dug a hole, while the girl painted beach pebbles to sell for a pound each, arranging them carefully on a small stool she'd commandeered to be her shop stall. Their mum and dad had their feet up on the deck, and were thumbing through the Sunday papers with a half-drained cafetière by their sides, a snapshot of parental bliss.

In the blink of an eye, Daisy whipped out her purse and bought three of the little girl's painted stones before she'd even had a chance to put her paintbrush down.

"Morning, Tom. Morning, Lucy," Frank called out.

Tom Segensworth jumped at the appearance of Frank, as did his wife, snapping their Sunday supplements shut, as if Frank were here for a surprise beach hut inspection.

"Frank, what brings you here?" Tom said it as a greeting, but it was laced with too much alarm to be classed as that. Both husband and wife got to their feet, almost standing to attention. Frank might as well have said, "Stand by your beds."

"I'd like you to meet Fiona, Sue and Daisy," Frank said. "They'd like to ask you a few questions about Malcolm and the fire."

Tom and Lucy Segensworth swallowed simultaneously, looking worried. Fiona was well aware that this probably wasn't an admission of guilt but was rather that middle-class, British reaction to being in the presence of an authority figure.

"Is that when the fire engines came?" the little girl said, not missing anything. "We're not supposed to talk about it."

Lucy's worry turned into mild alarm. "Well, I didn't say that. It's just not a nice thing to dwell on."

"I liked the fire engines," said one of the boys, not looking up from his digging.

"Yeah, really cool," agreed the other one. "But why aren't we allowed to talk about it? Did someone do it on purpose?"

"Gosh, no," Lucy replied.

"Please, come inside." Tom whirled his arm in a gesture to get them out of the way before the kids interrogated them further.

The three ladies entered the spacious beach hut led by the Segensworths and followed by Frank, who closed the French doors behind him. Sunny yellows covered the walls with dashes of sky blue here and there. A neat, narrow set of pine stairs led to a sleeping platform in the roof, where Fiona glimpsed dishevelled duvets scattered with children's clothes.

"You have a lovely beach hut," Daisy remarked.

"Yes, it's not bad," Frank added, implying that it was passable but not quite up to his exacting standards.

Tom and Lucy hurriedly cleared the small lounge area of middle-grade paperbacks and children's puzzle books, along with empty beakers of juice, half-eaten bowls of soggy Rice Krispies and plates covered in toast crumbs, butter drops and jam splodges. "Apologies for the mess," Tom said. "We haven't had time to clear up."

"Please don't go to any trouble on our behalf," Fiona said. "This won't take long."

"Yes," Frank agreed. "Please take a seat."

Fiona found it odd that Frank was giving the couple permission to be seated in their own hut. Just who did this guy think he was?

"Fire away," Frank said to Fiona.

Fiona removed her phone and placed it on the table, avoiding a glob of jam. "Would you mind if I recorded this on my phone? It's a lot easier than taking notes." They had a lot of huts to get through. Audio recordings would make this mammoth task far simpler.

The couple nodded. "As long as it's not posted anywhere," Tom said.

Fiona shook her head. "Gosh, no."

"Will the police listen to it?" asked Lucy.

"Only if you admit to murder," Partial Sue joked.

Tom and Lucy's faces drained of colour.

"I'm sure that's not the case," Fiona reassured them, switching on her phone's recording feature. "We're just trying to find information that might help us catch the person who did this. Now, how well did you know Malcolm Crainey?"

"Not at all, really," Tom answered.

"Had you heard of him?" Partial Sue asked.

"Oh yes," his wife replied. "Everyone knew of Malcolm down here."

"What did you think of him?" Daisy asked.

Momentarily, Tom and Lucy's eyes flicked in Frank's direction, as if seeking his approval to answer. Frank made an almost imperceptible nod. "Didn't really have an opinion," Tom replied. "Just knew him as the eccentric guy who lived at the other end of the spit."

"Did you ever hear him having a disagreement with anyone?" Fiona asked.

The Segensworths shook their heads.

"Was there any talk of him having a son?"

Again, they shook their heads.

"Did you ever overhear any conversations mentioning Malcolm's name, perhaps in a negative light?"

Tom and Lucy shot glances in Frank's direction again, only for the briefest of moments. Then they regarded each other, as if exchanging telepathic thoughts. "No, nothing," Lucy replied.

"Didn't anyone complain about his eccentricities?" Daisy asked.

Before they had a chance to answer, Frank butted in. "You must understand that Malcolm's hut is quite a way from this one. It's not really an issue to the folks up this end."

Fiona had wondered when this would happen, when Frank would hijack the questioning and start answering on behalf of the hut owners. Even before this, his mere presence had been disruptive, influencing the way the Segensworths answered, perhaps to fit with some pre-approved narrative Frank had furnished them with.

Frank leaned back, lacing his hands behind his head, a little too relaxed for Fiona's liking, seeing as he was in someone else's home. "Besides,' he continued, "gossip's not really a thing down here. We all get along, don't we?"

The Segensworths nodded eagerly.

Fiona nearly choked. She'd never heard such rubbish. Gossip was a thing everywhere. Put any two British people together from any far-flung corner of the country, and within a minute or two they'd be moaning about someone or other. She wasn't about to let that rather large whopper go unchallenged. "Frank, when we first met, if I remember rightly, didn't you say that Malcolm got away with things other people didn't? Not pulling over for the Noddy train, dumping his empties in the recycling at six in the morning. How did you hear about that, if no one ever gossips?"

Frank shifted to a more appropriate position. "I wouldn't say it was gossip, just people sharing rumours."

Partial Sue screwed up her nose. "Sharing rumours is the exact definition of gossip."

Frank's answer was equally weak and unconvincing. "Not so much gossip or rumours. More of an exchange of information."

Fiona ignored Frank and aimed a question at Tom and Lucy. "Did Malcolm get away with things that other people didn't?"

Their eyes drifted to Frank for guidance. He tried butting in again. "I would just like to say—"

Fiona cut him off. "I'd like to hear it from Tom and Lucy, if that's okay."

"We'd heard rumours that he could be a bit . . . unconventional."

"Unconventional how?" asked Daisy. "Not following the rules?"

Fiona desperately wanted to add 'not following Frank's rules' to the end of that question, but she bit her lip.

"Well, like Frank said, dumping his recycling when everyone was asleep," Lucy answered, not giving them anything new.

Still, it was something for Fiona to work with. "That must have annoyed some people."

Frank scuppered her answer. "Like I said, Tom and Lucy are too far away to be bothered by that sort of thing, so the answer to that would be a no."

Fiona wasn't going to get anywhere. She cut her losses. "Fair enough, we'll just ask the hut owners at the other end of the spit about that."

"Good idea. Right, I think that's it." Frank pushed himself to his feet.

Fiona wasn't done yet. "Just a few more questions. Before the fire, did you notice anyone hanging around in the daytime, acting suspiciously?"

"What do you mean by suspiciously?" Lucy asked.

"A shifty ne'er do well," Daisy suggested.

"Maybe someone who didn't have any business here," Fiona replied. Everyone we've seen today is clearly here for the beach. You can tell — shorts, sandals, cold boxes. I don't know, someone loitering, not dressed right. Checking everyone's comings and goings."

"Like a burglar casing a house," Partial Sue added.

"I can tell you that would never happen," Frank interrupted. "Nothing gets past me. Eyes like a hawk."

Fiona drew in what she hoped would be a slow, calming, patience-inducing breath. "Frank, you weren't here that day."

"True, but if I had been, I would have noticed anyone suspicious. I know the signs. Did I tell you I used to own a security company? There's no one more experienced than me down here when it comes to security . . ."

Fiona's eyes glazed over as Frank seized control of the conversation, seemingly for good, delivering his I-know-more-than-you monologue. The man was a bottomless pit of smug self-congratulation.

When he came up for air, Fiona jumped in, feigned a smile, thanking Tom and Lucy, despite it being a complete waste of time thanks to Frank ambushing their efforts.

Out on the sand, Frank said, "I think that went rather well. Right, who's next on your list?"

Frank intended to be a continuous and indelible blot on the day, making their questioning a futile exercise. No one would give them a straight answer while he made himself at home in their beach hut. Fiona had to put a stop to it or at least give them a fighting chance of getting some helpful information without ruffling his feathers. But how? An idea was slowly forming.

CHAPTER 36

Fiona examined the list and found the next highlighted name. She ignored it, flicking through the pages, dramatically flipping them over, then running her finger down them, becoming more and more agitated. "There are so many to get through. It's already half past ten and we've only done one interview. I don't know if we're going to do it at this rate."

"Better get your skates on. Time's a-wasting." Frank sounded a little self-satisfied, happy that he'd taken control of this particular situation and it was going in his favour. But that was all about to change.

Fiona nodded. "Yes, we'd better get our skates on if we're going to get all these interviews done by the end of the day. We should split up. Go three ways. Divide and conquer."

"That's a good idea," Partial Sue agreed.

Frank's face dropped. If they split up, he could only accompany one of them, which meant he wouldn't be there to supervise the questioning of two thirds of the beach hut owners, who'd be free to answer unfettered by his influence. "We should stick together," he demanded.

"Now that's not really an efficient use of time, especially yours, Frank. I'm sure you'd like to get back to your

178

grandchildren, er . . ." Fiona stopped short of calling them Judith and Gloria. "Mabel and Gracie."

"They'll be fine without me," Frank said. "I just think the hut owners will be more inclined to answer your questions with me there. They might refuse if I'm not."

"You can write a note we could show them," Daisy suggested.

"A permission slip," Partial Sue added.

"Yes." Fiona smiled. "That's a good idea. I'm sure your name has great influence down here."

Like grandmaster chess players, the three ladies had him in checkmate — the kind that you only see once it's too late. Frank had nowhere left to manoeuvre. If he refused to write a permission slip, it meant that his name didn't carry any weight. Something his male pride would never admit. However, if he said yes to writing the slip, then he would have to relinquish his grip over two thirds of the interviews.

His male pride won. "Fine. No need to write a slip, just say I've given you permission. That will be enough."

"Thanks, Frank." Fiona did a little happy dance inside her head.

"But I'd like to accompany you, Fiona."

"Of course, no problem." Fiona conceded to having him tagging along. Not ideal but a small price to pay for giving Daisy and Partial Sue free rein to get some better-quality answers from the hut owners.

They divvied up the names three equal ways and set off, going house to house, or rather beach hut to beach hut, performing separate interviews.

By the fifth interview, Fiona had become irritated by the pointless tedium of having Frank beside her. No matter who they questioned, Frank's presence skewed their responses, making one hut's answers indistinguishable from the next, adding into an ever-increasingly bland, homogenised glob of useless information. Her phone's audio files filled with repeats. No one had anything new or unexpected to say. They didn't see anything. They didn't hear anything. They didn't know anyone with a grudge against Malcolm. Nothing out of the ordinary. A repeating pattern. A well-rehearsed stage set with Frank the director, who had trained his actors well.

They had just finished another pointless interview and had stepped out on the sand when Frank heard his name being shrieked. Alarmed, they glanced behind them to see the shape of a small-framed woman desperately scuttling towards them, kicking up sand in her wake as her flip-flopped feet struggled to muster any sort of speed. With a bright polka-dot summer dress, she held a straw trilby hat down with one hand as it was in danger of slipping off the back of her head due to her frantic scurrying.

"Frank! Frank!" she panted. Underneath her hat, her red face glowed. "I'm so glad I've found you."

"Take your time, Lynne. Catch your breath," Frank said.

Fiona forgot all about her mission to question the hut owners and wondered what dreadful news this poor woman had to impart.

Lynne took several deep, rapid breaths. "Something terrible has happened. Simply awful. You must come immediately."

CHAPTER 37

Fiona pulled her water bottle from her bag and handed it to Lynne, who took several long gulps. "Thank you," she gasped.

"Whatever's happened?" asked Fiona, fearing the worst. An accident? A lost child? A drowning? Another murder? God forbid.

Lynne looked at Frank for his approval, as if seeking permission to divulge information in front of a stranger.

"It's okay, Fiona is with me. Now, what's happened?"

"Someone's been drying their washing outside."

Had Fiona heard right? The terrible calamity that this woman had nearly collapsed a lung for was down to a laundry misdemeanour?

Frank reassured her with encyclopaedic knowledge of beach hut rules and regulations, reciting them verbatim. "That's okay. A hut owner is permitted to dry items, providing they are within the confines of their deck or on a washing line, providing said washing line does not exceed the overall length of their hut."

Lynne swallowed hard and rapidly shook her head, sucked down more oxygen, then blurted, "You don't understand. It's a rotary dryer."

"What!" Frank bellowed.

Lynne flinched slightly. "Someone's brought a rotary dryer onto the spit. And stuck it in the sand out in front of their hut. Can you believe it?"

Frank huffed. "Rotary washing lines are not permitted on the spit. Rules are quite clear on that. Why didn't you come to me with this earlier?"

Fiona hadn't realised this washing faux pas could be such a time-sensitive issue. She couldn't fathom what horrendous crimes garments orbiting in the breeze had been inflicting on the visitors to Mudeford Spit. Had a slew of passers-by been hospitalised? Slapped in the face by circling wet swimming costumes?

Lynne became upset. "I've only just found out."

"Who is it?"

"That newish couple at number one hundred and twenty-two."

A flash of anger passed over Frank's face. "I should've known it. Thought they'd be trouble. I'm sorry, Fiona but you'll have to carry on without me while I sort this out."

This was the best news Fiona had received all day. Now she'd be free to question without his interference. "That's quite all right, Frank."

She watched the unofficial sheriff march towards the end of the spit with more determination than she'd ever seen, flanked by his polka-dotted, straw-hatted Stasiesque informer. Was the whole of the spit like this? A network of informants who were encouraged to grass on their neighbours any chance they got? Or was Lynne a one-off busybody? She hoped so, but something told her the former would be more likely.

Fiona flicked forward on her list and realised that hut number 122, which was owned by the Deans, Sarah and Greg, was only five huts away from Malcolm's. Instinct told her it would be in her interests to observe the interaction between them and Frank. An opportunity, perhaps. She didn't know what sort of opportunity, but her insides were telling her she needed to be there. There might be something useful to learn. Apart from anything, it would be entertaining to see how Frank dealt with this washing-line insurrection.

She took off after them, keeping a safe distance, feeling like she was in an espionage thriller. Up ahead the hut with the rotary washing line came into view, not really bothering anyone. Fiona edged closer, got within a comfortable observation distance where she could see without being seen, using the corner of an unoccupied hut to partially conceal herself.

The rotary line was hung with what looked like children's bedding. A muscular guy also with his shirt off and covered in tattoos was knocking a football back and forward on the sand with his young son. Unlike Frank, this man's tattoos were tasteful interlocking Celtic designs that swirled around his thick arms and torso. An attractive woman with a towel wrapped around her head and one around her midriff sat on the deck feeding a small baby from a bottle.

"Excuse me. Excuse me," Frank called out in a semi-threatening tone. Lynne had fallen behind a few steps, taking shelter in Frank's shadow as he approached the offending family.

Greg stopped kicking the ball and turned to face Frank. Clearly no stranger to conflict, he stood square on, planting his feet in the sand shoulder width apart. Alpha male versus alpha male. This should be interesting.

Frank halted a good six feet away, out of fist-swinging distance, the pair of them equally matched for size and height.

Greg spared any politeness. "Watcha want?"

Frank pointed to the washing line. "I'm going to need you to take that down."

Greg considered his request for a moment. Although it was really a command. Bluntly and economically, he replied, "No."

Even from where Fiona was hiding, she could sense the ripples of shock radiating off Frank's reddening back, the disbelief stunning him as if he'd been tasered. Someone had dared disagree with him. Frank, the don of the dunes, had had the gauntlet thrown at his sandalled feet. Not something you see every day.

How would this play out? The immovable object meeting the unstoppable bore.

CHAPTER 38

Fiona gripped the weathered edge of the beach hut for stability. Now she'd see just what Frank was made of — whether it was stern stuff or all bluster.

Frank took a step forward. "I beg your pardon."

Greg stood his ground. "You heard me just fine. I said no."

Frank took a further two steps forward, closing the gap between them. "I'm sorry, but you have to take it down. Rotary dryers are not allowed."

"Yeah, and like I said, I'll take it down just as soon as the washing's dry." Greg turned to resume his game of football with his son.

Frank stood directly behind him, an attempt at intimidation. "I'm afraid that's not good enough. You leave me no choice but to take it down myself."

Greg turned to face Frank once more, his face reddening. "Touch it and it'll be the last thing you do."

The volume rose in Frank's voice. "Now listen, we can't have one rule for you and one rule for others. It'd be chaos down here."

"But I'm not breaking any rules," Greg replied.

Lynne popped her head out from behind Frank's back. "Rules state that rotary washing lines are not permitted on Mudeford Spit. It's very clear."

Greg regarded the niggly woman hiding in Frank's shadow. Rather than becoming more aggressive, he smiled, in that way someone smiles when they know something that the other person doesn't. "You left a key word out of that sentence. But I'll let you off. Next time I won't be so forgiving."

Frank chuckled. "You're letting us off? You're the one that's in the wrong, pal."

Greg casually shook his head. "No. Rules are rules, right? And the rules clearly say that no *permanent* rotary washing lines may be erected. Like I keep saying, this is temporary. I'll take it down soon as the washing's dried. I don't want one of these things outside my hut any more than you do, but I've got to dry the baby's bedding."

Frank gave himself a slight shake.

Observing the showdown from her concealed spot, Fiona realised that the thought of a physical attack hadn't weakened Frank's resolve but a legislative one had. He was a stickler for rules. They were his refuge. His armour. No one was above the rules. Not even him. But he'd been outgunned. Defeated by someone who knew them better than he did. Outflanked, or — Fiona smiled to herself — out-Franked.

A tactical retreat seemed the best option. He backed away, but had to have one last word to save his pride. "Er, yes, well, er, just make sure that rotary dryer is stored away out of sight afterwards."

"I'll stow it under the hut." Greg's grin widened.

"Very good. Yes, er, as you were." Frank stumbled and mumbled as he edged away, Lynne in tow.

"You two have a nice day," Greg said. "Thanks for dropping by."

Frank and Lynne said nothing as they hurried off. Fiona slipped back, out of sight, down the gap between two beach huts, watching as they passed.

"We must get that rule changed," Frank blustered. "No rotary dryers, period. Can't have the likes of him lording it over other people, using the rules as a weapon to get his own way."

The irony was not lost on Fiona. Using the rules to lord it over other people was Frank's *modus operandi*.

Lynne galloped alongside him, nodding sycophantically as if he were the king and she were his courtier. Fiona checked her list. There was only one Lynne, surname Graves, hut twenty-seven, and it wasn't highlighted. She wasn't there the night of the fire. Fiona made a mental note to delve into her background. With Lynne's unhealthy obsession for grassing up anyone who didn't toe the line, even when they were following the rules, she deserved closer inspection. Perhaps she was part of the Frank cabal. If such a thing existed, maybe they had arranged it so that none of them were anywhere near Malcolm's hut on the night of the fire to avoid suspicion. But then, according to the CCTV, no one had been.

Aware that she was becoming sidetracked, Fiona shook it off and emerged from her hiding place, heading straight over to the Deans' hut, hoping to capitalise on the situation. Greg would have no loyalty to Frank after their little altercation. Fiona was angling for a bit of 'the enemy of my enemy is my friend' leverage. Truthfully, she wasn't sure if Frank was the enemy, but for now, she'd act like he was. Greg would certainly be in no mood to follow Frank's rehearsed questions regarding the fire if that were the case. Less inclined to cover for him, if indeed a conspiracy was afoot.

Serendipitously, the football came rolling towards her. She picked it up. Greg trotted over to retrieve it.

"Thanks," he said.

"Was Frank having a go at you for drying your washing?" Fiona asked. "He's unbelievable."

Greg waved away Fiona's concerns. "Oh, well, you know Frank. Retired, too much time on his hands."

"Careful." Fiona grinned. "I'm retired."

"Yeah, but I bet you don't go around giving people an earful for drying their washing."

"No. True, true."

"Dad?" Greg's little boy cried out. "Can I have the ball?"

"Sorry, duty calls," Greg said to Fiona.

He was about to turn away when she asked, "Sorry, can I ask you a question, very quickly?"

Greg chucked the ball in his son's direction. "Be with you in a second." He turned his attention back to Fiona. "Depends on what it is."

"My name's Fiona and I'm investigating the fire at Malcolm's hut."

"Oh, that was a horrible business."

Fiona stuffed the list of names in her bag. "Yes, it was. Were you there on the night?" She already knew he was.

"Yes, whole family was here. That's a night I'll never forget, I can tell you."

"I can imagine," Fiona replied. "Tell me, did you see or hear anything odd that day, or perhaps in the evening? Anyone hanging around or something out of the ordinary? Or anyone arguing with Malcolm? Maybe one of the beach hut owners?"

"You know, the police already asked everyone that, and as far as I know, nobody saw or heard anything, me and the wife included. I really wish I had something I could tell you, but no, it was pretty much like every other day we've had down here. Nice and easy. Well, apart from the odd moustachioed whiner with bad tattoos." Greg chuckled.

Fiona braced herself for the real question she wanted to ask. Greg seemed like the only person on this spit who could give her an honest answer, seeing as he wasn't intimidated by Frank. "I know I sound like the world's worst conspiracy theorist, but did Frank ever go around coaching people what to say about the fire? Give them an official line to follow?"

Greg laughed. "That does sound like something he would do. But no. Apart from anything, he didn't have time. Police interviewed us all, right here, straight after the fire was put out. Wouldn't let us leave until we'd given statements. Frank wasn't here that night. He didn't have a chance to throw his weight around or give us a script to follow."

187

Of course, she should have realised that. There was no way Frank could've got to anyone before the police had. "How about afterwards?"

"Not that I'm aware of. Why do you ask? Do you think Frank had something to do with this?"

"I'm keeping an open mind, but Malcolm's lifestyle did seem to be at odds with Frank's wishes. I mean, we just saw his reaction to your dryer. Think about how he must've felt about Malcolm's eccentric hut."

Greg folded his arms. "Much as I'd like to point the finger at Frank — I mean, he's an uptight killjoy who thinks he's superior to everyone — I think if he truly had a problem with Malcolm, he would've come out with it. I don't think murder's his style. He would have wanted it done by the book. Forced him out with red tape."

Greg's assessment made sense. All the evidence so far pointed that way. Yes, he'd wanted Malcolm out, but would've done it by the rules — well, he had done it by the rules, by introducing a new law, to stop Malcolm staying on the spit all year round, but that had backfired. Question was whether Frank was prepared to go as far as to break the rules, indeed to break the law in the worst way possible.

Greg continued. "We've not been here that long but the way I see it, Malcolm was like seaweed on the spit. It can be a little irritating, but it doesn't do any harm, and after a while you get used to it. The kids thought his hut was the best one here."

Fiona smiled at his assessment of Malcolm. "I'll let you get back to your football, unless there's anything else you can remember, anything odd at all."

Greg rubbed his chin. He called over to his wife, still feeding the baby on the deck. "Sarah, can you think of anything odd before the fire?"

Sarah shook her head. "No, nothing. Just a few mosquitoes, that's all."

Fiona thanked the Deans and went back to her original mission, questioning the rest of the beach hut owners. She couldn't help feeling like it was a fool's errand. She'd possibly found the one and only family on the spit who weren't under the doughy fist of Frank and his flunkies and had drawn a blank. She hoped Partial Sue and Daisy had fared better.

CHAPTER 39

Monday morning's cake stood on the counter untouched. The frosting that had put up a good fight was wilting in the heat, making a glacial descent down the sides of the sponge. The culprit? The laser-like sun outside had sent the mercury soaring to nearly twenty-two degrees, and it had only just gone nine o'clock. At this rate, by lunchtime the tarmac outside would be as soft as the frosting currently on its way to becoming a liquid. Fiona, Daisy and Partial Sue were loath to admit it, but it was too hot for cake. Far too hot for anything. The thing really should have gone in the fridge.

The front door had been wedged open for a cooling breeze, but the air barely wandered into the shop. Soon, they'd have to shut the door to keep the hot air out rather than let the cool air in, because there wouldn't be any.

The Wicker Man poked his head inside the door. "Hot enough for you?"

Fiona groaned inwardly, adding to her already irritable state of mind, a mind that felt as if it were being slowly pressure-cooked inside her head. It had been slow and sluggish since they'd come in early, continuing the process of comparing notes or, rather, recordings from yesterday's mammoth interview efforts. They'd started last night at Fiona's but had given up around twelve, opting to finish off listening to the remaining interviews this morning. Clues had been thin on the ground — non-existent, to be precise — and it hadn't got any better this morning.

"Would you like some cake?" Daisy gestured to the melting mass of cream, icing and sponge.

The Wicker Man shook his head. "Alas, no. I'm going to cool down and invest my shekels in an ice lolly. Just nipping to the newsagent now for a Fab. Toodle-oo."

Before any of them had a chance to put in an order for any of their own lollies, he made a swift exit, perhaps for that very reason.

That meant they were back to facing facts, standing around the counter in a hot shop listening to uncomfortable truths being played out of their phone speakers. Every interview without exception had nothing new to offer. The accents and voices changed but the story didn't. Before the fire engines had arrived, no one had seen or heard anything. Not one interview contained even the tiniest sliver of a lead. Nearly 200 dead ends clogging up the digital storages of their three devices.

At eleven o'clock, Fiona reached over and hit the stop button on the very last interview. "That was a complete waste of time."

"It had to be done," Partial Sue reassured her. "Crossed off our to-do list."

"Yeah, I know. I just wish we had something to show for it."

Daisy disagreed. "You have got something to show for it. You got to see Frank getting a taste of his own medicine. I'd love to have seen that."

"Me too," Partial Sue added. "Speaking of Frank, something's been playing on my mind. Are we missing a trick with him? An elephant in the room."

Fiona had no idea what they could have missed. She thought they'd been scrupulously thorough. "What do you mean?"

"He's always banging on about how he used to run a security firm. Seems to me the problem with this investigation is the security camera footage, namely that it doesn't show anything. How's that possible? If anyone would know how to fiddle with a security camera, it'd be Frank."

It was a good point. Frank certainly had the credentials but any question of his involvement on that score had already been neutralised. "We had the footage checked by Freya," Fiona pointed out. "Apart from our poacher friends, nothing was amiss. Nobody's fiddled with it at the time of the fire. I can't see how Frank could've got anything past Freya. He'd have to be one hell of an IT expert. She's the best there is."

Daisy got on her phone and began searching. "Ah, here we are. Says on this company-check website that Frank's the ex-director of a firm called Right Stuff Security. He resigned but the company's still active."

Partial Sue snatched up her phone and Googled the name. After surfing around the site for a few minutes she became despondent. "Ah, you're right. It's not that sort of security firm. They don't deal with CCTV or any technical stuff. They supply door supervisors."

"What's a door supervisor?" Daisy asked.

"Nightclub bouncers, I'm guessing," Fiona answered. "That would explain Frank's bullishness on the spit. He's used to deciding who's allowed in and who isn't. And he's had a lifetime of dealing with undesirables, which is why he doesn't want them anywhere near the place."

"Darn it!" Partial Sue vented her frustration. "He so fits the profile of someone who would murder Malcolm. Can you imagine Malcolm trying to get into a nightclub? Frank wouldn't let him anywhere near it."

"That doesn't mean Frank murdered him," Daisy disagreed.

Partial Sue had a rebuttal lined up when Sophie Haverford swept in off the street, Jackie O-style oversized sunglasses taking up most of her face and a long, flowing, floral summer dress billowing behind her. She paused dramatically in the doorway, clutching the frame with one hand for support, the back of her other hand pressed against her forehead as if she were a Victorian lady about to swoon. If there had been a handy couch or chaise longue, she would have undoubtedly collapsed on it, the teetering height of her wedges helping to accomplish that. Thankfully she remained upright, staggering into the shop. "Oh, Fiona, Daisy, Sue. Something terrible has happened."

Fiona wasn't buying her melodrama. Sophie was an expert at it, wielding it like a Jedi, bending people to her will whenever she desired. Besides, Fiona wasn't in the mood. Last time someone had said something terrible had happened, the source of the trauma turned out to be a rotary washing line. What would it be with Sophie? Too many substitutions in her Waitrose delivery? Can't find the end of the Sellotape? And Sophie was not in her good books — not that there was ever an instance when she was, but the woman had dropped to new depths with the way she'd manipulated Annie Follet.

Sophie tugged the sunglasses from her face. She had been crying. They were used to her producing crocodile tears, and had witnessed them summoned at will whenever she needed sympathy or leverage. Delicate little beads of moisture would appear in the corners of her eyes, then tumble down her cheeks without troubling her perfect make-up. However, this was different. Her eyes were raw from crying, her skin puffy and swollen, not from crocodile tears, but proper fat, ugly ones. The kind you can't fake. The kind that produce snot.

Without thinking, the three ladies rushed to her side, guiding her in and pulling up a chair for her.

"Whatever's the matter?" Fiona asked.

Sophie gulped down air, as a fresh set of thick tears appeared. "There's been another fire on the spit."

They all gasped.

"Oh my gosh!" Daisy cried.

"What, last night?" Partial Sue asked.

Sophie nodded rapidly, sobs punctuating each word. "That's only half of it. I can't get hold of Bitsy. The police won't let me go down there to see if she's all right. It's all blocked off with tape. I'm scared something terrible has happened to her."

CHAPTER 40

Daisy placed a cup of tea in Sophie's shaking hands. It was far too hot for tea, and she hadn't asked for one, nor did she drink tea, but Daisy hoped having something warm to hold might offer a modicum of comfort.

The news of another fire had them all on their toes, twitching with alertness. Had the beach-hut killer struck again? It would seem so. Fiona was hungry for details, chomping at the bit to find out what had happened, but that would have to wait. Right now, Sophie needed their comfort and reassurance. Not easy to muster when the woman spent most of her time belittling and humiliating them. But Fiona would help anyone in distress, even if it was her nemesis from across the road. It wouldn't be easy. Dread plunged in Fiona's stomach as she feared the worst.

She caught sight of her two friends, clearly sharing the same thought, dark shadows passing over their faces. Had Bitsy become the next victim of the beach-hut murderer? It was unthinkable. Their outrageous, fun-loving new friend seemed unbreakable. She had rock-star indestructibility.

Partial Sue held Sophie's hand, attempting to reassure her. "Oh, you know what Bitsy's like. She's probably sleeping off a hangover, or her phone's switched off."

"Or she's lost it," Daisy suggested.

Fiona tried ringing her, but it went straight to voicemail. Come to think of it, she didn't remember seeing Bitsy on the spit when they were interviewing yesterday. "We went past her beach hut on Sunday. It was locked up tight."

"It was?" Sophie dabbed her eyes with a tissue.

"Yes, that's right. We didn't see her all day, and we were there until about 6 p.m."

Daisy hazarded a guess. "Maybe Bitsy got the urge to go somewhere, er, like Portsmouth."

Sophie ceased sniffing and regarded Daisy curiously. "Why would she want to go to Portsmouth?"

Daisy's eyes flitted left and right, scouring her mind for a valid reason while regretting her choice of off-the-cuff destination. Just why would an ex-It girl of the Eighties from Richmond spontaneously visit Portsmouth?

Partial Sue clicked her fingers and supplied a highly improbable answer. "The Royal Historic Dockyard. HMS *Victory* is quite a sight, and they have a museum full of ships' figureheads."

Daisy shuddered. "I've seen those, they're really creepy. One of them looked like Michael Ball."

Sophie didn't look convinced, and Fiona couldn't blame her. "Ships aren't really her scene. Unless they're owned by billionaires and have a celebrity chef on board. Why would she go to Portsmouth on the hottest day of the year? It doesn't make sense. She would have told me. Would have asked me to come with her. Something's wrong. Something's very wrong." Sophie handed Partial Sue her tea, got to her feet and grabbed Fiona's arm. "What if she came home to her hut in the evening, went to bed and then someone burned it down, like that Nigel fellow?"

"Malcolm," Fiona corrected. "And you don't know that's what happened. There are over two hundred huts on that spit."

Sophie continued blubbing. "I can't take this. I have to find out. You know the police. You could talk to them. Get some answers. Maybe even get us past the tape."

Fiona wanted to help. "We'll do whatever we can but I'm not sure they'd listen . . ."

"But you're investigating the murder. Doesn't that count for anything?"

"Not really," answered Partial Sue. "We're just amateurs."

"Please, please. You have to try." Sophie held onto Fiona with both hands, almost shoving her against the counter. "I'll do anything. Anything. You know that musty smell all charity shops have and mine doesn't? I'll tell you the secret of how to get rid of it."

"That's okay, Sophie. You don't need to do that."

"I will, if it will mean getting answers. Please, please. Please . . ." Sophie worked herself up into a lather, a bubbling mix of hiccupping and crying, taking manic breaths in between sobs.

Fiona tried to calm her down. "Sophie, Sophie. Take it easy. Try to take some deep breaths. We'll shut up shop and go down there now. See what we can find out."

Sophie flung her arms around Fiona's neck and squeezed hard. "Thank you, thank you. I am in your debt, and a promise is a promise. It's dry-cleaning."

All three ladies looked confused.

"Sorry?" Fiona said.

"I dry-clean all our donated clothes," Sophie replied. "That's how I get rid of that musty smell. That's why our shop doesn't smell awful like yours does."

Only Sophie could manage to make them dislike her even more at a time when she was in dire need of their help.

CHAPTER 41

Sophie was in no fit state to drive, so Partial Sue took all four of them as far as automotively possible — to the very end of Broadway, the dead-end road leading to the start of Hengistbury Head and Mudeford Spit beyond. Parking the cramped Fiat Uno by the side of the road, Sophie hadn't complained once about the lack of room in the compact hatchback, nor the fact that it needed a clean, nor the sweet wrappers littering the footwell. She had bigger things on her mind.

Up ahead they could see the police presence, two officers and two police cars parked across the start of the tarmac path with tape stretched everywhere. The public had gathered in front of them — a small group, who didn't appear to be gawkers or nosy parkers, but rather walkers and beachgoers who'd planned a day out and were now wondering what to do, with all that hot sunshine going to waste.

As they exited the car, Sophie emerged a little unsteady on her feet, gripping the door post of the car for support. Fiona didn't like the look of her. Her face had become paler and her skin clammier, as if she were about to be sick.

"Why don't we go and check things out," Fiona suggested. "You stay in the car, Sophie, with the windows down."

"I'm not a dog in danger of overheating," Sophie snapped. Then her face softened. "Sorry, I'm a little tense at the moment. I couldn't bear staying here. I have to know what's happening."

"Of course," Fiona replied.

They made a short and hasty walk towards the police cordon.

"I'll do the talking," Fiona announced just before they reached the tape. She'd had no problem talking to police officers in the past but felt her anxiety rise with every step, worming its way up her throat and round her vocal chords, threatening to mute her. The nerves were getting to her, and she knew why. Fiona liked Bitsy. They all did. She'd go as far to class her as a friend, albeit a very new one that she hadn't known for long, but still a friend. Worry that something bad had happened to her threatened to drag her into the same anxious state that Sophie found herself in.

She smiled weakly at the two police officers. "Hot enough for you?" Wincing as the words passed her mouth, she wondered why the hell she had chosen those particular ones, especially when she hated them so much. Fiona's fear was making her spout meaningless drivel.

Strangely, the two police officers welcomed the odd comment. "I'll say," said the one on the left. "Gonna be a scorcher today."

"Already is," said the other one.

"I demand to know what's happened to my friend," Sophie blurted.

Fiona leaned in and whispered to Sophie. "It's okay. Let me talk to these gentlemen." She turned back to the police officers. "Sorry about that. She worried about our friend who's staying on the spit. We heard there was a fire last night."

The officer on the left became serious. "I'm afraid no one's allowed in or out at the moment."

"Would you happen to know which hut burned down?" Partial Sue asked.

"Who told you that a hut burned down?" the officer asked.

198

Truthfully, they didn't know and had only assumed that a hut had burned after what Sophie had said.

Fiona attempted to answer. "That's what we heard. But we really just want to know if our friend is safe."

The other police officer cleared his throat. "I'm afraid we can't give out any information at the moment. It's still a crime scene down there."

"Oh my God," Sophie cried. "A crime scene? That means murder."

"Not necessarily," Fiona reassured her.

"So is it a murder scene or a crime scene?" asked Partial Sue.

"Can't say, I'm afraid, ladies."

"Tell them," Sophie grabbed Fiona's arm, yanking her closer towards the officers. "Tell them that you know that ethnic policewoman and her scruffy sidekick."

"Their names are DI Fincher and DS Thomas," Partial Sue reminded her.

"You know DI Fincher and DS Thomas?" asked the officer on the left, clearly not believing a word any of them were saying.

Before Fiona could answer, Sophie barked, "Know them? I've been questioned by them for a crime I didn't commit."

The melodramatic outburst hadn't helped. The officers regarded Sophie and the rest of them as four batty ladies who really needed to move along.

"Well, if you know them," said the left-hand police officer, "why don't you give the DI a call? I've heard she's very approachable." The officers exchanged smirks.

"Call them. That's a good idea." Fiona pulled out her phone and flicked through her list of contacts. She still had DI Fincher's mobile number saved. She hit the call button.

The police detective answered immediately. "Fincher."

"Oh, hello. It's Fiona Sharp."

"I'm really busy right now, Fiona."

"Sorry, I just need to know if a beach hut burned down and if so, which one."

"Can't divulge anything at the moment. Now, if you'll excuse me."

"What did she say?" Sophie's eyes desperately searched for answers from Fiona's expression.

"Nothing. She hung up."

The policeman on the right adopted a more considerate tone, now that Fiona had proved she was telling the truth. "Well, I know they're very busy down there," the officer said. "So it's not surprising."

"Please, can't you tell us what's going on?" Sophie asked.

"I'd love to, but we can't. Police procedure, I'm afraid," he replied.

Sophie scowled at the pair. "This is outrageous!"

"They're only doing their job," Fiona said.

"Why don't we all go and have a nice cup of tea?" Daisy suggested.

Sophie stamped her foot as if she were eight. "I don't want tea! I don't like tea! And it's too hot! I want to know if my friend is alive."

A powerful diesel engine growled in the distance. From down the tarmac path, rumbled the hulking red shape of a fire engine, no doubt returning from the spit.

"Stand clear, please." One of the officers unravelled the police tape from around a lamp post and wound it back to let the fire engine pass.

The ladies did as they were told. As the vehicle approached their position, the driver throttled back and changed down through the gears, slowing the vehicle to a walking pace as it turned onto the road. Fiona got a glimpse of a familiar face. Sitting in the rear of the cab, his red hair was unmistakable. Fiona manically waved both hands to attract his attention.

The fire engine continued along the road briefly then rumbled to a halt. Fiona rushed after it. The cab door opened and Martin, her window cleaner and part-time fireman, leaped out, still clad in heavy-duty firefighting uniform, and met her halfway.

Breathlessly she asked, "Martin, what happened down there?"

"Really not supposed to say. Not until the police have finished."

"Please, we have a friend staying down there and we're all worried stiff."

Martin glanced around, checking they were out of earshot of the police officers and the other firefighters. He sighed heavily. "Another beach hut burned down. Identical to the last. Fire started on the side wall in the gap between the huts. Same burn pattern and everything."

"Wait, what number was it?" Fiona asked.

"Ninety-eight."

Fiona's knees buckled. Ninety-eight was Bitsy's hut. She managed to hold it together just enough to ask, "Was there a body?"

The driver of the fire engine banged the side of the door. "We need to go!"

Martin backed away, his face contorting sympathetically. "I'm sorry. That's all I can say at the moment."

He climbed back into the cab and was gone.

Fiona stood by the side of the road not moving, the horror of the news numbing and fixing her to the spot as if she'd been speared by a rod of cold steel.

How would she break this news to Sophie? Worse than that, would Sophie be strong enough to hear it? In her fragile state, Fiona feared that it would crush her completely.

CHAPTER 42

Sophie, flanked by Daisy and Partial Sue, caught up with Fiona. Sophie's eyes were large and vulnerable, but her mouth spoke rapid fire. "What did he say? What did he say? Please tell me."

Fiona looked around and spied a vacant bench. "Let's take a seat over there."

Sophie wasn't stupid. Being asked to sit down before being given news was never a good sign. "It's bad, isn't it?"

"Let's just sit down, shall we?" Fiona insisted.

They all collapsed onto the bench. Its painted wooden slats were hot and not particularly comfortable. Fiona closed her eyes, steeling herself for what was to come next, as if she were about to jump off something high. "Bitsy's hut burned down last night."

Silence. Nothing from Sophie. A delayed reaction as the terrible news sank in. Finally, a hiss of air issued from between her lips. Pure pain departing her body. Slowly, she doubled over, as if she had stomach ache. The three ladies threw their arms around her, holding her tightly. Sophie was their worst enemy, but they wouldn't wish this on anyone.

Quietly Partial Sue said, "Did they find a body?"

"I don't know," Fiona replied. "Martin wouldn't say. So there's still hope."

"Hope!" Still seated, Sophie suddenly bolted upright. "Hope! We all know that's not true. He's sparing us the worst. Why do people do that?"

"It might not be the case, Sophie," Fiona replied. "He might not be able to say. Not until the police and the fire investigation officer have made their assessment."

Sophie's grief suddenly switched to a stinging anger. "I think you'd know if there's a dead body in a beach hut. 'Oh what's that big, charred thing shaped like a person. It's a dead body.' My friend is dead. My best friend is dead." Her anger subsided as quickly as it had appeared, replaced by an expression of sorrow. Sophie collapsed back on the seat and began rocking back and forth, the grief and shock too much for her body and mind to bear. "I can't believe this has happened. Why would someone do this?"

There was nothing the ladies of the Charity Shop Detective Agency could do or say to alleviate her pain. They felt it too. They had all warmed to Bitsy instantly, and now it seemed she might have gone, just as quickly as she had crash-landed into their lives. A hot mess of money and mirth, an out-of-control thrill-seeker with a kind heart.

Sophie sobbed out her anguish on the bench, and the charity shop ladies sobbed with her. So many tears that even the hot sun couldn't dry them.

Ten minutes later, Sophie flipped the other way. The anger was back, her lips quivering with rage. She turned to Fiona and spat out the words, "You have to find the person who did this. Find them and bring them to justice. No, better than that. Find out who did this, give me their name and I'll pay for someone to stick them in a beach hut and burn it."

"I don't think that would be a good idea," Daisy said.

Two incendiary eyes fixed her. "Why the hell not?"

Daisy picked her words carefully, not wanting to ignite Sophie's volatile state of mind. "Because it wouldn't bring Bitsy back, and that would make you sadder."

"Plus, you'd be wanted for murder," Partial Sue said realistically. "And I don't think Bitsy would want that."

Sophie said nothing, staring at Daisy unflinching, unblinking. Daisy shrank slightly, anticipating a tirade of self-righteous anger. It never came. Sophie's resolve crumbled and she plunged once more into a helpless mess of tears, snot and sobbing. It was infectious, and within seconds they were all weeping again.

After the incessant tears had leached all the moisture from their bodies and they had no tears left to cry, they sat silently staring into the distance, zombie-like and dehydrated.

Fiona had no idea how long they'd been sitting in a stupor like that. Ten, fifteen, twenty minutes. Half an hour, perhaps. She'd lost all track of time. Gradually she emerged, awakened from her suspended state by a peculiar sound from behind the bench — a gentle licking, or was it slurping?

Fiona looked behind them. Someone had insensitively joined them, a woman facing the other way, perching her behind on top of the backrest of the bench, completely oblivious to their distress. She was demolishing the largest double ninety-nine Fiona had ever seen, licking around the two flakes pushed into the soft yellow ice cream. Dressed in a short-cropped jean jacket and white flares, she would have looked extremely chic had it not been for a ratty, grease-stained baseball cap pulled down onto her head and a mess of grass stains covering her. Whatever had this woman been up to? More importantly, why had she chosen this bench and this particular time to suck down a mountainous ice cream, while they were deep in grief? Fiona glowered at her, hoping she'd sense that she was not welcome and should move on.

Sure enough, the woman picked up on Fiona's laser-like gaze. She slowly turned her head in Fiona's direction. Beneath the filthy baseball cap, a rather worse-for-wear Bitsy stared out.

CHAPTER 43

Fiona blinked several times. Her mouth fell open, her tongue lolling around uselessly in her mouth, as it tried to issue words that wouldn't form.

Bitsy continued mindlessly gorging her ice cream, eyes half-lidded and not quite focused. After a beat, she croaked, "Sorry, I'm a bit out of it. Haven't eaten for twelve hours." Her voice had the texture of a gravel pit.

"Bitsy?" It was all Fiona could think of saying. She hadn't recognised her at first, presumably because of the baseball cap pulled low on her face, but also because it was the only time she'd glimpsed her not swathed in a garish oversized changing robe. She also didn't look her usual bright, hundred-watt self. Her skin was dull, grey and sleep starved.

The other three women came out of their grief hibernation and twisted around to see Bitsy leaning on the back of the bench, obliviously scoffing a flake.

Sophie nearly slid off the seat in a heap, her brain not coping well with the two opposing extremes of one moment thinking that her friend was dead and the next seeing the surreal sight of her alive and well, and scarfing down a double ninety-nine ice cream of all things. She leaped up and threw herself at Bitsy, bearhugging her with so much force that the ice cream dropped from Bitsy's hand and splattered on the ground.

"Hey, I was eating that!"

Sophie shrieked, squeezing her ever more tightly, tears of joy drenching her face. "Bitsy. Oh, Bitsy!"

At first Bitsy seemed amused at her best friend's sudden show of heavy-handed affection, but then she winced and tried to wiggle free. "Okay, this is becoming uncomfortable, not to mention a bit weird."

"You're alive! You're alive!"

"Course I'm alive."

Sophie's habit of switching from one emotion to the other resurfaced. Angrily, she shoved Bitsy away with both hands. "Where the hell have you been? I've been worried sick about you."

Bitsy's face became fierce. Not taking any nonsense, she shoved Sophie back. "What do you mean, where the hell have I been? I can go and do whatever I want. I don't need your permission."

Sophie shoved Bitsy again. "We thought you were dead!"

Before Bitsy had a chance to retaliate, Fiona got between them. "Ladies, perhaps we should all sit down and explain to Bitsy, very calmly, why we were worried about her."

"Fine," said Sophie.

"Fine," said Bitsy.

The pair of them took a seat grudgingly. Wisely, Fiona decided to slot herself between the two of them in case the shoving should resume. When Bitsy sat down they noticed she was shoeless, her feet blackened and dirty.

"What happened to your shoes?" asked Sophie.

Bitsy dismissed the lack of footwear as trivial. "Oh, lost them at some point last night. Probably when I was rolling down that hill in Christchurch, the one with the castle. That's how I got these grass stains."

The other three ladies regarded her, puzzled.

"I decided to go shopping yesterday afternoon in Christchurch," Bitsy explained. "They've got some great

206

boutiques. Got this outfit. Wore it out of the shop, and, well, shame to let it go to waste, I thought I'd go to the pub, show it off. Got talking to a couple of hairy bikers. One thing led to another, and we were out all night, getting up to mischief."

Sophie shot her friend a disapproving look.

"Oh, please," Bitsy snapped. "Don't you dare slut-shame me. It was nothing like that, you prude. But it wouldn't matter if it was. Independent woman and all that. But that's not what we did. We went on a playground crawl."

"What's that?" asked Daisy.

"It's like a pub crawl. Which we did earlier, by the way, but instead of going to pubs you find playgrounds and have a go on everything in the dead of night. Me, Dave and Spider invented it last night. It's a hoot. Dave and Spider are the hairy bikers I met. They're camping in the New Forest.

"Is that Dave's or Spider's hat?" asked Partial Sue.

Bitsy pulled the scruffy hat from her head and examined it. "Oh yes. Forgot I had this. He gave it to me for doing a hundred spins on the roundabout without throwing up." She put it back on. "Anyway, I've had quite the all-nighter so now all I want to do is go back to my beach hut and sleep it off."

"Er, that might be a bit difficult," Fiona said.

Sophie, having calmed down and switched back to sympathetic mode, reached across Fiona and gripped Bitsy's hand. "Someone set light to your beach hut last night."

"What?" Bitsy cried.

Sophie took a deep breath. "It burned down."

Bitsy sat perfectly still for a moment, absorbing the awful news. "Oh, well that's put a dampener on things."

Sophie snatched her hand away. "Is that all you can say? Bitsy, we were terrified that you were inside. That you'd been burned to a cinder."

"Take it easy, Sophie," Fiona said. "Bitsy's probably in shock. She needs our support."

"Sorry. I was just worried sick, that's all."

"She was," Daisy added. "We all were."

Bitsy's face softened and then saddened. "Well, I'm sorry I put you through that. Bit of a bummer, though. I liked that beach hut. I suppose I could get someone to rebuild it."

She didn't seem rattled by the incident, more irritated and inconvenienced that her beach hut had gone. Fiona couldn't tell whether this was down to being extremely philosophical about the whole thing, or if it was a bit of bravado covering up the real shock inside. More likely the former. Perhaps that's what money did for you. It insulated you from shock and trauma because nine times out of ten, there were no insurmountable problems when you were sitting on a mountain of cash. Or was Bitsy merely still drunk from the previous night, the alcohol cushioning her from the shock? After sleeping it off and sobering up, would she see things differently? If Fiona had to guess, she'd probably say no. Bitsy didn't seem the type to worry about anything. That cross was for the rest of them to bear.

"Bitsy!" Sophie bellowed, then calmed her tone. "Bitsy, someone possibly tried to kill you last night. Probably the same one that killed that Malcolm chap."

Bitsy's face contorted into one of confusion. "Are you sure? I mean, they didn't do a very good job of it. I was out. Place was empty. Not exactly what you'd call the work of a cold and calculating killer. More like random arson, I'd say. Anyway, it's not the first time someone's tried to kill me. This oligarch's wife had a go once, sent a hit man after me for having a fling with her husband."

"What happened?" asked Partial Sue, her eyes wide.

"Luckily, I'd also had a fling with the hit man the year before. Used the old charm to persuade him not to bump me off. But that was ages ago."

Fiona wasn't convinced. "People have long memories. Do you think she'd try again?"

Bitsy shook her head. "I doubt it. She's now on her fourth husband, and lives in the Hamptons."

"Anyone else that might have a grudge against you?" Partial Sue asked.

Bitsy snorted. "Only half the married women in Chelsea and Mayfair. That's why I moved to Richmond." Bitsy caught sight of Fiona's face, which must have appeared hungry for the names of possible suspects. "If you're thinking one of them did this, then don't. None of them know I'm here."

That last sentence gave Fiona the impression that Bitsy hadn't come down for a holiday but to escape someone. It had always struck Fiona that Mudeford Spit seemed a little quiet for someone who needed constant stimulation, and a little small to contain Bitsy's big personality. Had her beach hut been more of a hideout than a holiday home? Fiona remembered one of the first things Bitsy had said to them when they first met. That she was desperate to get away from all those stuffy people in London. Were those stuffy people also out to kill her?

"You're not running away from someone, are you?" Fiona asked.

Bitsy laughed. "Oh, please. Do I look like the sort of person who runs away?" She didn't, although, with those grass stains it looked as if rolling was her preferred method of escape.

Maybe the threat was closer to home. Bitsy was a non-conformist and a freethinker. Another bohemian like Malcolm, except she had money. The link between the two was obvious. They didn't fit the Mudeford Spit stereotype or add to its ambience — more like disrupted it, staying up late and making a noise. Had Frank Marshall and his network of beach hut informants decided that she had to go too?

"Has anyone been a bit snooty towards you?" Fiona asked.

"Snooty?" Bitsy questioned.

"Looking down their nose at you," Fiona clarified.

"Like who?"

"Frank Marshall."

Bitsy balked at this suggestion. "Frank and I get on like a house on . . ." Her voice trailed off as she realised it wasn't the most appropriate idiom, given the circumstances. "Frank and

I are besties. Bonding over our love of trains and such. He also enjoys old churches and my great uncle used to be the reverend of St Martin-in-the-Fields. We're always chatting."

It seemed that Frank might genuinely like Bitsy, but there was always the possibility that he was keeping his friends close and his enemies closer.

Bitsy let out a massive yawn. "Can I crash at your place, Soph? Seeing as I'm homeless?"

Sophie switched places with Fiona and hugged her friend tightly. "You can stay as long as you want."

"Careful," Bitsy winced. "I'm still a bit tender."

Sophie loosened her grip. "I'm just glad you're alive."

Bitsy smiled. "Me too. Being dead would be so tedious."

Fiona interrupted. "I know this is probably the last thing you want to hear, but you really should talk to the police. They'll want to hear everything you've just told us."

"And in a lot more detail," added Partial Sue.

"And know that you're alive and well." Daisy smiled.

Bitsy slumped, exhausted. "Really? I haven't had any sleep. Can't you just pass on the message?"

"Not really," Fiona replied. "They'll need to question you, sooner rather than later."

Bitsy slumped some more. "Okay, but first I'll need another ninety-nine, with a Bloody Mary chaser."

CHAPTER 44

They'd abandoned selling cake in Dogs Need Nice Homes. It just wasn't a viable product in this heat. The last lot hadn't sold and the ladies had had to take it home with them. Not the worst burden in the world. Mind you, nothing was selling at the moment. Intense heat and sunshine was not good for custom, as people abandoned shopping trips for beach trips. Footfall had dropped, and feet that normally entered the charity shop were now paddling in the sea at Southbourne. The pavements were empty, only troubled now and again by people stopping for provisions to take to the seaside, emptying its shops of pre-packed sandwiches, disposable barbecues, boxes of beer and chilled bottles of wine.

The ladies had switched to selling ice lollies. Daisy had stocked up the fridge's little freezer compartment, stuffing it with Strawberry Splits, Fabs and Rockets. They didn't exactly fly out of the shop. Trouble was, one, the lack of customers and two, the fact that buying ice lollies from a charity shop was not the most appealing proposition. This had not deterred the Wicker Man, who'd cottoned on to the fact that their lollies were being offered at a vastly discounted rate of just fifty pence.

He leaned over Daisy's model, admiring its detail while slurping on a Fab, red juice lining his sloppy lips. Daisy stood close by, a wet wipe poised and ready.

"This is quite the miniature marvel," he gushed. Next second, a bright crimson drip fell from his lolly. Before it had time to splash onto Daisy's model, her cat-like reactions had thrust out the wet wipe, catching the offending drip. The Wicker Man, completely oblivious, lolloped around the model, Daisy shadowing him, her face increasingly irritable.

Partial Sue was more vocal. "You might want a plate for that lolly. It's dripping everywhere like an old Morris Minor."

"Pfft," he scoffed. "What folly, using a plate to eat an ice lolly. If the good Lord had wanted us to eat lollies off plates, he'd wouldn't have created little wooden lolly sticks."

Fiona shoved a plate in front of him. "Well, the Almighty's not here to clear up after you. Daisy spent hours making that model, she doesn't want melted lolly all over it."

"Tis a moot point." He stuffed the remaining lolly in his mouth and placed the empty stick on the plate Fiona held in front of him.

She picked it up with her thumb and forefinger and handed it back to him. "Bin's over there by the till."

"Yes, of course." The Wicker Man took his lolly stick and disposed of it properly. "I'd better head back to ye olde furniture shoppe, and earn some coin." He left.

"What do you think?" asked Fiona.

Partial Sue tutted. "In Wicker Man language, I think that means he's going to find a cool dark spot in his shop, select an appropriate piece of comfy furniture, put his feet up and have a snooze."

"Sounds about right," Daisy agreed.

"No, I mean, any more thoughts about what happened yesterday?" They'd spent the day debating and discussing the fire and Bitsy's miraculous survival, circling around arguments and picking apart theories.

The three of them congregated around the counter. Partial Sue kicked off discussions. "I'm still of the mind that it's someone from London. By the sound of it, Bitsy does have a lot of enemies. She got defensive when Fiona suggested it might be one of them."

"I think it's far simpler than that," said Fiona. "It's obvious that it's the same person who set Malcolm's hut alight. Bitsy's hut had the same burn pattern. Remember what Martin the fireman said?"

Daisy had another theory. "What if it's separate killers? What if someone came down from London planning to kill Bitsy, knew she was staying on the spit, had heard about Malcolm's hut burning down, and decided to copy the murder technique to throw us off the scent?"

"A copycat killer is a distinct possibility," Partial Sue agreed.

Fiona grunted, not convinced. "There are big problems with that theory. Firstly, they didn't manage to kill Bitsy. A killer coming down from London or a hit man hired by one of her enemies wouldn't come all this way and go to all that trouble without first checking if she was actually inside. Unless they were the Mr Bean of hit men. Like Bitsy said herself, if they were trying to kill her then they didn't do a very good job of it. Secondly, if it was a copycat killer, they'd have had to figure out how to set fire to her hut in exactly the same way as Malcolm's — using the mysterious gravity-defying petrol technique. Pouring it on the wall without it running down. Not easy, considering no one's figured out how it's done yet. That's quite a big ask."

The three ladies went quiet, chewing over theories in their minds, hoping this latest attack might throw up a new angle or clue.

Partial Sue thought she had one. "I think the fact that Bitsy wasn't home during the fire might be key to all this."

"How so?" Fiona asked.

"All along, we've assumed that the goal here is murder. But what if it's not? What if the intention is to merely scare people away? Bitsy proves this. She wasn't home."

"But what about Malcolm? He died," Daisy pointed out.

"Yes, but what if that was an accident?" Partial Sue replied. "Never meant to happen. Scare tactics that got out of hand."

A ping-ponging sensation bounced around in Fiona's tummy, excitement at this new possibility. The fires were warnings, not attempts at murder. Heavy-handed and extreme hints, except their first attempt with Malcolm had gone awry, and he had died. But by the second attempt they had learned their lesson, been more careful. Lit the fire when Bitsy was out.

She smiled. "I like this new slant. It makes a lot of sense."

"I sense a 'but' coming," Partial Sue replied.

Fiona shook her head. "No 'but' coming. None I can think of. This is a much more plausible interpretation of events. They wanted these two off the spit because they didn't fit with its genteel atmosphere. They were both eccentrics. Destroy their huts and they can't stay on the spit. A solid deterrent. I don't know anyone who would want to go back there after that. The only thing that didn't go to plan was that Malcolm died. Perhaps the arsonists hadn't realised the smoke would knock him out."

"Bitsy did talk about rebuilding her hut," Daisy remembered. "They might not have scared her off."

"Yes, but once the shock sinks in, I doubt that will happen," Fiona replied. "She won't want to return. They will have ousted another non-conformist."

"*They* being Frank and his cabal of self-righteous guardians of the spit, I suppose," Partial Sue added.

Fiona nodded. "Maybe Frank had given up trying to do things by the rules and had resorted to extreme measures."

An unwelcome thought popped into Fiona's head, one that she didn't want to acknowledge because it would explode the nice, neat package they'd just taped up and sealed, making a mess and sending that horrible Styrofoam everywhere.

"There is one other theory. A possibility we haven't explored," she began. "Was there any connection between Malcolm and Bitsy, other than the fact that they were both a bit left field? I know it's a long shot but would they have shared a common enemy? I mean, apart from Frank and his cronies."

Something caught Daisy's attention outside. "Why don't you ask her? Here she comes now."

CHAPTER 45

From across the road, Bitsy strutted towards them. Her appearance had improved considerably from the last time they had seen her. Hair freshly slicked back, she wore a simple baby-blue playsuit, a little on the large side, with silver pumps. Sophie followed, equally glamourous in a white vest top and wide-leg linen trousers.

As the pair of them entered the shop, Bitsy's mouth formed into a huge oval. She dispensed with any formal greetings and turned to her friend, accusingly. "Sophie, why didn't you tell me how amazing their shop was? It's like Narnia in here. Look at all this lovely wood panelling, and all this amazing stuff."

Slightly offended, Sophie muttered, "Well, it's okay if you like that sort of thing. My clients prefer clean lines and the like."

"Hold my calls. What is this?" Bitsy spotted Daisy's model. She danced around it, clapping with delight.

"Daisy made it," Partial Sue announced.

"No, you didn't!" Bitsy almost exploded with excitement.

Daisy nodded eagerly, grinning.

"You are so talented, Daisy. What an amazing thing to make. Soph, why haven't you got anything like this in your shop?"

"Well, my edit is more . . ."

Bitsy held up her hand for her to stop. "Rhetorical question." She turned back to the model, pointing out familiar sights. "There's the little jetty, the ice-cream kiosk, the restaurant with someone drinking a tiny cappuccino — you've even added froth on top. There's Frank's hut. She edged around to the other side of the model. "Oh, and there's my hut before it burned down." The glee from Bitsy's face fell away.

Sophie was at her side in a moment. "You okay, Bitsy?"

"Yeah, just a bit down about it all. My lovely beach hut's gone, turned into charcoal, and all my stuff's gone up in smoke."

"We're so sorry," Fiona said.

Bitsy sniffed. "Yeah, I mean, it's fine, I can replace it. But I was really enjoying myself down there. Now I don't know what I'm going to do. Stick it out here or go back to Richmond."

"You can stay at mine as long as you want," Sophie reassured her.

"You could rent another hut," Partial Sue suggested. "I've heard there are plenty available."

Bitsy shook her head. "No. The fire's taken the allure out of the place. It'll never be the same again."

"How did you get on at the police station?" Fiona asked. "Do they have any idea who did this?"

Bitsy sighed. "None. Well, not that they told me. Kept asking the same thing you did. Anyone have a grudge against me? Like I said to you, only half the married women in London. I wish I hadn't said that. They wanted to know every single name of anyone's nose I'd put out of joint. I gave them a list as long as my arm. I don't envy them. Going to take them a month of Sundays to investigate that lot. But, I must say, I did like DI Fincher. She's smart, apart from being a bit strait-laced. She's got the same pair of Jimmy's as I have."

"Jimmy's?" asked Fiona.

"Jimmy Choos," Sophie sneered. "They're shoes, dear."

"I know what Jimmy Choos are," Fiona replied.

"Fiona prefers Crocs," Sophie said with a condescending cackle.

217

Bitsy threw her friend a filthy look. "Sophie, don't fashion-shame people. It's really not on. So what if Fiona prefers Crocs? I've been living in a changing robe the last few weeks and you didn't say anything."

Sophie gave Fiona a fake smile. "Soz and all that."

Fiona didn't really care what Sophie thought of her fashion sense. But it was an odd sight, seeing Sophie put in her place. They were all so used to her being the queen bee around here that it was a unique experience watching her defer to Bitsy's superior social status. The only time she hadn't was when Bitsy had appeared alive and well after thinking she was dead. Then Sophie had acted like an angry parent. Completely understandable given the circumstances.

"Anything else useful emerge from the questioning?" asked Partial Sue.

Bitsy thought for a moment. "No, nothing. But I did overhear a young detective speaking to DS Thomas about the CCTV."

"What did he say?" Fiona asked.

"He said they'd checked through it and had drawn another blank. DS Thomas got irritable with the poor lad. Told him to check it again. The young officer said they had, and there was nothing."

"Nothing?" asked Partial Sue.

"Yep," Bitsy replied. "Nothing. Apparently, the fire started all by itself, same as last time."

Fiona leaped up, grabbed her phone and called Tides Restaurant. "Marcus, it's Fiona. I need you to send me the CCTV footage from Sunday night. And I need Seb's copy from the Smuggler's House."

In the background, noises of plates clattering and frying pans hissing reached her ears.

Marcus laughed. "You've got to be joking. I'm far too busy at the moment, as you can hear."

Fiona hated doing this. Playing hardball was really not her style. "We need that footage ASAP, otherwise the next call I make will be to report an incident of poaching on Mudeford Spit."

The line went quiet, apart for the cacophony of the kitchen. A beat later, Marcus said, "Fine, but you'll have to come and get it. I can't leave the restaurant."

"Can't you just email it to me?"

"No way. File that big would never get through."

Daisy gestured to Fiona to give her the phone. "Hello, Marcus. It's Daisy here. There's this brilliant website called bigfilefanclub.com. Just upload the file and we'll be able to open it at our end." Daisy waited, then pulled the phone from her ear and handed it back to Fiona. "He hung up."

Despite Marcus's abruptness, half an hour later the files came through and the five ladies gathered around the shop's laptop, sifting through the different camera angles. As before, they chose four views, giving them two images along the fronts of all the beach huts — one from the restaurant, the other from the Smuggler's House — and the other two revealing the space behind the two rows. Fiona cued up the footage to 2 a.m. Before pressing play, she asked, "Bitsy, are you sure you want to watch this? It might be traumatic seeing your hut going up in flames."

Bitsy took a deep breath. "I'll be fine. Fire away. In both senses of the word."

Five faces peered closer. Fiona scrolled through the footage, hopping it forward in twenty-second bursts. Just after 3 a.m., a faint glow appeared at the edge of both feeds, a carbon copy of Malcolm's hut fire, growing ever larger, then eventually wrapping its flaming tentacles around Bitsy's hut.

Bitsy whimpered. No matter how tough you were, witnessing your property, where you had slept and partied and relaxed, going up in flames would traumatise the hardiest of souls.

Sophie placed a reassuring hand on Bitsy's. With her other hand, Bitsy cuffed a tear. "I wasn't there for very long," she sniffed. "But I still had some happy times there.

The happiest was sitting on the deck drinking G & T s, the evening I fell off the scooter. Good times. Can I use your loo?"

"Of course," Fiona replied. "It's in the storeroom on the left."

Bitsy hurried to the back of the shop.

"Poor Bitsy," Daisy said.

"That's a lot of trauma to deal with."

"Might take her a while to get over it."

"Oh, she'll be fine," Sophie remarked, not joining in with their sympathies. Either she knew Bitsy better, certain she'd bounce back or she simply wasn't bothered. Sophie turned her attention to the laptop screen. "I don't get it. Why didn't we see anyone? How did the fire start if there's no one there?"

"Welcome to our world," replied Partial Sue.

They wound the footage backwards and forwards, watching and rewatching. They tried all the things they'd done with the footage of Malcolm's hut, checking for the presence of anyone nearby earlier in the day, and just like before, it yielded nothing usable. The fire just seemed to start itself. One second it wasn't there, the next it was.

Sophie clicked her fingers. "Bitsy left the gas on. That's how the fire started."

"We'd have seen a huge explosion if it were gas," Fiona explained.

Sophie had another go. "A bottle of gin."

"How would the gin catch alight?" Partial Sue questioned.

"Bitsy had a lot of gin in there and it exploded."

"Again," said Fiona, "we'd have seen an explosion. This fire started gradually."

Sophie's suggestions came thick and fast, as if she were on a game show, answering against the clock in a quick-fire round. "A barbecue. A small comet. Stray fireworks. Matches. A magnifying glass. Solar flares. Hot lava. A ghost." Her answers quickly deteriorated into random things that popped into her head. Sophie may have been a formidable

220

PR maven and fashionista but when it came to solving crime, she was out of her depth, and not even the tallest pair of Jimmy Choo heels would help keep her head above water.

"Oh, I know!" Her eyes lit up with enthusiasm. "Someone fired a flaming arrow from afar, like a Viking."

This was becoming painful. Fiona sighed. "How would the arrow get down into the narrow gap between the two beach huts?"

"Well, it would take a very skilled archer. Like Robin Hood."

"We'll be sure to check the other camera feeds for the presence of Vikings or Robin Hood." Partial Sue smiled wryly.

Sophie regarded her with a critical eye. "I'm sensing a tone of cynicism towards my suggestions. You should be thankful I have great ideas."

The toilet door in the storeroom opened, saving them from having to explain that Sophie's ideas were not great and she wouldn't be getting any requests from the Met to help them bust open big cases any time soon.

Bitsy emerged, her face a little puffy but much happier. "Sorry about that. Had a bit of an episode. Feeling better now. Soph, I think I might need to go into town. Get some new clothes, seeing as mine have turned into ashes. Thanks for the lend, by the way." She tugged on the baggy playsuit.

Fiona hadn't thought of this. Bitsy had no clothes or belongings left and was having to borrow Sophie's, which would explain the slightly oversized garment.

"You could always buy some clothes here," Daisy suggested. "They're second-hand but we have some nice items, and it would help out the homeless doggies."

"No offence," Sophie said, "but I think my shop is more suited to Bitsy's discerning tastes."

"I'll be the judge of that." Bitsy wasted no time moving around the shop, examining every garment with the hawk eyes of someone who knows exactly what she wants and exactly what will suit her. After several circuits of the racks, and trying on a mountain of clothes, not bothering to use the changing room but instead preferring to strip off there and then, Bitsy dumped a pile of clothes on the counter.

Fiona totted then up on the till. "That will be twenty-seven pounds. Call it twenty-five."

Bitsy refused the discount. "No, no. Can't deprive the little orphan dogs of what's rightfully theirs. Full amount, if you please." She pulled out her credit card. "Lucky, I had my flexible friend on me the night of the fire. About the only thing I do have."

Fiona took Bitsy's credit card and rang the sale into the till.

Bitsy turned to her friend. "Don't worry, Soph. I'll spend the same amount in your shop too."

"Thanks, bestie."

Fiona handed back Bitsy her card and a receipt while Daisy and Partial Sue bagged up her purchases. "Oh, nearly forgot," Fiona said. "One last question. Did the police ask you about Malcolm Crainey? If there was any connection between you two? Any mutual friends, acquaintances or enemies?"

"Ha," Sophie scoffed. "Bitsy and Malcolm didn't know each other. They're like chalk and cheese. Malcolm being the cheese, the stale kind you find on the floor under a fridge."

Sophie received an acidic stare from Bitsy, her harsh description of Malcolm not going down well. "The guy is dead and you're criticising his social standing. Not very nice at all." She turned to Fiona. "Yes, the police did ask me that. But as far as I know our paths never crossed. Never heard of him until I'd bought the beach hut. They're looking into it though. Checking my list of contacts with his, I believe. Anyway, I must be going. Leave you ladies to get on with your day."

Bitsy looped her hand through her many shopping bags and exited the shop, chased by an apologetic Sophie. "I didn't mean that about Malcolm. You're still going to buy some things from my shop, aren't you?"

"Not in the mood I'm in," Bitsy snapped without looking back at her.

"I've got some pieces that would look great on you, and they're dry-cleaned. You don't get that at Dogs Need Nice Homes."

They watched Sophie sycophantically selling the benefits of her shop, while Bitsy ignored her.

"Those two have a weird relationship," Partial Sue said.

"Love-hate," Daisy suggested.

"More parent and child, I think," Fiona added. "But the roles keep flipping between them."

"What do we do now?" asked Daisy. "With the investigation, I mean."

Fiona pointed to the laptop. "First we send Freya the footage. Get her to check it for tampering. I highly doubt it's been faked and we know the police have already checked it, but we just need to be sure. Then, after we close up tonight, we head down to the spit. Take a look at the wreck of Bitsy's hut. See if it reveals anything."

CHAPTER 46

The police cordons had been removed from the entrance to Hengistbury Head. Further down the tarmac path, Mudeford Spit was back open for business. Although early evening, just after six, day-trippers lingered, frolicking in the shallows, soaking up the sun, and queuing to get an outside table at Tides Restaurant.

The three ladies stood on the hot sand in front of the sad sight of Bitsy's blackened beach hut. Tangled around it, sagging police tape fluttered in the warm breeze, warning them not to go any further or venture near the two huts either side of it, which had received nothing more serious than a slight singeing.

Partial Sue pointed to the neighbouring huts. "Do we know who owns these two?"

Daisy nodded. "The Smiths from Twickenham on the right. Weren't here on Sunday. Been out of the country since Easter. And on the left, we have the Petersons from Salisbury, who were out that night celebrating a birthday — pictures are all over Facebook."

Ignoring the police warning, they circled the remains of Bitsy's hut, examining the wreckage, poking and prodding, hoping for a clue to emerge. There wasn't much to see. Similar to Malcolm's, most of the damage was concentrated in a U-shaped area high up on the right-hand exterior wall, in the narrow gap next to the neighbouring hut. Undoubtedly the origin point, the fire had burned right through the cladding and supporting studs behind, extending onto the roof, of which a large portion had burned and collapsed. This hut had burned for a lot longer, presumably because there hadn't been an Annie Follet around to raise the alarm earlier.

"Weird," Partial Sue commented. "Bitsy's hut is higher off the sand than Malcolm's. But still the arsonist has chosen to start the fire just below the roof again. The most awkward place possible."

"Maybe Sophie's theory of a flaming arrow isn't so daft after all," Daisy suggested.

Partial Sue stepped away from the hut and gazed at the start of the spit and the headland beyond. "How far do you think an arrow can travel?"

Daisy Googled it. Scrolling through her phone, she shook her head. "All sorts of answers — some say it's five hundred metres, others say a thousand. Ah, here we go, current record is one thousand two hundred and twenty-two metres."

"That's a long way."

"Is that hitting a target though?" Fiona asked.

Daisy did another search. "Record for the furthest arrow actually hitting a specified target is three hundred and thirty metres."

Fiona shielded her eyes from the sun and joined Partial Sue squinting at the start of the spit. "How far is it from here to the dunes on the other side of the restaurant?"

"About two hundred and fifty yards in old money, I'd say," Partial Sue replied.

Daisy converted it into metric. "That's two hundred and twenty-eight metres. But why from the dunes?"

"Because if someone fired a flaming arrow, they'd need to be concealed from the restaurant's CCTV."

Partial Sue wasn't buying it. "That means the archer wouldn't be able to see the target and would need to be a Guinness World Record breaker. It's asking quite a lot."

"But it would answer why no one's been caught on CCTV so far," Fiona replied.

"Wouldn't the cameras have captured a flaming arrow flying through the sky?" Daisy asked.

"The cameras only cover the fronts and the backs of the huts. Not the middles, where there's a blind spot," Fiona answered. "Remember, when we watched the footage, we never saw the fire starting, only the glow as it spread out from the centre."

All three of them stood on the sand twisting their heads this way and that like meerkats, examining Bitsy's hut, then switching to the dunes at the start of the spit, weighing up the plausibility of the theory.

"What about the gravity-defying puddle of petrol Martin mentioned?" asked Partial Sue. "How did that happen if it's a flaming arrow?"

Daisy slowly expanded a theory. "Perhaps a small water balloon is attached to the arrow, filled with petrol. It breaks open on impact, splashing against the side wall of the hut. Before it has time to drip down, something ignites it."

"Mm." Fiona became cynical. "This arrow is getting a bit technical."

Partial Sue furrowed her brow. "Not to mention heavy. Would something like that even fly straight? Also, both fires started in the narrow gap on the side wall. It would be a hell of a shot to get an arrow between two beach huts, I imagine. Wouldn't it be more likely that an arrow would land on the roof? The shot would have to be perfect every time. Plus, wouldn't there be the remains of an arrow, even a burnt one?"

The three ladies looked at one another. Thinking the same thing, they dropped onto all fours and began digging at the sand alongside the hut where the fire started. When it yielded nothing, they switched to carefully picking through the remains of burnt wood for anything long, straight and pointy. After half an hour of searching they gave up and stepped away from the debris, dusting off their grimy hands. Daisy handed each of them a wet wipe.

Fiona took another wipe from Daisy, as the first one had barely scratched the surface. "This theory has too many drawbacks. Mostly lack of evidence and credibility. It's too much of a long shot, excuse the pun."

"I, for one, am relieved," Partial Sue said. "Imagine if it was true. We'd have to admit that Sophie was right."

The three ladies giggled.

"Can you imagine how big her ego would be?" Fiona said.

Daisy sniggered again. "It's a wonder she can get down Southbourne Grove as it is."

"I think we dodged a bullet there, or rather an arrow." Fiona glanced up and down the spit inquisitively. "You know, normally at this point Frank would appear, poking his nose into what we're doing and lecturing us." Fiona did a fair impression of Frank's authoritative drawl. "Did you know that the surname Fletcher is derived from someone who used to make arrows?"

"That's exactly what he would say," Partial Sue remarked.

"Is that really where the name Fletcher comes from?" Daisy seemed genuinely interested. "Well, I never knew that."

Fiona did a double take, her head swivelling rapidly up and down the spit. "Come to think of it, where are all the hut owners?"

They'd been so focused on examining Bitsy's hut, it had escaped their attention that all the beach huts were shut up tight. There were plenty of day-trippers, but no hut owners and not one beach hut open.

"Maybe they were scared away by Bitsy's hut burning down," Daisy suggested.

Partial Sue shook her head. "No, they're a defiant bunch."

Never a truer word had been spoken, as Fiona was about to find out.

Her phone rang. It was Antony Owens. "Oh, thank goodness I've got hold of you."

"Antony, what's the matter?"

"I need your help. I think I'm about to be eaten alive. The beach hut owners, led by Frank Marshall, have called an impromptu meeting at the community centre. After the second fire, they're demanding answers. They want to know why no one's been caught yet."

"Hang on, Antony. We'll be there ASAP."

In the distance they glimpsed the friendly shape of the Noddy train, arcing around its turning circle to make its return journey. The three ladies gave chase, waving furiously to flag it down and hitch a ride back to Partial Sue's car. They needed to save Antony Owens from the beach-hut lynch mob.

CHAPTER 47

As the three ladies pushed open the stiff metal doors of the community centre, a wall of sound assaulted their senses — aggressive, angry voices that talked over one another and had plenty to say, the kind that forced fists to shake and fingers to point.

From out of the cacophony, snatching words here and there, Fiona deduced that this meeting appeared to be more about finding someone to blame than someone to accuse. Without a doubt, that someone was Antony Owens, who looked like the loneliest man in the world, standing on a temporary stage facing the angry mob spread out among rows of plastic chairs that weren't getting much use as most people were on their feet, shouting at him. In his usual smart suit, he gripped the sides of the lectern for dear life, as if at any moment he might be wrenched away and burned at the stake. Malorie Granger stood off to one side, presumably arbitrating. But she didn't appear to be arbitrating anything, rather she was letting the assembled beach-hut owners verbally tear Antony to pieces.

Just as Fiona was debating whether to step in to rescue the poor man, Malorie took centre stage and raised her hands for calm. "Quiet, please, ladies and gentlemen. We need to let Mr Owens give answers to your questions, otherwise there is no point in having this hearing."

A hearing? That sounded serious and confirmed Fiona's fears: this was about finding fault, not finding the killer.

Antony Owens hooked a finger into the neck of his shirt, tugging it to relieve the heat or the tension. He swallowed hard. "We are doing everything we can to catch the arsonist."

The ceasefire didn't last long. Shouting resumed. Random accusations flew at him from every corner of the room.

"You're not doing enough!"

"It's not safe down there!"

"How soon before someone else dies?"

"How do you propose to keep us safe?"

This last question caught Antony's attention. He brightened a little. "Now, that I can answer." He shifted through his notes resting on the lectern and held up a map. Fiona couldn't quite make it out, but assumed it was a map of Hengistbury Head and Mudeford Spit. "I have proposed, pending council approval, for a network of more security cameras at regular intervals along the spit—"

Before he could finish, Frank Marshall stood up. "We already have cameras at the restaurant and the Smuggler's House. As far as I know, they didn't catch anyone. What do we need more cameras for?"

Fiona thought this a little odd coming from an ex-security professional who had wanted to gate off the whole spit. But everyone roared in agreement.

Antony attempted to salvage the proposal. "These would be different. These would be council run. Monitored twenty-four hours—"

Frank turned to his assembled beach hut brothers and sisters. "They want to spy on us. Control us. Take away our freedom. We're not going to let it happen, are we?"

Whipped up by Frank's *Braveheart* rhetoric, the whole room erupted into a storm of aggressive shouts of "No!"

"Classic fartlighting," Partial Sue muttered.

Fiona had to agree. Frank certainly knew how to say something incendiary to cause a stink. She became a little worried for Antony Owens' safety. "I think we should go up there."

"Are you mad? I'm not partial to being shouted at by angry mobs."

"But Antony's all alone up there," Daisy said. "He looks like he could do with some moral support."

Partial Sue scowled. "We'll get lynched."

"They can't lynch all of us," Daisy replied, then thought better of it. "Can they?"

"Nobody's getting lynched, come on," Fiona reassured. They followed her to the front, up the steps and onto the stage, where Antony rushed over to meet them, relief causing his whole body to sag. Away from the microphone he gushed, "Thank you, thank you. I don't think I would've lasted much longer."

"You look like you could do with a hand," said Fiona.

"I'll say."

Malorie stepped in once more, hands aloft. "Okay, okay. Quiet, please. Ladies and gentlemen, I believe we have some . . ." She glanced over at Fiona, Partial Sue and Daisy, struggling to find the right words to describe the three of them, seeing as there was no love lost between them. "These ladies may have some information about the case."

The room went quiet.

Antony addressed the crowd. "I'd like to introduce Fiona, Sue and Daisy, the private investigators whom I've hired to get to the bottom of this."

The assembled crowd stared back, some confused, some sniggering, the unlikely sight of three retirees not exactly fitting the stereotype of hard-nosed, no-nonsense private investigators.

Antony Owens stood back to let Fiona have the microphone.

"Good evening." The microphone squealed harshly with feedback so she moved back slightly. "We've been investigating the fire that took Malcolm's life and also the most recent fire on Sunday night—"

"Have you got any suspects?" someone shouted.

"No, not yet," Fiona replied. "But we're working on it."

A groan came back at her.

"Do you have any leads?" someone else asked.

"Several," Fiona replied.

"Let's hear them," Frank Marshall called out.

"We definitely know that both fires were started in the gaps between the huts, high up on the right-hand wall."

Frank Marshall got to his feet. "I don't mean to be rude, Fiona. I've been helping you with your enquiries, being very generous with my time and cooperation. But what you're describing is how the fire started. That's not a lead."

There were grumbles of assent.

Fiona could feel herself losing the room. Not that she'd had it in the first place. "We have interviewed a great deal of people on the spit—"

"Now, hold on a second," Frank Marshall interrupted. "Are you saying it's one of us? No one who owns a beach hut would ever dream of doing anything like this to one of their own. How dare you imply that we would."

Frank was back to fartlighting again. Stirring up anger where there really didn't need to be any. A roar of indignance filled the room, drowning out Fiona's voice.

"No, I didn't mean that. We have to interview everyone. It's standard procedure. The police did the same."

When it had quietened down, Frank said, "Now, once more, do you have any suspects?"

They did. Realistically, the one and only suspect was him, perhaps enabled by some of the audience. Whether it was a handful of them or all of them, she didn't know. However, there was no way she could reveal that. Not if she wanted to get out of there alive with her friends. Instead, she supplied a feeble answer. "We're working on it."

The whole crowd descended into a chaos of baying, jeering and booing. Not even Malorie's intervention could quell them. "Order! Order! I will have order!" she cried as if this were Prime Minister's Questions in the House of Commons.

Frank, already on his feet, strode with purpose to the front of the stage, climbed onto it and headed towards the lectern. Fiona expected Malorie to block his path, assert her authority and demand he leave the stage, her face boiling with rage. None of these things happened. She let him past unchallenged.

It became eminently clear that Frank intended to hijack the lectern. Fiona and her friends stood their ground. She held her hand over the microphone. "What do you want, Frank?"

"I need that microphone."

"I hope you're not intending to create any more unrest," Fiona replied. "This lot look ready to riot."

"Quite the opposite." Frank smiled. "I believe I can settle them down. Ensure a peaceful resolution. In any case, what choice do you have?" He nodded to the incensed crowd.

Fiona could see no other alternative. She, Daisy and Partial Sue stepped back to stand with Antony.

Frank tapped the microphone with his forefinger, testing it was still on. "Fellow beach hut owners. I believe the future of our safe haven is under threat. We need to do something, and fast."

There were murmurs of agreement.

"I propose that Antony Owens be relieved of duty, and instead, I will step in and represent our needs."

"Wait! What?" Antony cried, his voice small without the aid of the microphone.

Frank turned to him, still speaking into the microphone. "I'm sorry, Antony, you've had your chance and it hasn't worked out. No offence, but how can you represent our needs when you don't even have a hut?" Frank turned back to the gathered assembly. "I, on the other hand, am one of you. I know what we go through on that spit, our struggles, our trials and tribulations." Frank spoke as if having a luxury beach hut in one of the most idyllic and exclusive areas of the UK were akin to living in a besieged city. "That's why I propose that I become your official representative. By show of hands, who agrees?"

Every hand in the community centre shot into the air. "Motion carried."

Everyone cheered.

Antony confronted Frank. "You can't do that. You know very well any changes have to be voted for unanimously. Not everyone who owns a hut is here."

Frank beckoned for a woman Fiona recognised to approach the stage. It was Lynne, the washing-line snitch. In her arms she carried a stack of printouts. Frank came out from behind the lectern as she handed them to him. He held them above his head. "I have here endorsements sent by email from every hut owner who couldn't be here tonight, supporting me in taking over the role of liaison officer." He handed the stack of emails to a shocked Antony, who sifted through them, checking their validity. He cast a defeated look at Fiona. This whole meeting had been planned by Frank, a stitch-up to elbow Antony Owens out of the way and slot himself into the job.

"You'll need to make that official with the local authority," Malorie said.

"It will be the first thing I do tomorrow morning." Frank grinned.

Fiona put a commiserating hand on Antony's arm as he continued to stare at the printouts in disbelief.

But Frank wasn't done yet. "In my new role as beach-hut liaison officer, pending council approval, of course, I would like to propose that due to lack of progress, the current private investigators be removed from investigating the fires."

"*What!*" the ladies cried out in disbelief.

CHAPTER 48

Shaking his head, Antony Owens handed the printouts to Fiona, then stormed off the stage and out of the door.

The three ladies looked at one another, stunned, then at Frank, who did his best to feign sympathy, angling his bushy eyebrows like two sides of a lifting bridge. "I'm very sorry. But we can't rely on well-meaning amateurs. It's nothing personal."

Why did people say that, as if it somehow made everything okay? This was intensely personal. It was all about personalities and egos, mostly Frank's, who thought he was better than everyone else. Or did Frank feel threatened? Frightened that they were getting close to the truth that he was the killer, enabled by his beach hut cronies. Was this all a ruse to get them off the investigation? It was a strong possibility, apart from the fact that they had no tangible evidence against him. Or maybe he thought that they did.

Dozens of reasons why they should stay on the case flashed through Fiona's mind. Sensible reasons she could debate and argue into the microphone, if Frank would let her. However, this was not a crowd that would listen to sense or reason, not in the state they were in.

Her thoughts were confirmed when Lynne the washing-line snitch began shouting, "Out! Out! Out!" A second later, the whole room joined in. A sea of incensed, well-tanned faces, chanting and stamping feet, making the place shake.

Frank did nothing to calm them, enjoying the spectacle he had created, feeding off it. He glanced over at Fiona. She was sure she could detect a smirk under that bristling moustache of his as he luxuriated in getting what he wanted. Fiona appealed to Malorie for help, but she seemed just as shocked as them.

A tactical retreat was the only option. Fiona stepped off the stage followed by Partial Sue and Daisy, accelerating towards the door, the berating voices following them. For people who were all about preserving their peaceful haven, they were incredibly aggressive.

Thankful to be outside on the pavement, staggering away from the toxic atmosphere, the three ladies took deep breaths as if they'd just escaped from a collapsing building.

"I was not partial to that at all," Partial Sue croaked. "Let's find the car and get away from here as fast as we can."

They threaded their way along Southbourne Grove.

"I can't believe they kicked us off the case, in front of everyone," Fiona said.

"And sacked poor Antony," Daisy replied. "How humiliating for him."

"Speak of the devil." Partial Sue pointed. Up ahead, Antony Owens stood on the pavement, head bowed, his back against a smart, blue, metallic BMW parked by the roadside.

In front of him, his wife Olivia, immaculately dressed and made up to the nines, tried to console him. "Don't worry. We'll figure something out. I can go back to teaching at the technical college." They halted their conversation at the ladies' approach.

Antony Owens' face reddened. "I'm so sorry I called you here tonight."

"Don't be," Fiona said. "I'm glad you did. No one should have to face that on their own."

He continued to apologise. "Sorry for running out on you. I felt so humiliated back there."

"Completely understandable," Daisy reassured him. "What vile people."

Partial Sue shook her head in disgust. "It was a set-up from the start. That meeting was to get rid of us. Plain and simple."

Antony Owens cast his eyes down at the ground. "I've lost my job and they've kicked you off the case."

"Will you be okay?" asked Fiona.

He glanced up at her. "Well, I've still got my day job."

Olivia attempted to bolster the situation. "We'll make up the extra cash somehow. At least Antony won't have to put up with those whining beach-hut owners anymore, and you won't have to investigate those grisly fires."

"Oh, we intend to keep investigating," Fiona said.

Surprise jolted him. "You are?"

"We are?" Partial Sue asked, equally shocked.

"Why not?" Fiona replied. "We just won't get a donation at the end of it, but if Frank thinks he's put us off, he's got another think coming and, more importantly, we have a murderer to catch."

Fiona was desperate to reveal that she thought Frank was behind it, but she didn't have enough evidence. And the mental state Antony Owens was in, he might take that information and confront Frank with it or do something else he'd later regret. Bruised egos like nothing more than turning swiftly into angry, vengeful ones. Better to keep her theories to herself until they had solid evidence.

He shook all three ladies' hands one by one. "Well, I will wish you good luck. And thank you for all your hard work so far. I wish things could have turned out differently."

They returned his kind words with their own and watched him and his wife climb into their car and pull into the evening traffic.

When the car was out of sight, Fiona turned to her two friends. Time to nip any negativity in the bud. "We put this behind us. No dwelling on that childish nonsense we experienced in that meeting. As far as I'm concerned, we have even

237

more motivation to catch the killer than before. To prove to that pompous idiot Frank and his beach minions that he was a fool to sack us."

"It probably is Frank," said Partial Sue. "Especially after what he just did."

"A distinct possibility," Fiona replied. "But until we have anything solid to accuse him with, we have to keep an open mind."

Partial Sue tutted. "That guy is a master manipulator. He got everyone to agree to sack us and Antony pretty sharpish. Unless he'd been planning it for ages."

Daisy ventured a guess. "Maybe it's a bit like that stock-cube syndrome."

Partial Sue shot a confused look at her friend. "Stock-cube syndrome?

"You know," Daisy said, "where hostages start bonding with their captors."

"You mean Stockholm syndrome. I'm not sure it applies to people with beach huts."

"Oh, silly me."

But perhaps Daisy had inadvertently hit on something. "You know," Fiona said, "that's not such a crazy thought. Frank is a bit like their captor. Well, influencer. Once people are on that spit, sooner or later they agree to his demands. He got everyone to unanimously agree to get rid of Antony Owens. That's no mean feat." She forgot that she still had the printed-out emails of all the absent beach hut owners in her hands, pledging their support for Frank's proposal. There was one in particular that would help answer her question.

She flicked through them and found the one she'd been searching for. Greg Dean, hut number 122, the one who'd defied Frank over the rotary washing line had pledged his support for tonight's little coup. What had made him decide to do that? She needed to know how he'd been persuaded.

There was only one way to find out. Fiona handed Daisy the printouts and pulled her phone from her bag together with the contact details of all the beach hut owners. She dialled Greg's number and put it on speaker. He answered instantly. She could hear splashing sounds in the background. Baby's bath time.

"Oh, hi. My name's Fiona. I spoke to you on Sunday regarding the fires on the spit."

"Oh, yeah. I remember."

"Sorry, have I called at a bad time?"

"No, you're all right. Go ahead."

Fiona took a breath. "We've just been to a beach hut owners' meeting where Antony Owens was unanimously voted out."

"Sorry about that."

"Would you mind me asking what swayed your decision?"

"Not at all. Well, after I heard about the second fire, I wanted something done. Antony Owens hadn't been doing a bad job. It's just we didn't feel safe on that spit. As you've already guessed, I'm not Frank's biggest fan. He's an old fart. That said, he does get things done. Despite having cross words with him I know if we had a problem, he'd be on it like a Rottweiler on a dropped sausage. He's more tenacious than Antony."

He had a point. Frank had a zealous commitment to Mudeford Spit that was unquenchable. "Yes, I can imagine," Fiona agreed.

"Plus, he's doing the beach hut liaison job for free," Greg said.

"Sorry, *what?*"

Partial Sue's eyes widened.

Greg explained. "We all had to pay an annual subscription for Antony Owens. Whereas Frank doesn't want any money. So it's a win–win."

And there it was. No great mystery or sorcery afoot. Frank hadn't done some sort of mass Jedi mind trick on all the hut owners or threatened them with his Stasi network of informants. He'd simply saved them a bit of money. No matter who you were, if someone offers to make your yearly bill smaller, you take it.

Fiona thanked Greg and hung up.

"What now?" asked Partial Sue.

"This doesn't change anything," Fiona replied. "Frank is still our number-one suspect. We just need to prove he's responsible."

That had been the problem since day one. Theories abounded, as did suspects with one in particular popping his moustachioed head up more than any others, but evidence had eluded them. Fiona had reached the point where she doubted there was any to be found. Could this be the perfect crime? One that left behind no viable evidence?

No. That was unthinkable. They just had to try harder.

CHAPTER 49

Next morning, the heatwave had a brief, troublesome interruption. A thunderstorm gate-crashed summer like an angry drunk throwing its weight around at a wedding reception, except that instead of knocking over the finger buffet and insulting the bride's mother, it had blotted out the sun, blown rubbish along Southbourne Grove, and chucked rain against the shop like there was no tomorrow. According to the forecast it would be gone by opening time. Strangely, Fiona didn't mind the meteorological outburst. It suited her irritable mood as she sat behind the counter staring at Google, resorting to random searches, hoping they might throw something up — a stumbling, foolhardy method that relied on chance rather than detective skills. Fiona had to admit she was out of ideas, scratching around in the dust, or in this case, the search engine. Maybe Frank was right to have formally taken them off the case. They were getting nowhere. Hadn't been for some time. She hoped that when her friends got in, they might have something new they could bring to the table.

The doorbell tinkled. Fiona was about to raise her head above the laptop screen and inform the rather keen shopper that they weren't open yet, when she realised she knew the person standing in the doorway. Water dripped off the huge, tent-like cagoule that nearly touched her toes. A wax hat had been secured tightly around her chin by a drawstring, its wide brim buckling under the drenching it had received. The woman stared at Fiona through big, owlish glasses that were in the process of steaming up.

Fiona remembered those large sad eyes and the name of the sorrowful donor who previously came attached to a pushchair. "Mary, come in out of the rain. No child today?"

Mary stepped in, dripping water everywhere. "No, she's with my mum and dad."

Fiona gave her a sympathetic smile. She always wanted to give Mary a hug whenever she came in. Wholly inappropriate, of course. Or maybe she could offer her some other form of comfort. Perhaps when she'd finished going through her grandfather's things, if that's what she'd come in for, she'd make her a cup of tea and ask her how she was doing, if that wasn't too prying or painful.

Mary took a deep breath and steadied herself. "Sorry, could I just get something out of my grandfather's box?"

"Yes, of course. It's still behind the till, safe and sound. I'll get out of your way and give you a bit of privacy." Fiona made her way to the back of the shop and heard the parcel tape being carefully torn from the top of the box.

Just before she reached the storeroom, Fiona's phone pinged. A text message from Freya at the computer shop.

CCTV tot negs.

Fiona stared at the screen, not really understanding the message. Was 'tot negs' good or bad? If Fiona had to hazard a guess, she'd say it was short for total negative, but she couldn't be sure. With Freya and the Wicker Man, Fiona seemed to be stuck between two people who used indecipherable language, one from a bygone era, the other from an era yet to happen.

Fiona texted her back asking for more clarification. Her phone pinged almost instantly.

CCTV not faked. Triple-checked. No tampering.
But I did hit the target.
I am the axe queen!

Fiona was happy that Freya's axe-throwing skills had improved but it was another disappointment on the investigation front. Not that Fiona had been holding out much hope for the footage, but she'd had a sliver of optimism that this time the killer might have slipped up and left a clue behind.

She texted Freya back to thank her and turned to see that Mary had left as quickly as she'd arrived. Fiona shrugged and returned to her laptop. Mary's grandfather's box had returned to its position behind the counter, the tape stretched back over it, although it was beginning to lose its stickiness in places.

Taking a seat in front of the screen, Fiona drummed her fingers on the counter, resuming her incessant stare at the Google search panel, hoping for inspiration. Her fingers drummed harder as she became more desperate for a lead to follow, or even just something to type into the search bar.

By her feet, Simon Le Bon raised his head wearily, a questioning look in his big brown eyes.

"Oh, I'm sorry. Am I disturbing you, your highness?"

He glared back at her.

"Have you got any ideas?"

He yawned and went back to dozing.

"Yep, that's how I feel about this whole thing."

Half an hour later, the rain fled, seen off by a vengeful sun that dried up pavements and reclaimed its sovereignty over the skies. Daisy bustled in, huffing and puffing with red cheeks. "I think I have something."

Fiona nearly fell off her seat with relief. "I'm dying to hear it, because I've got nothing."

She dumped her bag and joined Fiona at the counter. "Well, I've been thinking about this killer and come to the conclusion that they're just like a magician. They've made themselves disappear. Both times, nothing on CCTV."

Fiona wondered if Daisy's theory might be plausible. "Freya texted me this morning. Confirmed no tampering of the latest footage."

Daisy nodded. "As we suspected. Well, I started to think of it like a trick or an illusion. You know, it looks real, but it can't be real because it's impossible. How can someone get onto the spit without being seen and start a fire. How would a magician do it?"

"Probably by distracting us, misdirection."

"Yes. So I did the lateral-thinking thingy and noticed this." Daisy showed Fiona her phone screen on which were two sets of tide tables and weather charts. "Remember when Marcus and Seb confessed to poaching? They always did it when the tide was low and there was no wind because it was easier. Well, both times there's been a fire it's coincided with super-low tides and no wind. Have you seen Christchurch Harbour at low tide, I mean a really low one?"

Fiona shook her head.

Daisy led Fiona over to the model and pointed to various points along the harbour's edge. "I've only created part of the harbour here, just to give an indication. If I'd added the whole thing, the model would have been huge. That's because when the tide's out, it turns into an eight-hundred-and-seventy-acre mudflat you can walk across from anywhere around the outside. You wouldn't need to come down the tarmac path or over the headland. You could avoid the CCTV completely if you trudged across the mud." Daisy's face became bright and wide with enthusiasm.

Fiona braced herself to be the bringer of bad news. "That's true, and it's a brilliant observation, but once you step out of the harbour and onto the spit, you still need to cross the sand to reach the beach huts, at which point you get caught by the CCTV." She pointed to the tiny cameras Daisy had recreated on the restaurant and the Smuggler's House.

Daisy paused, her face contemplative until her thought processes worked through Fiona's logic. "Oh." Her features dropped and her shoulders sloped as disappointment took its toll. "I am such a dimwit. Of course, the CCTV still picks you up. Why didn't I remember that?"

Fiona put a reassuring hand on Daisy. "Listen, don't be downhearted. This is the kind of thinking we need — lateral thinking. Keep that up and we'll crack this."

"But I feel so stupid."

"Not at all. That CCTV is outfoxing us at every turn. Everything we think of gets scuppered by it. But we can't lose heart now. This is how cases are cracked. There's no such thing as a bad theory, we just need to keep exploring them. Doggedly carrying on. One will eventually be true. Like you said, this person is some kind of magician. We just need to peek behind the curtain and discover how they're making the illusion work."

Partial Sue burst through the door, puffed out and flustered, not unlike Daisy a moment ago. "I think I've got something," she cried, her eyes glittering.

CHAPTER 50

They had to wait for the revelation, teased for a good five or six minutes because a major breakthrough couldn't be revealed until Partial Sue had a cup of tea in her hands. She made one for all of them and then joined them at the counter.

"So come on, what's this big breakthrough?" Fiona was eager to sink her teeth into something new and promising.

Partial Sue hesitated. "Er, I didn't say it was a break-through. I just said I had something."

"Is it evidence? A lead? A suspect?" Daisy enthused.

Partial Sue's eyes dulled, became doubtful. "Not really. More of an interesting twist. Actually, less of a twist, more of an observation after last night's performance."

Fiona bit the inside of her lip, hopefully concealing her disappointment. She didn't want observations. She wanted fresh leads, bursting with possibility and arrest potential. But she had to be patient and hear her friend out. Observations can lead to bigger things. "Let's hear it then."

Partial Sue pulled out her phone and showed them an article from the local paper five years ago. The headline read: *Tides Restaurant Plans Dashed*. Below this was an artist's impression of a new and improved Tides Restaurant, revamped and refurbished with a swanky bar and balcony added on top, illustrated with beautiful people in open-necked shirts and perfect hair sipping on cocktails while admiring the view.

Daisy and Fiona speed-read through the article while Partial Sue précised its contents. "Essentially, six years ago, Marcus put in an application to extend the restaurant to give it a second storey. It went through planning but when the beach-hut owners got wind of it, they were on it like a ton of bricks. Frank did what Frank does best, got every one of them to oppose it, unanimously."

Fiona read out a quote from Frank Marshall. "'We want things to stay as they are on our beloved spit. A safe, peaceful haven. Those who want disruptive night life can find it elsewhere. We don't need it down here making children and older people feel unsafe.'"

"Malorie was a councillor back then," said Partial Sue. "From what I can tell she put the kibosh on the whole thing. Listen to this quote from her: 'We have listened to the beach hut owners' concerns and decided that the current restaurant set-up serves their needs more than adequately. There is simply no need for a second storey on Tides Restaurant'."

Fiona thought back to Malorie's behaviour at the hearing last night. She didn't exactly enable Frank but she didn't exactly stand in his way either.

Partial Sue's voice brimmed with enthusiasm. "Hey, what if Malorie is part of Frank's extended cabal? A handy facilitator when he wants things done."

Daisy raised her hand as if she were in class. "But I thought Malorie couldn't stand Frank. Hated that he was always pestering her for things to be done on the spit, checkpoints and the like. And remember when he tried to get Malcolm made homeless — she made sure Antony Owens represented him and allowed him to stay."

Daisy made a good point. Traditionally, Malorie and Frank had been at loggerheads, and they'd heard this from several different sources. She didn't like him and had made sure he never got his way in the past.

"You're right," Fiona said. "I don't think she's helping Frank. Remember, she's not a councillor anymore. She manages the community centre, which Frank had obviously hired for his hearing slash planned coup last night. She hasn't got any authority. She couldn't have stopped him even if she'd wanted to. Plus, he did everything by the book — got the necessary number of votes to get rid of Antony. He didn't need Malorie. All he needed was a venue to make it happen. I think what we saw was her being a bit pompous, assuming control of the meeting, as if she were the chairwoman. Textbook Malorie. Has to pretend to be the most important person in the room. When in reality she was only there to unlock the place, put the chairs out and then put them back again and lock up afterwards. And she looked shocked at what he did."

Partial Sue pursed her lips. "Well, she wasn't in control of the meeting at the end. I'd say she lost control, and what about all that stuff she said about advising Frank to make his appointment official with the council?"

Daisy thought hard. "You can take the councillor out of the council, but you can't take the council out of the councillor — no, that doesn't quite work."

"I know what you mean," said Fiona. "Old habits die hard. She can't help being the authoritarian, even though she doesn't work at the council anymore."

Silence fell over the charity shop. Three minds sifting and searching for anything that could be of use, that might lead to something else.

Fiona spoke up first. "The way I see it is we're back to square one. We have a main suspect — Frank — and possibly several hut owners supporting his regime."

"If he is behind this all," Partial Sue said, "he'll think he's scored a victory. Got his nemesis fired and us off the case. Probably thinks he's got us out of his hair, that we'll stop investigating."

Daisy smiled. "It's only going to make us more determined."

"Never a truer word spoken," Fiona added.

The three ladies looked to one another, their jaws firm and their fists clenched, eyes of steel-hard determination.

Over the next two weeks that steely determination reduced by daily increments, dulling then collapsing, until it became a ball of scrunched-up tin foil. Progress eluded them, robbing them of motivation, not helped by the ever-rising temperature outside.

CHAPTER 51

The hottest day of the year so far. When newsreaders, papers and social media liked to keep reminding you how hot it was, as if you didn't know already by your feet sinking into soft tarmac or the grass turning into hay before your eyes. Forgettable statistics flew around the airwaves and on phone alerts: the hottest day since the last time we thought it was the hottest day.

Fiona was fed up with it. Her head was swelling up as if it might pop off at any moment, and no quantity of Fabs, Rockets or Strawberry Splits would assuage the feeling. After closing up at the end of the day and saying cheerio to Daisy and Partial Sue, she decided only a dip in the sea would chill her hot skin and soothe her irritability. Simon Le Bon could come in with her. He could do his cute little breathy doggy paddle around her and cool down his hot furry body.

However, when she reached her road, she was reminded of the perils of living by the beach on a swelteringly hot day. Grand Avenue resembled a scrapyard. Cars were parked in a cavalier fashion, abandoned everywhere and at every angle. What was it about hot weather that made people forsake the highway code and shun the feared authority of single and double yellow lines? But today, desperate to cool off, drivers had gone one better. Those who couldn't find illegal parking on the road had resorted to illegal parking on the pavement. Fiona found herself chicaning around cars strewn across her path. Many already had yellow cellophane-wrapped parking tickets tucked neatly beneath their windscreen wipers.

Undeterred, Fiona pushed on past her house and onto the clifftop, that was usually a wide-open stretch of grass, perfect for dog walking. Not today. It too had been commandeered by beachgoers, their chaos of cars parked with abandon, leaving Fiona to wonder how half of them would get out. Walking to the fence at the edge of the cliff, she peeked over at the beach below. It resembled an ants' nest by the sea. A wriggling mass of bodies elbowing one another for space. The sea wasn't much better — a bubbling stew of humanity, not cooling or relaxing.

She couldn't face it and turned back to the calming refuge of home, opting instead for a cold shower for her and a stint under the garden hose for Simon Le Bon, followed by her feet up under the shade of her veranda and copious G & Ts with crushed ice — the only way to have a G & T in her opinion.

By midnight, the heat of the day had refused to subside, enabled by a blanket of cloud that had stretched over the sky just as the sun retreated, trapping and intensifying all that sticky warmth.

A stuffy, fitful night's sleep ensued. Sweat from Fiona's top lip continually drained into her mouth, salty and bitter, waking her from what slumber she could briefly snatch. The still night made everything more claustrophobic. Unfamiliar sounds from miles away carried across the heat-saturated air. She couldn't tell what was real from what was imagined. Laughter, conversations, foxes barking, and trains in the distance clattering through her mind. On hearing sirens, she woke with a start to find that they were real — booming and terrifying, accompanied by straining engines rushing impatiently down Southbourne Grove from what her dozy brain could deduce.

Fiona glanced at her clock: 3.45 a.m. Groaning, she turned away, back to the challenge of falling asleep. Corkscrewing in the sweaty sheets several times, she came to the conclusion that sleep would elude her, probably until tomorrow night or until this blasted heat subsided. Adding to her discomfort, her gut did not feel right. She thought back to what she'd eaten last night. A cheese salad, hardly the scourge of upset tummies. She realised it was nothing she'd eaten, but rather what she *felt* — an uncomfortable sensation that spelled trouble.

Snapping back the covers, she slid out of bed, leaving Simon Le Bon snoring. In the bathroom she splashed her face with cold water, relishing the shock of the cool liquid on her parched skin. But still her mind echoed with the noise of sirens, even though they'd long since faded into the distance.

Fiona knew from experience never to ignore gut feelings. Whether by chance or some sixth sense at play or a spurious branch of science that had not been fully understood, gut reactions were almost always right. Leaving Simon Le Bon asleep in a fluffy semi-circle, she got dressed, headed downstairs and grabbed her bicycle from the shed. Riding out into the dry, early-morning air, she pointed her bike east towards Mudeford Spit and the dull light leaking into the corner of the sky, heralding the new day.

The incessant hum of her bicycle chain echoed off buildings as she pedalled through an eerie and deserted Southbourne Grove, its shop windows dark, their doors locked up tight. Fiona didn't glimpse another soul. Not even a car passed her as she pedalled into the Broadway, past its well-kept, slumbering houses, their curtains pulled across tightly.

However, up ahead, at the end of the cul-de sac, blue lights pulsed in the muted glow of the fledgeling morning. Pedalling furiously, she could tell her gut had been right.

Three police cars were shunted together to form a blockade across the road and whatever gaps were left had been sealed off with police tape.

Dripping with sweat, Fiona screeched to a halt, garnering the attention of the officers on guard duty, two females and a male, although they must have seen her from miles down the road, a lone cyclist frantically pedalling towards them.

One of the female police officers approached, leaving her two colleagues leaning against one of the cars, chatting.

"Can I help you?" the officer asked.

"Can I get down on the spit?" Fiona asked breathlessly. She already knew she couldn't but thought playing innocent might lead the officer to be more loose-lipped.

"I'm afraid that won't be possible."

"Why not?" Fiona asked.

"There's been an incident," the officer replied, poker-faced.

"What sort of incident?" Fiona stared across the harbour at the stretch of sand in the distance. It was hard to make out any clear details, but a plume of dark smoke merged into the dusky morning, and she could just make out the block-like shapes of a couple of fire engines. "Has there been a fire?"

"I'm afraid I can't give out any details at this point," the officer robotically replied.

"I can see fire engines down there. Has anyone been hurt?"

"As I said, we're not giving out any information until we know more."

Fiona climbed off her bike and wheeled it closer to the tape. "I know someone down there. Please can I just see if they are all right?"

A second female police officer approached to support her colleague, noticing Fiona's increased insistence. "I'm afraid the whole place has been sealed off until further notice. No one's coming in or out anytime soon."

"But what about my friend who's down there?" Fiona didn't have any friends down there, but if they pushed her on this, she had a stack of names and beach hut numbers she could drop into the conversation to convince them that she had.

"Yeah, another crew was called to Branksome Chine. Nothing serious. Just a beach bonfire that needed to be put out."

"Do you know what time?"

"I think it was roughly about the same time as the hut fire, about three in the morning."

"Thank you, Martin." Fiona hung up and turned to her friends. "Well, that backs up Bitsy's story. All the partygoers would have scarpered at three-ish, when the police and fire engines arrived. Branksome Chine is probably about an hour-and-half walk along the sand to Southbourne beach where Sophie lives."

"More like two hours if you've had a few," Partial Sue remarked.

"Which would put her coming home at five in the morning, as Sophie said. Bitsy must have been at that party — otherwise how would she have got those timings right?"

Daisy had gone strangely quiet, head bowed, fiddling with her phone. Bitsy's story had checked out, more or less, yet she didn't seem very happy about it. Slowly, she lifted her head. "I hate to play devil's avocado or whatever it is, but there is another explanation. A way Bitsy could have known the exact timing of everything happening on the beach while not actually being there." She turned and raised her phone screen.

Fiona and Partial Sue peered in, not really believing what they were seeing. Grainy footage of the beach at Branksome Chine, in black-and-white night vision — a fire ablaze on the beach and people scattering while police tried to corral them and firefighters attacked the bonfire. The time stamp in the corner read: *3.07 a.m.*

"Where did you get this?" Fiona asked.

"My neighbour's a surfer. He's always going on about checking the webcams before he goes surfing, to see what the waves are like. I thought I'd see if there was one at Branksome Chine. There is. You can watch it live or scroll it back, in ten-minute intervals, up to twenty-four hours, so you can see

"I'm sorry, we can't give you any more information at this point. This whole area is a crime scene."

Okay, Fiona wasn't getting on the spit anytime soon, and she wouldn't be able to wheedle any more answers out of them, but at least she'd acquired the most important answer she needed: the place was a crime scene.

Before the police officer had let this slip there was always the chance it could have been an accidental fire — a barbecue that had been knocked over, or even a controlled detonation of an unexploded World War Two bomb, which had happened here before. But they'd classified the situation as a crime scene, and that meant only one thing: the beach hut killer had struck again.

CHAPTER 52

Fiona's phone had been placed squarely on the counter, face up, home screen showing a picture of Simon Le Bon, irresistible and cute — hair its usual dishevelled mess, pink tongue lolling to one side. The real Simon Le Bon snoozed at their feet — the furry one, not the popstar one (if the latter had been snoozing anywhere, it would probably be in a hammock on a Caribbean beach, not on the floor of a charity shop). The three ladies had gathered around the phone, staring at it, willing it to ring.

They'd been in this meditative state for some time now, after Fiona had filled them in on the events of the early hours of this morning. The police had not been forthcoming with any more information, despite Fiona making a nuisance of herself and ringing them several times. DI Fincher's and DS Thomas's phones had gone straight to voicemail, leaving Fiona to wonder if they were off duty or had just anticipated that Fiona would be pestering them and had screened her calls.

There was nothing about the fire on the news either, so the ladies had resorted to their one and only reliable resource of information: Martin the fireman. He hadn't been on duty last night but had promised to call them as soon as he knew anything. For now, without any more details, all they could do was stare at the phone.

The doorbell chimed, breaking them out of their trance. Slightly dazed, they turned to see the Wicker Man wandering in. Noticing the glazed looks in their eyes, he asked, "You three okay?"

They nodded in unison.

The Wicker Man eyed them curiously. "You look like Shakespeare's Weird Sisters. Except you're looking into a phone instead of a cauldron. Hope you're not planning to do me in like that murderous Scottish king." He took a sharp intake of breath, his eyes bright and twinkling. Fiona knew the signs, the tics and tells of an incoming am-dram monologue. She simply didn't have time for this.

He cleared his throat. "Fair is foul, and foul is—"

"What can we do for you?" Fiona interrupted.

The Wicker Man flustered. "Oh, er, I was just hitting my stride. The Scottish Play is a passion of mine."

Partial Sue's eyes narrowed. "Sorry. We're just waiting for an important call. Whatever you need, could it possibly wait?"

"Do you perchance have any lollies left?" He knew full well that their fridge was stuffed with them. "That dastardly heat last night has left my mouth drier than the inside of a pharaoh's tomb."

Fiona nodded in the direction of the storeroom. "Just leave the money on the side."

"Oh, right, yes." He patted himself down. "I seem to have misplaced my wallet."

Fiona didn't have time to haggle. She smiled. "Have one on the house."

"Much obliged." He disappeared into the storeroom and emerged with one lolly in his mouth and another in his hand. "One for the road." He winked, did a circuit of Daisy's model and was gone.

"He's getting a bit cheeky with the freebies," Partial Sue complained.

"And we are a charity," Daisy said. "He's taking out of the mouths of homeless dogs."

"While filling his own," Partial Sue added.

Fiona was about to add to the displeasurable discourse when her phone pinged. She snatched it up. A text message from Martin. She read it to herself then swivelled the screen around for her colleagues.

Sorry I didn't have time to call, I'm not on a shift today but here's what I found out:
Another beach hut fire
No. 163
Owned by the Bradleys
They got out alive. Just.
Same burn pattern as before
No one caught on CCTV
Police have no suspects

A shocked silence fell over the three ladies. They'd known it was coming, having had prior knowledge, but it always hit home the hardest when confirmed beyond all doubt. The killer had struck. Thankfully, the victims had narrowly escaped death.

Daisy broke the silence. "I can't believe the killer's targeting people with young children."

Partial Sue and Fiona swung their heads in her direction. "Th-they had children?" Fiona stuttered.

Daisy nodded vigorously. "I remember interviewing the Bradleys that Sunday when we blitzed the whole spit. They have two girls."

Partial Sue let out a slow, trembling breath. "This is terrible. Not that it wasn't terrible before, but going after people with kids. How old are they?"

"Both under ten if I remember rightly," Daisy replied.

Fiona rested her head in her hands. "Jeez. Lucky they got out or we might be looking at . . ." Her voice trailed off. She swallowed hard and didn't want to say the words out loud. The reality of what could have happened was far too upsetting.

Silence. This time longer. Contemplative.

Fiona banged both palms on the table, making her friends jump. "We need to nail this sick individual. Daisy, tell me about the Bradleys. What are they like?"

"Let me guess," Partial Sue said. "They were slightly bohemian. A bit left field. Handmade shoes. That sort of thing. Square pegs like Malcolm and Bitsy. Didn't fit in with the other genteel beach hut owners down there. Hence why the killer, or Frank, as he's better known, set light to their hut."

Daisy shook her head. "Well, no. That's just it. They were a very quiet, mild-mannered family. Unmemorable, I'd say, in the nicest possible way."

"So how come you remember them?" asked Partial Sue.

"Because they'd won their beach hut in a competition," Daisy replied. "In a newspaper."

"I don't remember hearing that when we listened to the interviews on your phone," Partial Sue said.

"They mentioned it as I was leaving, after I'd pressed stop."

Partial Sue glared at Daisy. "Why didn't you tell us this before?"

"Well, it didn't seem relevant. We were asking people about the night of Malcolm's fire. Not how they came by their hut. Plus, I'd questioned dozens of people that day. It just slipped my mind."

"How did they win it, Daisy?" asked Fiona.

"In the *Daily Express*, I think," she replied.

Partial Sue reached for her phone and found the newspaper article in seconds. "Here it is." The story had been published just over a year ago with a big, brash headline: *Beach Hut Winners!* Below, a corny grip-and-grin image showed Mr Bradley shaking hands with the editor-in-chief of the paper while he handed over a set of keys. Mrs Bradley and their two daughters stood beside them, sweet, smiley and inoffensive.

Dressed in plain, practical clothes, the two girls had identical hair to their mum's: shoulder-length and mousey, clipped to one side.

Fiona scanned the article. "They're from Wiltshire. David Bradley is a radiographer at a hospital, Verity Bradley is a doctor's receptionist, and their two daughters are at junior school. They said they wanted to win the beach hut so they could have a special family place where they could all be together, quietly read their books by the sea and birdwatch."

Daisy cooed.

Partial Sue scoffed. "Well, they don't fit the victim profile of our killer. That's Frank Marshall's ideal family, right there. Nice and conventional and in bed before 10 p.m."

Fiona pushed out a large, irritable breath. "The killer's moved the goalposts and wrongfooted us with a nice big stumbling block."

Fiona always knew when stress had got her in its grip because she'd mix her metaphors and come down with a dose of tinnitus. She ignored the whining in her ears, but the metaphorical stumbling block had landed squarely on the one and only theory that made any sense, smashing it to smithereens — that the killer had been targeting people who didn't fit with the spit's small 'c' conservative aesthetic, ousting oddballs and the unconventional in a bid to preserve the peaceful haven. These latest victims personified that aesthetic. "The connection between the victims has gone. Evaporated."

"Now what do we do?" Daisy wailed.

"Find a new connection," replied Fiona. "If there even is one. This rules out Frank and his cabal, though. He'd never target anyone like this. He'd welcome them with open arms."

"Well, let's not jump to any conclusions until we know more about the family. Looks can be deceiving."

Fiona knew this was a long shot, unless there was some darker, rebellious side to the Bradleys, and they became party animals the second they'd covered up their patio furniture and closed their net curtains. Somehow, she doubted it.

Silence descended over the trio still gathered around the counter. Minds locked in thought, wondering how they would move forward from this setback. Daisy scratched her head and Partial Sue's eyes darted around the room as though searching for inspiration.

They had to disperse as a couple of customers came in. Clustering by the till never gave a good impression to potential buyers, in this case a lady in her seventies with a young grandson, a sweet little pre-school boy in a stripey T-shirt and dungaree shorts. Making a beeline for the toy section, he knew exactly what he wanted, pointing his delicate index finger up to a purple My Little Pony.

"Are you sure that's what you want?" his grandmother asked.

He nodded, sending his fringe into his eyes.

Fiona thought the woman would talk him out of it, persuading him to buy a truck or a spaceship, but she didn't.

"Well, that's the one we'd better have then." The grandmother lifted it off the shelf and handed it to him. Gleefully, he examined it all over. She handed him a two-pound coin and said, "You take it to the till now and pay the ladies."

He didn't have to be told twice, his little legs waddling towards Fiona, holding up the money in his pudgy hands.

"That will be one pound." Fiona smiled and took the coin from him. "What are you going to call her?"

"Jess," he said in a soft voice.

"You know, in the past, purple was the colour of kings and queens," Partial Sue pointed out.

"You could call her Queen Jess," Daisy suggested.

"I like that name." He hugged the purple pony. "Queen Jess."

Fiona handed him his change. He thanked her and turned to give it to his grandmother.

"That's okay." She smiled. "You can keep that to buy an ice lolly."

"We have ice lollies," Daisy blurted. "They're fifty pence each."

"But we're doing a special deal — buy one pony, get two lollies free." Fiona winked.

"Oh, that would be lovely," the lady replied. "It's hot enough to fry an egg on the pavement out there."

"I reckon you could cook a full English," Partial Sue suggested.

The grandmother laughed. "Don't tempt me."

Daisy fanned out a selection of lollies from the fridge. The little boy picked a Fab while his grandmother chose a Strawberry Split.

They watched the two happy customers leave, stepping out into the hot morning sun, licking their ice lollies hard. Before they were out of sight, the little boy threw them a hearty wave through the window. The three ladies waved back.

"What a nice, polite, little boy," Daisy enthused.

Partial Sue rubbed her hands together. "Yes, and he's just given me a belter of an idea."

CHAPTER 53

Daisy decided not to return the remaining lollies to the fridge, reasoning that they all deserved something to cool down their overheated brains.

Fiona took a bite off the top of her Strawberry Split. The cold mainlined straight into the nerves of her teeth, forcing her to gasp. When she'd recovered, she said, "So come on. What's the new idea?"

Partial Sue paused. "That grandmother and her grandson made me think of it. She gave him the money to buy his pony. He didn't pay for it himself." She said it as if the little boy had committed some gross retail misdemeanour.

"Well, he only looked about three, I doubt he has his own income," Daisy said. "I thought it was lovely — a grandma treating her grandson."

Fiona had to agree. Her observation did seem a little harsh. "What are you getting at, Sue?"

"I'm just drawing a parallel with Malcolm, Bitsy and the Bradleys."

Fiona drew a blank, not seeing the connection, and neither did Daisy judging by the way she bit the side of her lip. They both stared at their friend, confused.

Partial Sue sighed. "Like the little boy's purple pony, none of our three victims paid for their own beach huts. Someone else footed the bill."

This was an unexpected angle, taking both Fiona and Daisy by surprise. One that deserved to be held up for further scrutiny.

"How do you figure that?" Daisy barked. "I mean, Bitsy bought her beach hut, all cash, remember?"

Partial Sue smiled mischievously, her accountancy brain forensically flexing. "Everything Bitsy owns comes from an inheritance, a trust fund. I love her to pieces but, let's face it, she's never worked a day in her life. All her money is really her parents' money. And she's loaded. Buying a beach hut for her was like buying a pair of shoes."

"Not the sort of shoes she buys," Fiona snorted.

Partial Sue ignored the comment. "Then there's Malcolm. He got given his hut. Well, indirectly. His aunt left him the Sea Garden, but he didn't want the responsibility of a big place, so he swapped it with his cousin Seb for the beach hut. In a roundabout way, he didn't pay for his hut either."

Fiona had a tingling sensation building in her stomach. "And the Bradleys won theirs. A prize from a newspaper."

"Exactly," Partial Sue said. "All three had their beach huts handed to them, sort of. They didn't do anything to earn them."

"That's it! That's the connection! Well done, Sue." The excitement radiated out from Fiona's tummy into her arms and legs. A new angle on a case often did this, especially when it was a good one. Fidgety energy took over her body. She found herself unable to remain still and paced around the shop, thinking out loud. "If this is true, then surely the motive behind the fires must be jealousy. Has to be. Someone envious that these three have been handed the country's most desirable and expensive beach huts on a plate."

"Sour grapes," Partial Sue added.

Daisy frowned. "But if the motive is jealousy, that could be anyone. Hundreds of day-trippers go down there every day and look enviously at the people in those huts, wishing they could be them, sitting on their verandas, sipping white wine watching the sun go down over the harbour. I know I do."

"Yeah, but you wouldn't burn someone's hut down because of it," Partial Sue replied.

Daisy crossed the shop and examined her model, eyeing up each hut one by one. She stood upright. "Does this mean Frank and his cronies are off the hook?"

"No," Partial Sue said. "Well, maybe. Actually, I'm not sure. I haven't thought that far ahead."

Daisy pulled out a wet wipe and started giving the roofs of the miniature huts a little clean. "I'd say it could still be beach-hut owners. What if they were miffed that they'd had to work hard to buy their huts while these three just had them dropped into their laps, as it were."

Fiona and Partial Sue joined Daisy at the model, helping her dust it.

"I'd say it's more likely to be a non-owner," Fiona said. "They'd be more motivated than someone who already owns a hut. But let's not rule anyone out."

"What about an ex-beach-hut owner?" Partial Sue proposed.

The other two ladies ceased their cleaning, their silence loud and incendiary, as they thought the unthinkable.

"You don't mean Antony Owens?" Daisy gasped.

Partial Sue jutted out her chin. "Someone who's had the joy of owning a beach hut and then lost it. That's got to sting. Had to sell it, presumably because of financial problems, as we already know. Frank and a few of the other beach hut owners look down on him something terrible because of it. Constantly reminding him that he's not a hut owner anymore. The bitterness must be unbearable, especially with that job he's got. Sorry, I mean with the job he had. Plenty of motive there, I'd say, even more so now they've given him the boot. Jealousy is one hell of a toxic emotion."

Daisy stared at Frank Marshall's miniature beach hut. "But if that's true, surely Frank's hut would have been first to go up in smoke."

"Too obvious," Fiona said. "Antony and Frank have a track record of being at loggerheads. They tense up at the mere mention of each other's names. It's common knowledge they don't like each other. Antony Owens couldn't burn down Frank's hut without having the finger pointed at him."

"So he turns to the next best thing, or worst thing," Partial Sue replied. "He targets people who he feels don't deserve to have a beach hut. Bitsy, Malcolm and the Bradleys."

Daisy smeared away a layer of dust off the roof of the Smuggler's House. "I can't believe Antony Owens would kill people. He's so smart and clean."

"I don't know what personal hygiene has to do with it," Partial Sue remarked.

Daisy was clearly finding it difficult to believe that Antony Owens could murder anyone. "Maybe it was just a warning. Like we said before, to get them to leave the spit."

"Hm," Fiona mused. "I think that theory about the fires being warnings is out the window. According to Martin, the Bradleys only just made it out alive."

Partial Sue's face paled. "We should tell DI Fincher about this new connection between the victims. In case there's anyone else on that spit who's been given a hut. They could be the next target. I mean they've probably already put two and two together, but it can't hurt."

Fiona clicked her fingers. "You're right. I can't imagine there'd be many people who have been gifted a beach hut. But if there is, they could be next on the list."

Fiona retrieved her phone and rang DI Fincher. It went straight to voicemail so she relayed everything they'd just discussed into her recorded message, missing out their theory that the killer could be Antony Owens. She wasn't ready to drop him in it until they had more evidence and, like Daisy had correctly pointed out, there could be thousands of people who'd be jealous of beach hut owners. To be sure the message got through she also sent it as a text, thumbing away on the screen. She had just hit 'send' when Sophie Haverford burst through the door with all the drama of a bad soap actress.

"Oh, Fiona, Sue, Daisy. I'm so glad you're here."

"Where else would we be?" Partial Sue scoffed.

Sophie almost threw herself at Fiona, grabbing both her hands. "Please! You have to help me! I'm begging you."

It was at that point that Fiona noticed that Sophie didn't look her usual impeccable self. Bags sagged beneath her eyes, her hair was lank, and her clothes appeared to be poorly matched — normally a heinous crime in Sophie's eyes. Whatever could have happened?

CHAPTER 54

Never one to turn away anyone in distress, even a relentlessly rude harpy such as Sophie Haverford, Fiona led her to the chair by the till and sat her down. Daisy and Partial Sue joined them.

"Would you like an ice lolly?" Daisy asked.

Sophie nodded.

Something was definitely wrong. Sophie would never normally accept anything edible that came on the end of a stick unless it was an hors d'oeuvre offered by an impeccably dressed waiter within the context of a swanky summer garden party held by someone with influence.

Once more, Daisy returned from the storeroom, fanning out a selection of lollies. Without hesitation, Sophie snatched a Rocket from her hand, making short work of the syrupy lolly, almost eating it whole, reminding Fiona of those snakes that unhinge their jaws. The sugar hit relieved the tension on her face somewhat and she calmed down enough for them to try to tease out the details of her distress.

"Sophie, tell us what's wrong?" Fiona asked as gently as she could.

Sophie snapped the spent lolly stick in half and flicked it towards the bin, where it missed. "It's Bitsy," she shrieked.

All the tension returned at the mere mention of her friend's name, the tendons in her neck standing out so much that they could be plucked like the strings of a double bass.

Daisy's face dropped. "Oh, no. Has something happened to her again?"

"No, nothing's happened to her. She's absolutely fine and dandy. It's me who's suffering. It's been absolute hell ever since she moved into my beachfront penthouse." Sophie never referred to her home as merely her home, her place, or even her apartment or flat. No, she always had to speak its full title as if she were reading from an estate agent's sales literature, for the benefit of anyone in earshot so that they'd know she resided in not just a penthouse, but a beachfront penthouse.

"She's driving me crazy. I haven't slept for days, and my beachfront penthouse looks like orcs have been living in it."

"How come?" asked Partial Sue.

"Because of Bitsy!" she snapped. "She never wants to go to bed. She doesn't have an off switch. Never runs out of energy. She's up all hours of the night trying to get me to go on her 'missions of fun', as she calls them, which usually involves me driving her to some mysterious house where she's heard there's a party. Either that or she wants me to stay up drinking or do something childish like climbing trees at three in the morning. I'm normally a lights-off-by-ten gal. But she won't let me sleep. It's like living with Keith Moon. Luckily, I don't have a swimming pool — I mean I could've had a pool but it's not necessary when one owns a beachfront penthouse what with the sea being so close — but if I did, she would've probably driven my SUV into it by now. And she got butter all mixed in with the jam."

Fiona didn't know what was more shocking, that or the fact that Sophie ate jam. Partial Sue tried unsuccessfully to supress a snigger. The normally unflustered, indefatigable, Teflon-covered Queen of Southbourne, Sophie Haverford had a weakness, an Achilles heel called Bitsy.

"It's not funny! And if I don't get my nine hours sleep, I'm like . . . I'm like — well, just look at me. I'm wearing the same clothes each day, like you three do."

"Ah, good to see the same old Sophie is still in there somewhere," Fiona remarked.

Sophie attempted an apology, which popped out as another insult. "I'm sorry, but it's true, and it's all because of her." She jumped up and grabbed Fiona by the lapels. "Can I hire you to get rid of her? Is that part of your detective work? I can pay."

"We're not assassins for hire, Sophie. And I don't think you really want to kill your friend. I think you're sleep-deprived and it's making you emotional." She knew the torture of being sleep starved. She wouldn't wish it on her worst enemy, who also happened to be Sophie Haverford.

Sophie collapsed back into the chair, head bowed, sighing heavily, managing to hold back the tears. "I just don't know what to do. She's my best friend but she's driving me insane."

"Couldn't you just ask her to move into a hotel?" Daisy suggested. "Tell her you need your space. I'm sure she'd understand."

Sophie glanced up at them. "I couldn't ask her to do that. Thing is, she's helped me out so much in the past. Supported me through thick and thin. If it wasn't for her, I wouldn't be the PR maven I am today. Without her contacts and connections, I'd be just another schmuck."

Fiona had always assumed that Sophie had come from money, had everything handed to her by Mummy and Daddy. Clearly, she'd struggled like the rest of them.

It was tempting at this point to indulge in a spot of schadenfreude, to delight in the downfall of her nemesis from across the road. To enjoy that karma had caught up with her, and she was getting what she deserved as payback for the large debt of nastiness she'd been running up all her life. But try as she might, Fiona couldn't bring herself to celebrate Sophie's discomfort, even though she knew that if it were the other way around, Sophie would be dancing a merry jig right now. This was the second time she had turned to Fiona for help. Maybe she had realised that cultivating friendship was more important than winning battles over her rivals.

Who was Fiona kidding? This was Sophie. As soon as her problem had gone away, she'd return to her spiteful ways, badmouthing and abusing them every chance she got. She really didn't deserve their help, not after all the horrible things she'd said and done. However, Fiona was better than that, and wouldn't turn away someone who was clearly suffering, even if it was someone as vile as Sophie. She knew her friends would feel the same.

Partial Sue sniffed the air. "Can anyone smell smoke?"

They all sniffed, everyone apart from Sophie, who shrank in her seat and became even more miserable.

"It's me," she confessed. "Bitsy came in last night stinking of smoke, and now my beachfront penthouse smells like a cigar room."

"She smelled of smoke last night?" Fiona threw a worrying glance at Partial Sue and Daisy, who returned concerned looks. "What time was this?"

"Usual story. Early hours of the morning, about five."

Sophie would have no idea that another beach hut had burned down last night. Nothing had appeared in the news yet. She'd be completely oblivious to the fact that her words had unwittingly inserted Bitsy into the position of a possible suspect. Fiona's heart became heavy while her head spun erratically. She didn't want to believe it of Bitsy. Everyone liked the woman and there was probably a completely rational explanation for her having smoke-infused clothes. However, she told herself to be cold and dispassionate and not let her affection for Bitsy cloud her judgement. They would need to get to the bottom of this, which meant questioning her. Maybe not in a harsh 'slap you around the face with a phonebook' kind of questioning but something gentler and more conversational, that didn't feel like she was being accused.

From having no new suspects, in the space of minutes they now had two: Antony Owens and Bitsy.

"Where had she been?" asked Daisy.

"No idea," Sophie replied. "I've given up asking."

"We can ask her now," Partial Sue said. "Here she comes."

Bustling across the road, Bitsy fizzed with limitless energy like a human perpetual-motion machine.

A mournful groan like whale song rose from the depths of Sophie's lungs as the source of her pain bounced its way towards them.

CHAPTER 55

Dressed in a bright orange vest, equally bright lime-coloured shorts and canary-yellow sandals, Bitsy blasted through the door like a citrus tornado. "Hey, ladies." She spied Sophie seated by the counter. "Aha! There you are. Gail told me you'd be here. You thought you'd got away from me, didn't you?"

Sophie let out a small, almost imperceptible whimper.

Fiona wanted to help Sophie with her Bitsy-shaped sleep problem. However, there were more pressing issues. Namely, the revelation that Bitsy had come home smelling of smoke on the same night that a beach hut had burned down and a young family had narrowly escaped death. Coincidence? She had to find out, sooner rather than later.

As Bitsy came closer, she caught sight of her friend, weighed down by anxiety and lack of shuteye. She put her arm around Sophie's shoulders. "Hey, what's up?

"Nothing, bit tired that's all. I have to have my nine hours, otherwise I can't function."

Bitsy didn't take the hint. "What you need is cheering up. Hey, what say we all go out to brunch or, even better, how about afternoon tea? My treat. Somewhere fancy with a terrace overlooking the sea. We could have a G & afternoon

T — it's all the rage in Pall Mall. Just like afternoon tea with cucumber sandwiches, jam and scones but instead of cups of tea we quaff G & Ts. We could start early. Drink till the sun goes down and then see where the night takes us."

Daisy jumped in enthusiastically. "Oh, that sounds fun."

"I hate to be a killjoy," Fiona said, "but we have to work."

Sophie nodded manically.

Bitsy huffed. "You sound like this one here." She flicked her eyes in Sophie's direction. "While I'm out living my best life, she's living her mediocre one, going to bed at ten. You all need to come on my missions of fun."

"Did you have a mission of fun last night?" asked Partial Sue.

"Yes, she did," Sophie answered. "Tell them what you got up to."

Bitsy's face froze momentarily, her features in a holding pattern as she mulled over the question. Surely there wasn't much to mull over. It wasn't a difficult question. Unless she needed an excuse to cover up what she was really doing and didn't have one to hand right this moment. She shook her head as if dislodging her thoughts. "Do you know, I can't remember. Brain's drawn a blank. Old memory banks aren't what they used to be."

"You came home smelling of smoke, if that's any help," Sophie sneered.

"Oh, yes." Bitsy snapped her fingers. "I remember. There was a huge bonfire on the beach."

They needed to gauge whether she was telling the truth or not. The easiest way to test that was with details. Big lies are easy to make up on the spot, but little detailed ones are harder to come by on the spur of the moment. The police did it all the time and so did the Charity Shop Detective Agency. "Which beach?" asked Daisy.

"No idea. Nowhere near Southbourne. Further down the coast, closer to Poole, I think."

"How did you get there?" Fiona asked.

"You know, I can't remember," Bitsy replied. "Maybe got a taxi." This wasn't looking good. But then she redeemed herself. "But I can tell you, you missed out, Soph. You all did. Atmosphere was fab. Guitars, people singing and dancing. Like an early Glasto, I imagine. But then the bizzies turned up and we had to leave."

Okay, so Bitsy had an alibi, except she'd taken a sliver of time to think about it. Was it the truth and she'd just needed a moment to recall the information, or were those few seconds enough for her to concoct a plausible story — one that didn't need much evidence to back it up? Beach parties usually went hand in hand with bonfires and guitars, perhaps even a visit from the police. Not a massive stretch of the imagination. Either way, it was too flimsy. Not enough to hold Bitsy up as a suspect or let her off. Fiona needed to know more, while simultaneously persuading Bitsy not to burn the midnight oil and let Sophie get some sleep. An impromptu plan leaped into her head. Two birds, one stone.

"Anyway!" Bitsy clapped her hands, making Sophie jump. She didn't look like she could take much more of this. "It's settled then. We're all shutting up shop early for G & afternoon Ts long into the night."

"Trouble is, Bitsy, we have charity shops to run," Fiona said.

Bitsy dismissed the excuse with a wave. "Oh, work schmerk. You can take an afternoon off. You're always shutting your shop early to go investigating."

She had a point. Clearly, Bitsy wouldn't take no for an answer. Fiona put her plan into action. Bitsy lived her life like a young child, care and consequence free, which is probably where she got all her energy from. She had no responsibility and unfathomable financial resources. Therefore, Fiona had to treat Bitsy like a parent would treat an energetic child. On the occasions when Fiona had had her nieces and nephews for weekends as youngsters, the key to getting them to sleep at night was to tire them out during the day. Swimming, bowling, roller skating in Hyde Park, hide and seek, hikes

274

in the woods, pulling up weeds in the garden, organising treasure hunts — anything to burn off all that phosphoric juvenile energy. She had to do the same with Bitsy.

"Tell you what," Fiona replied. "We'll come out with you."

Sophie panicked. "We will?"

Bitsy jiggled on the spot. "Wonderful!"

"But we can't leave until we sort out our storeroom," Fiona clarified. "It's about to explode and spill into the shop."

Bitsy stopped jiggling.

Fiona wasn't making this up, apart from the fact that the storeroom was always in that state, with more donations than they knew what to do with. "We've got bags and bags of clothing that need sorting. The dirty ones washed, dried and ironed, then put on hangers. If we can make a dent in that then we'll come out."

"Why don't I help you?" Bitsy asked.

Yes! Bitsy was on the hook. Fiona's plan was a go: tire Bitsy out in the storeroom and use that time to subtly question her about last night's alibi to see if it held any water, while Sophie sloped off back to her shop to escape and possibly find somewhere to have a stealthy snooze. Two birds, one stone.

Sophie made a swift exit and Bitsy was put to work. Surprisingly, she went to the task with great gusto, feeding dirty clothes into the washing machine, transferring them to the dryer and ironing them. Piles of donations appeared in neat, folded stacks — shirts, trousers, tops and dresses.

"This is fun," said Bitsy, attacking a button-down shirt with the steam iron. She thrived on new experiences, but the novelty of domesticity wouldn't last. Soon it would have the same effect on her as it did on everyone, becoming crushing drudgery.

Fiona needed to strike while the steam iron was hot and step up her questioning. "Talking of fun, how did you hear about that beach party last night?"

Bitsy paused and propped the iron up on its end. Was she recalling information or preparing another lie? "I was in

the George in Christchurch, having a drink, and I got talking to a bunch who said they were heading over to a beach
party after closing time. I think I must have tagged along
with them."

"Was it Spider and Dave, the hairy bikers?"

Bitsy shook her head. "No, they were students."

"Oh, what university did they go to?"

"You know, I never asked. Probably a bit rude of me."

"Was the party in full swing when you got there?"

"Oh, yes," she said. "Big bonfire going, lighting up the
sky."

"How did you get home?"

Bitsy thought for a second. "Can't remember. But I
think I must have walked along the beach back to Sophie's
because I had sand in my shoes this morning."

Fiona slid subtle question after subtle question into the
conversation throughout the day. All the answers that came
back were plausible, if a little light on detail. It appeared to
be nothing more than a simple night of frivolity. A mission
of fun, as Bitsy put it. Fiona felt awful for even thinking
that Bitsy would have anything to do with setting beach huts
alight, including her own, but she had to consider anyone a
suspect in their line of work.

By late afternoon the yawns coming from the storeroom
were getting louder and longer, Bitsy dropping some unsub-
tle hints at how tired she was. She'd only been at it a few
hours. At least the second part of Fiona's plan was bearing
fruit.

Bitsy appeared in the doorway to the storeroom, her
head tilted wearily against it, her face glistening with sweat.
"You know what? I'm plumb tuckered out. This charity lark
is hard work."

"Well, we thank you for all your help," Fiona said.
"That's helped us immensely." The other ladies joined in,
congratulating her on a job well done.

Fiona had never seen Bitsy so coy or bashful. "I know
I'm going to sound like the world's worst lightweight—"

Bitsy yawned — "but would you mind if we knocked the G & afternoon T thing on the head? Do it another time?"

In her mind, Fiona gave herself a well-deserved slap on the back. Mission accomplished — a mission of *no* fun. "Of course. Not a problem."

Relief seemed to lighten the gravity around Bitsy. "I think my nights out are catching up with me. Need to join old boring Bagpuss Sophie and have an early night."

"I love having early nights," Partial Sue commented.

Daisy remained silent, clearly not happy about being denied a fancy evening out overlooking the sea, sipping G & Ts and gorging on sweet and savoury delicacies, no doubt served on three-tiered fine-china cake stands — her idea of heaven.

"We'll do it another time," Fiona suggested.

"What about tomorrow?" Daisy was desperate to prevent this cakey gift horse from galloping away.

"Can I see how it goes and get back to you on that?" Bitsy sagged with fatigue as she wandered through the shop and out of the door. She turned just before leaving. "I'll nip over to Sophie. Tell her tonight's cancelled, then it's a bath and I'm going to try one of those early night thingies that's all the rage with you guys." She smiled and left.

Fiona turned to her two friends. "What do you think? Her story sounds reasonable."

Daisy nodded in agreement.

Partial Sue rubbed her chin. "I'm not buying it."

Fiona's face tightened into a frown. Whatever could have made Partial Sue doubt Bitsy's story?

CHAPTER 56

Arguments about the validity of Bitsy's story flew back and forth across the charity shop between Partial Sue and Daisy — a kind of crime-debating tennis over a rack of shirts instead of a net, with Fiona as the unelected, unwitting umpire for some reason.

"She'd been out to a party with a bonfire," Daisy protested. "I always smell of smoke after I've been to a bonfire on firework night. Even though I stand well back and follow the firework code. Although I do like to have a sparkler or two. But this is Bitsy we're talking about. She's our friend. She's not a murderer."

"I'm not saying she's a murderer," Partial Sue replied. "All I'm saying is we should be open-minded and not swayed by our friendship. We've only just met her. We don't know anything about the woman."

"What makes you doubt her story?" asked Fiona.

"It's too simplistic and extremely convenient. Her story sounds plausible until you analyse the details. There aren't any. She's left out times and places, and the names of the people she was with. All things that could confirm her story."

Daisy's face twisted with annoyance and Fiona didn't think it was entirely to do with her missing out on a swanky

G & afternoon T. "If Bitsy made up her story because she was busy burning down a beach hut with a family inside it, that also means she burned down Malcolm's hut, and then her own. Why would she do that?"

Rather than quashing Partial Sue's argument, it strengthened it. "That gives her the ultimate alibi. Burning down her own hut makes her look like a victim. Puts her above suspicion so she can continue her spree of arson. Think about it, Bitsy's one of the very few people who could afford to destroy a five-hundred-thousand-pound beach hut without it making a dent in her bank balance. And we've only got her word for it that on the night in question she was out with a couple of hairy bikers called Dave and Spider."

"She did have one of their hats," Fiona reminded her.

Partial Sue gave her an I'm-not-going-to-dignify-that-with-an-answer stare.

Daisy had a counterargument, a proper one. "If she's the killer, why did she help Fiona get the CCTV footage from Seb and Marcus?"

Partial Sue began straightening out a rack of men's shirts. "Because if she's the killer, whatever staying-invisible technique she's using would mean she'd already know there'd be nothing on the footage that would incriminate her. Plus, it adds to her cover. Look, I'm not happy saying these things about Bitsy. I'm just playing devil's advocate."

Fiona cleared her throat. "Which brings us to the elephant in the room. No CCTV again. No one was seen setting light to the Bradleys' hut, which means no one was there to smell of smoke. Unless the Predator lit the fires."

"Who's the Predator?" asked Daisy.

Putting her hands to her mouth and wiggling her thumbs and forefingers, Partial Sue said, "A sort of invisible crab-faced alien. It's a film."

Daisy's eyes darted back and forth, confused. "How do you know it has a crab face if it's invisible?"

"Well, sometimes it appears unexpectedly at the most inconvenient times."

"Like a traffic warden when you're on double yellows dropping back a library book," Fiona added.

Partial Sue agreed. "Yes, except extremely violent with stabby things and throwy things."

Daisy shuddered.

"Okay, I take your point, Sue," Fiona said. "But we still don't have any motive. What would Bitsy have against a mild-mannered family like the Bradleys, and a loner like Malcolm who never troubled a fly and hardly ever set foot off the spit?"

"And don't forget, Malcolm was killed before Bitsy came to the area," Daisy added.

"That doesn't mean anything," Partial Sue replied. "She could have killed him before her official arrival, to establish an alibi." She thought for a moment, sliding shirts along the rail so they were spaced evenly. "Maybe there is no connection between the victims. Maybe it's more about arson than murder. A lot of people commit arson for the thrill. They get a kick out of it, and Bitsy is definitely a thrill-seeker. She can have anything and go anywhere she wants. She's rich and bored. What's left for someone who has everything? Breaking the law."

"She does fit the profile," Fiona agreed.

Daisy got on her phone and started tapping and scrolling. "Says here the five most common motives for arson are: fraud to get the insurance money or to escape financial obligations; terrorism for political or religious reasons; crime concealment to cover up a murder or a burglary; jealousy and revenge; and lastly vandalism for either excitement, or to vent anger."

"We can discount fraud, financial obligations and burglary," Fiona said. "Bitsy's not short of cash. Not terrorism either, she's neither political nor religious — she's as hedonistic as they come. And, as I just said, what would she have against Malcolm and the Bradleys? So, it can't be jealousy or revenge. That just leaves two: vandalism — doing it for kicks, which I think is the most likely; or concealment of murder

— bit of a grey area, that one. The fires didn't exactly conceal a murder, they caused one."

"Hey!" Daisy became excited. "Says here that like serial killers, serial arsonists operate in a well-defined area or community."

"You couldn't get more of a well-defined community than Mudeford Spit. But why that particular place?" Fiona asked.

Partial Sue shrugged. "Maybe she has a thing for seeing beach huts burning. Causing destruction."

Daisy put her phone away. "But from the CCTV, no one's ever around to see it go up in smoke. Unless Bitsy is a superhuman Viking and is extremely good at firing flaming arrows from miles away."

"She'd still smell of smoke if she were handling flaming arrows," Partial Sue said.

Fiona needed to put a stop to this. They were stumbling in the realms of Nordic conjecture, which sounded like something from Dungeons & Dragons. While it was good to explore theories, they were irrelevant without hard facts to give them integrity and to stop you straying into some surreal areas — in this case, the top of Hengistbury Head in the dead of night with Viking-goddess Bitsy shooting burning arrows into the darkness.

Fiona reached for her phone.

"Who are you calling?" asked Partial Sue.

"The George pub in Christchurch. I think what we're lacking here are hard facts, times and names. It's the only way to verify Bitsy's story before we go off on tangents." She put her phone on speaker. "Oh, hello, sorry to bother you. My friend Bitsy was in your pub last night and lost her—"

"Oh, yes. We know Bitsy," the landlord replied, clearly smiling down the other end of the phone.

"You do? Oh, wonderful. So she was in your pub last night?"

"I'll say. We love having Bitsy in. Always a good night for us and our customers when she's around."

"How come?"

"She lights the place up and the cash register never stops ringing. Always buying rounds of drinks for everyone. I'll be able to retire soon if she keeps it up."

"That sounds like Bitsy, generous to a fault. Did she stay until closing time?"

"Oh, yes, then left with a bunch of students."

"Did they say where they were going?"

"No idea. Er, what was it you said she'd lost?" A suspicious tone crept into his voice. She was losing him.

"Oh, don't worry, we've found it, but thank you for your time." Fiona hung up. "That's one half of her story confirmed."

"Still doesn't mean she's innocent," Partial Sue said. "She could've met the students in the pub. Heard they were off to a beach party, decided to seize the opportunity to go off and commit arson, knowing she could use their beach party as a cover story."

Daisy folded her arms defensively. "Sounds far-fetched to me. How would Bitsy know there was a bonfire?"

"The students might have mentioned it before they left. And what beach party doesn't have some sort of fire?"

Her friends were edging too close to the borders wild of conjecture again. Fiona needed to get them back on the straight and narrow. "Okay, let's check the validity of the beach party. If the police were called and there was a bonfire, then fire and rescue would've certainly been involved."

She made a call to Martin the fireman. He answered on the first ring. "Hi, Fiona."

"Hello, Martin. Sorry to bother you. Can you speak?"

"If you're quick. Got a ton of windows to clean today."

"Thank you for the information about last night's beach hut fire."

"You're welcome. Sorry I didn't have more for you. It's too early yet."

"That's okay. Tell me, were there any other fires last night?"

if you've missed any good waves that day. Or in this case, a bonfire beach party."

Bitsy now had the means to be in two places at once, virtually. "She could've just looked at the webcam," Fiona said. "To get the timings right for her alibi."

Partial Sue swore. "She could've heard about the bonfire from the students in the pub, then decided to use it as an opportunity to make out she was at Branksome Chine while she was actually down on Mudeford Spit setting light to a beach hut — somehow unseen."

They re-examined the footage again and again, desperately checking to see if they could spot Bitsy in the fleeing crowd to prove her innocence. But there were too many people moving erratically and the footage was far too grainy to make out individuals.

The three ladies went silent. Bitsy was back to being a suspect.

The mechanism was there, but that still didn't mean she'd done it. Trouble was, no one wanted her in that position. They liked the carefree, generous, fun-loving Bitsy, not the one who could be putting on an act to cover up the fact that she was a serial arsonist.

Reluctantly, they put a pin in it for now. Before they could come to any firm conclusions, they had another possible candidate who needed to be investigated: Antony Owens.

CHAPTER 57

Next day, Antony Owens sat in front of the counter bedecked in a perfectly tailored linen suit creased in all the right places and paired with a jaunty Panama hat. Though he appeared calm and collected, as if he were about to value a rare piece of china on the *Antiques Roadshow*, he gave away his discomfort by tugging at his cuffs, and he had the impatient expression of someone with better places to be. "I'm not exactly sure why you've asked me here. I'm not working for the beach hut owners anymore and neither are you."

Fiona, Daisy and Partial Sue sat on the other side of the counter. It felt a little too formal for Fiona's liking. They'd invited Antony Owens in for a quick, friendly chat, not an interrogation.

"Would you like an ice lolly?" Daisy asked.

He declined. With his reddening face he really looked as if he could do with one, but probably didn't want to risk lolly drips ruining all that tasteful linen.

"We're still working on the case," Fiona clarified. "On our own time, as it were."

"Okay," he said, in that way people say 'okay' when they really mean 'not okay'. "But I feel like I'm in an interview."

"Or an audition." Daisy attempted a joke to lighten his mood.

"For the part of the man from Del Monte," Partial Sue added.

Antony Owens didn't see the funny side and scowled at them both.

Fiona tried to salvage the situation. "Sorry, we would sit around the table, but it's still occupied with Daisy's lovely model."

Antony Owens gave a tiny shrug, not bothering to turn around and acknowledge or admire Daisy's handiwork. "Could we get on with this? I have a ton of work. I shouldn't even be taking a lunch break."

"Yes, of course." Fiona had to tread carefully. They all did. This wasn't going to be easy. "We just wanted to pick your brains about beach huts."

Antony Owens regarded her inquisitively. "There's not much to them, they're not complicated. What do you need to know?" His replies were curt and offhand. After the humiliation of being booted out of his second job as liaison officer, the last thing he probably wanted to do was talk about beach huts.

Fiona smiled. "Not so much the technical aspect. More the emotional one."

Antony Owens didn't seem any more enlightened. She had to broach the subject at some point — it might as well be now. "When you sold your beach hut, did you feel a sense of loss?"

"Of course."

Fiona waited for more embellishment to that answer, but it never came. She pressed on. "Giving up a place like that must have been hard."

"Yes, it was." More monosyllabic answers. He wasn't making this easy, or perhaps he was just impatient, hence the economy of his responses.

"Do you ever think you'd made the wrong choice?"

"With hindsight, yes. But at the time it was the right thing to do."

"How so?" asked Partial Sue.

"A few years ago, my wife set up an engineering consultancy business. At first it went well, but then business began to drop off. We had a choice. Abandon it and write off our losses, or persevere and put more money into it. We chose to persevere, so the beach hut had to go."

"Do you regret that decision?" asked Fiona.

Antony Owens cast his eyes at the floor and sighed. "Every day. Beach hut prices have gone insane over the last few years. Our hut would have been worth double compared to what we sold it for. I heard one went for half a million recently. Half a million! For nothing more than a glorified garden shed by the sea! Selling that hut was probably one of the worst decisions I've ever made." As if sensing his regret, Simon Le Bon got out of his bed and licked the man's fingers to console him. Antony flinched and withdrew them.

Fiona waited a beat then asked, "When you go down on the spit and see the other beach hut owners, how does that feel?"

"How do you think? I only went down there for the job, but now that's ended at least I can avoid the place. Out of sight and out of mind."

Fiona braced herself, preparing for the awkward question she'd been working up to. "But when you do go down there, how would you describe your exact feelings? Is it a sense of deep loss? Disappointment? Or does it make you annoyed and angry? Maybe even jealous of the other hut owners?"

That last sentence caught his attention. His eyes locked with Fiona's, anger flaring in them. Antony Owens wasn't stupid. He could read between the lines. "Oh my God. You think I did it, don't you? Set fire to those beach huts. Killed Malcolm."

"We don't think anything," Partial Sue said. "We have to explore all possibilities, which means asking some difficult questions."

Antony Owens twitched all over, unable to contain his anger. "This is unbelievable. How dare you accuse me of such a thing?"

"We haven't accused you of anything," said Daisy.

"No, you've just heavily implied it. You're not even supposed to be investigating this anymore."

The ladies were silent. He glared back at them, possibly wanting to goad them. Then his demeanour changed, a new thought colliding with his brain. Anger fled, replaced by forced laughter. Not the happy kind, more the mocking kind. "Would you like to hear a confession from me? A shocking revelation for your investigation."

The three ladies remained silent.

He grinned impishly. "You'll like this. I only hired you to shut up those beach hut owners. To stop their pompous whining — 'When are you going to do something, Antony? This is not acceptable, Antony.' You three were just a sop to keep them quiet. I never seriously thought you'd solve the case. You were just a bunch of well-meaning amateurs, a pantomime horse to distract them because I couldn't afford proper private investigators with the budget I had." The anger returned to his face. "You know, what's funny is that you took it seriously. There's nothing more pathetic than a bunch of Sunday leaguers who think they're playing in the Premiership."

Antony Owens stood. "I really think you should take a good look at yourselves and think about your choices in life, because at the moment you're wasting your time, playing dress-up detectives. No one takes you seriously. You look like fools." He smoothed his linen suit. "I have to go. My head feels like a volcano that's about to explode."

"Maybe you'd like that ice lolly now," Daisy offered.

He ignored her and stormed out.

CHAPTER 58

Three days later, the mood hadn't improved, and a crisis of confidence had set in. Antony Owens' words had hurt, skewering the three ladies with uncertainty and holding them fast with doubt. Their self-belief as amateur sleuths, which was never an unshakable tower of strength to begin with, had been irrevocably undermined by the knowledge that he had never expected them to succeed. They had been mere place-holders designed to keep the beach hut owners off his back by providing fake reassurance that something was being done. Stopgaps until the real professionals could catch the culprit.

It wasn't the first time in this investigation that their confidence had been knocked. Frank Marshall had done a pretty good job of it when he'd sacked them after dismissing Antony Owens. But somehow, this felt worse. Frank was being Frank. An overcompetitive busybody with a superiority complex, it hadn't come as a massive surprise and, crucially, they didn't respect him. However, they had respected Antony Owens, which was why it hurt all the more.

To make matters worse, an oppressive Saharan breeze had wandered up from the south, forcing itself on an already sweltering country. The temperature had become unbearable. Lethargic and hot, but not particularly bothered, the ladies shuffled around the shop, not particularly doing much of anything.

The Wicker Man popped his head around the door that had been propped open for ventilation, although with the temperatures outside it was more like having an oven door open. "Hot enough for—"

"Yes," Fiona snapped, fanning herself with a copy of the *Southbourne Monitor*. "Yes, it's hot. We know it's hot."

"My car seats were so sticky driving in this morning," Partial Sue moaned, "I nearly stuck to them."

"Your car seats are always sticky," Daisy said.

"What's that supposed to mean?"

"Cleaning them once in a while wouldn't go amiss."

Before a full-scale argument broke out about the hygiene levels of Partial Sue's car, the Wicker Man waded in. "Ladies, ladies. What's the matter? Why are you all so grumpy? Is it the heat?"

They exchanged humbled glances. "Someone said nasty things about us," Daisy informed him.

"What scoundrel did that?" he asked. "Why, you're the sweetest, smartest, most generous people I know."

"That's kind of you to say," Partial Sue replied.

"Well, when you're not biting my head off for saying 'hot enough for you'." He grinned.

"Sorry about that," Fiona said. "We're just feeling a bit down at the moment."

"Quite understandable given the circumstances. Seriously, tell me who offended you. I know someone in London, a gentleman thug." He tapped the side of his nose. "Could teach this miscreant some manners and then some."

Fiona nearly fell off her seat. "No. That's really not necessary."

"Well, just say the word and this cad will get a good walloping."

"It's just a silly matter," Daisy said.

"Well, if it's a silly matter, why the long faces?"

Fiona didn't have the energy or the inclination to get into this. She cut to the real reason why the Wicker Man was here. "Did you want an ice lolly?"

"You read my mind," he replied. "Shall I help myself?"

Fiona nodded.

He wandered into the storeroom, checked the fridge, then emerged empty-handed. "There are only Rockets left. Do you have any Fabs?"

Fiona didn't mince the look she gave him, not impressed that he was complaining about the stock levels of ice lollies he never paid for.

He took the hint. "A Rocket will more than suffice." He retrieved said ice lolly from the storeroom, stripped off the wrapper and did his usual circuit of Daisy's model, as he did every morning like a small child enchanted with a train set on Christmas morning.

He leaned in closer for a better look, and then the inevitable happened. "Oops." He looked up guiltily.

Daisy didn't hide her concern. "What?"

"Must be hotter than I thought. Bit of lolly's fallen off and wedged itself between huts twenty-nine and thirty. I'll see if I can get it out." The Wicker Man went at it, prodding his thick saveloy fingers between the two miniature beach huts, trying to dislodge the shard of ice. "Oh dear. I think I'm making it worse. Do you perchance have a cloth?"

On her feet in seconds, Daisy snatched up a kitchen roll by the till and tore off several sheets in one slick motion. In the blink of an eye, she folded over a portion again and again, transforming it into an elongated rectangle so she could slot it between the two huts, blotting up the chunk of ice lolly that was swiftly becoming a puddle.

"This is going to leave a stain." Daisy switched from kitchen roll to wet wipe with the speed of a gunslinger. "It's not coming out."

The Wicker Man backed away. "I do apologise. I believe a tactical retreat may be the best course of action, so I don't do any more mischief." He made a hasty exit, leaving Daisy vigorously going at it, the stain not shifting.

"How's it looking, Dais?" Partial Sue wandered over to the model.

"Not good."

The red juice made it appear that one of the buildings had been bleeding. "Oh no. It's *The Shining* but in a beach hut instead of the Overlook Hotel."

"That would have been a very different movie," Fiona remarked. "Is it ruined?"

"Not completely but it's soaked in. I can't get it out. I might have to rebuild this section."

"I think we might have to ban food in here," Fiona suggested.

Partial Sue glared at Fiona, horrified. "Steady on, Fiona. We're not savages."

Daisy ceased cleaning. This was too important to ignore. "No eating means no elevenses, no brunch, no afternoon tea and no having cake when we feel like it."

"Well, maybe we ban the Wicker Man," Fiona replied.

"We couldn't hurt his feelings like that. How about no food to be eaten around the model? I'll make some signs."

They nodded in agreement at Partial Sue's proposal.

Attracted by the melted strawberry ice, a fly zigzagged in through the open door and proceeded to do buzzing circuits of the shop. Simon Le Bon came to life, leaping out of his basket, heroically chasing it, his jaws clacking together every time it came within biting range.

Partial Sue grabbed the copy of The *Southbourne Monitor*, rolling it up tightly. "That's all we need, a blessed fly. I am not partial to flies in any form."

The Charity Shop Detective Agency thus became wholly engaged in the pursuit of fly catching. They expected the insect would have a brief nose around the shop and then leave the way it came, out of the open door. But the fly being a fly darted everywhere except out of the shop. Tantalisingly, it would head straight for the open door, appearing to leave, then divert at the last second, much to everyone's annoyance.

Repeatedly the creature circled the model, then Stuka-dived between the huts to feast on the spilt lolly juice before it was shooed away. The ladies were forced to employ this tactic, as they couldn't risk swatting the thing without damaging Daisy's creation.

After ten minutes of unsuccessfully ousting the winged foe, the trio gave up in a cloud of sweat and hot, heavy breathing, deciding to let nature have its way. Collapsing by the till, and drinking copious amounts of water, they watched as the insect circled the model, yo-yoing every now and then to land on it briefly. Lured by the sugar, it would vertically descend, grab a quick hit, and then ping back up again, never lingering too long in case the ladies changed their minds and came after it.

No chance of that happening. The ladies were spent. However, Simon Le Bon hadn't given up and he patrolled the base of the model growling and occasionally getting up on his hind legs.

"Look at it," Partial Sue said. "That smug fly knows it's won."

"Don't they live in a different time zone or something?" Daisy remarked, nonsensically.

"I think you mean they see everything in slow motion," Partial Sue replied. "That's why they're impossible to catch. We must be like lumbering giants."

"That's it. I knew it was something like that."

Fiona had gone quiet, mesmerised by the fly's repeating pattern: drop down; feed; vertical take-off; orbit the model; then do it all again. It duplicated its manoeuvres with robotic precision, a complete master of flight.

"We'll give it five minutes then we'll have another go," Partial Sue suggested.

"How about we get another lolly, a decoy to tempt it out of the shop?" Daisy said.

"That's a good idea. What do you think, Fiona?"

Fiona said nothing, still enrapt by the self-assured winged insect.

"Fiona? Fiona?" Partial Sue attempted to break her out of her trance.

She turned her head slowly towards her two friends. "I think I know how the fires were started."

CHAPTER 59

By the looks on both their faces, Fiona could tell neither of them was convinced by her theory. They wore strained, uncomfortable expressions, as if they were trying their hardest to make something fit that really didn't want to.

"A drone?" Partial Sue questioned.

"Yes. We've been looking at this all wrong." Fiona led them over to Daisy's model, whereupon the fly, almost as if on cue, zipped into the air and flew off towards a rack of hats. "That fly gave me the idea. We've been thinking about this too literally. Fires have been started, therefore, logically, you need someone to start a fire. Arson needs an arsonist, right? However, the CCTV tells us no one's there. They're invisible. How can this be? But what if, like our friend the fly, a drone flies in high above the spit, then drops down vertically in the camera's blind spot between the two huts and starts the fire."

Partial Sue's brow bunched up. "Wait, wait, wait. I'll admit a well-controlled drone could possibly make that manoeuvre. I've seen people flying them, they're pretty precise. But how does a drone start the fire? It hasn't got any hands to light a match or carry petrol — remember Martin said that was the fuel used."

Daisy piped up. "Maybe it carries the petrol in a little container. Like that thing Amazon did a few years ago when packages were going to be dropped off by drone."

Partial Sue shook her head. "I can't see how that would happen. It'd have to fly down, somehow splash petrol against the wall, then set light to it and fly off again."

"Maybe the fire's already lit," Daisy replied. "Slung beneath it in a little basket."

A bizarre image popped into Fiona's head of a hanging basket from a garden centre hooked to the bottom of a drone, except instead of fuchsias and begonias it was full of flames. She had to admit, her theory was beginning to sound absurd.

Partial Sue wasn't buying it either. "Okay, let's assume you're right. That it somehow managed to carry a miniature fire pit or barbecue or something. It then has to sling the fire against the beach hut side wall, where there's not much space, without setting itself alight, plus it would make one hell of a mess, dropping evidence everywhere on the sand. Surely it would be easier to have a release mechanism and drop the lit fire onto the roof, like a bomb. But we know that's not what happened. I like your theory, Fiona, I really do. It solves a lot of problems with the case. But it's too tricksy to work. Too much to go wrong. Plus, I think someone would notice a fire flying across the night sky. It's too conspicuous."

"I'll admit it, the theory does have a few issues," Fiona confessed. Her idea felt more and more outrageous with every breath, bordering on silly. Childish, even, and not worth further inspection.

The three ladies stood in silence, staring at Daisy's model, heads deep in thought. The fly made a return journey, whining and circling above them before darting down to snaffle another slurp of the good stuff. Fiona waved it away with the back of her hand before it had a chance to land. It whizzed past her ear, causing her to flinch.

"You know," she said, "when I interviewed Annie Follet, I asked her if she noticed anything out of the ordinary that night and the only thing she could think of was a mosquito buzzing around."

"A few people mentioned that to me too," Partial Sue replied.

Daisy agreed. "Remember the CCTV of the night of Malcolm's fire? Annie swatted something away when she left her beach hut, like you just did with that fly."

Fiona did remember. Then there was Greg, who'd had the disagreement with Frank about the washing line. His wife had mentioned a mosquito. "Are mosquitoes common down there?"

"If they were common, then it wouldn't be out of the ordinary," Partial Sue remarked. "What are you thinking?"

"I know you don't believe my drone theory but is there a chance the engine of a drone could be mistaken for a mosquito?"

"I'll say — those things are just as irritating," Daisy agreed.

Partial Sue looked doubtful. "But they do sound a little bit different. Or maybe that's all it was — a mosquito." She got on her phone, searching 'drone engine noise levels'. "Says here that the average drone is about eighty decibels at a distance of five feet. But you can buy special quiet, stealthy drones. Noise level goes down to sixty decibels."

"How loud is a mosquito?" asked Daisy.

Partial Sue did another search. "Forty decibels at five feet. Little bit quieter, and I'd argue their pitch is much higher."

"However, the drone that night would have been a lot further away from Annie Follet," Fiona pointed out. "It would have been hovering above Malcolm's hut, a few metres away. It would have sounded quieter."

Partial Sue grunted to herself. "I'm not convinced. Drones don't sound like mosquitoes, regardless of how far away they are."

Daisy decided to do her own Google search. "Let me see if I can track down a drone with a forty-decibel engine."

"In the early hours of the morning when you're half-asleep, you might be mistaken," Fiona said.

Partial Sue wouldn't budge. "It's just not the same thing."

Fiona attempted to convince her. "I've heard whining sounds when I've been walking Simon Le Bon on Southbourne beach and thought it was an insect, only to look up and see a drone hovering above me."

"But mosquitoes sound more like dentists' drills." Partial Sue made a high-pitched squeal that went straight through Fiona's skull. "Whereas drones have a lower tone. Either way, we're still stuck with the practicalities of the crime. How does a drone start a fire?"

"Like this," Daisy said.

Her announcement halted Partial Sue's and Fiona's debate abruptly. They leaned in to get a closer look at her phone screen.

Fiona drew in a breath. She wouldn't have believed it if she hadn't seen it.

CHAPTER 60

Daisy's phone showed a flashy website, all bursts of reds and oranges, for a company called Future Burn Technologies. A stars-and-stripes flag in one corner and a mean-looking bald eagle in the other gave away the fact it was an American company that manufactured flamethrowers. Big, ferocious-looking things sending out plumes of destructive fire. A grid of images below advertised their individual products with dramatic names like the Reaper, Stinger, the Great Leveller — they sounded like a line-up for a heavy-metal festival. However, in the lower right-hand corner, one stood out from all the others: the Little Dragon. The subheading read: *This mini flamethrower packs a punch and attaches to most drones.*

"Well, I never," breathed Partial Sue. "A flamethrowing drone."

"Didn't I say it could be a flamethrower right at the beginning?" Daisy announced proudly.

She had mentioned it, Fiona remembered, and Martin had dismissed it. They all had. That's because they had been too literal. Thinking in straight lines, they'd assumed a big, bulky flamethrower like the ones you see in war films with a massive tank strapped to the soldier's back and a huge nozzle linked by a flexible tube at the other. They hadn't considered it could be a lightweight, micro-flamethrower, and never in a million years one that bolted directly to the underside of a drone.

* * *

The Charity Shop Detective Agency was not good at waiting. Patience not being their greatest virtue, the ladies paced around the shop, a nervous excitement infecting all of them since they'd encountered the Future Burn Technologies website — rather different from the start of the day, when defeat and lethargy had dominated their collective moods. Now they bristled with energy that had nowhere to go just yet.

Continually glancing at the big clock on the back wall of the shop, Fiona urged its hands to spin faster. Time was holding them back from moving forward. Specifically, the time difference between Southbourne and Thomasville in North Carolina, where Future Burn Technologies resided in an old furniture factory on the outskirts of town. They needed information about the Little Dragon flamethrower, but they could only get it once Future Burn Technologies was open for business. Fiona had tried calling, but all she'd heard was a polite recorded message informing her that no one was available to take her call, but to have a nice day, all the same.

They'd searched the internet, scoured websites for anything resembling the Little Dragon that could be bought in this country or in Europe or even the rest of the world. Their efforts came up empty. The diminutive flamethrower that fit snugly to the underneath of a drone was unique to the States, and there was only one place that manufactured it: Future Burn Technologies. They had to wait. They stood by the model of the spit, a natural centre of operations, as if it were a World-War-Two plotting table for mapping the positions of aircraft.

The seconds moved painfully slowly. While they waited, Partial Sue played the company's product video. Daisy and

Fiona joined her to watch the spectacle. A big, brash guitar soundtrack opened with a gritty voiceover that seemed more suited to an action movie. "The Little Dragon from Future Burn Technologies." Flying through the air came a drone, four spinning props on outriders attached to each corner, while slung underneath was a long, thin, black nozzle attached to what appeared to be a fuel tank. The drone hovered in the air as the voiceover continued. "Airborne firepower for all your burn needs." The footage cut to a man in a field wearing safety goggles, standing next to the drone on the ground with the Little Dragon fixed to its underside. With a remote control around his neck, he launched the drone. It flew ahead of him then fired out a plume of flame about three metres long, incinerating a nearby bramble bush.

"Why couldn't he just walk up to it and set it alight?" Partial Sue asked.

"Why would anyone need a flying flamethrower for that?" Daisy added.

As if answering her question, the voiceover continued, "Makes easy work of those hard-to-get-to places." The video cut to the drone hovering near a dead branch, high up in a large oak tree. A second later, the Little Dragon did its thing and turned the branch into a ball of flame.

"I think that tree's a goner," Daisy said.

The video cut to a rotating CGI image of the Little Dragon. "Only from Future Burn Technologies. The Little Dragon — where fire flies. Fits most drones with a three-pound payload and takes regular gasoline."

"Gasoline, that's American for petrol." Partial Sue said. "The more I play this the more I think your drone theory is right. A flamethrower would fit the burn pattern. A circular pool of petrol that burned up into a 'U' shape. The petrol never had time to drip down because it was already lit. Sprayed onto the wall."

"How big would you say that drone was?" asked Daisy.

"Not massive, easily under a metre wingspan," Fiona replied.

"It would need to be," Partial Sue said. "The gaps between beach huts are barely a metre wide. Can drones fly through small gaps like that?"

Daisy did what Daisy did best and began Googling. "I've found a site with tips on precision drone-flying. It says with practice you can fly between buildings but never fly too low below the roofline or you risk losing signal."

Fiona's heart raced. "That explains why the fires are started so high up. Our murderer didn't want to risk losing control of their drone. But at the same time they needed it to stay hidden."

"You think that's good, listen to this," Daisy said. "Precision-flying can be performed in windy weather but is more challenging. Better to wait for windless days to practice your manoeuvres. Remember I had that daft theory that all the fires coincided with low tide and thought someone had walked across the harbour?"

"It wasn't daft," Fiona replied.

"Well, every time there was a fire it also coincided with windless nights — perfect for precision drone-flying."

Fiona couldn't stop a smile forming on her face. "It's starting to tick all the boxes."

"Hey—" Partial Sue pointed to the coastguard station on the model — "that couple on top of the headland, the one with all the home comforts, deck chairs and biscuits and such."

"Beryl and Steve," Fiona confirmed.

"Yes. Didn't you say they had radar? We should take a trip up there. Get a look at it, see if it picked up a drone."

"Oh, that sounds like a good idea," Daisy agreed. "A nice walk up to the headland followed by a cup of tea. I bet it's a lot cooler up there."

"Yes, they do have radar," Fiona replied. "I already asked them, but it's marine radar. Picks up boats and ships, not things on land or in the air. They said you need specialised radar for that kind of thing."

"That's right," said Daisy. "I read a piece in the paper about it. The local airport had to install special radar to detect drones because these idiots kept flying them over the runway, making all sorts of mischief for the airline pilots. Normal radar doesn't pick them up."

"We should still double-check to be sure."

Fiona found the number for the coastguard station and called them, expecting to hear the cheerful voice of Beryl or Steve. But a chap called Kevin answered. Apparently, it was their day off. Nonetheless, she posed the question, and just as Fiona had thought, Kevin confirmed that the only radar on the station was marine radar for ships and boats, and not designed to pick up drones.

"What shall we do now?" asked Partial Sue.

"Nothing to do but wait for Future Burn Technologies to open," Fiona replied. "That's going to be our link to the killer."

CHAPTER 61

Finally, the clock dragged its sluggish hands around to the one o'clock position, the equivalent of eight o'clock on the Eastern Seaboard of America. Fiona inhaled nervously, attempting to push down the butterflies ricocheting in her stomach like cooking popcorn. She made the call to Future Burn Technologies and put it on speakerphone.

A chirpy woman answered, "Gooood morning. You're through to Future Burn Technologies. I'm Violet. How may I help you today?"

Fiona became tongue-tied and self-conscious compared to the self-assured American receptionist. "Oh, yes, er, hello. My name is Fiona Sharp. I'm calling from the UK."

"I love your accent by the way."

"Oh, yes. Thank you. Yours is very nice too. I was phoning regarding one of your products. The Little Dragon."

"Yes, that is a wonderful model. I believe we are doing a discount this week. Would you like to know more about our special deal?"

"Well, I wasn't looking to buy at this particular moment. I was after some information."

"Yes, certainly, ma'am. Go ahead. What would you like to know?"

304

Fiona cleared her throat. "It's actually information regarding a customer. I need to know if anyone from the UK has bought—"

"I am very sorry to butt in," Violet said, "but I'm afraid we can't give out customer details or information. As you can understand, it's private and confidential and wouldn't be professional."

Fiona knew it would come to this. She changed tack. "Yes, I completely understand. I'll be honest with you. I'm a private investigator and we have reason to believe one of your Little Dragons may have possibly been used in several local arson attacks. So it is very important that we know if any individuals in the UK have purchased a Little Dragon recently—"

The receptionist interrupted once more. However, the friendly Southern hospitality had evaporated. "Ma'am, I really don't care for your tone or your accusations. We are a family business, hardworking and honest, providing high-quality products for the farming community. I'm afraid I will have to terminate our conversation. Y'all have a nice day now."

"No, please wait—"

The line went dead.

Fiona swore. "I'm so stupid. I shouldn't have mentioned the arson attacks. No company's going to give out information if they think they're somehow involved in breaking the law."

Daisy reassured her. "Well, I think you did brilliantly."

"Me too," Partial Sue agreed. "That's a tough phone call to make. Thing is, they're not going to give us what we need immediately. We might have to try several times before they give us what we want. Let them cool off for a bit and we'll try again later."

"We should cool off too," Daisy suggested. "Who fancies a Rocket?"

After nervously scoffing the ice lolly, Fiona sat wondering how long she should leave it before phoning back.

She felt like a dizzy, lovestruck heroine in a romcom, wondering how big a gap to leave before asking to go on a second date, because she didn't want to come across as needy. Except Fiona wasn't dizzy or lovestruck. She was definitely needy though. Her desire to know if they'd shipped a Little Dragon to the UK had her pacing the shop. The waiting was unbearable, knowing that a flamethrower manufacturer in North Carolina could quite possibly have the name of the killer sitting in its database right this second.

She glanced at the clock. It had been two hours. Long enough. She reached for her phone, startled when it buzzed with an incoming call. Fiona answered. "Hello?"

Another female American accent. This time more formal and serious. "Hello, am I speaking to Fiona Sharp?"

Fiona frantically waved at her friends, who immediately dropped what they were doing and came over. She put it on speaker. "Yes, that's correct."

"My name is Willamina Prescott, I work for a firm called Doyle, Dane & Prescott in Thomasville. We represent Future Burn Technologies' legal needs."

"Oh, okay." Fiona did her best to hide the shock that she had provoked them so much that their lawyer had got involved. Though it shouldn't have surprised her. The States was the land of suing and countersuing, where even the mere hint of wrongdoing had people snatching up their phones to get legal representation.

"Can I confirm that you made an enquiry this morning regarding the usage of one of their products, the Little Dragon."

"That's correct."

"I have a prepared statement I would like to read on behalf of Future Burn Technologies regarding this matter, which I will email to you after our conversation is over." She cleared her throat. 'Future Burn Technologies would like to state that their products are designed purely for agricultural use, including but not limited to weed removal, snow and ice clearance, grassland management and pest control. Future Burn Technologies' products are not intended for damaging

306

property or harming individuals. Future Burn Technologies can take no responsibility for the misuse of said products in any form. Any such misuse is entirely the responsibility of each individual owner. Each product is shipped with a set of safety instructions. All products are sold on the understanding that these instructions are adhered to. Furthermore, Future Burn Technologies would like to state for the record that no product has ever been shipped or exported to the United Kingdom. Licensing and export laws prohibit such a transaction from occurring. All Future Burn Technologies sales to date have originated from within the United States."

Fiona wasn't bothered about all that guff at the beginning. She knew that it never stood up and was only designed to dissuade people in the first instance. However, the last part snagged her attention. "So, let me get this straight — no one living in the UK has ever bought a Little Dragon and had it sent to Britain or requested one be sent to Britain?"

"That is correct. As I said, export and licensing laws prevent it."

Partial Sue piped up, leaning into Fiona's phone. "What about if someone flew to the States, bought a Little Dragon, then brought it back in their suitcase?"

Willamina Prescott replied, "That would be against the law and not the responsibility of Future Burn Technologies. However, from my limited knowledge of airport security, it would never make it. Since nine eleven, luggage scanners have become extremely advanced. It would be detected instantly and that person would be arrested for bringing a flamethrower on board a commercial airline and charged, without a doubt."

"Even if it were dismantled?"

"Especially if it were dismantled. Security staff closely monitor anything that resembles the parts of a bomb or weapon." She quickly changed her tone, conscious that she had been sidetracked. "But, as I said, Future Burn Technologies do not manufacture weapons. Their products are solely designed for agricultural purposes."

Willamina Prescott stayed on the line while Fiona waited for her email to come through, attached with the statement she had just read out, containing the crucial declaration that no Little Dragon flamethrower had ever been sold to anyone in the UK. The woman then promptly hung up.

Fiona exhaled deeply, not used to having a brush with the US legal system. "Well, that was unexpected."

"And disappointing," Partial Sue remarked. "I was hoping they'd have a name for us."

The three of them went quiet as another promising lead bubbled, fizzled and dried up like water spilled on a hot pavement.

Daisy broke the silence. "What about if someone over here bought it second-hand on eBay, and had it sent here in a parcel."

"Same problem," Partial Sue replied. "Parcels still have to go through Customs, where they get scanned and x-rayed. Anything banned for export won't make it through."

"What if you posted it back, piece by piece?" Daisy asked.

Fiona frowned. "That's a distinct possibility. Probably the safest way to get it here undetected, but then you'd have to rely on the seller not having a problem sending it that way. They might get cold feet. They'd be putting themselves at risk for exporting something illegal. But it does give me another idea. We need to go to the Cats Alliance."

"How come?" asked Partial Sue.

"There's another way to get hold of a flamethrower without having to buy one."

CHAPTER 62

After Blu-Tacking a hastily scribbled *Back in five minutes* note to the door, the three of them trooped across the road to Sophie's lair, or the Cats Alliance as it was better known.

In the heat of the afternoon, the tarmac surface had an unsettling adhesive quality underfoot, and by the time they'd reached halfway, sweat had beaded on their foreheads and soaked into their eyebrows.

The door to the Cats Alliance was firmly shut, leading Fiona to believe that they were closed for the day. However, the sign said they were open, and she could see Sophie's unmistakable slender silhouette through the window. Her hair appeared to be propped up in some sort of Amy Winehouse beehive, presumably to keep her neck from becoming sweaty.

Fiona tried the door and as she opened it a wave of soothing cool air slammed into the three of them, causing them to gasp.

"Hurry up! Close the door! Close the door!" Sophie barked, clearly back to her abusive, polished self. She was wearing a long, flowing, white gown with slits high up the sides of her legs and arms. "You'll let in all that devilish heat."

Stepping in and closing the door hastily behind them, a groan of delight came from the three ladies as the frigid air enveloped their heat-swollen bodies.

"You have air-con!" Fiona cried.

"Of course, don't you?" Sophie knew they didn't. None of the shops along Southbourne Grove did. "I had it installed last time we had a refurbishment. I don't think one can properly shop unless one has a cool head. Affects the judgement." She eyed up their outfits disdainfully.

"A frozen water bottle in front of a fan works just as well," Partial Sue pointed out.

"But it does look rather vulgar." Sophie's horrified tone did little to mask her smirk.

Fiona noticed Gail toiling away in the storeroom, sweat dripping off her nose as she fixed a pretty Tiffany lamp. "The air-con budget didn't stretch to the storeroom, then?"

"Oh, Gail's fine, aren't you, Gail?"

Gail looked up at the mention of her name and gave a brief wave, then went back to work.

"I see you're feeling better," Fiona said to Sophie. "Getting your nine hours, I take it."

There was no word of thanks from Sophie for helping her get a decent night's sleep during her Bitsy-shaped meltdown. No word about anything. Just a blank poker face.

"Where is Bitsy by the way?" asked Daisy.

"London. To straighten out some affairs."

Fiona still considered Bitsy to be a suspect. Had she slunk off to lie low for a while? The timing couldn't have been more incriminating, especially as last time Bitsy mentioned London, she was trying to avoid the place having put more noses out of joint than an East-End thug. Or was that all a fabrication?

"Is she coming back?" Fiona asked.

"She assures me she will," Sophie replied. "Not, I hasten to add, to my place. She'll be staying at the Chewton Glen. It's one of the most exclusive hotels in the area. We'll see how they like her coming back at four in the morning." Sophie cackled. "Now, what do you want? I am a very busy lady, as you know."

She didn't look very busy, her white ensemble almost merging with the slick, white, marble counter she leaned against. What charity shop had a white marble counter, for heaven's sake? It even had matching white marble coasters for her coffee.

"It wasn't actually you we came to see," Fiona said.

"Wait, what?" Sophie gave her the filthiest of looks. This didn't compute in her self-centred universe. How could anyone be in the presence of the mighty Queen Sophie of Southbourne and not want to commune with her? "Well, who on earth have you come here for?" She looked around at the cool interior of the vacant shop.

"Gail," Fiona replied.

Gail looked up again at the mention of her name.

"Gail?" Sophie sneered.

"Yes, can you spare her for five minutes?"

Sophie swished around the shop dramatically, as if wounded by their request. "I simply don't know. Gail has important tasks to do."

Fiona couldn't believe she was playing hardball with Gail's time after all the help, comfort and support they'd given Sophie lately.

"Please, Sophie," Daisy wheedled. "We just need to ask her a few questions of a technical nature."

Sophie closed her eyes as if it were all too much to bear, not sparing the melodrama. "I'm afraid I simply cannot allow this."

Partial Sue scowled. "Sophie, you were in a right old state over not getting enough sleep the other day, and we came to your aid. The least you can do is let us have a word with Gail."

"Did I? I don't remember that."

Fiona had had a feeling Sophie would return to her old vindictive ways the second she'd got a decent night's sleep. Did she regret helping her? Not really. Showing kindness to someone in need was a good thing. Plus, she'd seen a human, vulnerable side to Sophie. It was nice to know she had one and wasn't some lizard-person in human skin.

However, Partial Sue wasn't so forgiving. "Let us have a word with Gail or we'll tell Bitsy she was driving you crazy and you wanted her out of your flat."

Sophie laughed. "Go ahead. How's that going to look? Like you're a bunch of petty telltales. Besides, who's she going to believe, you or me? And it's not a flat, it's a beach-front penthouse."

A stirring at the back of the shop distracted them momentarily. Gail emerged from the storeroom, a traditional canvas rucksack over one shoulder and her trusty hiking cane in one hand. As she walked quietly towards the door, Sophie said, "Er, where do you think you're going?"

Gail ignored her and pushed the door open.

"Looks like Gail's taking her lunch break," Fiona said.

"'S'right," Gail mumbled.

Sophie stuttered some random words, attempting to form a plausible reason to prevent Gail leaving but nothing coherent made it past her lips.

The ladies followed Gail out of the shop to a small café a few doors up, where Fiona bought them all bacon sandwiches and bottles of ice-cold cloudy lemonade.

When they had finished noshing, Daisy played Gail the promotional video for the Little Dragon on her phone. She watched it twice, hardly blinking, engrossed by the miniature flying incinerator.

Fiona posed the question they'd been dying to ask. "Gail, how difficult would it be for someone to make one of those from scratch — the flamethrower bit, not the drone?"

Gail's eyes wandered, deep in thought. Then, quick as a flash, she delved into her rucksack and pulled out a pen. She snatched up a napkin and drew a series of boxes linked by lines, a simple schematic. She annotated each box, pausing now and then, touching the pen to her lips as she mentally constructed the constituent parts of a miniature flame-thrower: fuel tank, fuel hose, pump, ignition coil, nozzle, battery.

"Is that it?" asked Partial Sue. "It's not particularly complicated."

"'S'right." Suddenly, Gail remembered something else and drew a separate box off to one side: remote control.

"Is that so you can operate the flamethrower while its flying?" asked Daisy.

"'S'right."

"Could anyone build that with a bit of engineering skill?" Partial Sue asked.

"'S'right."

"And could you get the bits from a plumbers or electrical suppliers?"

Gail mulled it over, then frowned and shook her head. She wrote *three pounds* on the napkin and underlined it — the maximum payload weight mentioned in the video that the drone had to carry.

Partial Sue hazarded a guess. "The parts would be too big and bulky for the drone to lift."

"'S'right," Gail said.

Keeping the weight down would be crucial. Not only would the drone have to get off the ground, but it would also need to retain its precise manoeuvrability. The parts would need to be small and light yet functional enough for the drone to negotiate the narrow gap between two beach huts.

"So where would you get the bits?" Partial Sue asked.

"Internet, I suppose," Fiona replied. "But unlikely. It would leave an incriminating trail for our would-be suspect. Easy to trace."

Daisy's eyes became wide. "What about a model shop?"

Gail clicked her fingers. "'S'right."

Partial Sue flinched with excitement, nearly sending posh lemonade all over the table. "You saw Antony Owens' wife, Olivia, in the model shop."

"I did," Daisy replied. "And the model shop in Southbourne is like stepping back in time. I don't think they keep records of sales or anything judging by the antique till they've got. It's cash only."

"What was she buying?" asked Fiona. "She said it was a train for her nephew."

Daisy scratched her chin. "Yes, but thinking back, it could've been anything. It was in a paper bag. It could've been parts for a miniature flamethrower. Who knows? That's what we need to find out."

"She ran an engineering consultancy," Partial Sue remarked. "She has the know-how."

"She lost a beach hut," Fiona added. "She has the motive."

A wave of positivity spread around the table, quietly confident grins on faces. Another highly promising suspect had materialised before their eyes. Perhaps the most unlikely of all. Dapper Olivia Owens went straight to the top of their list.

CHAPTER 63

After thanking Gail profusely, they hurried up the road to the model shop, desperate to know what Olivia Owens had been buying, and if it fitted Gail's inventory of parts. Of course, it all depended on whether the owners would part with that information.

After the initial euphoria of adding another name to their list of suspects, they had conceded that there were a couple of snags with the evidence against Olivia Owens. Firstly, Daisy had seen her in the model shop well after the first beach hut had burned down. If a flamethrowing drone had indeed been employed to devastating effects, it would have already been built at that point, its parts already sourced and constructed, which meant she could have been telling the truth — she was there to buy a train for her nephew. However, as Partial Sue pointed out, there was always the possibility that Olivia Owens had been there to buy replacement parts, either to fix or maintain her equipment. Olivia was still in the picture, just.

Secondly, as they walked along the pavement, hugging the shade in a bid to avoid the laser-like sun and stay cool, they decided to use the time to make a quick search online of Olivia's engineering credentials. They weren't difficult to find. LinkedIn and various other business sites still held brief records of her now defunct company, the Liv Consultancy. Not exactly what they were expecting.

"Chemical engineering?" Partial Sue said.

"Isn't that all test tubes, Bunsen burners and laboratories?" Daisy asked.

Partial Sue screwed up her face. "Sounds like it. I was expecting electrical engineering or mechanical engineering. That would be a better fit. Could a chemical engineer even build a flamethrower?"

"I don't see why not," Fiona said. "According to Gail, an amateur with a bit of technical know-how could probably build one. And a device that squirts and ignites petrol — that's got to be right up a chemical engineer's street."

Daisy continued Googling the subject. "I think Fiona's right. Listen to this — chemical engineers design and construct equipment and machines for industry that solve problems and create products. A flamethrower is both a machine and a product, isn't it?"

"And not a particularly complicated one," Fiona remarked. "I'd say someone like Olivia Owens could do that with her eyes shut."

"Do you think her husband is in on it?" asked Partial Sue.

Fiona nodded. "Strong possibility. He shares the same motive. They lost their beach hut. But I think at this point, we shouldn't assume anything until we know more."

Up ahead, the model shop came into view, conspicuous by its time-warp aesthetic compared to the more modern shop fronts around it. The place appeared to have remained unchanged since Harold Wilson was prime minister.

"I see what you mean about going back in time," Partial Sue said. "They've still got that orange stuff covering the windows from the fifties. Always reminds me of that crinkly wrapping around the old Lucozade bottles."

Daisy got a hit of nostalgia. "Oh, I remember that. Mum used to give me Lucozade when I was ill off school. Bed made up on the sofa, still in my pyjamas watching *Programmes for Schools and Colleges*. Only time I was allowed to watch TV in the daytime, glass of warm Lucozade in my hand. Back then you used to get it from the chemist. Big glass bottle with bobbly bits around it and orange plastic wrapper. You're right, Sue, it's just like that stuff in the window. What's it for exactly?"

"I think it blocks the sun's rays," Fiona said. "Stops the merchandise fading."

They reached the outside of the model shop and peered in, only to discover that the orange plastic's UV-defensive capabilities had long since been exhausted. An array of boxed models formed a hodgepodge window display that appeared to have remained unchanged for at least the last two decades, judging by the bleached-out artists' impressions of the models contained within each one: the *Golden Hind* and HMS *Ark Royal*; a Harrier jump jet; a Scalextric set and various train sets, both steam and diesel. The boxes had also crumpled slightly, deformed by years of neglect, sun damage and gravity.

Before entering the shop, Daisy issued a warning about the owners. "Ken and Nigel are twins, not identical, but they act more like an old married couple." She pushed the door open, and they entered the hot, dusty, to-scale realm of planes, trains and automobiles, stacked on sagging shelves all the way up to the stained suspended ceiling, in no particular order. The place smelled of singed plastic and irritation.

A long glass cabinet ran the whole length of the shop, filled with a mass of bits and bobs, little drawers sprawling with electrical cables, small electric motors and various accessories bagged up in cellophane. Ken stood behind the counter next to a hefty till that appeared to be made of Bakelite with buttons so hard to push you were in danger of dislocating a finger every time you used it. He had a miserable face with pallid skin and a bald head. His brother Nigel had a similar appearance except he'd won the genetic lottery, retaining a full head of salt-and-pepper hair, although it was a little on the lank side. Nigel stood atop a low stepladder, attempting to pull out a large model of Concorde without causing all the other boxes to come crashing down on his head, as if he were playing giant Ker-Plunk.

Stating the obvious, Ken said, "Be careful you don't bring that lot down."

"Oh really?" Nigel replied. "I didn't think of that. So glad I have you to point that out. Instead of standing there, why don't you help me?"

"It was you who decided to stack the civil aircraft among the radio-controlled cars. You have to own it."

They brightened a little when they noticed Daisy. "Hello," they chorused.

"You've bought some friends," Ken said.

Nigel wedged the Concorde back into a gap it clearly wasn't meant to fit into and backed down off his stepladder. "How's your model of the spit going?"

"It's finished. Do you want to see it?"

They nodded enthusiastically. Daisy brought up some images on her phone.

"Oh wow," Ken gushed, examining each image in great detail. "This is exceptional model-making, Daisy."

Nigel agreed. "We get a lot of people in here showing off their builds, and don't get me wrong, they're good, but nothing like the quality of your work. You've even got the yellow shade of Portland stone on the coastguard station just right."

Daisy blushed. "Thank you."

Ken contradicted his brother. "The coastguard station's built of Purbeck stone. That's why it's yellowy."

"It's Portland stone."

"No, it's not. It's Purbeck stone."

Nigel's face glowed red. "Any fool knows Portland stone is yellow."

Ken's lips became thin, almost baring his teeth. "Oh yeah, well how come all the buildings in London are grey? It's because they're built from Portland stone."

The ferocious sibling rivalry over nothing in particular continued, until Fiona cleared her throat. "Er, actually, we have a very important question — well, questions — that need your expertise."

The ego-flattering silenced the pair. They turned to Fiona.

"What is it you would like to know?" asked Ken.

Fiona pulled up Olivia's LinkedIn page and showed them her profile picture. "Do you recognise this woman?"

"Oh, yes," Nigel said. "She's been in here a few times. Buys model trains. Hornby double-O."

From the schematic Gail had drawn on the napkin, Fiona read out the constituent parts required to build a homemade flamethrower. "Has she ever bought a small fuel tank?"

"No," Nigel answered.

"A fuel hose?"

"No."

"A fuel pump?"

"No."

"An ignition coil?"

"Don't sell them."

"A nozzle?"

"That could be any sort of piping or cylinder. We have all sorts of sizes."

"Okay," Fiona replied. "Has she bought any sort of piping or cylinder?"

"No."

"A battery."

"No."

"There's one more." Partial Sue pointed to the corner of the napkin.

"Oh, yes. A remote control?"

"We sell a lot of them," Nigel said. "What type?"

"Not sure," Fiona replied. "But did you sell one to her?"

"It's possible," Ken said.

"But can you be sure?" Daisy asked.

"No," Nigel replied.

"Could you check your transactions?" Fiona asked.

"I'm afraid we're all cash," Nigel explained.

Ken rolled his eyes. "I told you we should start accepting credit cards. But you didn't want the extra bank charges."

"I'm not giving the bank more of our money."

"Yes, but we would sell more, don't you see? It's a false economy."

Before another argument erupted, Fiona stepped in. "So, this lady never bought any of the items I've just mentioned."

"No, very sorry. What's this about anyway?" asked Ken.

"I'd rather not say at this point." Fiona knew they wouldn't get any further with these two. They'd exhausted all current possibilities, not helped by their haphazard approach to retail. Time to move on and get out before they had to answer any awkward questions themselves. "If you remember anything else relating to that customer, could you let us know?"

"Yes, of course." Nigel smiled.

"Just call Dogs Need Nice Homes," Daisy informed them. "That's where we all work."

"Righto," Ken said.

They'd drawn a blank at the local model shop in the first instance, but that didn't mean anything. A smart woman like Olivia probably wouldn't have sourced the parts to build a weapon at a local model shop where she'd easily be recognised, especially not one where she regularly bought trains for her nephew. She'd have covered her tracks, gone elsewhere. Somewhere out of town where she could be anonymous, possibly obtaining the individual parts from several different outlets.

Just as they reached the door, Nigel said, "Oh, I do remember one thing."

All three ladies turned to face him.

"I think I sold her a drone a while back."

CHAPTER 64

Now they had the ladies' attention.

Fiona attempted to hide the desperation in her voice. "Can you remember what type of drone you sold her?"

Nigel's face went blank. He looked to his brother.

"Don't look at me," Ken said. "I didn't sell it."

Nigel's face contorted as he tried hard to recall exactly what Olivia Owens had purchased. "You know, I definitely sold her a drone. I remember that much."

"Was it one that could carry things?" Daisy asked.

"I mean we do sell heavy-lift drones that can lift one and a half kilos or more."

"What's that in old money?" asked Partial Sue.

"About three pounds," Ken answered.

The three ladies exchanged excited glances. "Was it one of them?" asked Partial Sue. "It would be really helpful if we knew."

Nigel rubbed his temples with both hands, attempting to tease out the memories. "I can't remember. We sell a lot of drones."

Fiona noticed the cameras in the corner of the shop. "Perhaps you have it on CCTV. A recording of what she bought."

"Footage is only kept for thirty days," Nigel informed them.

"But none of our cameras work," Ken said.

Nigel became cross. "I told you we should have got them fixed."

"We don't get any shoplifters in here. Nobody shoplifts packets of moss and tiny tins of paint. What's the point?"

"I'll tell you what the point is, situations like this—"

Fiona cut short another argument between the pair. "Do you know when she bought it?"

"Mm." Nigel gave it some thought. "I'd say at least six months ago. Or was it a year?"

"You could try the Drone Pilot's Registry," Ken suggested. "Anyone who flies a drone over 250 grams has to register with the Civil Aviation Authority."

Daisy had her phone out and was on the registry in seconds. "It says here I need the pilot's ID number before I can check their details."

Ken and Nigel stared at each other blankly.

"How would we get that?" Fiona asked.

The siblings shrugged.

"I suppose we'd have to ask her for it," Partial Sue said.

If Olivia was the beach-hut murderer, there was no way she'd be giving up that information in a hurry. And registering with the Civil Aviation Authority wouldn't be at the top of her to-do list if she was burning down beach huts with a drone.

Fiona decided to give up asking about things they could only speculate on, instead focusing on what they knew. Might as well use the opportunity to pick their brains instead. "What's the range on an average drone?"

"How long is a piece of string?" Ken replied.

Nigel was more informative. "It varies. Horses for courses. A toy drone would only be a hundred feet. Whereas a long-range drone would be nine, maybe ten miles. I'd say average drones would be two or three miles, possibly four, depending on the model, which we obviously can't remember." He cast his eyes down guiltily.

"Which *you* can't remember, not we," Ken snapped.

"So you don't have to be near the drone to control it?" Fiona asked. "Or see it in the sky above you?"

"Oh no, not at all," Nigel answered. "HD cameras mounted on the top or bottom show you what the drone sees. You could be sitting in your car controlling it. Wouldn't matter where you are, as long as it stays in range."

"What about at night?" asked Partial Sue.

"A good camera will have night vision," Ken said. "Plus, they come with all sorts of optional extras and add-on gizmos these days — GPS controllers that show you where you are on Google Maps, software that lets you programme a set flight path so you don't even have to fly the thing."

Nigel continued, "Like a car satnav, it takes you straight to a pinpointed destination. Except the drone takes care of the driving or flying, as it were. Then home again, completely hands-off."

But how feasible would it be to slot a drone between two beach huts, Fiona wanted to know. "When you say pinpoint accuracy, how pinpoint are we talking?"

The two brothers ruminated, then Ken said, "In a built-up area with high buildings, I'd say about two or three metres."

"But if you're flying in clear open space with nothing to get in the way then it can go down to under a metre," Nigel said.

The skies above the spit and Hengistbury Head couldn't be clearer. Apart from the Smuggler's House at the end, there was nothing above a single storey to cause any obstacles. If the drone stayed high, then its accuracy would be at a maximum. Once in position, it could drop vertically, plummet straight down as sure as a lift in a shaft, right between the two huts.

"What about precision-flying, between small buildings?" Fiona asked.

"Oh, piece of cake." Nigel pulled a small box from one of the drawers behind the counter and held it up. "Drones can be retro-fitted with these — obstacle sensors — if they don't have them already. They can fly through tight gaps without bumping into anything and, if the drone has advanced GPS controls, it can hold a given position perfectly. Everything can be automated with a drone, pre-programmed, even the take-off time. Like setting a video recorder."

"It just depends on how much you're prepared to spend," Ken added.

The more Fiona heard, the more she was convinced that a modified drone had been used to set fire to the beach huts. It could perform precision attacks, regardless of how inexperienced the pilot was and, crucially, undetected. She needed to be sure of this last part. Even though she'd already had a second opinion, it didn't hurt to have a third.

"Tell me, would radar pick up a drone, retrospectively? Say one flew over my house a few weeks ago, would there be a record of its flight pattern and the source of the signal?"

"Only if you'd set up specialised drone-sensing radar equipment in the first place," Nigel said.

"But if it was a pre-programmed drone," Ken pointed out. "There would be no signal to trace back to the source — they don't use controllers. The drone does everything."

They headed back to their own shop with a lot of unanswered questions about Olivia, but feeling a whole lot more secure about Fiona's drone theory.

"So I think that this drone as a means of committing the crime is not just a flight of fancy, pun intended." Partial Sue chuckled.

"Me too," Daisy agreed.

"They're an ironic pair, aren't they?" Partial Sue said. "Ken and Nigel know all about technology but choose to live in an analogue world."

"Not sure if that's more to do with saving money," Fiona replied.

"Yeah, I suppose that makes sense," Partial Sue said, being partial to avoiding unnecessary expenditure herself.

Halfway back to Dogs Need Nice Homes the trio of ladies were already melting, their clothing damp with sweat.

They took respite from the evil sun by huddling under the generous canopy of a greengrocers. He glared at them from within the safety of his shop, not happy that they were there to shelter rather than to buy, but he didn't say anything because, well, that's what British people did. Similarly, the ladies found themselves compelled to buy something even though they'd initially had no intention of doing so, opting to purchase three nectarines to assuage the guilt and discomfort of standing beneath the greengrocer's canopy rent-free, because, well, that's what British people did.

Fiona sank her teeth into the fruit's juicy flesh, realising how parched her mouth was. "What do we think about Olivia as a suspect?"

Partial Sue made short work of her fruit, gnawing it down to the stone. "I am partial to a good nectarine," she said. "What else would a glamour puss like her want with a drone? Unless it was to burn beach huts because she was jealous."

Fiona disagreed. "She could be completely innocent. I mean, she's an engineer and loves gadgets, don't you remember what Antony Owens said? And Ken and Nigel backed up her story about buying trains for her nephew."

Daisy took her time with her nectarine one small mouse-bite at a time. "I think it could be a case of the mother is the invention of necessity."

"Necessity is the mother of invention," Partial Sue corrected.

"That's the one."

"What do you mean, Daisy?" Fiona asked.

"Well, the crime, if she did it, fits her personality."

"What, because she's an engineer?" Partial Sue said.

Daisy shook her head. "Well, I was thinking more because she's a germophobe. Hates touching things. You've seen her in our shop. She moves around it as if something might leap out and bite her. This is a perfect way to commit a crime for a germophobe. The drone does all the dirty work. She doesn't have to go anywhere near the crime scene. Can do it all from her house, or car, or whatever."

Fiona hadn't considered this. It made perfect sense. A germophobe's dream. A crime where you don't have to be there, don't have to touch anything. "You're right, and it doesn't leave any evidence behind."

Olivia was fast overtaking all their other suspects to become their number one. Everything they had discovered thus far clicked into place. She had the motive. She had the know-how, and now with Daisy's brilliant observation, she had the means that fitted her profile in more ways than one.

"Well done, Daisy," Fiona congratulated her. "That's a great bit of reasoning. She may have arrived at that method, as you say, out of necessity because she doesn't do touching."

Rather than looking pleased, Daisy's face darkened. "There's just one thing. Would you mind holding this?" She handed her barely nibbled nectarine to Partial Sue, who clearly did mind, judging by her grimace.

After wiping her hands, Daisy dug out her phone. "Olivia friended me on Facebook after she saw my model. Just out of curiosity, I checked her posts on the dates of all the fires. Every one of them shows she was out of town. She has an alibi."

Fiona and Partial Sue gathered around her phone screen, while Daisy scrolled through Olivia's photos on Facebook. They were treated to shot after shot of her in swanky bars with her equally glamorous friends in short dresses, having long drinks and small bites to eat.

"The night of Malcolm's death she was out on the town in Bath with her girlfriends. When it was Bitsy's fire, she was in a country hotel in the Cotswolds, and when it was the Bradleys' turn, she was in London."

Fiona enlarged one of the shots. "I thought they were short of cash."

Partial Sue tutted. "Expensive tastes — no wonder they've got money troubles. But more importantly, social media posts can be faked, right? You can add the times and locations yourself. She could've thrown those pictures up there and lied about where she was, because she was down here committing arson."

"Her friends all have similar pictures." Daisy brought up the corresponding shots on Olivia's friends' pages. "It'd be difficult to get all these people to agree to do that unless they were in on it as well."

"But I thought she was a germophobe," Partial Sue protested. "Look, she's got her hands all over glasses that some waiter or barman has touched."

"Maybe she's fine with restaurants and hotels where everything's cleaned regularly and staff hygiene is strict," Daisy replied.

"Or that could be a whole charade as well. Who knows?" Partial Sue said.

"Doesn't matter," Daisy said. "All those locations are too far away to launch a drone attack."

"But she doesn't need to be there." Fiona felt nectarine juice trickling down her hand. She ignored it and continued. "According to what Nigel and Ken said, an advanced drone could have flown all by itself on a pre-set course, at a pre-set date and time. She doesn't need to be anywhere near it. She could've prepped and primed it, then left it in her garden or behind her garage, then went off on her jollies. Or, if she didn't want Antony to know about it, she could've hidden it somewhere, say, deep in the forest. She sets a timer. Thing takes off by itself in the dead of night, does the deed. Flies back. She's nowhere near it and then she retrieves it when she gets home."

"What about operating the flamethrower?" asked Partial Sue.

"I'm sure that could be achieved automatically," Fiona replied. "It's not outside the realms of possibility that the second it's hovering in exactly the right position and at exactly the right height, it activates the flamethrower for a controlled burn, especially with her engineering skills."

"But if the whole thing's automated, then any one of our suspects could've done it," Partial Sue said.

Fiona went to speak, her mouth opening and shutting like a goldfish's. The possibilities of the technology had changed the dynamics of the crime. It had become remote and detached. Premeditated to such an extent that the perpetrator could have been miles away when it happened, raising a glass with friends or, more likely, tucked up in bed. They didn't need to be anywhere near the spit, in the same town, or in the same county for that matter. A heavy-lift drone could do all the heavy lifting of the crime, as it were. An anonymous automaton to do the killer's bidding. Not quite the terminator, but perhaps something less sophisticated, like the robots from the Seventies' Cadbury's Smash adverts.

Fiona sifted through what she knew. "Okay, for me Olivia's the most likely candidate, still top of the list. It's a bit convenient that she was out of town for every single fire. However, as you rightly said, with this technology, anyone could've done it, wherever they were. Traditional 'where were you on the night of the murder' is not relevant anymore. It's no longer about someone's proximity to the scene of the crime. But one thing is certain, we know how they're doing it. The method of arson. And if we know their method then they can be caught."

"What do you suggest?" asked Partial Sue.

"I think it's time we share what we know with DI Fincher and DS Thomas."

Daisy and Partial Sue nodded.

Fiona made the call.

It went straight to voicemail.

CHAPTER 65

As Fiona spoke, DI Fincher never tore her gaze away from Daisy's model, while her colleague DS Thomas stood in his usual spot by the door, chewing gum with his weight-trained arms folded as if he were providing security for a low-level VIP. Smart cop, scruffy cop, Antony Owens had called them, because the young female DI was always immaculately dressed, while the older DS preferred well-worn casual sportswear. Today, the DI wore a loose-fitting white blouse that contrasted sharply with her dark skin, and a pair of matching slacks, while she silently padded around in ballet shoes. DS Thomas had mismatched his sports brands: a shiny Adidas vest top paired with Nike cotton joggers that had gone baggy at the knees, and a pair of battered Converse.

Neither of them uttered a word. They had been like this for the last forty minutes, patiently listening. Using the model as a prompt, Fiona carefully outlined everything the three ladies had deduced — that a drone had set the fires with the possibility that the culprit had not even been in the same postcode.

When Fiona had finished, the DI remained silent. She stood still and sighed heavily. Fiona couldn't tell whether she was cross, sad, disappointed, or thought the whole theory was childish nonsense.

Eventually she inhaled deeply. "This case has had us foxed. No evidence, no CCTV, no one anywhere near the huts at the times of the fires. None of it made any sense. How did we miss this? A drone of all things."

"Probably because you didn't have a model," Partial Sue said.

"What?" DI Fincher looked puzzled.

Fiona attempted to clarify. "It wasn't exactly deductive reasoning that led us to this conclusion. I stumbled upon the idea. Someone dropped an ice lolly between the model huts and a fly swooped down. If that hadn't happened, I doubt I would have thought of a drone."

DI Fincher smiled, possibly relieved that serendipity had been responsible, and that she and DS Thomas weren't losing their deductive powers.

"How many people know about your drone theory?" DS Thomas asked.

"No one, just us," Partial Sue replied.

"But you talked to Gail about the homemade flame-thrower, and Ken and Nigel about drones," the DI said.

"Only generally," Fiona replied. "We didn't mention anything about them being used in connection with the fires on the spit."

DI Fincher glanced across at her colleague. "Okay, we need to see them straight after this. Make sure they don't speak to anyone about it."

"How come?" Fiona asked.

"We don't want to tip off the killer that we know their technique. Same goes for you three — you can't mention this to anyone. It could sabotage what I have in mind."

"What's that?" asked Partial Sue.

"As you've correctly informed us, the only way to detect a drone is with the right surveillance equipment. I'm proposing we set up specialised radar to detect the drone before it gets anywhere near the beach huts, block its signal, stop it setting another fire and trace the signal back to the source — the person pulling the strings."

Fiona and Partial Sue smiled. DI Fincher had not only taken them seriously, she was proposing countermeasures that would stop any more huts burning down and catch the killer.

Daisy wasn't smiling. She raised her hand. "What if they're using a pre-set flight programme? There'd be no signal to trace. The killer can do everything anonymously without a controller. We might never catch who's doing this."

DI Fincher rubbed her chin. "Yes, that might be a problem."

"I highly doubt they're using a programmable drone." Everyone turned to regard DS Thomas, who pushed himself off the wall and took a few steps forward. "You'd have to have a lot of faith in the accuracy of its flight program. That drone has to slot between two beach huts – a gap of about a metre. If it's out by a centimetre or two, you can't correct the mistake."

"But what if it has obstacle sensors?" Daisy asked. "To stop it crashing."

"True, but if the situation changes, if something unexpected happens, there's no room for error or contingencies. I tell you, if it is a drone causing these fires, I'm ninety-nine per cent sure it's being controlled by someone."

It was the most words they'd heard the detective utter. They were good words too. Wise words. Would anyone risk a drone flying on autopilot when there was so much that could go wrong? So much at stake? Not to mention the fine tolerances of the deadly mission.

"I agree," DI Fincher replied. "Whoever's doing this will want to be in control at all times, to be able to improvise. But we have to explore all avenues. We'll talk to our superiors. See if we can scrounge some budget to set up a drone radar system."

DS Thomas gave a cynical snort. "They won't agree to that. Not before we've traced drone sales and any parts that could construct a homemade flamethrower."

"That's going to be fun," DI Fincher added, "and tracking down registered drone pilots."

Fiona didn't envy them that tedious task. "That could take a while. Another attack could take place during that time."

DI Fincher brightened. "That's the argument I'll use to get them to sign off on this ASAP. Protect lives and property, but we also need to follow procedure. Starting off with the drone that was sold to Olivia Owens."

CHAPTER 66

The police officers got their budget.

The counter-drone system, to give it its official title, was erected in an undisclosed location. DI Fincher couldn't tell them exactly where, but Fiona did manage to prise a few details out of her. A fake tradesmen's van had pulled up somewhere in Christchurch. Two technicians in overalls had lugged unmarked packing crates inside a building and up to the top of the roof. To the casual passer-by it appeared as if someone were having solar panels fitted or a new boiler installed. Up on the flat roof, the equipment was hidden from view behind a high parapet, swiftly erected and fired up, ready to catch the drone killer, as they were now being called.

Everything about the operation had to be stealthy and camouflaged. Radio silence for the radar. If the killer got the merest whiff that their actions were being monitored, they'd back away. However, DI Fincher couldn't help showing off some of the system's credentials. It had a ten-mile operating radius, allowing for it to be set up a few miles away from the spit, which was just as well. With all the wagging tongues and poking noses down there, word would get around, and they couldn't risk tipping off the killer. The skies were now safe, being monitored twenty-four seven by rotating shifts of radar technicians in the contractor's control room, deep inside an industrial estate in Somerford.

When the charity shop was customer free, Fiona passed on what she knew to Daisy and Partial Sue. "Now the equipment's up and running, the police will be notified of any drone flying within a two-mile radius of the spit. They'll track its signal, and the owner will get an unexpected visit. And if it flies too close to the spit, the drone will be disrupted and brought down before it can do any harm."

"But what if it is a pre-programmed drone?" asked Partial Sue. "How will they track it if there's no signal?"

"They've thought of that," Fiona replied. "If the drone is sophisticated enough to be pre-programmed it will almost certainly have a fly-home feature."

"What's that?" Daisy asked.

"It's a safety feature that kicks in if the drone has a problem. Last thing you want is an expensive piece of kit flying off into the wild blue yonder. At the first sign of trouble, it automatically sends the drone back where it came from. The contractor said they could disrupt the drone, make it think it was malfunctioning. The fly-home feature would kick in and send it back to where it took off. The police could then follow it until it lands and lie in wait. Hopefully, the drone killer would appear at some point to retrieve it. That's the plan, anyway."

Everything seemed to be lining up for a perfect sting operation, except for one thing. Fiona had the nagging feeling that DI Fincher and DS Thomas had made a mistake. Perhaps not a mistake, more painting themselves into a police procedural corner (which sounded like a regular show on Radio Four where the public got to quiz a nice, friendly police officer about their methods). However, this particular tight corner had to do with Fiona informing them that Olivia Owens had purchased a drone. The police had had to follow up the lead. Olivia Owens had to be questioned.

DI Fincher and DS Thomas had opted to call round at her house for a 'friendly chat' rather than a formal police interview and all the technicalities that would have come with that. They needed to establish what sort of drone she'd bought in the first place before they could start throwing accusations around, especially as Ken and Nigel's memories of her purchase were a little sketchy.

Olivia confirmed that she had indeed bought a drone, and proudly presented it to them: a little recreational camera drone with four small propellers at each corner, about the size of a small sandwich box. She had, she claimed, bought it for her husband's birthday. It wasn't exactly a toy, but it wasn't what you'd class as a flying killer robot either, and certainly not big enough to warrant a drone pilot's licence. Controlled by a simple app on his phone, it had fifteen minutes' flying time and a range of 150 metres. Restricted to supporting its own weight, the lightweight gadget was incapable of anything nefarious, aside from annoying the neighbours. DI Fincher and DS Thomas had left, satisfied that Olivia Owens was not the drone killer.

Fiona had no idea if Olivia was the killer or not. Actually, that wasn't true — she was their number-one suspect. What she did know was that Olivia was smart. Assuming for argument's sake that she'd somehow hidden her purchase of a sophisticated drone and controller, or simply paid cash, Olivia had established tight alibis on the night of every fire, placing herself elsewhere. If she'd used a pre-programmable control system, although DS Thomas believed this was highly unlikely, the drone could've carried out the attacks while she was living it up with her girlfriends in another part of the country. But she would also have the smarts to know that the police would also suss this out and come knocking on her door. So she would have made a big deal of buying a simple drone locally, a decoy to throw them off the scent. But there was another, more important reason for doing this — perhaps the main reason. She may have purchased a harmless, innocent little drone to serve as her early-warning system, alerting her that the police were getting close. If she knew police procedure then she'd know that they would follow up the purchase of all drones bought recently, including hers. The second they came knocking at her door, she would realise they were onto her technique, sending a signal that it was time to halt her attacks. It would be a fail-safe wake-up call unwittingly provided by the police.

Which is exactly what happened.

The attacks ceased.

CHAPTER 67

The school summer holidays ended abruptly and with it the jam of cars searching for parking spaces near the beach. No more processions of dawdling small children dripping ice lollies down their fronts following weighed-down parents, already exhausted before their feet had even touched the hot sand.

Instead, a procession of a new kind took over. Fresh-faced children starting school for the first time, rattling around in their new uniforms with plenty of room for growth, walked hand in hand with Mum or Dad to their first day at school. Some were overexcited, jacks out of their boxes, bouncing around at the thought of starting school as if their limbs were elastic. Others were inconsolable. Hot tears streaked down flushed faces, hands clinging onto their parents for dear life. Fiona felt a pang of sympathy for them. She remembered her first day, still traumatising her all these years later. That feeling of dreadful separation from your cosy, loving world, the shock like plunging into an arctic lake.

By late September the sun hadn't given up its hold over the thermometer. It continued its merciless assault on the country, turning bird baths into dust bowls and flat roofs into shallow tar pits, with a hosepipe ban still in place.

Fiona checked the messages on her phone, a habit that had become more and more frequent. Her eyes were never off her screen, seeking any indication that a drone attack had been detected, thwarted, and someone brought to justice. But it remained blank on that front. Nothing had occurred since they'd first hit on the idea of a drone being used.

Of course, there had been plenty of false alarms. Holidaymakers and hobbyists mucking around flying drones over or near the spit. They had turned out to be nothing more sinister than flying cameras capturing the landscape and the unspoilt beaches for posterity when the sun was bright and the sea glittered. But nothing had occurred at night. No flights, no flames thrown and certainly no beach-hut infernos.

Fiona couldn't help thinking that the killer had been tipped off and had backed off. The only suspect that had been questioned about drones was Olivia Owens. It had to be her. None of the other suspects knew that the police had drones at the top of their list as a murder weapon, giving her the ultimate heads up to cease and desist. Fiona couldn't understand why the police hadn't hauled her in and asked to search her house. Not that she would have been stupid enough to store a killer drone on her property or left a financial trail for the purchase of one. Maybe that was the reason. They simply didn't have enough evidence.

A text popped up from Partial Sue. The strangest message she'd ever read.

Act normal when you come into the shop.

Fiona didn't like the sound of this. Nothing was ever okay when someone advised you to just act normal. She texted back: *Why? What's wrong?*

Nothing. Just be normal when you come in.

Fiona's tinnitus squealed. It hadn't played up in a while but now it sounded like a seven-year-old blowing a tuneless recorder in her ear. Dashing along the pavement she became terrified that Partial Sue had a gun pointed at her head this very minute, and was being forced to empty the till, which would have very little in it at this time of the morning. Actually, being a charity shop, it had very little in it most times of the day. Also, what sort of thieves would be robbing the shop but letting Partial Sue send a text?

Not taking any chances, Fiona spotted a chunky branch by the side of the road. She snatched it up to use as a make-shift weapon. Simon Le Bon bounced up and down on his front paws, assuming the stick was for him. Judging by the size of the thing, he'd barely be able to lift it, let alone fit his little jaws around its girth.

Bursting into the shop, stick held aloft, Fiona expected to find Partial Sue in peril, tied to a chair with a weapon being waved in her face while several not very bright thieves carted mountains of second-hand clothes out of the shop, believing they could fetch hundreds for them.

No such scenario presented itself. Although the one that did appeared equally unsettling and bizarre. Partial Sue, not normally in before Fiona, stood behind the counter, arms wide, fingertips resting on its surface. She grinned artificially, as if she were an alien pretending to be a human. "Oh, hello, Fiona. What a lovely morning. Hope you're well." For someone who'd just advised her to act normal, Partial Sue's behaviour was bordering on strange.

Fiona was lost for words, her curious mind leaping ahead, wondering what on earth was going on. She caught sight of Partial Sue mouthing the words, "Act normal", her eyes wide and pleading.

Fiona did her best. "Morning, Sue. Another sunny day again."

"Yes indeed. A fine day ahead. I shall have a stroll along the promenade later."

Why had she started speaking like the Wicker Man? Stiffly, she came out from behind the till, her eyes flicking towards the storeroom. "Come, join me in the back, where we shall make tea."

Fiona followed her, eager to get to the bottom of this. When the door was firmly shut, she barked, "What the hell's going on?"

Partial Sue thrust a stiff index finger to her lips to shush her. "Keep it down or she'll hear."

Fiona reduced her voice to a whisper, concerned that her friend had become some tinfoil hat-wearing conspiracy theorist. "Who will?"

"Mary," she hissed.

"Mary?" Fiona replied.

"Yes, Mary, you know. The sorrowful donor. She's listening."

Was Partial Sue, her sharp, quick-witted friend finally losing it? "Are you feeling okay? You haven't had a bump on the head or been eating Stilton before bed again?"

The disappointment on Partial Sue's face made Fiona feel bad for suggesting such a thing.

Still keeping her voice low, Partial Sue spoke fast and manically. "No, I haven't been at the late-night Stilton. Just listen. You know that box the sorrowful donor brought in?"

Fiona nodded. "The one behind the counter."

"Well, I noticed the flaps had come unstuck the other day and, well, I couldn't help myself. You know what I'm like with new donations — well, they're not exactly new but, you know what I mean. So I came in early today. I didn't disturb anything because you hadn't given the all-clear for the stuff to be put out yet, but I just wanted to have a peek inside. And then I saw it."

"Saw what?"

"A listening device. A bug."

Did Fiona hear that right? A bug? Why would anyone want to listen to what they had to say?

CHAPTER 68

"Are you sure?" Fiona asked. "Maybe it was a bit of her grandad's old electronic junk she'd decided to donate."

Partial Sue took out her phone and pulled up a picture, revealing the contents of Mary's box captured from above. A mess of old shoes, ties, cufflinks, some books on cars, a table tennis bat, and various odds and ends.

"I can't see anything," Fiona said.

Partial Sue enlarged the shot. In one corner, tangled with all the other junk and pushed up against a small, dog-eared hole in the cardboard was an anonymous black box, slightly larger than a box of matches. A lead snaked out the top, connected to another larger plain black box about the size of a hip flask.

"It's difficult to see. That could be anything," Fiona remarked.

"It's not. I know my spy equipment. Got the catalogue at home and everything. I love browsing through it. Find it relaxing. I know all the products inside out, and I know a bug when I see one." She flipped away from the picture and onto a saved internet page for the online version of her spy catalogue. "It's this model here. It's exactly the same."

341

Fiona peered in at the image of another nondescript black box. "I mean, it looks the same, but then it's just a plain black box. Lots of things are plain black boxes."

"Not really. Listening devices have no logos, markings or serial numbers. Have to be anonymous, like the one in the cardboard box."

"Bit difficult to see without getting it out," Fiona said.

Partial Sue panicked. "No, we can't move it. She'll hear the commotion and know it's been discovered."

"But how can you be sure it's a bug?"

Partial Sue pulled up the photo on her phone again. "Look where it is. Underneath everything and shoved right up against that little hole in the cardboard. That's no coincidence. They advise bugs to be placed where the microphone isn't covered. And that other box it's attached to is a battery booster." Partial Sue switched back to the online spy catalogue and scrolled down the web page to a section entitled *Items often bought together*. The bug was advertised with a larger device, a battery booster, the same proportions as the one in the cardboard box of donations. "The battery in the bug only lasts for a hundred hours according to this, but when it's attached to that booster, it can last a lot longer."

Fiona felt the colour drain from her face. She swallowed hard. "How much longer?"

Partial Sue shrugged. "Not sure. This particular model is voice-activated, to save on battery, only records when there's something to hear, so it could vary. But I would say, maybe two or three weeks. Why do you ask?"

Fiona sighed. "Because Mary, whoever she is, has been in since she first dropped that box off. She said it was to take things back from her box of donations — things she decided she didn't want to part with. What if it wasn't that? What if she was—"

"Changing the battery booster. How often has she been in?"

Fiona rubbed her temples. "At least a couple of times."

"How far apart were they?"

342

"Can't be sure, but she's definitely been in twice since she dropped the box off."

Partial Sue's eyes became wide and incensed. "That works out about right, roughly. She's been coming in to change the battery. But why would she want to listen to our conversations? Do you have any idea who she is, where she comes from?"

Fiona shook her head. "None whatsoever. I don't know her second name, or if Mary is even her real name. But I do know that as soon as we hit on the idea of a drone being used, the attacks suddenly stopped. We had that conversation about it right here in the shop. Told DI Fincher and DS Thomas all about it. She would have heard everything."

"You think she's behind the fires?"

"Why else would she bug this shop?"

"Sounds like the sort of thing Sophie Haverford would do. Snoop on us."

"Sophie thinks we're beneath her. She wouldn't stoop so low. But word got around on the spit that we were investigating the death of Malcolm Crainey. The killer must have heard and decided to install it as a bit of insurance. Keep tabs on how close we were getting. I mean, they can't exactly bug the police, but they can bug us. The attacks stopped the second we discovered the method."

"Unless the killer had had enough by then. Was satisfied they'd burned down all the huts owned by people they thought didn't deserve one."

"That's a possibility."

The two women stood in silence for a while, the shock slowly creeping through them like poison. Their cosy safe haven had been violated, infiltrated by a possible murderer who had listened to every word they'd uttered. But desecration of their privacy was the least of their problems. This Mary knew everything about them, getting blow-by-blow accounts of their investigation, and they knew nothing about her apart from the fact that she was a good actor. Utterly convincing at playing the part of the bereaved granddaughter.

Even shunting her child into the shop to add to the panto-mime. It had worked. Fiona had had sympathy for the poor woman, wanted to give her a shoulder to cry on.

She tried to recall her face but even that was difficult. Mary had made herself look as bland and unmemorable as possible, make-up free and totally anonymous behind her oversized glasses and hat pulled tightly down to her eye-brows. She could be anyone. Conveniently, she'd also worn gloves every time she'd been in, leaving no fingerprints. She doubted the police would get any usable DNA off the box or any of its contents. They probably weren't even hers and would no doubt lead to an innocent individual who'd had a clear out at a car boot sale.

Repulsion that they had been well and truly hoodwinked ignited Fiona's synapses. The shock that had ensnared her moments earlier flared into a searing anger. Fear became energy and unstoppable motivation. Somehow, they would catch Mary.

"How does she actually hear our conversations?" Fiona asked. "Does she have to download them each time she comes in to change the battery?"

Partial Sue pulled up the details on her phone. "This particular bug connects to your phone, it says here. Relays everything. Sends an alert when there's something to hear. According to that green light on the booster, it's still got power. She's listening right now. We should take the bug to Freya. Maybe she could track down the phone number it connects to."

Fiona shook her head. "No. If Mary is smart enough to plant a bug, she'll be smart enough to use an untraceable burner phone with no strings attached. And, like you said, we can't risk moving it. If we do anything different, she'll cut the connection and we'll never know who she is. We just have to continue as if everything is the same. Make her think nothing has changed."

"So what happens next?" asked Partial Sue.

Fiona drew a blank. The pair of them felt trapped in the storeroom, not daring to venture out.

"Oh, this is ridiculous. We can't stay in here all day," Partial Sue said.

"No, you're right. We have to try to act normal."

"So that's all we do. Keep letting her listen to our conversations?"

"That's exactly what we do. But we're going to do something else. Wait there a second." Fiona left the storeroom, closing the door behind her. A second later she returned, clutching a well-used Ordnance Survey map that had just been donated, although it wouldn't stay that way for long. The folded-paper version of a stiff upper lip, Ordnance Survey maps were reliable in a crisis and reassuringly accurate, and for those reasons were always in demand, even the ones that were a few years old. Its pink cover announced in no-nonsense typeface that it was a Landranger 195, 1:50,000 scale.

"How are your map-reading skills?" Fiona asked.

CHAPTER 69

Draining her tea, Fiona placed her cup carefully back on the saucer. Across the table, Marcus, the owner of Tides Restaurant, gave her the briefest of smiles, barely troubling his laughter lines.

Though it was late in the afternoon, the sun still rouged Fiona's cheeks. The spit was busy with pre-schoolers, parents and retirees, hopping in and out of the shoreline, or floating around in bright inflatable watercraft, making the most of the Indian summer. Simon Le Bon sat under the table in the shade tethered to one of its legs, stretching his little body now and again to snaffle morsels of food that had fallen on the decking.

Fiona pulled her purse from her bag.

"It's okay, Fiona. This is on the house," Marcus said.

"Oh, that's very kind of you."

"Not at all."

She closed her notebook and patted the cover several times. "Thank you so much for this. It's very helpful for what I have in mind."

"You're welcome."

Fiona rose to her feet, making a big deal of waving her notebook. "I'd better get back to the shop with this."

"Let me know if you need anything else."

"Will do." She watched Marcus disappear into the restaurant then checked her watch, realising she'd underestimated the time. There'd be no gentle stroll along the tarmac path under the leafy shade for her. She needed to get back before closing time.

Up ahead the Noddy train waited as a slow-moving conga of young families, dragging pushchairs and cool boxes, queued to get on board. Fiona made a dash for it along the sand. It'd probably be the last train of the day.

Her progress was halted by the big, round, smiley, bearded face of Steve the coastguard with a pretty blonde child clutching his hand. Still in his uniform, with rolled-up trouser legs, the pair of them had wet, sandy feet. "Hello, Fiona. What a nice surprise. This is my granddaughter, Dina."

Fidgeting on the end of her grandfather's arm, she managed a delicate, "Hello."

"Well, it's very nice to meet you, Dina."

"We've been paddling," Dina boasted. "In the sea."

"That's the best place to do it, so I've heard." Fiona snatched a glance over their shoulders at the Noddy train slowly filling up. Never one to be impolite, she would have to cut this conversation short with all the deftness of a seasoned diplomat.

"Dina loves it down here," Steve said. "Beryl's back at the coastguard station but she'll be down soon, once her shift's over."

Dina grinned. "We're getting ice cream, aren't we, Grandad?"

"We are indeed."

"I'm getting two scoops," Dina announced.

"Well, that's only if you're a good girl. You're very welcome to join us, Fiona."

"I'd love to but—"

"Can I stroke your dog?" Dina unhitched her hand from her grandfather's and squatted down on her little haunches.

"Oh, yes. He's very tame."

Right on cue, Simon Le Bon played his cuteness card and began licking Dina's face.

"It tickles," she shrieked in delight. "Is he a puppy?"

"Well, Simon Le Bon is six, but he looks like a puppy, since he's had his fur trimmed for the summer."

"He could have a paddle," Dina replied.

"Yes, that's a good idea. But I'd better get back because my friends will be wondering what's happened to me. Tell you what, I'll come past the coastguard station next time and you can have a proper play with him."

Dina pogoed up and down with glee. "Could I take him for a walk?"

"Of course."

They waved their goodbyes and Fiona bustled as fast as she could towards the Noddy train. By the time she reached it, the queue had dissolved, and everyone had slotted themselves inside. She checked along its length for a vacant seat. Weary bodies and hot, relieved faces were wedged into each one, many children sitting on parents' laps, and not an inch of available space. Reaching the front, it became apparent that she would not be travelling by this particular mode of transport today.

A jolly-faced driver popped her curly head out of the cab and waved. "Room for a small one up front," she said. "If you don't mind sharing."

Fiona smiled. "I'll take that offer." She slid in next to her, Simon Le Bon hopping onto her lap. "Thank you."

"Not at all. You had the look."

"The look?"

"The I-can't-face-the-walk-back-to-the-car-park look." The driver chuckled. "Seen it a million times. That walk along the path is lovely on the way here but on the way back, it can be a bridge too far."

The driver started the engine. Surprisingly there were more controls than Fiona would have expected. "You drive this every day?" she asked as they clunked and wobbled forward, gradually picking up speed.

"Oh no. Just part time. I've been doing it for over fifteen years now. Best job in the world. Look at that view."

The train curled around the silvery lagoon beside the harbour, the clatter of the engine sending birds flitting up from their perches like fireworks. Simon Le Bon growled at them. Fiona jolted up and down on the less than comfortable bench seat. "Gosh, you need a strong back for this."

"I'll say, and a good sports bra. With this suspension, the old jubblies take a bit of a hammering."

Fiona had a dropping sensation in her stomach, hollow and uncomfortable, and it wasn't the shuddering Noddy train or the thought of wearing a sports bra all day. It was the same feeling she got when she thought she'd left the gas on. More specifically, an oversight. Sitting here in the cab, she realised they hadn't questioned any of the Noddy train drivers. She reassured herself that the police probably had this covered but that wasn't the point. They were supposed to be detectives and they had missed several people who could have valuable information. "Tell me, were you driving on the day before Malcolm's hut burned down?"

"No, I wasn't thankfully, but I heard all about it. What a terrible thing to happen. And those other fires. I tell you, it hasn't been the same since. A lot of hut owners haven't returned. Sold up. A few empty huts on the market now. I'm so glad those fires have stopped, though, touch wood." The driver searched around the cab for something wooden to tap. There wasn't anything so she patted the top of her head.

"Did you know Malcolm at all?"

The driver changed gear. "Oh yes, everyone knew Malcolm. Eccentric, one-off. I liked him. He was a character, you know."

The same story she'd heard from everyone. Would this conversation be any different? "Was there anybody who didn't like him?"

"Well, if there was, I never heard anything, but then I never do. It's mostly holidaymakers and day-trippers I get on here. Hut owners don't really use the Noddy train."

"Do you think it was a hut owner, rather than a visitor?"

"Well, I don't know about that. But I do know they like things to be just so down here and, well, Malcolm wasn't a just-so kind of person. For example, I don't think some of the owners ever got over the old, British-racing-green train being replaced by this new white one. There was a lot of tutting and shaking heads when that happened, I can tell you. Still, it had to happen. The old one kept breaking down. It's no good having a traditional Noddy train if it doesn't work properly. It's not them that have to put up with a load of grumbling parents stuck halfway. Did you know, this used to have a face painted on it, until they kicked up a fuss? Got it painted over."

"Yes, I'd heard that," Fiona replied. "Did Malcolm ever use the Noddy train?"

"Oh gosh, no. He push-biked everywhere. Could never afford the fare — for anything. Although I do remember when I first started, I gave his kid a lift once."

Fiona nearly fell out of the cab. "You mean Malcolm's son?"

"His son? Oh, no. Malcolm didn't have a son. He had a daughter. Only met her the once, then never saw her again. Bright little thing, she was. Very curious. Sat up here with me in the cab. Wanted to know what every button and dial was for. How the engine worked. Never stopped asking questions. I think it was the only time she visited Malcolm. He put her on here to send her back to her mum, who was waiting at the car park. She and Malcolm didn't want to see each other, so I took her. Never saw her again."

Fiona's hands shook as she pulled her notebook from her bag. "Can you remember what her name was? Where she lived?"

"Mm, long time ago. The old noodle's not what it used to be. Have no idea where she was from. Not local, I can tell you that. Now, what was her name? Maybe Maggie, Maisie."

"Mary?"

"Mary — that's it. Her name was Mary."

Fiona gripped the seat to steady herself, almost putting her fingernails through the vinyl, urging the Noddy train to go faster.

CHAPTER 70

Fiona stood poised outside the door of Dogs Need Nice Homes, taking several slow and deep controlled breaths. Sifting through her thoughts, she attempted to order them and calm her mind. Bit difficult when she had new, rather large information occupying any spare space in her head.

Malcolm had a daughter, not a son. Mary. Question was, what should she do with this information? Fiona had been chewing this over every second of the journey back. Her brain was working overtime, causing her tinnitus to shriek in her ear like a factory whistle at knocking-off time. What to do? *What* to do? Did it really change their plans? No, not really. The only difference was now they knew who she was. Knew her motive, sort of. She'd wanted to kill her estranged father for not being around, possibly, or maybe she just wanted his beach hut. Even in its charred state it would be worth a small fortune, but then why did she try to kill Bitsy and the Bradleys? Fiona had to stop herself falling down the rabbit hole. She was becoming distracted, losing focus. She had to keep moving forward. Stick to the meticulous arrangements they'd made.

Fiona unlocked the door. It was past closing time and she'd missed Daisy and Partial Sue, who had already left for the day. Following the pre-planned script in her head, she moved over to the till, dropped the keys on the counter and pulled out her phone to make a call that went straight to Partial Sue's voicemail.

"Oh, hi, Sue. Sorry I missed you. Got waylaid. I know you and Daisy had to get away on time tonight. I'm guessing you're both on the train, hence the voicemail. I'm back at the shop now. Just got the train myself — the Noddy train, that is, not a real one. Anyway, thanks for locking up. I just popped back in to get my glasses and to pick up something important.

"Listen, I've got some good news, some bad news and some big news, really big news. Bad news is the counter-drone equipment was dismantled two days ago. Just got a call from DI Fincher. I know what you're thinking, but it wasn't her decision. It was a budget call. Money ran out, and it didn't help that the attacks had stopped. It doesn't matter though, because I have some good news. Fantastic news, in fact. I know for certain who's behind it all. Got it all here in my notebook. Guess you're dying to find out. It's someone we know or, well, I know. I don't think either you or Daisy met her. It's Mary, the sorrowful donor, who left a box of her late grandfather's things behind. Just having a look through them now." Fiona tucked her phone under her shoulder, grabbed a pen and prodded around, shifting things about, purposefully ignoring the elephant in the room — or box in this instance — the bugging device and its charger.

"Hmm, it's all fairly innocent stuff. Some shoes, books and various bits and bobs. But you're not going to believe who she really is. It will blow your mind. Anyway, I'll stick this box in the boot of my car. Take it with me tomorrow morning. I've got a meeting first thing with DI Fincher. That's the earliest she could see me. Going to lay it all out on the table for her. Then I'm ninety-nine per cent sure she'll arrest her. Because I've just acquired some damning evidence. Sue, we've got Malcolm's killer. We did it! Sorry, just getting a bit overexcited. Anyway, I know you'll be out of mobile phone range for the next couple of days, but ring me back as soon as you get this. Oh, and say hi to Daisy and make sure you tell her the good news."

Fiona hung up, put her phone away, then sought out a pair of rubber gloves with which to move Mary's box of donations into the back of her car. After locking up the shop, she made the short drive home with Simon Le Bon, while the butterflies in her stomach rioted.

CHAPTER 71

Fiona sat on her kitchen floor, her back pressed up against its wooden, stable, side door. Split in two, the bottom half was firmly shut, but the top was slightly ajar, just enough so Fiona could hear what was going on outside, but to all intents and purposes, it appeared closed. It led to her side alley, which faced the blank, windowless wall of the house next door, forming the boundary with Fiona's property. Turning left out of the stable door would lead to her tall side gate and the front of the house, turning right to her back garden and the shed. The stable door and alley were probably the most secluded, private part of the house, not overlooked by anyone, which is why she'd chosen it as the most probable target.

Fiona checked her watch: 2.33 a.m. Time had become glacially slow, not helped by the fact that she kept peeping at her watch. Incessant glances, a nervous tic. Fiona's mind kept flip-flopping between doubt and fear. Maybe she'd got this all wrong and was on a fool's errand, ridiculously sprawled on her cold kitchen floor in the middle of the night with nothing for company except a flask of tea. Simon Le Bon had been packed off to a neighbour down the road with his basket and a Tupperware box of treats. She thought it would be better if he weren't here tonight. However, she dearly missed him.

The absence of her little furry comforter felt as if she'd had a limb removed. By this time of the morning the pair of them would be fast asleep on her bed, his little warm body pressed against hers. But not tonight. The cocktail of adrenalin and anticipation kept her jittery and slumberless. She found the waiting unbearable. Inevitably, her mind drifted towards the irresistible pull of fear.

In the cold light of day, Fiona's plan had seemed smart and logical, confident even. But right at this moment, in the dead of night, it seemed downright reckless. It was only now she realised that if this went wrong, she could lose everything. Fiona shivered, terror seizing hold of her mind. Her tinnitus screeched, as if berating her. What had she been thinking?

The next hour felt as if each second were a week, each minute a year. It dragged so much that Fiona worried the hands on her watch might slow down and stop altogether. At least her tinnitus gradually retreated, and she'd had the foresight to make herself a flask of tea to comfort her through the long, torturous hours, although she had to be frugal with her tea consumption. A full bladder would mean leaving her post, and that wouldn't do. She had to stay vigilant at all costs and weigh up whether it was safe to have another couple of mouthfuls. Yes, it was. Her hands shook as she unscrewed the top of the small tartan flask. The reassuring aroma of hot, milky, sugary tea reached her nostrils. Normally she didn't take sugar, but these were exceptional circumstances calling for exceptional measures — two and a half teaspoons to be exact. She was about to pour when a faint humming danced around the periphery of her hearing.

At first, she thought it was her tinnitus, back for more. She concentrated hard, almost straining. No, this definitely originated from outside. Slowly and soundlessly, she placed the flask back on the floor.

She listened again, needing to be sure of what she was hearing. There were plenty of odd, inexplicable noises at night. Nocturnal creatures, snuffling and scratching around, which would quickly move on, fading as soon as they had appeared. However, this subtle noise was too constant. A high-pitched squeal, only just audible. It could be a mosquito. Or it could be a drone.

Her heart sped up, her breaths sharp and short. She had to keep calm. Had to be ready.

Leaning over to the right, her trembling fingers coiled around the handle of a hefty red fire extinguisher. Martin had recommended it — a four-kilogram powder model, suitable for class A, B and C fires. A good all-purpose model that would work on a multitude of materials including wood, paper, flammable liquids and electrical equipment. Naturally he was pleased when anybody decided to improve the fire safety of their home. Fiona hadn't ventured to tell him what it was really for.

She felt around the lever at the top of the extinguisher, double-checking that she had pulled the safety pin so that it was ready to snatch up and use. With her other hand, she reached for the base and unclipped the long, thick, liquorice-like hose, gripping and holding it up like the end of a rifle.

Slowly, she rose to her feet, lifting the fire extinguisher as she did so, keeping it close to her chest while ignoring the strain on her knees. Stepping to the left and keeping her back to the wall, she peered through the tiny gap in the door. Out in the darkened alleyway there was nothing to glimpse. Instead, she angled her ear to the gap and listened.

The whining continued, sometimes louder, sometimes softer. If she'd had to guess, she'd say that whatever it was had decided to slowly circle her house, performing a recce of the situation below, which sort of ruled out a mosquito. She didn't think insects, especially mosquitoes, were that picky. That only left one option: a drone, and not just any old drone. A drone with a miniature DIY flamethrower bolted beneath it, seeking out a suitable place to start a fire, which Fiona had calculated would be millimetres away from where she currently stood – the other side of her wooden stable door. The only drawback was that the drone would have to fly very low between the two buildings and risk losing signal, but Fiona had that covered should it try to start a fire elsewhere.

The whine faded away and she feared it may have given up and abandoned its mission, or that it had actually been a mosquito and had buzzed off to find an open window so it could fly in and bite some unsuspecting victim in their sleep. The irritating noise completely disappeared.

A false alarm.

The still silence of the warm night returned. Fiona stood absolutely still, playing it safe until she was sure the noise had ceased completely.

She couldn't tell how long she stayed like that. A minute? Five? Maybe ten? Eventually, she turned away from the door, ready to resume her position on the floor. As she did so, the whining returned.

Fiona froze, not daring to move an inch. She listened hard, cocked her ear to the crack in the door. Extremely faint, it appeared to be coming from directly above, high over the house. The humming never changed in pitch or tone, holding its position, hovering. She imagined it levitating between her house and the neighbour's fifty feet up, held on pause while its night-vision camera surveyed the scene below like a timid bird, not daring to make a move until it was absolutely sure it was safe. Fiona resumed her position to the left of the door, back against the wall, head turned sharply to the side, allowing her the tiniest glimpse through the gap in the top half of the stable door.

The tone of the whine altered. A descending chord not unlike the engine of a plane, throttling back before landing, except barely audible, dropping vertically, just as she had predicted when she'd first conceived the theory.

She didn't have time to congratulate herself. Fiona gripped the extinguisher tightly in both fists, her palms slippery with sweat.

Down and down it came, closer and closer.

Now the humming was outside her door. Though still not that much louder than a mosquito, it sent her heart into overdrive. Through the gap, in the dimmest of light, she glimpsed a mechanical object, hovering at eye level, striking fear into her heart. She could make out at least one rotor blade spinning not more than a couple of feet away from her. The experience was almost mesmerising, like staring into a cobra's eyes just before it struck.

She had to act.

It was now or never.

CHAPTER 72

Fiona threw back the top half of the stable door and came face to face with the killer drone. With barely enough light to see properly, she could make out that it was about the size of a large, square biscuit tin. Hanging in the air like a giant mechanical insect, it was held aloft by four spinning blades, creating a menacing low-level hum, not unlike her tinnitus. Extending horizontally from the shadowy mass, a single, long, proboscis-like tube extended beneath the main body — the nozzle of the homemade flamethrower.

Gripped by the shock of seeing her theory manifested in front of her, Fiona became paralysed. Unblinking and unable to move, she stared at this strange DIY angel of death, barely visible in the blur of darkness.

A click and a whirr came from beneath the main body, bringing her back to her senses. In the next millisecond it would deploy its flame, and she would be engulfed in fire.

Hand on the extinguisher's trigger lever, hose pointed directly at it, Fiona squeezed.

The speed and ferocity of white powder that shot from the nozzle surprised even Fiona, who'd never once fired an extinguisher in her life. Engulfing the drone in a thick, massing cloud, she lost sight of it for a second or two.

Like an angry wasp, the drone emerged wobbling and jerking upwards, its rotor blades stuttering and failing to gain enough height to escape. It veered sideways, to the right, into her back garden towards the shed.

Fiona followed it, continuing her assault, keeping the nozzle trained on the fleeing drone. However, it managed to evade her, staying just out of reach of her aim and making a shallow ascent, hoping to clear the roof of the shed.

As it neared the small building, the shed door flew open. Partial Sue leaped out, fire extinguisher in hand. She unleashed a fresh torrent on the escaping drone, mercilessly enshrouding it in a suffocating cloud.

From the opposite direction, Fiona joined her, their extinguishers converging on the failing drone in a pincer movement. With a double onslaught to contend with, the drone jerked erratically, complaining as the deluge of powder fouled up its delicate machinery, working itself deeper and deeper. The thing failed to gain height. It would only be a short matter of time before it came crashing down to earth.

The plume of powder from Fiona's extinguisher grew smaller — diminishing by the second, it coughed and spluttered, then ran out. A few seconds later, Partial Sue's was also depleted. The drone broke free, wobbling and faltering as it gained height towards freedom.

As it rose into the night air, now certain of escape, it almost reached the guttering of Fiona's house, until a back bedroom window shot open. Daisy, also armed with an extinguisher, blasted it, sideswiping the drone with such force it was like the Abominable Snowman swatting a fly.

The drone nearly flipped over. Recovering briefly, it never had a chance. Daisy's aim was relentless, never giving it a second's respite. Its blades became fitful and then useless, unable to support its weight. It dropped, clattering onto Fiona's patio, lifeless.

The two ladies in the garden gathered around it, cautiously holding their extinguishers to their chests. If the thing should attempt one last escape, they'd bring the heavy cylinders down on it, smashing it to smithereens.

Daisy joined them. "Is it dead?"

"Not sure." Fiona tapped it with her foot. The drone was caked in white gunk, as if it had been caught in a blizzard.

"What do we do now?" Partial Sue asked.

Fiona tried to think. But her mind, rather like the drone, had become clogged, not with white extinguisher powder, but with adrenalin and stress. The whine of the drone had been replaced with that of her tinnitus. The trauma of the event was sending her into shock. Someone, most probably Mary, had wanted to set fire to her house, with her in it. Though she had been expecting it, and even planned for it, the reality of a situation could never prepare you for what it felt like to have your life threatened.

A voice came from behind them. "I'll tell you what you can do now. You can all get inside."

"Move now," said a second voice. "Or we'll put fifty thousand volts into you."

CHAPTER 73

Fiona, Daisy and Partial Sue took up the whole of the couch with only the dimmest of table lamps throwing long, sinister shadows across the lounge. Not daring to move, they'd had their extinguishers and their phones taken off them by their captors.

Steve and Beryl looked very different out of their coast-guard uniforms. Dressed identically in the gloom, matching his-and-hers fleeces had never been so menacing. Perhaps it was because the cute, wholesome couple who normally kept mariners safe were pointing stun guns at them. Beryl also had a large drone controller slung around her neck.

"What are you going to do with us?" Partial Sue asked.

"Finish the job." Steve smiled warmly, his round ruddy face not really fitting with that of a murderer.

"Oh, yes," agreed Beryl, equally chirpy.

"What about Mary?" Fiona asked.

"What about her?"

"She's Malcolm's daughter. What's her part in all this?"

Beryl and Steve locked eyes, then they burst into fits of laughter.

"She's not Malcolm's daughter." Steve smirked.

"She's ours," Beryl said. "I thought you three were supposed to be expert detectives."

"But your daughter's called Molly," Fiona pointed out.

"Yep, that's our pet name for her."

One of the contrary quirks of the English language was that some nicknames were slightly longer than the original and sounded nothing like them. Mary, a case in point, became Molly or even Polly.

"She's really not Malcolm's daughter?" Partial Sue asked. "You didn't adopt her or anything?"

Beryl looked horrified. "Gosh, no. Gave birth to her myself. I have no idea who Malcolm's daughter is. Don't care either. Just someone who happens to have the same name, I suppose."

"Lots of people are called Mary." Steve picked up Fiona's flask. He'd noticed it when they'd led the three ladies into the house. He unscrewed the lid and poured himself a cup of tea. *Her tea.* This annoyed Fiona no end. It was one thing to invade someone's house and hold them captive but quite another to help yourself to their tea without asking, or even offering them a cup. She felt violated.

He took several gulps before handing it to Beryl who drained the rest. "I can tell you one thing for certain," he added. "We'd do anything for our daughter and our granddaughter. When we heard that you were planning to tell the police about Molly, well, we couldn't let that happen. Had to act."

Beryl nodded. "She's completely innocent. Had nothing to do with this. Has no idea what we've been up to."

Partial Sue spoke up. "But Mary, sorry, Molly, bugged our shop. She kept coming back in to change the batteries. She must have been in on it."

"She had no idea we planted a bug," Steve explained. "My father really did pass away recently. That bit of the story is true. He and Molly were close. It really affected her. She wanted to drop off some of his unwanted things at a charity shop. We'd heard on the grapevine that Antony Owens was planning to ask you to investigate the case, to shut up the whingeing hut owners who kept pestering him to do something, and we knew about you keeping stuff back for grieving relatives. Seemed too good an opportunity to pass up, so we planted a bug in the box and suggested she take the donations to your shop. Meant we could keep tabs on you, see if we were in any danger of being caught. It all worked out rather well — I mean, here we are."

Fiona got a chill, shocked at their lack of remorse and warped morality. They'd used Steve's dead father's possessions as a means to plant a bug, and their own daughter as the one to do it, setting her up as an unwitting and innocent mule, not worried in the slightest that they were putting her at risk.

"So why did Molly keep coming back into the shop, and how did you get over the problem of the battery running out?" Partial Sue asked.

Beryl answered. "She was genuinely taking things back for sentimental reasons. She's a sensitive soul, our Molly."

"We found a battery booster in China," Steve said. "Triple the battery life of the ones you buy here. We had to get it imported though. The only thing we didn't account for is someone spotting what it was. Thought it was fairly innocuous. When did you discover the bug?"

"Only a couple of days ago," Partial Sue replied. "I'm a bit of an amateur expert on spy gear."

"We carried on as if nothing had happened," Fiona said. "Obviously, we had no idea who Mary was when we found the bug. Had no address or second name. But we knew if she was listening, we could flush her out. Make her think that we had something on her, some incriminating information we could use to force her hand."

Steve clicked his fingers. "That was when you went to see Marcus on the spit. We saw you from the coastguard station. Very handy having such powerful binoculars at our disposal."

"We see everything that goes down on that spit." Beryl's voice was cold and monotone.

"What did he tell you about her?" Steve asked.

Fiona shook her head. "Nothing. It was all a ruse. All part of feeding you false information. I had no idea if anyone was watching or not. But just in case, I set up a meeting with him to make it look as if he was giving me something important. The whole thing was a pantomime. We were simply discussing options for a dinner party I'd booked."

"Then Sue and I pretended to go on a trip," said Daisy. "So it looked as if Fiona was alone. That she was the only person in possession of evidence that would lead to Molly's arrest."

"Fiona was the bait in the trap," Partial Sue added.

Steve had a smug grin on his face. "Backfired, didn't it? Looks like we turned the tables. Well, apart from you ruining our drone." His face dropped. "Do you know how expensive that was? And I had to build a flamethrower for it, all from scratch. I used to be an engineer in the Navy, you know. Maybe it can be salvaged."

Beryl waved her stun gun at the three of them. "Well, now that's all cleared up, it's time we were going, and time you three said your last farewells to one another — and this life."

365

CHAPTER 74

The ladies fidgeted on the sofa, terrified expressions contorting their faces as Steve and Beryl edged closer, guns raised.

"Wait!" Fiona cried. "Hold on. You haven't told us why you killed Malcolm."

"And tried to kill Bitsy and the Bradleys," Daisy added. "Why those three?"

Steve and Beryl halted their advance, exchanging expressions, silently debating whether to answer their questions or not.

Steve sighed and lowered his weapon. "You know why. That's the one part of the investigation you got right."

Fiona sifted through the many theories in her head, trying to fathom which one had been true. She couldn't think straight. Nearly having your house burned down by a flying automaton and then being held captive by two volunteer coastguards with stun guns will do that to a person.

"I'll put you out of your misery," Steve said. "Sue cracked it. The link between all three victims. None of them had earned the right to have a beach hut. I have no problem with someone who's worked for it. But people being handed them on a silver plate — that's not right. Why should they have that privilege and not us?"

"We've always loved the spit," Beryl said. "Loved seeing the little kids running around being kids, happy and free, having dream childhoods. We wanted that for Molly when she was little, but we could never afford it. When Dina was born, we wanted it for her too, especially as she's never met her father. He disappeared the second she was born. They both deserved to have something nice in their lives — a beach hut on Mudeford Spit to make wonderful childhood memories, but we still didn't have the money."

"That's why we took the volunteer jobs at the coastguard station," Steve said.

This sounded completely counterintuitive. The coastguard job didn't pay anything. But then Fiona thought of the little touches they'd added — the comfy chairs, tables, parasols and the mini fridge stuffed with food. The home-sweet-homeness of the whole place. "The coastguard station was your surrogate beach hut," Fiona said. "A substitute for the real thing."

"That's right." Steve paced up and down in front of the sofa, getting his thoughts in order. "It was the nearest we could get to beach hut life. We tried to make it the same for Molly and Dina. You've seen what we've done to the place. But it's a pale imitation. We can't sleep in it for a start, and it's not like being down on the spit. Part of that little community with all the other children and families. At the end of the day, it's still a coastguard station on a lonely, windswept headland."

Beryl chimed in. "When Steve's father died, he left us some money. At last, we thought, we can afford the real thing. Molly could give her daughter that idyllic childhood that we weren't able to give her. But the prices had become ridiculous. Even further out of our range, and they were going up each month. As soon as one came on the market it'd be snapped up. So we had the idea of devaluing the properties while getting rid of a few people who didn't deserve a beach hut in the first place."

Steve stopped pacing. "Start some fires. Commit a few murders. Frighten people into leaving, create a surplus of beach huts to drive the prices down. Make them more affordable, so we could get what we wanted for Molly and Dina."

"We started with Malcolm. He was the worst of the lot. You saw the state of his hut. That layabout didn't appreciate what he'd been given, free of charge. He had to go first."

Fiona winced at their cold heartedness.

"What happened with Bitsy's fire?" Daisy asked. "Did you want to kill her too?"

Steve nodded. "That was the intention, but we got cocky after getting away with Malcolm's murder. Became sloppy. We should've checked the spoilt brat was in. That was amateurish, I'll admit. We didn't make the same mistake with the Bradleys."

Daisy was shocked. "But they had young children."

"So what?" Steve replied. "Why should their kids get an idyllic childhood and not our granddaughter?"

Fiona was having none of it. Their reasoning was weak and misplaced. "Didn't work though, did it?" she pointed out. "They got out alive and, from what I can tell, your actions have hardly made a dent in beach hut prices. But what would Molly make of all this? Do you think she'd be proud of what you've secretly done on her behalf? Actually, sounds like you were doing this for yourself. Using your innocent daughter and granddaughter as an excuse for arson and murder, to get what you've always wanted. Did you ever ask her if this is what she wanted? I think she'd be ashamed and horrified."

Fiona had hit a nerve.

Steve rushed at her, holding the stun gun inches from her face. "Shut up! This is all for her! And she's never going to find out, because none of you will be alive to tell her." He straightened up and took a step back, waving the weapon between them. "Which brings us back to you three. We're going to stun you unconscious then set fire to your house with all of you in it."

Beryl stood next to him. "Now you've destroyed our drone we'll just have to do it the old-fashioned way. Don't worry, you'll be dead of smoke inhalation before the place burns down — just like Malcolm."

Steve kept his stun gun pointed on them while Beryl crouched before the fireplace. Fiona always kept it prepped with a Jenga-like stack of kindling precariously perched on a generous mound of scrunched-up newspaper, ready to light when the mood took her fancy. Beryl unpicked it piece by piece. Then she remade it, arranging some of the sticks and paper so they extended out of the fire, down onto the hearth, reaching across to the rug like a rustic fuse. She took a couple of small logs from a basket beside the fireplace and positioned them on top of the trail of wood and paper. "After you're unconscious, we'll put a match to this lot, then it will look like you've lit a fire, dozed off and a couple of logs have rolled out and set your rug alight, burning the house down."

"Lighting a fire in September? Who's going to believe that?" Partial Sue sneered.

"Lots of people light fires in September," Beryl replied.

"What about my smoke alarms?" Fiona said.

Steve jiggled his trouser pockets, making the contents rattle. "Thought of that. We'll put dead batteries in them."

"It'll show up in the autopsy that we've been stunned first, even if we do die of smoke inhalation," Partial Sue said.

Steve thought for a moment. He rounded the back of the sofa and shoved it forward with them on it, so they were now level with the trail of wood and paper. "Not if your bodies burn first."

Beryl tucked some more wood and paper under the sofa, just to make sure it was certain to catch alight. She stood up and dusted off her hands. "There, that should go up nicely."

Fiona tried to swallow but her throat had tightened, garrotted by fear.

CHAPTER 75

Steve and Beryl exchanged self-satisfied glances, pleased with their work and how everything was turning out so hunky-dory.

Steve tossed his gun from one hand to the other. "Now the nasty part. We'll have to stun you one by one, so we can light the fire and make our escape."

"Remembering to grab our drone on the way," Beryl reminded him.

Steve slapped his head. "I am such a dunce. Yes, we can't leave evidence lying about. I suppose we'd better take the extinguishers as well. Might look weird if we leave them."

"Good idea. Have to be thorough. Make it look like an accident."

But they weren't nearly as thorough as they thought. Any decent fire investigation would discover that the blaze had been started deliberately. Not to mention all the residual foam outside from the fire extinguishers. Then there were the ladies' phones. Steve and Beryl had taken them, but the police would check all their call records, including Fiona's voicemail to Partial Sue pointing the finger at Molly and her box of donations which currently resided in the back of Fiona's car along with the bug. But it would all be academic if the ladies were already dead.

Steve became impatient, his hands fiddling with the stun gun. "Come on. Who's going first? You need to pick, or we'll pick for you."

"No," Fiona said.

"What? You want us to choose?"

Fiona leaned forward, fixed them with an icy stare. "No. I mean, no one's going to be stunned by either of you."

Steve stepped forward, gun raised. "Oh, I think you are, and I think I'll start with you."

Fiona spoke quickly. "No, you won't, because I can tell you something that will make you forget about killing us and make you want to get away from here as fast as possible."

Beryl laughed. "I don't think so, sweetheart. You're bluffing."

"I'm not and you won't be calling me sweetheart afterwards."

"No, it'll be more like harpy," Partial Sue said.

"Or horrible cow," Daisy offered.

Fiona stared at her two friends, wondering where they were going with their thesaurus of potential insults Beryl might use on Fiona when she became more enlightened.

"Sorry, continue," Daisy said.

Fiona attempted to restore some gravitas to the situation. "Believe me, you'll want to hear what I have to say. If you'd rather stun us first and never know, go ahead, be my guest. But you'll be looking over your shoulders for the rest of your short lives." Fiona sat back and crossed her arms.

The fleece-wearing pair grew silent, considering the proposition. But they were unable to resist. "Go on," Steve said.

"We told you about feeding you false information," said Fiona. "About pretending to know who Mary was and having evidence against her. But that was only half the ruse."

"It was a *ru*." Daisy chuckled, pleased at her bit of word play.

"I really don't like lying," Fiona continued, "and this was a big lie, but sometimes—"

"The end justifies the means." Partial Sue grinned.

"You heard me leave a message on Sue's phone. Picked it up through your bug. That's what brought you here. Us knowing the identity of Mary wasn't the only lie in that voicemail. I lied about something else. Something very big. Something that's going to be a bit bothersome for you two."

"That's putting it mildly," Daisy said.

Beryl and Steve stood absolutely still, anticipating Fiona's next words. She kept them waiting on purpose. The more time she could waste, the better. Plus, it didn't hurt to see these two psychopaths squirming in their sensible shoes.

Steve came out of his stupor. "What? What wasn't true?" He waved the stun gun in Fiona's face again.

She casually pushed it away. "Stop waving that thing at me or you'll never know."

Beryl's eyes became wild and anxious. "Steve, stop pointing the gun at her. Fiona, tell us what it is."

Fiona cleared her throat dramatically. "In that message I said that the counter-drone surveillance equipment had been dismantled two days ago. That was a lie. It's still up and running."

"Fully functional," Partial Sue added. "Anything that flies within a two-mile radius of the spit immediately gets tracked and investigated by the police. Especially one flying in the early hours of the morning. Fiona's house is exactly one point seven five miles from Mudeford Spit."

"We checked it on Google Maps," Daisy said.

"And on an Ordnance Survey map," Partial Sue said. "Just to be on the safe side. Not that we don't trust Google Maps but there's nothing better than a good old Ordnance Survey map when it comes to accuracy."

Daisy gave a warm smile. "I like how they show you the difference between a church with a steeple and a church with a tower."

Beryl and Steve shifted uneasily, swallowed hard. Steve tightened his grip around his stun gun.

"The police will disrupt any drone that flies dangerously close to the spit," Fiona continued. "We're too far away for that to happen, so we knew we'd have to do that ourselves, hence the fire extinguishers. However, this house is within the drone exclusion zone. Which means ever since your drone took off and flew here, it's been tracked. Right to this very location."

Partial Sue pointed to the controller hanging from Beryl's neck. "Same goes for the source of the signal. Lucky for us you're not using a pre-programmed drone. We took a bit of a calculated risk there, but it paid off. The police are going to trace the signal right here. They'll be arriving any second."

Steve's face grew red and inflamed as he tried and failed to keep a lid on his bubbling rage. "You're bluffing. The police would never agree to a sting operation like this. Far too dangerous."

"Isn't that entrapment?" Beryl asked.

"Yes, it is," Fiona replied. "But the police don't know about it. We know DI Fincher and you're right, she'd never agree to allowing a flamethrowing drone to target a home in a suburban area with people in it. But we had to lure you out somehow."

"She'll be cross with us," Daisy said. "Very cross."

"But not half as cross as she'll be with you two," Fiona added.

Beryl and Steve exchanged looks of confusion and fear. Best laid plans falling apart. Although, their plans hadn't exactly fallen apart. The three ladies had just had a better one. From the frustration on his face, Steve couldn't accept that they'd outsmarted him and his wife. His eyes narrowed as he sifted through the evidence in his mind. "Wait a second . . . But how did . . . When was . . . Who was?"

Partial Sue didn't look impressed. "Are any of those sentences going to have endings?"

"You're wasting precious escape time," Fiona said.

Steve pointed an accusing finger. "Ah-ha! That's it! This is all another ruse, isn't it? You made all that up, to make us think the police were on their way here to get us to leave. Well, it's not going to work. We'll stick with the plan thank you very much." He raised his stun gun, pointing it at Fiona. "Starting with you, smartarse."

Beryl tried to get her husband's attention. "Steve."

He didn't hear her. "Gonna stun you unconscious, then the other two."

"Er, Steve?"

"And set light to your house."

"Steve!"

"What?" He turned to his wife, who pointed up at a corner of the lounge, near Fiona's curtains, which were tightly drawn. A smudge of blue light flashed on and off at regular intervals. Then another appeared on the ceiling, and another in the opposite corner.

"I think it's too late for any of that, my love."

CHAPTER 76

September was coming to an end. A lot of things came to an end at this time of year. The month stood at the crossroads in the calendar between the conclusion of summer and the descent into autumn and winter. All the signs were there. The air had turned, an almost imperceptible shift. Not exactly a chill or a nip but it was as if it were preparing itself for one. Still warm, but the air smelled different, fresher. The light too had changed. Muted somehow, less yellowy, more bronze.

Fiona felt the cool hand of winter beckoning, or was it the melancholic mood that had set in now that the investigation was over and the culprits caught? She feared her depression wasn't far away. The 'It' that haunted her would come creeping back. She could sense it testing the borders of her mind, prodding here and there to see if it was safe to trespass.

"What are you having?" asked Partial Sue, the vast menu nearly covering her small head.

Fiona was glad of the distracting question. She hadn't so much as glanced at the menu yet. "I can't decide, it all looks fabulous."

They'd booked a table on the decking at Tides Restaurant for Bitsy, who'd returned just for the weekend to say a sad farewell to everyone. She'd be returning to London, for good. Initially, they'd planned on something lavish, hence Fiona's meeting with Marcus to discuss options. But in the end Bitsy just wanted a small, intimate dinner with her friends, which unfortunately meant inviting Sophie.

Frank Marshall had joined them too as he'd just 'happened to be passing'. Fiona didn't want him there, but Bitsy insisted. She wasn't aware of just how nasty he'd been. How he'd humiliated the ladies in front of all the beach hut owners, sacking them on the spot. But this was Bitsy's evening and Fiona didn't want to make a fuss, so she kept quiet as did her colleagues. It annoyed her that people like Frank never seemed to get their comeuppance.

He hadn't apologised for his awful behaviour and neither had Antony Owens, even though both of them knew by now that the 'well-meaning amateurs', as they'd called them, had caught the culprits. Fiona regularly saw Antony Owens skulking around Southbourne, avoiding eye contact. If it was any consolation, he didn't seem particularly happy.

Olivia, on the other hand, looked happier than ever and was always pleased to see them. Daisy bumped into her regularly at the model shop, where she'd taken a job as manager to help pay the bills. After the ladies had questioned Ken and Nigel, the pair of them had agreed on one thing, which was a miracle in itself. They'd realised they needed to modernise so had brought in Olivia to shake things up. After a thorough deep clean, of course, she'd transformed the place. It was now a slick and well-organised retail environment, with a new computer system to keep track of stock and offer every conceivable way of making modern purchases. Even that horrible orange stuff in the window had gone.

"I'm absolutely starving," Partial Sue said. "I could eat a jacket potato the size of a man's shoe, covered in potato salad."

"Isn't that a bit like wearing double denim?" Fiona remarked.

"I'm having the soup," Daisy said. "I wonder if it comes with cretins."

"They're called croutons," Sophie smiled with smug superiority.

Bitsy wasn't happy about their conservative food choices. "You need to dream bigger than jacket potatoes and soup. Everyone have what you want. This is on me."

There were outbursts of "Oh no" and "You can't" and "Let's split it".

Bitsy was having none of it. "I insist. My treat."

Sophie closed her menu. "Gail and I will just have a green salad."

Groans came from every corner of the table. Gail's face grew downcast.

"Nonsense," Bitsy snapped. "This is a fun, indulgent evening. Gail, don't be a boring Bagpuss like this one. How about a nice lobster paella?"

It was one of the most expensive things on the menu. Gail nodded eagerly. Nobody saw the ladies of the detective agency swap secretive glances. Hopefully this lobster would have been bought and paid for, not snatched out of a fisherman's pot in the early hours of the morning.

"What are you having, Daisy?" Fiona asked.

"The sea bass. I'm thinking about becoming a Presbyterian."

"I think you mean pescatarian," Partial Sue said. "Unless you're thinking of joining a Scottish reformed church."

"My father was a Presbyterian," Frank blurted. "Nothing wrong with being a Presbyterian. We should get some drinks in."

"Aren't Presbyterians teetotal?" Partial Sue asked.

"I'm not a Presbyterian, but I am thirsty." Frank grabbed Marcus, who had just finished delivering food to a nearby table. "We'd like some drinks. A pint of Bishop's Finger, if you please."

"I'm sorry, we don't have Bishop's Finger," Marcus replied. "Dorset Knob?"

Marcus looked wounded. "I beg your pardon?"

Frank rolled his eyes. "It's a real ale."

"Oh, no. We don't have that either."

"Fiddler's Elbow?"

"No."

"Warlock's Forelock?"

"No."

"Yeoman's Tickle?"

"No."

"Betty's Dishwater?"

"No."

Fiona was sure he was making these up now.

Frank tutted as Marcus shook his head to more and more bizarrely named brews. "I've got more real ales back at my beach hut than you've got here."

Fiona could tell Marcus was itching to say, "Well, why don't you go back there, then?" But he remained professional. "I'm afraid it's only what's on the menu: Peroni, Fosters or Guinness."

Frank harrumphed. "I suppose a Guinness will suffice."

After the short delay, thanks to Frank, the drinks began to flow, as did the conversation, peppered with plenty of laughs of the belly and eye-watering variety. There were even a few guffaws in there too, almost all of them fuelled by tales of Bitsy's antics. She regaled them with story after story of posh and famous people she'd rubbed shoulders with and then done something very naughty with, most of them ending with her walking home in wet clothes or losing her shoes or waking up on the other side of the world with no idea how she'd got there. "So I'd only planned to go out for a quick snifter or two, down my local, then somehow I woke up covered in soot in the brig of the *QE2*, heading for the Bahamas."

"Magnificent ship," Frank commented, not really catching the main thrust of the story.

"How did you get there?" asked Daisy.

"Well, the last thing I remember, I was with someone from Spandau Ballet? No, it was one of their roadies. We'd dared each other to climb up into one of the chimneys."

"Funnels," Frank corrected.

Daisy became worried. "Did you get into trouble?"

"I'll say. Got a lifetime ban on all cruise ships. Word spreads like wildfire with that lot. The roadie lost his job. Works in Timpsons now."

The food came out and so did the phones. Daisy, Sophie and Bitsy snapped shot after shot of the colourful dishes to upload onto social media.

"Marcus, darling, this looks absolutely divine," Bitsy gushed. It smelled divine too.

"My pleasure," he replied. "*Bon appétit.*"

Plates clattered and cutlery jangled as everyone tucked in. Fiona speared a scallop with her fork and ate it whole. She couldn't help emitting a blissful groan as the tender shellfish, pan-seared in garlic butter, melted in her mouth.

Inevitably the conversation steered towards Beryl and Steve.

"I was shocked, I don't mind telling you." Frank pushed his plate away, after demolishing his steak and chips in about three mouthfuls. "I've known those two for years and never once would I have suspected them."

"How is life down here now?" Fiona asked.

"Well, we're a hardy bunch," he replied, as if they were troops at Dunkirk. "Nothing gets us down for long."

Several debates erupted, mostly led by Frank extolling the benefits of increasing security, loudly repeating his idea for the umpteenth time of having a checkpoint on the spit. "It would stop a lot of nonsense because you'd know exactly who was here at any given time."

Partial Sue spotted a flaw in his plan. "Unless it was a flamethrowing drone."

"No, but—"

Before he had a chance to finish his rebuttal, Daisy, acting quite out of character, spoke over him. "You know, it's Molly and her little girl Dina I feel sorry for. Her parents weren't who she thought they were. That must feel terrible."

"How is she coping?" asked Bitsy.

"She's distraught," Fiona replied. "Hasn't visited or spoken to them since they were arrested. DI Fincher said it's like a form of grief, finding out someone you're close to is a criminal. She's mourning the loss of the people she thought she knew."

"Ironic, isn't it?" said Partial Sue. "They were doing it all for her."

"I don't see what all the fuss is about." Sophie snorted. "Her parents are criminals and that's that. She needs to get over it and move on."

Bitsy gasped at her friend's insensitivity. "It's not that easy, Soph. Imagine if your parents had turned out to be psychopaths, obsessed with burning down beach huts. Would you get over that?"

"I would. I must be made of sterner stuff."

The growl of an engine interrupted the conversation. A vast black Range Rover with blacked-out windows and flashy chrome wheels rumbled past, inches from where they were sitting, jiggling the plates and cutlery on the table.

Frank's eyes bulged. "What the devil does he think he's doing? Vehicles are not permitted on the spit. What makes him think he's so special? See, this is why we need a checkpoint."

"Oh, just, leave it, Frank," Bitsy pleaded. "We're having a nice time."

But Frank couldn't leave it. His moustache twitched and his head kept swivelling in the direction of the Range Rover as it ploughed through the sand towards the end of the spit. He shook with indignation, his face reddening. "It's no good. I can't sit here while someone breaks the rules." He wiped his mouth to clear away the angry spittle that had gathered at the corners, threw down his napkin and trotted off after the offending SUV, shouting and waving his arms.

Maybe Fiona had been wrong about Frank not getting his comeuppance. Perhaps he already had. Fiona was reminded of the old Chinese curse: *May you get what you wish for*. He certainly had. He'd realised his ambition and was now the official, democratically voted guardian of his beloved peaceful haven. Ironically, this haven would never give him any peace, not while he was its protector, constantly fretting over every inch of sand and worrying about every misdemeanour, no matter how small. His blessing had become a curse. A demon that would never cease tormenting him.

Frank's departure stunted the conversation. A long, barren silence descended. There were several shivers around the table and it wasn't just the sun losing its heat as it hovered over the horizon.

Bitsy stood and raised her glass. "Here's to Fiona, Daisy and Sue. My newfound friends and kickass detectives who caught the drone killers."

Everyone cheered and smiled, apart from Sophie, of course, who was never happy when she wasn't the centre of attention.

Normal socialising resumed, more drinks were ordered, and the chatter increased in volume.

Fiona leaned over to Bitsy. "So I've been dying to ask, how come you're moving back to London? I thought you had enemies there."

"After my hut burned down, it was a sort of near-death experience. Well, not really *near* death. More in the neighbourhood of death. It made me depressed, I don't mind telling you. But then I thought, sod depression, I have good friends and that's all that matters. Life's too short. So I went back and apologised to all the people I'd wronged in London, mostly wives of husbands who I'd had flings with. Said sorry and made amends. Turned out I needn't have worried. They'd all been having affairs behind their husbands' backs before I came along. But they appreciated the gesture, and I felt better about myself. Bit of forgiveness goes a long way. Cleared the air, so it's safe to go back to my beloved city. But it's changed me, you know. Made me think about what's important. And that's having friends and being kind, which reminds me . . ." She called out to Marcus.

He hurried over. "Is everything okay?"

Bitsy showed him a post on her phone. "It's more than okay, darling. Just to let you know, I uploaded a shot of my butternut squash risotto to Instagram. Heston and Nigella have already liked it — that should get your till ringing."

Marcus nearly flew into the air with delight and surprise. "Oh my gosh. Thank you, Bitsy, thank you. I'll knock some money off the bill."

"Don't you dare. Full price, if you please." She turned to everyone around the table. "Listen. I am so flattered you all came tonight. I've had such an amazing time down here, well, apart from my beach hut burning down, but I've made some wonderful new friends and got to spend time with some old ones. I wanted you all to know, I've bought a little place in London and you are all invited to come and stay with me. It's dead central so is very handy for going out on the town."

"Whereabouts?" Sophie asked.

"Bloomsbury. The Chatsworth Hotel."

Jaws fell open, some of them mid-chew. They all knew Bitsy was rich but not buying-whole-hotels rich.

Bitsy clocked the shock on their faces. "What are you all looking at me like that for? Is there something wrong with the Chatsworth? Or is it the area — I knew I shouldn't have bought in Bloomsbury, too many hotels there already."

"You bought a hotel?" Daisy asked. "A whole one?"

"Yes, but it's just a tiddler. Nineteen rooms. One of those boutique thingies. I've always wanted to own a hotel, mostly so I can live in it and don't have to worry about food or cleaning or doing laundry. However, important thing is, there's plenty of room for all of you to stay, completely free. Whenever you want. Although I can't guarantee a balcony room. Manager gets snotty when I give them out to my friends. What do you say?"

"Are you sure, Bitsy? That could get expensive," Partial Sue remarked.

"Friends are more important than money." She stretched her hands across the table, giving theirs a squeeze one by one.

"Gail's never been to London," Sophie said.

"'S'right," Gail muttered.

"Well, that's settled then. We're all taking Gail out on the town. We'll do dinner at The Ivy, watch a show, then shots at the Groucho — the full works, all on me. Then maybe see if we can crash a celeb's party."

Gail's face nearly exploded with joy. Everyone's did at the thought of staying in a luxury hotel with Bitsy as their host, opening doors that would never normally open for them.

Fiona felt a warm glow of happiness enshroud her. She had more than one reason to be happy. Bitsy had given her something of great value, and it wasn't just the offer of a glitzy weekend in the capital. From now on she'd try to adopt Bitsy's attitude. Focus on her friends. As long as she had them close by, she knew she'd be just fine.

EPILOGUE

A lone figure stood in the shadow of the coastguard station, which had been locked up and abandoned for the night. The whole place was different now. Peering in through the window, it pained the woman to see that all of Steve and Beryl's effects were absent. The new pair of volunteers had removed them, hiring a small van to do so, and with it the memories of how it used to be. A jolly place, full of warmth and fun. Now it was just a cold empty shell, stacked with utilitarian electronic equipment.

It didn't make her sad, just angry.

She turned once more, fitting the heavy-duty binoculars to her eyes. Observing the spit below, she focused on a table with six rather excitable women and one large man. She'd watched them spend the night laughing and drinking and eating. Through her earpiece she could hear them, as if they were standing right next to her. It hadn't been difficult to bug their table — she'd placed it before they'd arrived. There was only one outdoor table reserved for six people, seven if you counted the addition of Frank. The reserved sign was already on the table when she'd passed by. Sitting down briefly and leaning over, she had pretended to dislodge a stone from her flip-flops, while her other hand slipped the bug under the table. The whole thing had barely taken a second.

She listened to their sycophantic claptrap, her hands ever tightening around the shafts of her binoculars. Essentially, the whole evening was a schmaltzy session of back-slapping and congratulating one another at how wonderful they were. It made her sick to her stomach. From the moment they'd arrived, it hadn't ceased. *Talk all you want*, she thought. It only made her more determined.

Her parents had made the ultimate sacrifice. They'd made sure the finger of justice never pointed towards her. Steve and Beryl had kept her off the police radar. Ringfenced her from anything criminal, guaranteeing her innocence by paying for everything and doing everything themselves. Molly had not been involved in any of it. However, in reality, she'd been the driving force behind it all. They'd do anything for their little girl, including helping her achieve her lifelong ambition: to own a beach hut for her and Dina.

They'd tried their hardest in the past. Thought that the coastguard station would sate her, but it was nothing like the real thing. She simply had to have a proper beach hut for Dina to grow up in and had persuaded them to get it for her by any means necessary. They had initially thought that the money Steve had inherited from his departed dad would be enough to buy Molly's dream, but the prices of huts had become stupid, unattainable. They would need to break the law to bring the price down. To kill.

But, before any of this had happened, they had taken steps to protect Molly. If they were caught, they'd claim she had no part in it. It had to be this way. They couldn't risk Dina growing up without a mother. So they'd peddle the story that they'd planted the bug in the box without her knowledge, slipping in the little white lie of the triple-strength battery booster from China. The reality was, there was no such thing. This was the only part of the crime where Molly had been involved. She'd had to go into that god-awful charity shop and change the battery booster every few weeks so they could monitor if they were in any danger of getting caught. Of course, there was always the small risk that the police would check the device and find out it only lasted weeks rather than months. Then they would deduce that her parents had been lying to protect her. But it was a minor detail that had got lost in the furore of the drone killers being apprehended. The police had two culprits who'd been caught red-handed and they had confessed. A perfect, textbook take-down.

The only downside, apart from her parents being convicted, is that Molly would have to play along with it, pretending to be shocked and outraged at her parents, disowning them to make it appear convincing. Bit harsh, but her parents had known the risks before they'd agreed to help her.

One thing was sure, she'd make those three lady detectives pay for ruining her dream of owning a beach hut — oh, and putting her parents behind bars, of course. Yes, they'd be sorry.

"Mummy, who are you looking at?"

She'd almost forgotten Dina was by her side, playing on the steps.

"Why can't we go inside the coastguard station like we used to?"

"Because of the people Mummy is looking at."

"Are they the ones who made Grandma and Grandad go away?"

"Yes."

"I don't like them."

"Mummy doesn't like them, either. Don't worry, we're going to get them."

"When will we do that?"

"Soon, darling. Soon."

THE END

ACKNOWLEDGEMENTS

Biggest thanks, first and foremost, must go to my publisher, Steph Carey. Without her I wouldn't have had the opportunity to write these books and a great deal of fun along the way. Although it's also difficult writing a book, having Steph's support and guidance makes it a whole lot easier, and makes every book immeasurably better. The same goes for my editor, Cat Phipps, whose sharp skills turn my manuscript into a cleaner, leaner, more pleasurable read. In fact, I need to thank the whole team at Joffe Books who work tirelessly behind the scenes to make every book a success.

You can't start writing without getting the research right and for that I really appreciated the help I got from the volunteers at the National Coastwatch Institution, who patiently answered all my questions, especially about radar. I must also thank Rich and Julie Carey, and my sister Jane, who gave me a real insight into life on Mudeford Spit and the quirks of beach hut etiquette, many of which I included in the book.

When it comes to police procedure, I get the best advice from Sammy H.K. Smith. She's a real-life police detective and a great writer — what more could you ask for? I also rely on some of the best beta readers out there to tighten up my manuscript, spot pesky typos and correct any silly mistakes I've made. They are Suze Clarke-Morris, Kath Middleton and Paul Lautman, plus Julia Williams. I must also thank Nick Castle who has done another cracking job on the cover.

Family is so important to me, and I am so lucky to have the best. Many heartfelt thanks to my wife Sha for all her help and support, and reassuring me when I lacked confidence. Also, to Dan and Billie, who are always so positive and enthusiastic about my writing.

Lastly, a massive, massive thank you to everyone who takes the time to read my books, and all the lovely things you've said about them. You can't believe how much of a buzz it gives me. I can't thank you enough. It's because of you that I am able to enjoy this wonderful privilege. It also ensures that the ladies of the Charity Shop Detective Agency will be back, sipping tea and bringing more killers to justice.

THE JOFFE BOOKS STORY

We began in 2014 when Jasper agreed to publish his mum's much-rejected romance novel and it became a bestseller.

Since then we've grown into the largest independent publisher in the UK. We're extremely proud to publish some of the very best writers in the world, including Joy Ellis, Faith Martin, Caro Ramsay, Helen Forrester, Simon Brett and Robert Goddard. Everyone at Joffe Books loves reading and we never forget that it all begins with the magic of an author telling a story.

We are proud to publish talented first-time authors, as well as established writers whose books we love introducing to a new generation of readers.

We have been shortlisted for Independent Publisher of the Year at the British Book Awards three times, in 2020, 2021 and 2022, and for the Diversity and Inclusivity Award at the Independent Publishing Awards in 2022.

We built this company with your help, and we love to hear from you, so please email us about absolutely anything bookish at feedback@joffebooks.com

If you want to receive free books every Friday and hear about all our new releases, join our mailing list: www.joffebooks.com/contact

And when you tell your friends about us, just remember: it's pronounced Joffe as in coffee or toffee!

ALSO BY PETER BOLAND

**THE CHARITY SHOP
DETECTIVE AGENCY MYSTERIES**
Book 1: THE CHARITY SHOP DETECTIVE AGENCY
Book 2: THE BEACH HUT MURDERS